The Incomplete Manuscript

By Kamal Abdulla

Translated from Azerbaijani by Anne Thompson

Strategic Book Publishing and Rights Co.

Strategic Book Publishing and Rights Co.
12620 FM 1960, Suite A4-507
Houston, TX 77065
www.sbpra.com

ISBN:978-1-62212-442-8

Typography and page composition by J. K. Eckert & Company

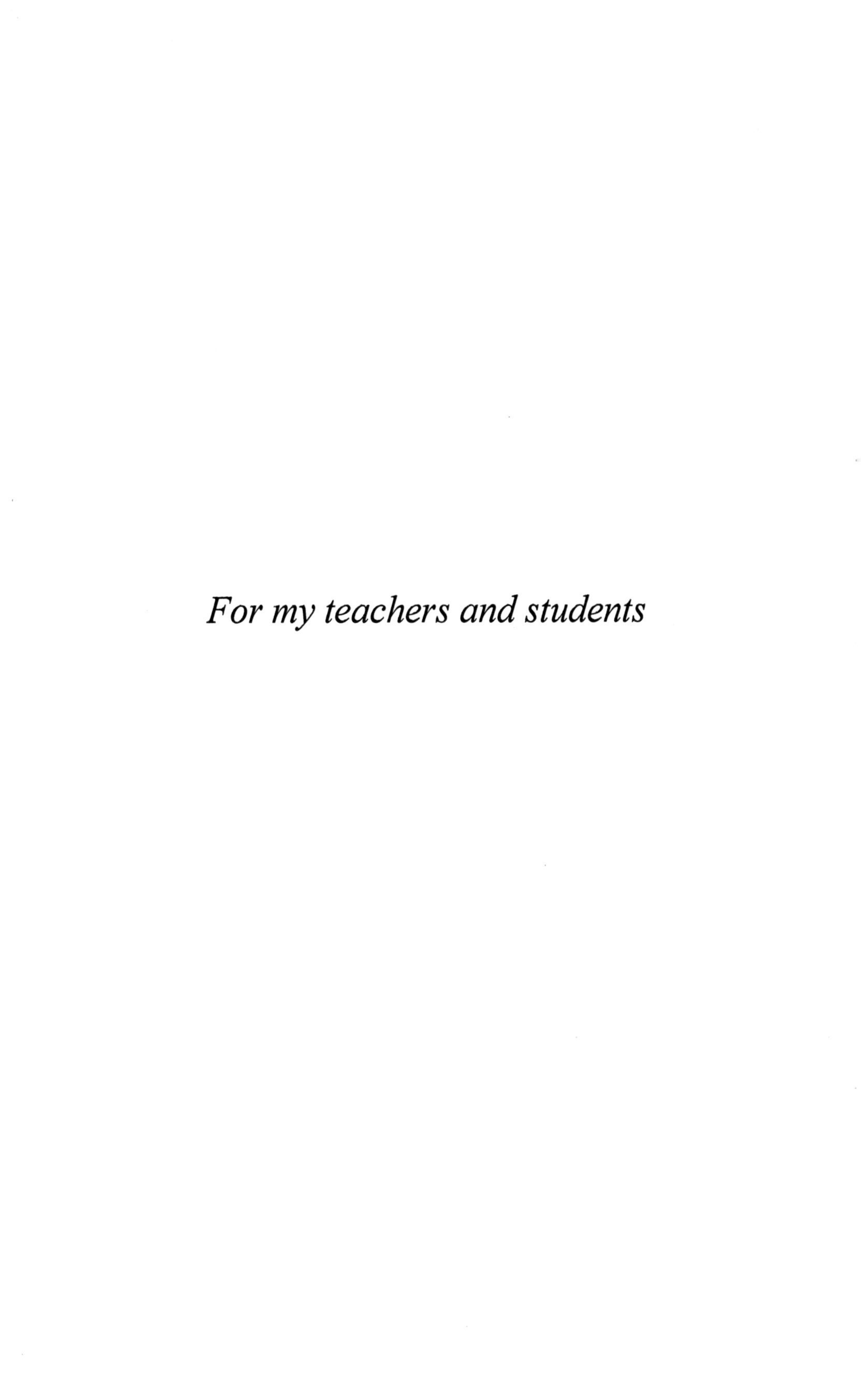

For my teachers and students

Contents

Preface:

From Incomplete Manuscript to *The Incomplete Manuscript*

(or Writing vs. Epic) by Prof. Max Statkiewitz, UW-Madison, USA . . . vii

Acknowledgments xix

Prologue I:

The Incomplete Whole. 1

Prologue II:

Do the Differences in the World Matter to God? 11

Prologue III:

The Right to Say, "I Don't Know" 15

The Manuscript 17

Epilogue:

The Mark of Incompleteness 187

Preface

FROM INCOMPLETE MANUSCRIPT TO *THE INCOMPLETE MANUSCRIPT* OF KAMAL ABDULLA OR WRITING VS. EPIC

The ambiguous relationship between the genre of the novel and that of the epic constitutes one of the important aspects of the development of modern literature in the West. *Satyricon, Don Quixote, Eugene Onegin, Ulysses,* are examples of such novelistic confrontation with the tradition of the epic. *The Incomplete Manuscript,* a novel by Kamal Abdulla presents arguably the most radical, most self-conscious confrontation with this tradition—to a large extend a tradition of the separation of genres, periods, and cultures—as well as with the hermeneutic mode that accompanies it, that is, the mode of the "reconstitution" or "recovery of meaning" of an authoritative text (Paul Ricœur). Indeed, the ostensible topic of *The Incomplete Manuscript* is such hermeneutic process, a patient reading of an ancient manuscript, supposedly preparatory notes for a great epic: "Perhaps you have realised that I am talking about the ancient Azerbaijani epic, *The Book of Dada Gorgud,*" writes the narrator at the beginning of the novel . He provides an informative scholarly note, presenting the Azerbaijani epic, and marking its importance for all the Turkic peoples. *The Incomplete Manuscript* as a whole will claim the important place for this tradition, for the epic, and on the other hand will offer its novelistic ("dialogical," "interrupting") comprehension, well beyond the strict generic, ethnic, and cultural boundaries.

At the outset of the novel, the narrator-reader introduces the title hero of the epic text and its supposed author: a bard, a soothsayer, and a holy man, Dada or Father Gorgud, the pivotal figure in the epic, and even more so in the incomplete manuscript (and in *The Incomplete Manuscript*). One can say that the novel of Kamal Abdulla enacts and problematizes this confrontation between the ancient epic mythical tradition and its modern "deconstruction." Indeed, in the words of the narrator, the novel is based on the comparison between "the text of the literary version of the Epic and the Incomplete Manuscript" , that is, the "notes" and the "observations" "written in the first person" The two modes of writing are professedly juxtaposed; they are nevertheless included in another first-person narrative (besides being "hidden" within a historical description of the Ganja's earthquake) in what we might call, with Mikhail Bakhtin a "polyphonic" novel.

The reading of the ancient manuscript within the plot of *The Incomplete Manuscript* is apparently conducted as a scholarly work in an academic setting of the Medieval Department of the National Manuscripts Institute. there is also a brief description of the condition in which our manuscript has been found; it bears some marks of time: fire and earth, human carelessness, the result of which is certain incompleteness and partial illegibility. Still it is pretty clear that the manuscript originates from the 12th century CE and refers to the Ganja earthquake in 1139, even though it does not give much new information about this event. This is in fact the reason why there is apparently not much interest in the study of this manuscript among scholars-historians.

In spite of the impression of a detailed scholarly procedure already early in the novel, its reader receives an impression that the reader of the manuscript, that is, the narrator of the novel, might be a stranger to the strictly academic preoccupation, to the scholarly truth, and that his curiosity might be of a different kind: "perhaps these academics, and this young Orientalist too," he writes "think they have lost an interesting dissertation subject? Perhaps they see me as a rival? In any case, I was an outsider, and these thoughts disturbed my peace of mind"; and towards the end of the novel he still worries that the librarians and other researchers "might get the wrong end of this stick and think that [he is] planning some investigative research. God forbid". Neither does the apparent commentary-structure of *The Incomplete Manuscript* impose a scholarly rigor in the ordinary sense of the term on the process of reading: "A prior commentary has claims to be a scientific introduction and we are a long way from making any such claims". On the contrary, the narrator-reader claims to focus on and to problematize "the places where the Incomplete Manuscript is cut off or leaves something unsaid". In this way, the reader of the manuscript, and hence the reader of the novel, will soon find themselves in a position of re-writing (the text turns out to be eminently "*scriptible*" or "writerly" in Roland Barthes' sense), that is, attempting to complete what turns out incomplete in the manuscript, even if with the awareness of the difficulty, perhaps of the impossibility, nay, of the hermeneutic hubris of this task.

It is a scholar—the librarian of the Institute—who, in the beginning of the reading adventure of the narrator, affirms: "the manuscript is incomplete. It doesn't have a beginning or an end"; and he adds, peremptorily, obviously in order to discourage his research: "You won't find it of any interest". The narrator confirms the incompleteness after the first rapid reading of the manuscript, but it is precisely this particular incompleteness that arouses his interest—to be sure a different kind of interest, poles apart from the strictly scholarly one. He is fascinated with the enigma and the uniqueness of his text (even among the genre of incomplete manuscripts). This two-sided incompleteness appears to the narrator as the distinctive mark of the manuscript: "Maybe our Incomplete Manuscript has one main difference from all other incomplete manuscripts—our Manuscript has neither beginning nor end". Only after the careful rereading, "rewriting," of the Manuscript another, ontological, existential explanation of its incompleteness will appear to the narrator: "Everything now bears the mark of incompleteness, like our Incomplete Manuscript". The Manuscript is incomplete because it reflects (exemplifies) the essential incompleteness of the world, or rather *worlds.* Indeed, towards the end of his adventure the reader of the manuscript realizes that paradoxically the heroes of the epic do not live in a common world, and that "each of them is talking to the other in their own world ; Bayindir Khan had his own Gorgud in his world, while Gorgud had his own Bayindir Khan in his world. They are not in the same place for one another".

This strange discovery of the narrator-reader is para-doxical, of course, in respect to the epic tradition because it is the unity of the world, "the world of myth" that characterizes the genre of the epic. In Mikhail Bakhtin's influential opposition between the novel and the epic, for example, the latter is distinguished by the unity and the coherence of its world, "the world of the epic" (мир эпопеи), which is "the world of memory" (Mikhail Bakhtin), located in the "absolute past,"[1] and walled off from the historical, "modern" temporality—the novelistic temporality, in Bakhtin's view. The world of the epic has always already been "past," enclosed in the national, ethnic tradition (in the Book), it has never been "contemporary," opened to (ex)change as the novel has been: it presents a unified world of the fathers and the founders of families), who are "first and best"; their time is the summit of the national history that will always remain the model and the standard of comparison, to which the

---

1 Bakhtin refers to "Goethe's and Schiller's terminology as the source of his notion; in *Über epische und dramatische Dichtung,* Goethe opposes indeed the action in epic as *vollkomen vergangen* to the action in drama, which is *vollkommen gegenwärtig*— Goethe, *Sämtliche Werke,* vol. 36, 149–152.

descendents could hardly live up.[2] The essential characteristic of the epic is its concentration on the past as an ideal, a unified ideal past.

Thus, the proper reading of an epic text has to be carried out within the hermeneutic of the recovery of meaning, the meaning of the Father; and it has to combine the reverential distance with a certain sense of community between the descendants and the "fathers." The narrator of *The Incomplete Manuscript* is confronting these requirements of the hermeneutic of recovery when he expresses his admiration and the seeming nostalgia of the reader of the epic (who feels, however, somewhat estranged from the mythical tradition) after his third, definite reading of the manuscript. His "surprise and admiration" for the author of the manuscript (and of the epic) and for the world that he described (created) "had no limits," he is sorry that "this society no longer exists," that it "remains in antiquity, far away and out of reach," and he complains that "little today connects us with antiquity."

Some of the "commentaries" of the narrator which accompany his reading of the manuscript seem to express the same nostalgic mood, related to the incompleteness of the manuscript in its role of a testimony of the epic events ("epic truth"). They mark the ostensible failure of the hermeneutics of the recovery of meaning, at least in its straightforward version: "… and unfortunately we will never know what it was that Dada Gorgud remembered"; "here two or three pages written in Dada Gorgud's hand can be considered lost to us forever"; "does Aruz really say this or not? We shall never know"; "here, at this sad moment the text about Shah Ismail breaks off for the last time and ends … Nobody can ever say for certain whether what is described here truly happened or is simply the product of the imagination". The latter eventuality—the imagination of the author, the artistic imagination, the imagination of art and literature—will tend to impose itself as the novelistic confrontation with the epic, historical and mythological tradition progresses in *The Incomplete Manuscript.*[3] It will end by dominating the reception of this tradition in the conclusion of the novel.

To be sure, in modern times, the awareness of the loss of the world of the heroes does not lead to the abandonment of historical research and of an attempt at the reconstruction of the past. Even though nobody would ever

---

[2] No reader of The Iliad or The Book of Dada Gorgud, for example, would fail to notice the pertinence of this remark as to the stature of the heroes in the epic; see e.g., Nestor's speech in the first book of The Iliad, Agamemnon' review of troupes and his comparison of Diomedes to his father Tydeus in the fourth; as well as Dada Gorgud's naming of Bamsi Beyrak, Bamsi the Bold, and Basat the Dominant, the emphatic admiration of Gazan for Bayrak's courage, etc. (the latter are presented in the epic and reiterated in The Incomplete Manuscript).

know for certain "how it really was" (*wie es wirklich war)*—in the words of the founder of modern historiography, Leopold von Ranke[4]—one feels that one could still obtain an independent historical verification of the heroic deeds from epic tales and thus carry out the "completion" of "incomplete manuscripts." Other manuscripts can be discovered (in libraries, in the sand, or anywhere, for that matter, for example "on the security guard's table," as in our novel). Archeological searches have unearthed traces of the downfall of the Mycenaean culture around the turn of the 12th century BCE ("the fall of Troy"), or of the crisis of the Oghuz culture in the 12 century BC (around the time of the Ganja earthquake). But such founds could not really interfere with the history of the origins, a "monumental history," as Nietzsche calls it, or with the epic that it has produced (the epic, which has confirmed, and to a large extent, produced it in return). Nietzsche is right to question the possibility of a clear distinction between the monumental history, on one hand, and myth, on the other: "there have been ages," he writes in chapter 2 of the second *Untimely Meditation,* "quite incapable of distinguishing between a monumental past and a mythical fiction, because precisely the same stimuli can be derived from the one world as from the other."[5] Those stimuli have always been the ones directed toward the foundation and preservation of a unified world, the world of a national, cultural unity. And it has been Memory , rather than science/knowledge or history in the strict sense, that presided over this process of unification.

The status of writing in this confrontation with myth and history has often been seen as ambiguous. On the one hand, the written texts have often fixed the mythic tradition and allowed its preservation and transmission (for exam-

---

3 For an insightful discussion of Kamal Abdulla's *The Incomplete Manuscript,* from the point of view of the complex relationship between the truth of historical chronicle and that of literary fiction, see Rahilya Geybullayeva, "History, Myths and Recycling Cultures and K. Abdulla's *Uncompleted Manuscript,*" in *Interlitteraria* (Tartu University), Issue 13 vol. I, 2008, pp. 148–163.

4 Leopold von Ranke, *Geschichten der romanischen und germanischen Völker von 1494 bis 1514* (Leipzig: Verlag von Duncler & Humblot, 1885), p. vii: (" *wie es eigentlich gewesen*"). The incomplete manuscript refers to this ideal of modern historiography but transposes it into the framework of the structural incompleteness and the artistic/literary response to it; see p. 14 below and p. 9 of the novel.

5 Friedrich Nietzsche, "On the Uses and Disadvantages of History to Life," in *Untimely Meditations,* trans. R. J. Hollingdale (Cambridge: Cambridge University Press, 1997), p. 70.

ple, the Homeric text in 6th century BCE and *Oghuz Namah* in 14th century CE); on the other hand, writing threatens the tradition by hardening it.[6] It might be considered inimical to the Truth of Memory and to the mythic tradition. Plato disclosed and stigmatized the illusory claim of writing to support memory in the *Phaedrus,*[7] and in our time the narrator of Mikhail Bulgakov's novel—to whom the narrator of *The Incomplete Manuscript* refers in his Prologue–seems to express the same view when he shows the inutility of the manuscript for the support of the Master's true novel (which might be in a sense considered a kind of "true myth"). To be sure "manuscripts do not burn" (рукописи не горят), but even if they did, the word would be preserved since the Master, just like an ancient bard—Homer or Dada Gorgud—remembers his "novel" by heart (To Margarita's question about his remembering the *word,* the Master replies: "Don't worry! Now I shall never forget anything."[8] Thus the Master attempts to preserve (create) the divine, epic word of myth.

Dada Gorgud, agrees that "in the beginning was the word,"[9] but he seems to foresee a particular power of the written word when he says/writes in one of his aphorism: "Nothing happens if it was not already written in the beginning."[10]And Kamal Abdulla draws all the consequences of the deconstructing potential of writing, the potential to confront the authority of the epic word, of the *logos* and *muthos* of the absolute past and monumental history in *The Incomplete Manuscript.* Indeed, writing might be viewed not only as useless in the case of living epic memory; it might be considered dangerous (a "dangerous supplement" in Derrida's words),[11] and unsettling the rigid legality of

---

[6] The narrator of *The Incomplete Manuscript* refers to this phenomenon as the "frozen immobility" of the "statuesque" epic characters (p. 15).

[7] Plato, *Phaedrus,* trans. Alexander Nehamas and Paul Woodruff, in *Complete Works,* ed. John M. Cooper (Indianapolis/Cambridge: Hackett Publishing Co., 1997), pp. 506 ff.; *Phaedrus,* in *Platonis Opera,* ed. Ioannes Burnet (1901; Oxford: Oxford University Press, 1986), pp. 227 ff.

[8] Bulgakov, *The Master and Margarita,* p. 314; М. А. Булгаков, *Мастер и Маргарита,* p. 452: "Но ты ни слова... ни слова из него не забудешь? … Не беспокойся! Я теперь ничего и никогда не забуду."

[9] It is this opening of the Gospel of Saint John that (in some of its interpretations) came to epitomize the logo-centrism (or epo-, mytho-centrism) of Western culture: *The Greek New Testament,* Institute for New Testament Textual Research (Münster/Westphalia, 1966 by United Bible Societies), p. 320.

[10] *The Book of Dede Korkut,* trans. Faruk Sümer, Ahmet E. Uysal, Warren S. Walker (Austin: University of Texas Press, 1972), p. 4.; *Le livre de Dede Korkut: Récit de la Geste Oghuz,* trans. Louis Bazin, Altan Gokalp (Paris: Gallimar, 1998), p. 55: "*Nul accident n'atteint les créatures, qui n'ait été écrit de toute éternité.*"

the tradition. Manuscripts neither simply burn nor are ever preserved intact. We have always to deal with pages marked by "scorched marks," by "stains," even pages "torn to shreds," or altogether missing. Of course, in a simple sense some of these *lacunae* can be completed in the process of a scholarly research. But in ontological sense—the sense of Derrida and Kamal Abdulla—they are marks (traces) of the essential indecidability and incompleteness (finitude) of human life and of its representation. In this sense, incompleteness is *inscribed* in human existence.

Kamal Abdulla develops the thought of essential inscription of human finitude when he brings together writing and secrecy under the common notion of what Derrida calls "ichnography," and Dada Gorgud's manuscript is particularly "secretive" in this respect since it is mysteriously joint to another manuscript—that of the story of Shah Ismail[12]—both being hidden within the remains of a description of Ganja earthquake. When the narrator rejects his identity as a writer—together with that of a scholar-historian—he certainly distinguishes, just like Derrida does, between two kinds of writing: one ("good"), an inscription in the soul according to the mode of (epic) memory (*anamnēsis*); and the other ("bad" or badly slighted, as Nietzsche would say), disrupting, secretive writing in the mode of (supposed) aide-memoires, "notes" and "observations". The "good writing" tends to form a book:: "The idea of the book, which always refers to a natural totality, is profoundly alien to the sense of writing."[13] Thus, it would be tempting to oppose the wholeness of *The* Book *of Dada Gorgud*—the recorded text of the epic, the image of the closed mythic world of the ancient Oghuz society—to the incompleteness of both the ancient and the modern manuscript (the writerly novel). The ideal continuity and wholeness of the book could thus be undermined, "interrupted" by the essential, "original" *lacunae* of the manuscripts (essential, "arche-writing" [*archi-écriture*] as "arche-trace" [*archi-trace*]).[14] And indeed, the phenomenon of the "interruption of myth" is one of the possible definitions of literature (Jean Luc Nancy). But Kamal Abdulla's novel seems to thwart this

---

[11] Jacques Derrida, *Of Grammatology,* trans. Gayatri Chakravorty Spivak, Baltimor and (London: The Johns Hopkins University Press, 1974/6), pp. 141ff.

[12] Shah Ismail Khata'i, was the ruler of Azerbaijan and Persian the first half of 16th century; he was also a poet

[13] Jacques Derrida, *Of Grammatology,* p. 18; *De la Grammatologie,* p. 30–31. Cf. *Dissemination,* trans. Barbara Johnson (Chicago: Chicago University Press, 1981), p. 149; *La Dissémination* (Paris: Èditions du Seuil), 1972, p. 187; and Jacques Derrida and Maurizio Ferraris, *A Taste for the Secret* (Cambridge: Polity, 2001), p. 8.

[14] Jacques Derrida, *Of Grammatology,* p. 60ff; *De la Grammatologie,* p. 88ff.

definition when it displays a text that is at the same time more "original" and more writerly—indecidible, secretive, incomplete, that is, always already "interrupted"—than the epic, namely, the "notes" and "observations," "preparatory work for an epic that is to be written". In fact, Nancy's eventual formulation of the relationship between myth and literature does not contradict this view: "In the work, there is a share of myth and a share of literature or writing. The latter interrupts the former, it 'reveals' precisely through its interruption of the myth (through the incompletion of the story or the narrative) ...."[15] But this "interruption of myth is no doubt as ancient as its emergence or its designation as 'myth'" . The relationship between myth and literature, as well as the question of the "origin" is extremely complex, and it would be difficult to imagine a text better displaying this complexity that *The Incomplete Manuscript.* Indeed, the original event of composing an epic is here always already marked by the inter-ruption and in-completion of the "tentative" notes and observations. And, as we have already noted, the epic itself may contain—in its introductory aphorism—the seed of its writerly deconstruction. Of course this "aphoristic energy" (Jacques Derrida) can only appear after the work of (un)veiling, performed by the narrator and the readers of *The Incomplete Manuscript,* is (provisionally) "completed."

When Kamal Abdulla's narrator emphasizes his greediness for a secret, he does display a certain "dis-ruption of writing," an "aphoristic energy," of which Derrida speaks.[16] And in this sense he might be considered an offspring of Dada Gorgud, or rather the character of Dada Gorgud in the novel might be considered to be his writerly projection. Indeed, in the novel of Kamal Abdulla, Dada Gorgud is not only the secretary of Bayindir Khan, he is also a *secretary* in the strongest sense of the term: not only the writer-narrator but also "the keeper of the secrets"; everyone in Oghuz society "knows that a secret told to Dada will be kept safe". In that sense, not only the secret of Beyrak's heroism is revealed to Bayindir Khan, and thus to the reader of the ancient incomplete manuscript—and to the reader of *The Incomplete Manuscript* , an "unveiling" of the secret happens each time when a certain incompleteness of the manuscript manifests itself. The veil is in fact the crucial image for the incomplete manuscript, both the novel and the epic notes—the

---

[15] Jean Luc Nancy, *The Inoperative Community,* p. 63; *La communauté désœuvrée,* p. 159: "*Il y a dans l'œuvre la part du mythe et la part de la littérature ou de l'écriture. La seconde interrompt le premier, elle 'révèle' précisément par l'interruption du premier (par l'inachèvement du récit ou du discours).*"

[16] Cf. Jaqcques Derrida, "Cinquante-deux aphorismes pour un avant-propos," in *Psyché, Inventions de l'autre* (Paris: Galilée, 1987/2003).

veil as the image of the play between concealment and unconcealment of the secret, that is to say, the image of its/their truth, or the truth of the emerging artistic image: "Dada Gorgud's preparatory notes, observations and sketches open like a gauze curtain to reveal ideas and meanings that have lost their true outline and become the invention of the artist—when the clouds disappear from the sky, the blue depths of infinity look greater, and you come nearer to God, to the greater, higher Truth".

This work of truth as veiling/unveiling or the essential "original" incompleteness–constitutes then a major difference between Dada Gorgud's preparatory notes for the epic and the final, "familiar text of the epic." The latter would not differ from the former so much by the content of its political view, the ideological content that might better suit the need of the patron of the epic, as by its incompleteness, that is, its openness to unveiling in the process of constant rewriting. The dramatic question of the narrator as to the connection between the two historically disconnected texts within the same manuscript, namely the tales of Dada Gorgud on the one hand, and the story of the Shah Ismail, on the other hand, might thus be answered—incompletely, to be sure—with the reference to the same play of veiling/unveiling of the process of political (Machiavelian) expediency, that is, to its truth.

Given the major difference between the preparatory notes for the epic and the final "text" of the epic, that is, the difference between the mythological, establishment of the world on one hand, and its writerly, novelistic play between familiarization and defamiliarization, on the other hand, one might wonder—as the narrator of *The Incomplete Manuscript* does—why the preparatory notes and observations have been preserved (how such a preservation is possible at all?), rather than the text of the "complete" epic. After all, the forms of the latter have always had better chances to be preserved by the powers that be (cf. for example the fate of Homeric epics or Virgil's *Aeneid* in comparison with that of the so-called Menippean satires). Kamal Abdulla's narrator, in a sense an offspring of Dada Gorgud—a *secretary*—says that this is "God's secret!" But is this not the devil's (or rather the artist's, Mikhail Bulgakov's, Kamal Abdulla's himself) secret as well—the secret concerning the persistence of writing (and of art), namely, the claim that "manuscripts do not burn" in its "divine" sense?

As we have already noted, manuscripts neither burn entirely nor ever remain intact; they always leave *traces,* the traces of the epic desire of wholeness, on the one hand—"a complete whole in our imagination" says the narrator of *The Incomplete Manuscript* (p. 13)—and of its "original" frustration,: "the preparatory notes and observations," on the other hand. Once again, Kamal Abdulla's stroke of genius consists in situating the incompleteness of writing at the very origin of the epic endeavour, which is supposed to found, to "establish" a culture. Indeed, Dada Gorgud is discovered/imagined in *The Incomplete Manuscript* as the author of *both* the epic and the notes and observations, and it is in the latter that the truth is revealed: "'This is really how it was!' the Incomplete Manuscript says". The truth of the ideological, mythological function of the "complete" epic is revealed at the same time as a strict, dogmatic hermeneutic rule: "'But future generations must understand and accept it like this,' the Epic seems to say". And, most importantly, the authority of the notes and observations as to the historical and mythical truth of their affirmations is ultimately undermined on the authority of a great Azerbaijani poet Huseyn Javid (an authority to end all authorities): "But the reality presented by this text can also be doubted. Huseyn Javid's saying 'a man is right to doubt' lives today and will live on in future". The serious "political" function of the incomplete manuscript (and of *The Incomplete Manuscript*) is not so much an affirmation of the hermeneutic of suspicion, as the patient *unveiling* of the hermeneutic process (with its constant "self-interruption")[17]. Thus incompleteness is shown to be the very principle of interpretation. To paraphrase Nietzsche's famous aphorism: there are no complete manuscripts—only (incomplete) interpretations[18]; for (incomplete) manuscripts are always calls for interpretations. And in order to preserve the "incomplete manuscripts" from falling (back) into the epic unity and completeness, a great interpretive/artistic force is needed. Only such force is able to release the epic heroes from their "frozen immobility," so that they "begin to live—to love, to hate, to be faithful, to cheat, to scheme, to laugh, to cry". Displaying their living (and mortal) nature (as opposed to the quasi-divine nature of the heroes), Kamal Abdulla transports the "noblemen and sons of noblemen, khans and sons of khans" from the epic world of myth to the "untimely" world of the novel. The past loses its "absoluteness," but gains its contemporary relevance: "Ancient Oghuz society begins to be seen in its real, spiritual context". Thus the counterpart of the re-vitalization of the traditional, "statuesque," epic heroes must be the re-activation of the reader, who (re)discovers his/her spiritual affinity with them: s/he ceases to be a passive receiver of the tradition or a

[17] It is in this sense that *The Incomplete Manuscript* is "literature (writing) and not myth." Jean-Luc Nancy, *The Inoperative Community*, p. 72; *La communauté désœuvrée*, p. 179: "*littérature (écriture) et non mythe.*"

[18] Friedrich Nietzsche, *The Will to Power*, trans. Walter Kaufmann and R. J. Hollingdale (New York: Vintage Books, 1968), p. 267 (481, 1883–1888): "No, facts is precisely what there is not, only interpretations"; *Der Wille zur Macht* (Stuttgart: Alfred Kröner Verlag, 1996), p. 337: "*nein, gerade Tatsachen gibt es nicht, nur Interpretationen.*"

dispassionate scholar, and becomes a participant, a writer—a "secretary"—eventually an offspring of Dada Gorgud.

One might be tempted to say of the novel of Kamal Abdulla what its narrator says of the ancient, incomplete manuscript, that "despite its deceptive incompleteness, [it] will make great changes to Gorgud studies" , except that it is as much—if not more—"because of" its *incompleteness* that *The Incomplete Manuscript* will have this impact—and not only on Gorgud studies, but on the reading and study of modern literature and its relationship to the ancient (epic, mythical) tradition, as well as its affinity with other traditions.

—Prof. Max Statkiewicz,

University of Wisconsin-Madison

Acknowledgments

This book grows out of long years of comprehension and six months of writing. The gravity of the first part falls on the shoulders of the teachers; the second part of it falls on the students. I express my deepest gratitude to all my teachers and students, without whom this book couldn't have been written: *Docendo discimus!*

I would like to give special thanks to N, who was both a teacher *and* a student to me in this whole process. It takes incredible talent and patience to play both roles.

Prologue I: The Incomplete Whole

The new manuscript, registered in the catalog as being in box No. A 21/733 and housed in the third section of the Medieval Department of the National Manuscripts Institute, immediately captured my interest. It appeared to be straightforward and easy to understand—exactly the kind of manuscript that usually didn't attract much attention, according to the librarian.

Sensing my surprise, the librarian looked at me and smiled. "This manuscript is no different from any other. It hasn't been studied in detail yet, but it is thought to be from the twelfth century. It deals with the Ganja earthquake[19], which everyone knows about—historians, scientists, and the general public alike," she said simply. "The author's language and style are clear, simple, and intelligible. But there's a 'but.'"

"A 'but'?" I asked curiously.

The librarian nodded. "Yes, you see, the manuscript is incomplete. It doesn't have a beginning or an end. This is probably a result of the earthquake; it had been passed from hand to hand, rescued from fires, buried under earth and rubble. Eventually, it became illegible. In fact, some pages have been torn to shreds; some pages are only half there; and some are missing altogether. Some even bear scorch marks," she explained. Then she shook her head. "You won't find it of any interest."

On the contrary, her words only made me want to read it more. Considering what it had been through, I found the whole idea of reading it incredibly inter-

[19] Azerbaijan's second city, Ganja, was badly damaged by a powerful earthquake in 1139.

esting. We started walking past rows of bookcases, their shelves stacked with dusty manuscripts, old and new. As we walked down the marble steps toward the exit, I turned and looked sideways at the librarian. "Can I see the manuscript?" I asked hopefully.

The librarian hesitated. "You won't find it of any interest," she repeated. She sighed quietly to herself and then continued. "It has just come into the Institute's possession. Somebody left it on the security guard's table. We put an announcement in the *525th Newspaper:* Please come forward, whoever you are. Tell us where you found it. You will receive a financial reward." She shrugged, adding, "You know, the Institute gives rewards to people who find ancient manuscripts. But we didn't hear a thing. And the security guard? Well, he's a security guard. He doesn't remember anything."

"Can I see the manuscript?" I patiently asked again.

The librarian grinned, realizing how persistent I was. "Why not? But it is being restored right now," she replied. "Actually, I think the manuscript describes the Ganja earthquake. It gives some details about it." She fell silent for a moment and then looked at me again. "Some people think that the details of the Ganja earthquake are like a miniature painting that contains something quite different inside. What do you think?"

I raised my eyebrows, slightly caught off-guard by her question. Not knowing what to say, I simply shrugged quietly. *What a bizarre question to ask,* I thought. With that, I thanked the librarian for her time and told her that I'd be back soon.

A few days passed, and something had drawn me back to the Manuscripts Institute. This time my purpose was clear, though, and I knew I needed concrete help. I knew that manuscripts keep their own secrets in their script. In fact, even someone who knows Arabic script perfectly cannot always read ancient manuscripts.

§ § § § § §

The young Orientalist was a skinny scrap of a girl. I could tell from her expression that she had taken on her current job without enthusiasm; perhaps, she had been told to do the job. The director's ready response to my earlier request—"Of course! Come whenever you'd like, and I'll find someone competent to read for you"—did not sit well with the girl. I could sense it in her mute protest.

The young Orientalist filled out an order sheet. Soon after, she retrieved the manuscript from box No. A 21/733. The pages seemed to belong to a genuine, ancient manuscript—pale, rough, and yellowing. In some places, they were torn; in others, they had clearly been blackened by fire. We then gathered the manuscript and entered a small room. With that, the Orientalist, her face still registering mute objection, got down to business. She hardly paid any attention to me the whole time.

Our slightly awkward meetings took place for three days. Finally, the Orientalist had finished reading through the entire manuscript—or as much of it as she could comprehend. When she turned the last page, she looked at me blankly. ""If you'd like, I can write out the text in Latin script and give it to you in three or four days," she offered.

What more could I want? It was as if she had read my mind. (To be honest, I hadn't been able to follow the young girl's reading of the manuscript all the way to the end.) I nodded excitedly. "That would be excellent!" I exclaimed.

A few days later, the Orientalist handed me a second version of the manuscript in neat Latin script. I thanked her profusely, and she mumbled something incomprehensible, which I took as a secret reproach. She turned sharply to walk away, but before she left me alone with the new manuscript, she turned and looked at me. "If you're interested in the Ganja earthquake, there's nothing about it in there," she blurted, pointing at the manuscript in my hands. "It's about something else." With that, she turned and walked quickly away, her high heels clacking on the tiles.

Finally, I was left alone in the room. We had already agreed that I would study the text in the small room; I wouldn't ever take it out of the Manuscripts Institute. At the same time, *The Incomplete Manuscript* would stay in the room, too. I thought I might need to compare the two texts to each other. Later, when I was reading the story as it unfolded before me, I would look at those yellowing pieces of paper—hardly pages anymore—and see a living witness.

It's about something else, I thought. *But why would the subject change?* I imagined that I was close to a source on the history of Ganja, not such an important source in the sense that the events are now common knowledge—for example, everybody knows that Georgian troops attacked Ganja soon after the earthquake and sacked the city—but maybe a source with some new information. *Perhaps, the academics, and the young Orientalist, too, think they lost an interesting dissertation subject? Do they see me as a rival?* I wondered. In any case, I was an outsider, and these thoughts disturbed my peace of mind.

After hearing the Orientalist's odd remarks, I suddenly felt that I was at the door to a secret. I felt strangely agitated. I tried to get a grip on myself and calm down. *Never mind,* I thought. *Time will pass. They will see that my research is disinterested. I will read some of it here and there, and then I'll return it and go. I have work to do, anyway. I'm not a historian or a writer, or even a seismologist. Well, who am I? Oh, God. Why am I so greedy for a secret?*

I ended up reading the manuscript three times in three days. The Orientalist had been right. Suddenly, I found that the more I wanted to speak calmly, the less I felt able to do so. In fact, the hair on the back of my neck would stand on end—always a sure sign for me that something important was afoot.

After the first reading, without paying attention to the torn, damaged pages, I was able to understand the general meaning of the ancient manuscript: why had it been written, what for, and who wrote it. I also realized who the manuscript belonged to. The second reading cleared up the other obscure points. There had been quite a few of them, and they mainly concerned the content. The third reading was done to satisfy my thirst for spiritual pleasure. I believed in the greatness of the author, his eminence as a man. My surprise and admiration at what he did for a great and ancient society had no limits. I was only sorry about one thing: The society no longer existed. It remained in antiquity, far away and out of reach. I do not know if we can say that it is "lost" or not; however, it is difficult to deny that little today connects us with antiquity.

After reading *The Incomplete Manuscript* for the third time, I bumped into the young Orientalist in the corridor. One point still remained unclear to me, and I was interested in knowing what her thoughts were on it. The incomplete text that she had given me was inside another larger text. The two texts were interwoven. Had this not been the case, it would have been possible to identify *The Incomplete Manuscript* at first glance. But it was not like this. The beginning of the text confused everyone.

When I asked the Orientalist about it, she reluctantly said that the beginning of the text really was about the Ganja earthquake, or to be more exact, *referred* to it, and then referred to events that everyone today knows about—or at least scholars do—while very quietly and calmly moving seamlessly into another tale.

After two or three illegible pages, *The Incomplete Manuscript* begins its life with an incomplete sentence: "…day Bayindir Khan wanted me at his side again, and I came to Gunortaj, the Khan's residence, and greeted him with a courteous bow." In fact, this was the second sentence of *The Incomplete Manuscript.* The preceding sentence referred to the Ganja earthquake; strangely, that sentence, too, was incomplete: "The wise men of the city saw that the people were suffering after the calamitous earthquake in Ganja just on the . . . day Bayindir Khan wanted me at his side again. I came to Gunortaj, the Khan's residence, and greeted him with a courteous bow. Bayindir Khan asked me, 'Do you know why I have summoned you, Gorgud, my son?'"

So, with one subject incomplete, another began. *Is there a reason for hiding The Incomplete Manuscript inside, under the cover of the Ganja earthquake?* I wondered. I followed my thoughts, but quickly got nowhere.

Hmmm. Maybe I'll try to follow the trail that I have already found. Eventually, you, the reader, will see how far I got.

First of all, let me say that the main part of *The Incomplete Manuscript* has been written in the first person. This part of the manuscript can be called "Notes," or "Observations." It is impossible not to see that the notes are preparatory work for an epic that is to be written. Perhaps, you have realized that I am referring to the ancient Azerbaijani epic, *The Book of Dada Gorgud.*[20] We do not have another epic that so accurately reflects the ancient history of our nation, its way of life, or the roots of its joy and pain.

At the beginning of the work, its author, Dada Gorgud, is described as a true prophet of the Oghuz world. The spiritual branches of this magnificent twelve-part work can be traced back to ancient times. We can even say from some of the "itinerant" plots that well-known adventures in the epics of Homer are projected onto the Oghuz world. Which characters are older—Polyphemus or Tapagoz, Odysseus or Beyrak, Agamemnon or Salur Gazan, Penelope or Banuchichak? These are questions raised in the research of nineteenth century scholars, celebrated German romanticist, Von Diez[21], legendary Turkish linguist, Hatipoglu, and that giant of Russian oriental studies, Kazim Bey.

Today, these questions are less relevant; they can be answered or not. The main point is that if the characters listed above can coexist side by side, and if the name of one reminds you of another, then you have your answer. There will be no need to research into "who is older." In essence, *The Book of Dada Gorgud* consists of pages from the life of the strong, ancient Oghuz society. This society arose in mythological times and established a stable state based on a system of independent public and political relations. It fought its neighbors and made peace with them. It created internal discipline in its land. It put the principles of justice at the basis of its way of life. It suffered raids and made raids of its own. It can't be denied that Oghuz society has its place in history. Unfortunately, however, historians have yet to give it the place it deserves. This is close to the truth.

---

[20] *The Book of Dada Gorgud* is a collection of twelve stories about the heroes of the Oghuz Turks, narrated by Dada Gorgud. The Turkic people consider the epic to be part of their literary heritage. Dada, or Father Gorgud, is a bard, soothsayer, and holy man who may or may not have existed. The Oghuz are a Turkic tribe, the precursors of today's Azerbaijanis.

[21] H. F. Von Diez discovered one of the two extant manuscripts of *The Book of Dada Gorgud* in the Royal Library of Dresden in 1815.

The ancient Oghuz created their own remarkable culture like the ancient Khazars, the ancient Indians, the ancient Egyptians, the ancient Armenians, and the ancient Greeks who have all vanished, leaving just their names and tales of their exploits. *The Book of Dada Gorgud* is a brilliant artistic expression of the culture of the Oghuz.

And now there is *The Incomplete Manuscript,* too! It is a great monument with preliminary notes and observations. It outlines sketches of every event and every character, which were then later fleshed out in *The Book of Dada Gorgud* itself. Comparing the text of the literary version of the epic and *The Incomplete Manuscript,* we can see some big differences. For example, there are noticeable differences between Beyrak in the text of *The Book of Dada Gorgud and* Beyrak in *The Incomplete Manuscript.* The differences are often unexpected, like the very different, unbelievable relationship between Lady Burla and Salur Gazan, and like the revelation of the real reason for the conflict between Old Aruz and Salur Gazan. All of these, of course, do exist.

It cannot be denied that Dada Gorgud, the single author of *The Book of Dada Gorgud* and *The Incomplete Manuscript,* and *The Incomplete Manuscript*'s Notes and Observations sections, has fulfilled a very serious, complex, and I would even say political mission. *The Incomplete Manuscript* says, "This is really how it was!" Meanwhile, *The Book of Dada Gorgud* seems to say, "But future generations must understand and accept it like this."

This prompts a question: Why did the author not destroy his draft notes in *The Incomplete Manuscript* after he had finished *The Book of Dada Gorgud?* Who knows? Maybe he meant to? It would be logical. Anyone who reads the Notes section would probably be confused by the difference between the draft notes and the main text. Perhaps, someone wanted to hide the notes in *The Incomplete Manuscript* and hide the manuscript itself in another text on the Ganja earthquake in an attempt to lose it? It is hard to say for sure. But I am certain that the author had to destroy one of the two manuscripts—*The Book of Dada Gorgud* or *The Incomplete Manuscript*—and *The Incomplete Manuscript* was doomed to destruction. Then it didn't get fully destroyed. This is God's secret!

Here's a question that puzzles some of the best minds: How can a human being learn, by heart, the grand epics—the likes of *The Iliad, The Odyssey,* and *The Book of Dada Gorgud*—and pass them on to future generations without forgetting a single line? All kinds of scientific theories are put forward to answer this question. But important as it is to remember and pass on these great works, the principle of writing down the oral epics is no less important. Clearly, any text starts off as notes—the output from the writer's laboratory. *The Incomplete Manuscript,* tagged with No. A 21/733, is studded with notes by the author, who we can now say with confidence is the people's sage, Dada Gorgud.

Maybe it would be more accurate to call these notes observations. Why not? What does this change? Maybe those who doubted the unlimited powers of recall of an ozan, a shaman, or a poet were right. (Remember Russian academic, Fomenko,[22] and his group?) Regardless, *The Incomplete Manuscript* proves that the author, in seriously recording day-by-day, hour-by-hour what he witnessed, was preparing for a great examination. He was preparing to write the magnificent *Book of Dada Gorgud* that we know so well. This is confirmed by the style of those Notes and Observations sections in *The Incomplete Manuscript.* Later, we see how the separate sketches, sayings, and thoughts on style are made visual in *The Book of Dada Gorgud.* To be more accurate, though, it's actually the other way around. Today, we know that the descriptions of scenery, the stylistic twists and turns, and the quirks of speech in *The Book of Dada Gorgud* originated in the Notes section of *The Incomplete Manuscript.*

A wise man once said that Dada Gorgud will return to us. I don't know how, but I believe that he will definitely return. Another wise man said that manuscripts do not burn; they emerge unscathed from the flames. Earlier, we briefly mentioned only the first part of *The Incomplete Manuscript.* Why? What is the second part? Of course, what we refer to as the second or parallel part is in no way connected to the earthquake in Ganja. What is it then? One more secret emerges from within the secret. Studying *The Incomplete Manuscript,* readers will find that the main text presented as the Notes section breaks up in places, and the gaps are filled with content that, at first sight, seems incredible. The first piece gives no information on its origin; it leaves only a strange feeling, an odd doubt. However, all doubts are later dispelled.

The second parallel part of *The Incomplete Manuscript* concerns a period in the life of Shah Ismail Khata'i, Ruler of Azerbaijan and Iran.[23] It is an extraordinary story—more literary tale than historical record. It is important to note that the story of Dada Gorgud and the story of Shah Ismail have been

---

[22] Russian mathematician, Anatoliy Fomenko, supports a revision of chronological history. He says that the dates on which historical events are believed to have occurred do not correspond with a mathematical analysis. He says that much ancient history (such as the history of ancient Greece and Rome) in fact took place in the Middle Ages.

[23] Shah Ismail (1487 to 1524), founder of the Safavid dynasty, ruled Iran from 1502 to 1524. A Shia Muslim from Ardabil, Shah Ismail initially ruled over Azerbaijan only, but by 1510, he controlled the whole of Persia. Shah Ismail made Shia Islam the religion of his state. Under the pen name Khata'i, Shah Ismail wrote poetry in Azerbaijani Turkish.

conceived differently. (Dada Gorgud's section is much larger.) Although each text speaks in its own language, the two texts follow and complete one another. Shah Ismail, Lele, the Vizier, Lady Tajli, and Khizir take the reader into another world and shake the foundations of our imaginations.

At the same time, one of the main questions rises up like a column before our eyes: Why does *The Incomplete Manuscript,* carefully framed within the Ganja earthquake, divide into two? Maybe the two manuscripts are interlinking combs? Why? Is one hiding within the other?

Something was bothering me, not about the Shah Ismail story, but about the Dada Gorgud Notes section. Was it not a sin to touch the secret, virgin notes? Is it right to reveal this secret? If *The Incomplete Manuscript* consisted of only notes and observations, then perhaps, it would not be so bad. But the notes were wrapped around an enigma. Maybe it would be better to say that these notes, scattered throughout the text, accompany the main subject.

In modern parlance, this subject is a real investigation process—a real investigation into the ancient Oghuz community, into the ancient Oghuz state established by the Khan of Khans, Bayindir Khan, and an investigation recorded by the secretary, Dada Gorgud! Readers will see that both the investigated and the investigators will later become the primary and secondary characters in *The Book of Dada Gorgud.*

Maybe the primary characters in *The Book of Dada Gorgud* are incidental in *The Incomplete Manuscript,* or perhaps, the heroes in *The Incomplete Manuscript* are secondary and tertiary characters in *The Book of Dada Gorgud.* In fact, this investigation casts light on some obscure passages in *The Book of Dada Gorgud.* Without getting ahead of ourselves, we can say that the investigation reveals the main reason for the outbreak of war in the *The Book of Dada Gorgud* between the Inner Oghuz and the Outer Oghuz.[24]

Readers will be plunged into a situation that is both complex and terrible, as well as simple and comical. People in that distant time lived with the same feelings that we have today; they breathed like us; and they had the same anxieties and concerns. It is almost as if such a long period of time never separated us. While style changed, the actual substance remained the same. Obviously, one can't say that life was exactly the same as it is today, but it really has not changed very much.

It wouldn't be a bad idea to mention the reason that led to the investigation. Like all significant events, this story begins with a minor detail that is

---

[24] The Inner and Outer Oghuz are two branches of the Turkic Oghuz tribe, which migrated west from Siberia and Altay via Central Asia to the Caucasus and eastern Turkey.

instantly forgotten: Salur Gazan is informed that there is an enemy spy among the Oghuz. This spy is a real saboteur, passing state secrets to the enemy. For example, Salur Gazan goes hunting. The enemy is informed that it is an opportune moment to go and plunder the Oghuz. In this instance, I think that the author is predicting (with amazing foresight!) the earthquake that happened many years later in distant Ganja. Additionally, he foresees the attack of a ruthless enemy on this ruined city.

This is not the thought of an ordinary man. Later, Beyrak is preparing to get married. The spy does his work again. This time, according to *The Book of Dada Gorgud,* enemies kidnap Beyrak and hold him captive in Bayburd[25] for sixteen years. In another instance, Bakil breaks his leg, and the spy reports the information and so on. Over time, the spy's activities badly hurt the Oghuz, and Salur Gazan is resolute in his intention to find and arrest the spy.

The spy is arrested, but the problems do not end there; on the contrary, that's when they really begin. *The Incomplete Manuscript* reads: "Foaming at the mouth, the Oghuz noblemen insist that the spy be chopped in two." Instead, they completely change their position once the spy has been arrested and do their best to set him free—and they manage it. A council is held, and the noblemen cast their votes. Ultimately, the spy is released at midnight. He is told to leave the Oghuz and to disappear completely.

The investigation begins shortly after the spy's release. The Khan of Khans, Bayindir Khan, finds out about the story and begins to try and figure out exactly who released the spy. He sets up a real investigation and involves the splendid Oghuz noblemen, Salur Gazan, Shirshamsaddin, Bakil, and Old Aruz. Soon, other noblemen and women bring news to and from the Khan of Khans, sometimes helping, sometimes confusing the investigation with their information.

Dada Gorgud is the only secretary, or reporter in other words, of the first investigation in Oghuz society. The Notes and Observations sections he recorded during the investigation can be seen as sketches for his future great work, *The Book of Dada Gorgud.* It is another question whether or not he planned from the start to write the epic. The nature of his notes taken during and outside the investigation implies that he did.

The nucleus and spirit of *The Incomplete Manuscript* rest on a tightened rope. As the various heroes twist over and under this tightrope like acrobats, they reveal themselves, their inner worlds, and their essence. All the while, Dada Gorgud, standing on one side of the tightrope—or perhaps, sitting

---

[25] Bayburd is a city in modern-day Turkey. In *The Book of Dada Gorgud,* it is a place from which the heroes start military campaigns.

beneath it—closely watches their every action and inscribes all that he sees and hears. Most importantly, he writes everything down on paper, ultimately crafting his words into *The Incomplete Manuscript.* This incompleteness makes a complete whole in our imaginations today.

Doubts will eat away at me. Tell me, am I right to publish this work, *The Incomplete Manuscript,* so that I can present it to the reader? Admittedly, the whole concept is a bit strange. However, as much as I sought out an answer to this question, I couldn't find one.

Prologue II: Do the Differences in the World Matter to God?

A separate manuscript looks out of the original manuscript. What did it remind me of? I remembered Islamic script, hidden cravenly behind Christian decorations in Alcazar Palace in Seville, scarcely visible today. It looks as though the victors thought that the writing of the Christian era would be nearer to God when it stood bravely on the letters of the enemy. But maybe that Muslim writing, lost to view but reawoken by time, is also addressed to God? Maybe both pieces of writing are an expression of the same desire? Are they both addressed to God?

This rarity, recorded as *The Incomplete Manuscript* in all bibliographic sources, is in fact something very different: The manuscript harbors a secret. It bears hidden within itself a culture different from the one it describes. This may seem ridiculous at first sight. The existence of another manuscript within the original manuscript creates new questions. From what and from who is this deeply buried writing being protected? Furthermore, is there a reason why this carefully protected writing has survived to our day? Will the value of this protection be known?

I feel like I am inside some kind of incomprehensible horror—that I am facing inadmissible reality. I remember the words of physicist, Niels Bohr, to Wolfgang Pauli, "Your theory is crazy, but it is not crazy enough to be true!" In closing the invisible circle of higher logic, the Great Impossible without fail turns into the Great Truth. There must be something in it.

I think that *The Incomplete Manuscript,* despite its deceptive incompleteness, will make great changes to studies about *The Book of Dada Gorgud.* It will cast light on some of the obscure meanings. But the reality presented by this text can also be doubted. Huseyn Javid's saying, "A man is right to doubt," lives today and will live on in the future.[26] But one thing is clear: From now on, everything will no longer look frozen, monumental, or lifeless. Many characters, who were created in accord with the laws of mythical poetry and are in some way statuesque, are suddenly released from frozen immobility in *The Incomplete Manuscript.* In fact, they begin to love, hate, be faithful, cheat, scheme, laugh, and cry. In other words, they begin to truly live. Above all, readers will see them as ordinary people. They are living, breathing people before they are noblemen and sons of noblemen, khans, and sons of khans.

Additionally, ancient Oghuz society begins to be seen in its real, spiritual context. Dada Gorgud's preparatory notes, observations, and sketches open like a gauze curtain to reveal ideas and meanings that have lost their true outline and become the invention of the artist. When the clouds disappear from the sky, the blue depths of infinity look greater, and you come nearer to God, to the greater, higher truth.

We do not have to note all the meanings in *The Incomplete Manuscript* that require explanation; there is no need. The reader, I am sure, will not get lost inside the text. A prior commentary has claims to be a scientific introduction, and we are a long way from making any such claims. It would be more appropriate to leave our personal, subjective interpretations at the places where *The Incomplete Manuscript* is cut off, or where it leaves certain things unsaid.

We thought it would be more effective if these explanations were given throughout the text and decided to provide them in a very specific script within the text of *The Incomplete Manuscript.* Readers will see this in the change of font. Readers will also see some text that is set apart from the regular text in this book. This text consists of notes from *The Incomplete Manuscript*'s own author.

Another important point must be taken into consideration. We have already noted that the main part of *The Incomplete Manuscript* actually leads in two different but parallel directions that complement one another. One direction is the record of the investigation carried out by Bayindir Khan (written down by the secretary Dada Gorgud) into an extraordinary event in Oghuz society. The second direction is the special notes, observations, and sketches of the author, also known as Dada Gorgud. The investigation process in itself probably pushed this wise man to a deeper understanding and better appraisal of many "good people of the Oghuz."

---

[26] Huseyn Javid was an Azerbaijani poet and playwright. During Stalin's purges, he was exiled to Siberia, where he died in 1941.

Nothing stops seeing Dada Gorgud's notes as a kind of stenographic record of the investigation. Besides, these notes are an undeniable statement of his intent to write *The Book of Dada Gorgud.* It would be impossible to create this laborious, magnificent work without such notes. The reflections of the author on characters and heroes, moments, or events can be considered to be as close to objectivity as possible. This is how it is in *The Incomplete Manuscript.* We often come across acute transformations in the literary text that is the *The Book of Dada Gorgud.* From this viewpoint, *The Incomplete Manuscript* differs quite a lot from the familiar text of *The Book of Dada Gorgud.*

Why have the objective (or maybe subjective)—let's keep it simple for now—relevant notes of *The Incomplete Manuscript* been so transformed in the text of *The Book of Dada Gorgud?* Is it the author's indifference, or is it the requirement of the client who is directly showing his adherence to the concept of statehood that is so fashionable today? Was it seen as promoting the spiritual development of the people? Personally, I think that the major differences between the people in *The Book of Dada Gorgud* and *The Incomplete Manuscript* and the reason for these differences have no importance to the Highest Truth—the Supreme Being who bears the name of God.

Prologue III: The Right to Say, "I Don't Know"

Maybe *The Incomplete Manuscript* has one main difference from all other incomplete manuscripts: It doesn't have a beginning or an end. Maybe it is a souvenir of the time of the Ganja earthquake. It may also be because Dada Gorgud didn't conceive the text as a linear novel, orderly and systematic, with a meaning that we could understand. In fact, it has both a beginning and an end for the author. Many passages in *The Incomplete Manuscript* make it clear that there *was* a beginning. If that's so, then the text appears incomplete only to us.

Sometimes, I wonder if I am doing something immoral—as if I am picking someone's pocket, spying on someone through a keyhole, or reading someone's private, intimate letters, revealing a big secret. Throughout my reading, these anxious feelings did not give me any peace. But the answer ultimately came by itself. If God knew what was required and sent this to my brain, my job is small; this has nothing to do with me. If *The Incomplete Manuscript* tells me to speak, I do not have the right to be silent.

Now, you decide: Am I right to present *The Incomplete Manuscript* to you or not? I am still seeking an answer to this question. Strangely, however, shortly after I had written this prologue and asked if I should share *The Incomplete Manuscript* with the world, I suddenly drifted off to sleep. My head rested on the writing table, and as I started to dream, I began to view myself from afar. This took a very short time. I saw a man in my dream. The appearance—the face and the figure of this man—disappeared from my mind the moment I woke up. But I clearly remembered the following short dialogue between us:

"Why did you do it?" the man asked.

"I don't know," I replied.

May God protect those who do not know from the wrath of those who do. Amen.

The Manuscript

...the wise men of the city saw that the people were suffering after the calamitous earthquake in Ganja just on the...day Bayindir Khan wanted me at his side again. I came to Gunortaj, the Khan's residence, and greeted him with a courteous bow. Bayindir Khan asked me, "Do you know why I have summoned you, Gorgud, my son?"

I replied, "I know not, majestic Khan."

"Gorgud, my son, only you can do it. I have chosen you," Bayindir Khan said. "We shall work together. I have heard news. I have heard that all is not well amongst the Oghuz; maybe you have heard something, too. There was a spy. He was captured, but then his dungeon was opened, and the spy was set free. Tell me whatever you know. Let's get to the bottom of this together." Bayindir Khan fell silent.

Although I had heard of the matter of which Bayindir Khan spoke, I kept my counsel and waited. Bayindir Khan's face slowly began to redden, and I sensed that he was struggling to keep his temper. He looked at me intently. "So you have truly heard nothing? Nothing? Yes, you!" He said nothing more. Instead, he just stood and stared at me, waiting for my answer.

Can I tell a lie to Bayindir Khan, the Khan of Khans? I wondered, trying not to panic. *He has troops, the blackest of slaves, an executioner, a prison, and a torture chamber.* Finally, I spoke up. "I heard, my Khan, I also heard some bad things," I confessed. I held my breath, wondering what he would say next. *The Khan suspects something, but his asking me means that he does not know everything. What should I say? God, help me! How can I know how much he knows before he hits the blank wall of unknowing? How should I lead him through that wall? Almighty God, you are my inspiration.*

"What did you hear? Speak! What has clouded your clear gaze? Aren't you here? Gorgud!" The Khan's voice was gradually getting louder.

"My Khan, I was thinking. Whatever you say, whatever you think can come to pass in this mortal world, my Khan, whatever comes to your mind, you may see in this life," I replied quickly and apologetically. My words seemed to please Bayindir Khan. He smiled. *I need to remember these fine words,* I thought, *breathing a sigh of relief. I may use them again.*

Suddenly, Bayindir Khan turned his attention away from me. I followed his gaze to see what he was looking at out the palace window. A small bird was caught in the thorns of some rose bushes in the palace yard, struggling desperately to free itself. As Bayindir Khan continued to watch the bird, I, too, studied it for a few moments. It looked as if it would be able to get free.

"Gilbash, go and take that poor bird out of the thorns!" Bayindir Khan ordered in a very low voice. I thought the Khan's request was strange; there was nobody else in his chamber. Seconds later, however, Gilbash was outside, dutifully lifting the bird free of the thorns.

"Then come here, Gilbash," Bayindir Khan added quietly.

I was puzzled. *How did Gilbash hear the whispered words of Bayindir Khan from the opposite side of the yard?* But a little later, Gilbash was back in the Khan's chamber with us.

Gilbash was Bayindir Khan's shadow—his breath, his soul, and his mind. Nobody among the Oghuz could gainsay him. Indeed, Gilbash had no words of his own. He said only Bayindir Khan's words. Gilbash would bring a message. Gilbash would take a message. Gilbash would speak to the Oghuz nobles and require them to take action. In a word, Gilbash was close to the Khan. True, Bayindir Khan had a Vizier, and it was not Gilbash. The Vizier was a man by the name of Old Gazilig. The Khan would discuss affairs of state with Old Gazilig. But when there were important, confidential matters needing resolution, Bayindir Khan would tackle them with the help of Gilbash. Such was Gilbash.

Once, Salur Gazan told me the story of Gilbash. Bayindir Khan took Gilbash to his palace when the latter was a child. Gipchag had captured his family, and he had been born in captivity. With great trouble, his father and mother sent word to the Khan that they needed nothing for themselves; they only wanted Bayindir Khan to redeem their son from captivity. After this message, they cunningly freed the child from bondage. He went to Bayindir Khan for protection. As Bayindir Khan knew his father, he became the child's patron. And now, Gilbash keeps all the secrets and mysteries of Bayindir Khan. But...

Bayindir Khan did not move away from the window that overlooked the yard until Gilbash approached the throne. Even in the worst of times, I had never seen him like this—stretched taut as a bow. I assumed that Bayindir Khan was about to raise some matters of importance; he had summoned Gilbash, after all.

> *When I got this far in* The Incomplete Manuscript, *I agreed with the Manuscripts Institute staff; it didn't seem very interesting. Furthermore, the young Orientalist was right.* The Incomplete Manuscript *was definitely about something quite different.* What are Bayindir Khan, Gilbash, and Dada Gorgud talking about? *I wondered.* What has happened among the Oghuz? What language are they speaking? *My next thought was that the young Orientalist had "massaged" the text for me, so to speak, in an attempt to make it sound strange on purpose. Deep down, however, I thought that was pretty unlikely. I continued reading...*

Bayindir Khan sensed that Gilbash had already entered the room; he was inside. Turning to us, he studied us both intently. "You will unravel this mystery, both of you," Bayindir Khan said. He gestured toward me, his gaze now flashing with anger. "Gorgud, you will write everything down. Whatever happens in this room, whatever words are spoken, you will write them down one by one." Then Bayindir Khan turned to Gilbash. "Gilbash, no man or woman can leave the Oghuz until this matter is resolved. Raiding, hunting, traveling—they must all wait. Whomsoever I summon must come here immediately, and then we will see. One more thing: Do whatever you must, Gilbash, but be sure that our words and discussions stay here," he said. "They must be buried here. No man can pass our words to another—no man, not even Old Gazilig. This affair should not grow. Do you understand?"

Gilbash and I stood there solemnly. We didn't say a word.

Bayindir Khan continued. "We must find the culprit," he said quietly. "Whatever it may cost." With that, he stared at us intently again for a few moments before turning toward the yard and going up to the window. "Gilbash will explain whatever you did not understand," he added. "Now go." The last words were addressed to me. Gilbash and I immediately left the Khan's chamber.

As we walked down the long passage, I quickly looked sideways at my companion. "Tell me, Gilbash," I said with urgency in my voice. "What was Bayindir Khan talking about?"

A few minutes later, we entered the yard of the Khan's palace. The elm tree in the middle of the yard had spread its shade over the green grass. We sat down on the carpet of shade, and I waited for Gilbash to fill me in. Gilbash was calm and serious. He looked me directly in the eyes and began speaking.

"Our Khan, of course, has great trust in us," he said slowly. "So we must be faithful in return. What do you say, Gorgud?"

"What can I say? I agree with you," I replied. "So the Khan is going to hold an inquiry, Gilbash?" At last, I could express what had been bothering me.

"Yes, the Khan will organize the inquiry," Gilbash answered. "The spy did not escape by himself. You know this; I know this; a babe-in-arms of the Inner Oghuz knows this. He did not turn into a bird and fly away into the sky, nor did he turn into a mouse and burrow his way out through the earth. He was freed from captivity and helped to flee the country. Of course, someone is behind this. Our duty is to find that person to satisfy the Khan…"

I had been agreeing all along with Gilbash. Do I have any other way out? I wondered, knowing that I didn't. Gilbash looked at me intently while he was speaking. His small eyes wanted to look right into my heart. A thought raced through my mind. No doubt, someone has reported this news to Bayindir Khan. But who? If only I could trick Gilbash into revealing that information. I knew there was no use anymore; the arrow had already been shot from the bow. It didn't matter who the informer was. Terrible events were about to take place. Who can withstand Bayindir Khan's interrogation, or his bloodshot, piercing gaze? I wondered. Oh, noblemen, what days await us? Help us, almighty God!

"Where have you flown off to, Gorgud?" Gilbash's voice brought me back to the shade of the elm tree.

"Me?" I asked, startled. "I am with you, Gilbash."

Gilbash shook his head. "You were miles away. Pay attention. Listen to me," he replied. "I think we should begin with Gazan. Let no one say among the Oghuz that Bayindir Khan tried to spare his son-in-law."

"So we start with Gazan?"

"Yes, we do. Then Shirshamsaddin, Bakil, and Old Aruz."

"And Beyrak," I added carefully.

"What could Beyrak do? He is beyond doubt," Gilbash said coldly, attaching no importance to my interruption. It was clear that he wanted to change the subject immediately. His voice softened. "Gorgud, Beyrak is still Beyrak. To spend sixteen years in captivity—and in a place like Bayburd…" his voice trailed off as he thought for a moment. "Not every warrior can enjoy a comfortable life there. That Beyrak is very cunning. Where does he get this intelligence from?"

"Beyrak is Bamsi Beyrak, the Gray Stallion. He has been clever since he was a small child," I said as simply as I could, thinking, *Of course, all his tricks will fade one day, like the mist when the sun breaks through.* "I heard that not long ago, Beyrak entered Bayindir Khan's service. Didn't he, Gilbash?" I then asked innocently.

Gilbash nodded. "He did, but this has nothing to do with it."

I realized Gilbash was not interested in discussing Beyrak at all, and this was a serious sign. Gilbash stood up and so did I. We crossed the yard toward the Black Gate. Seeing me off, Gilbash said, "Gorgud, come tomorrow at first light. Bring your pen and paper. I have one request of you: For the love of God, don't breathe a word to anyone of what you have heard here. You saw yourself that this is the order of the Khan."

"You said not to speak about this, and I will not speak," I said quietly.

"Yes, do not speak about this. We will do as our Khan advises," Gilbash said.

"I agree," I replied.

"Then, good luck! May your way be clear. Go. Come tomorrow," Gilbash said, turning away to go back toward the palace.

"Almighty God, protect you! Until we meet again," I said, adding, "Be in good health, Gilbash." With that, I mounted my horse and left the Khan's yard. Galloping away, I quickly left Gunortaj Palace behind.

I don't know how I reached the cave at the foot of the Red Mountain. I dismounted and my horse went to graze. I sat at the entrance to the cave, leaning my elbows against the base of the Stone of Light.[39] I sat like that for a long time. Thoughts were running through my mind like racehorses, none of which I could catch. Dark uncertainties gnawed at my heart. *What is to be done if Bayindir Khan is aware of the spy affair?* I wondered. *It will go ill with us. Ashes will be thrown upon our heads.*

Night had already fallen. I began to doze. As every night, the moon completed its course across the skies. *What good can come of the night?* I wondered. Finally, I entered the cave. I lay my head on a bed of stone and covered myself with a cloak of camel skin. But no matter how hard I tried, I could not fall asleep before midnight. Different questions began spinning around, tangling up my mind: *What am I to do? Suddenly, Boghazja Fatma will close her eyes and open her mouth? No, of course not. It wouldn't be a bad idea to meet her and tell her what to say if she is summoned by the Khan, but the hennas do not match. Bayindir Khan, not to mention Gilbash, will carefully examine every hair. They may spot something. Of course, they will be difficult. Beyrak, this Beyrak, Beyrak the informer? Did you inform on us to the Khan? Has Lady Burla turned you from the right path, Beyrak? Is it possible without Lady Burla? Did you slaver like a young bull?*

---

[39] This is the author's invention.

> *When does a young bull salivate? It's obvious—like scoundrel sons of scoundrels who see a beautiful girl for the first time and cannot stop themselves slavering at the mouth. "Slavering bullock" does not apply only to Beyrak; it applies to all the young noblemen of the Oghuz, too.*

Beyrak, take care now. After this, not even almighty God can protect you. Who else is there? Gazan, husband of the Khan's daughter, Lady Burla? Every day sent by God, they quarrel and fight. However, Gazan is Salur Gazan. Gazan would never be an enemy to Bayindir Khan. The Khan knows this full well. The Khan has infinite faith in Gazan. In that case, investigating Gazan is like drawing a veil over people's eyes, isn't it? On the other hand, Lady Burla will calm down a little. Will it be so bad if Gazan's nose is rubbed a little, and all the Oghuz see that the Khan is just, and then they'll express their thanks to him? Not bad at all, I thought.

During the inquiry, though, what if Gazan says that I told him to release the spy? What if Old Aruz says the same? Or Shirshamsaddin? No, he doesn't have the brains, and Bakil won't act against me; he would be afraid to cause me harm. Old Aruz? Yes, he may sing! Old Aruz and Boghazja Fatma are the weakest link—the link most likely to snap in the Khan's interrogation. Boghazja Fatma is a woman; it will be easy enough to confuse her. But Old Aruz is a wily fox. He would scatter the whole world to the winds without a sigh of regret. His arrogance is too great for the earth and sky. No one loves the arrogant. This is the truth.

Dump it all on Old Aruz, I thought. *This is the best way: Boghazja Fatma, Old Aruz, the spy. This link will suit everyone. Salur Gazan, yes. Lady Burla, yes. Shirshamsaddin? It will make no difference to him as long as his father, Gazan, is not troubled. Bakil? What could Bakil say in the inquiry? Gazan has offended Bakil. They cannot stand one another.*

> *Gazan explains the offense in one way; Bakil explains it in another way. Blessed is he who can make sense of it.*

Setting Bakil against Old Aruz will be the most important. If we can do it, Old Aruz's testimony will be worthless. Bayindir Khan will not listen to him at all. But this will not be easy to achieve, I thought. *Bakil will sooner tackle Beyrak and Gazan than do battle with Old Aruz, and Gilbash will see the ruse immediately. Well, let him see it. He will not defend Old Aruz; he has no cause to go against Gazan. Everyone is against Old Aruz, except for Bakil. The Oghuz have had enough of Old Aruz's scolding and arrogance: "Basat did this, Basat did that; Basat defeated the sly one-eyed ogre..."*

We must be incredibly careful. Old Aruz is crafty. We must not let this chance slip through our fingers. Beyrak is like game caught in a trap. Old

Aruz must suspect only Beyrak, I thought. *After all is said and done, the Khan truly needs the head of Old Aruz.* Half-sleeping, half-awake, I was lost in my thoughts for a while. I don't know how I slipped into slumber, but eventually I did.

§ § § § § §

When I woke early the next morning, the sun was already rising above the mountaintops. I hurried back to Bayindir Khan's court at Gunortaj. Pacing back and forth, Gilbash was anxiously waiting for me in the palace garden. Two tall, broad-shouldered warriors were standing nearby, ready to carry out orders. They bowed courteously in greeting.

Gilbash greeted me. "Good morning, Gorgud. The Khan has given the order: Salur Gazan must appear at court today. He will answer questions. Are you ready?" he asked, getting down to business.

"I am ready," I replied. *I guessed right in the night,* I thought. *Gilbash knew. The Khan has decided to begin with Gazan.*

Gilbash nodded and then turned to the warriors. "Go and call Lord Gazan to the Khan's court. Bayindir Khan has declared that he must appear immediately," he ordered.

Bowing, the warriors left without a word. They led two horses from the stables, mounted them, and galloped off through the Black Gate, soon disappearing from view. People were gradually gathering in the Khan's courtyard. Servants began bustling around the cattle shed—some busy milking cows, others lighting fires. The stalls and pens had been emptied, and the sheep and camels were being driven to pasture.

I saw two servants each leading a horse by the bridle through the Black Gate, and I recognized the horses immediately. I also remembered Beyrak. One of the horses was called Kechar, the Goat-Headed Stallion, and the other was Duru, the Sheep-Headed Stallion. They were the fastest horses in the Khan's stable. I had ridden one of the horses to arrange Beyrak's marriage. *May all the plans of Wild Gajar come to nothing,* I thought.

"Gorgud, come into the shade," Gilbash's voice brought me back to the Khan's courtyard. The sun was steadily approaching its place atop the high elm tree. We went into the shade of its boughs. Gilbash looked at me. "What do you think, Gorgud? Should we wait for Gazan or go and tell the Khan that we are here?"

"You know best, Gilbash," I said, feeling guarded.

At that moment, a manservant appeared and answered Gilbash's question. "The Khan summons you both," he said solemnly. Gilbash and I looked at each other and went to Bayindir Khan's chamber. When we entered the chamber, the Khan was sitting on his throne, lost in thought. He was downcast as before.

We bowed courteously in greeting and were greeted in return. Bayindir Khan then gestured to us to sit. We sat. "Do you know, Gorgud, my son, what is troubling me?" the Khan asked. Deep sorrow filled his eyes. "I am troubled because the famed and honorable noblemen of the Oghuz are today indifferent to the fate of the Oghuz—even Gazan. I did not expect Gazan to have a hand in this affair, too."

"Too," he said. If the Khan is testing me, then I better keep silent. If he is not, then it is still advisable to keep my counsel. If I say anything, it might arouse doubts and leave a mark on the Khan's heart, I thought. I remained silent.

Suddenly, Bayindir Khan turned to Gilbash. "Gilbash, has Gazan come yet?" he asked.

"He will come soon, my Khan. He has been sent for," Gilbash replied.

"Treat him with respect. He is our grandchild's father," Bayindir Khan said quietly. Once again, he turned his piercing gaze on me as if to silently ask what I thought about everything. I did not say a word. Instead, I fixed my eyes on the floor and bowed courteously. We stood in this pose for some time without speaking.

Suddenly the manservant came in. "My Khan, Lord Gazan has arrived with his son, Uruz. He seeks leave to enter," he said.

Gilbash and Bayindir Khan looked at one another. Bayindir Khan seemed surprised. "Uruz has come?" he asked. "Why has Uruz come as well?"

> *I was impressed by Gazan's presence of mind. Clearly, he foresaw it. By bringing his son along, he would inspire mercy in the Khan's heart—beautifully done.*

Gazan is lucky to get out of it. Now it is our turn, I thought. *God willing, he will not mention my name to the Khan.*

Gilbash gave the manservant a sign to leave the room. The servant left. When it was just the three of us again, Gilbash turned to face the Khan. "What should I do, my Khan?" he asked.

Bayindir Khan thought for a moment. "Do not let Uruz in yet. Let him go to the slaves in the courtyard and choose a new slave for himself. Tell the guards that he has my permission to visit the female slaves. It doesn't matter; he is still a child," he replied. "And then tell Gazan to come in."

Gilbash nodded. "As you command," he said. With that, he turned and left.

Bayindir Khan looked at me. "Stay in your place. Do you have a pen and paper?" he asked.

"Yes, my Khan," I replied. I sat cross-legged and made myself comfortable.

Bayindir Khan continued to look at me intently. "Gorgud, my son, write both my words and his. Do not miss a single word; put everything on paper. I want whoever may read it today or tomorrow to be fully aware of our affairs," he said. "What do you think? I do not think that Gazan is guilty. He has acted either out of naivety or tender-heartedness, compassion, or whatever else—I'm not sure."

The Khan was testing me without hiding it. "My Khan, Gazan is a brave man. His loyalty to you knows no bounds. Gazan is the pillar of the Oghuz," I responded. I had scarcely finished my words when Gazan came in. He had heard me, God willing.

Gilbash came in immediately after Gazan. Gazan dropped to his knees, crawled up to Bayindir Khan, and covered his hand in kisses. "Glory to the magnificent Khan," he said, bowing courteously. He threw a glance at me as though to ask, "What has happened?"

"Come, let me look at you, Gazan. Be seated. Tell me how you are. What news is there among the Oghuz? You have brought Uruz with you, haven't you? That was good of you," Bayindir Khan said. "Sit down, Gazan." He glanced at me. "Gorgud, my son, sit closer to Gazan. You keep doing your work, your writing." Then he pointed at Gilbash. "Gilbash, you come over here, too."

I saw that Gazan had not worked out what was going on. He clearly suspected something, or he would not have brought Uruz, but it seemed to me that he did not fully understand. After he had settled in his place, he stared at me again. There were a thousand questions in his eyes. I noticed that his hands were shaking a little; his fingers trembled. When he saw me looking at his hands, he quickly put them under a cushion.

Gazan looked up at the Khan. "My dear Khan, Uruz would not let me go without him. He said, 'You are going to see Grandfather? Take me, too!' I brought him to kiss your hand. What else was I to do?" he asked.

"You did right. You are welcome in my court. But you could have also brought Lady Burla with you," Bayindir Khan replied.

Everyone felt the mockery in the Khan's words, but Gazan did not respond. He took a deep breath. "Lady Burla bade us farewell, my Khan. She asked me to convey her warmest greetings to you, her father," he said calmly. "She said she visited you a few days ago and kissed your hand." Gazan was shrewd. He wanted the Khan to know that he knew that she had visited and conversed with her father. They were playing games and now they were equal.

Bayindir Khan frowned. Without further ado, he proceeded to the heart of the matter. "Gazan, do you know why I have summoned you?" he blurted.

Cloaking his face in astonishment and surprise, Gazan shook his head. "I know not, my father, my Khan," he said softly. "I was not told. I am ready to carry out any order from you, with my mind or my sword. Give me the honor of dying in your service! What has happened? Are you planning a raid? Will you not tell me?" When the Khan didn't immediately answer, Gazan looked around.

Without stopping writing, I glanced at the Khan, who was slowly stroking his beard. He nodded. "Gazan, all the world has heard of your bravery, your loyalty," he began. He paused for breath and looked at me to see if I was writing or not. I bent lower over my quill and, seeing that I was busy writing, he began to speak again. "I know well your loyalty to me, Gazan. There is no need to speak of it. I know that you are of noble lineage. The bird of Salur is your trusted friend. I have faith in you. I rely on you, Gazan. You are my son-in-law."

"Thank you, my father, my Khan," Gazan replied. "May your years be many and long. I beg you, give me the chance to lay down my dark head for you."

> *Look at this! What made him say "my dark head"? It was the first time I had heard it. Bravo, Gazan! My dark head, eh? But why "dark"? He should have said, "I sacrifice my dark head for you." No, that won't do. "I bring my dark head to you as a sacrifice," or "Accept as a sacrifice, my Khan," or "My Lord, my dark head..." That's much better, isn't it? I won't forget, God willing.*

Gazan continued. "Let me lay down my head for you, my Khan, I beg you!" he said. Suddenly, he began striking his forehead against the ground again and again, worshipping Bayindir Khan.

"Stand up, Gazan!" Bayindir Khan demanded. "Stop it! Do you think I take you for a stranger?" He glanced at Gilbash, confused by his son-in-law's strange behavior. "What is wrong with him, Gilbash?"

Gilbash quickly stepped forward and put his arms around Gazan, gently but firmly making him stop what he was doing. Gazan finally stopped hurting himself, but he continued to mumble. "My Khan, my father, who is dearer to me than my own father..." Finally, he composed himself and took his place again, sitting with his legs crossed.

Once he was sitting upright again, the Khan continued. "Gazan, my son, the sorrows of the Oghuz have not given me a moment's peace," he said. "The sorrows of the Oghuz are terrible. We had a spy amongst the Oghuz, Gazan—a spy!"

"Really, my Khan, a *spy?*" Gazan asked in disbelief. His surprise sounded so genuine that I almost believed him. I was amazed. Suddenly, I felt a sharp pain. Something made me turn and look at the Khan. His eyes were boring into my soul.

"Don't stop writing, my son, Gorgud," Bayindir Khan said forcefully. His voice had changed, and his words were cold as river water. He turned back to face Gazan. "See, Gazan, even Gorgud was struck by your sincerity. You are sure you know nothing of this matter?" he asked slowly.

"Nothing, my Khan, nothing," Gazan said quickly. "There was a spy, and he received his due. We caught him, yes, and we threw him in a pit and held him prisoner. We showed him the taste of blood. We drove him out of Oghuz. He has disappeared without trace, gone far beyond our borders. God willing, he will never return. We crushed him, my Khan. We destroyed him."

"Really?" the Khan asked, raising his eyebrows. "You say you destroyed him. How? Did you chop him in two? If so, may that be an example to all. Did you behead him? I am pleased with you, Gazan, if that's what you did. Or wait, maybe you threw him head first down a cliff, and the wolves and the vultures ate him up? That would be no evil. You did say you destroyed him, though, Gazan? Have I understood you right?"

Gazan hung his head like a guilty child, his body tense. I think he was inwardly trembling. "No, we did not chop him in two," he mumbled, forcing out the words.

"You did not chop him in two?" the Khan thundered.

"No, my father, my Khan. But I would have you know that I am not guilty!" Gazan cried. He was in shock.

"Gazan, can you assure me of this?"

"My father, my Khan," Gazan whispered.

The Khan took a deep breath, trying to remain calm. "Gazan, I am asking you again. Do not make me angry, Gazan. Can your tongue speak the truth?" he asked.

"Yes, my father, my Khan. I swear by your life that my tongue will not lie," Gazan answered. "It will tell only the truth."

What do you call the truth, Gazan? If you were to tell the truth, you would bring fresh disasters upon your dark head. Was that the truth that you spoke? Who knows the truth but almighty God? You say you will speak the truth. Then speak! Say that Boghazja Fatma came. She told me that the spy—the wretch you put in prison—is my son and your son, Gazan. Say the truth! But then forget me, Gazan. Forget about me once and for all. But when disaster befalls you, do not come looking for Gorgud...

"No, do not swear on my life," Bayindir Khan said.

"On my young son, Uruz," Gazan said quickly.

"No!" bellowed the Khan, now furious.

Gazan hesitated. "So what shall I do?" Suddenly, feeling inspired, he said, "Very well, my Khan. I swear on the life of my white-haired, old mother. I am not guilty on my mother's life."

Bayindir Khan's anger spread its wings and flew away, like the little bird freed from the thorns earlier. He nodded. "Now I believe you. All the Oghuz know the worth of your oath. You love your mother very much. This I know," he said.

At this moment, Bayindir Khan smiled slightly. He was probably remembering Gazan's deal with King Shokli. The story was well-known. All the Oghuz knew about it. King Shokli raided Oghuz, captured women and warriors, and then took them away. At that time, Salur Gazan, the Oghuz's Lord of Lords, was away on a hunting expedition with the best warriors from the army. He had left his lands defenseless. He had to answer to Bayindir Khan for this. The enemies combed through Oghuz.

But most memorable was the message that Gazan, preparing his revenge, sent to King Shokli: "Keep all that you have plundered. Have my wife and my son for servants; only give back my mother." Afterward, giving an account of himself to Bayindir Khan, Gazan said he had sent the message as a "trick." Whether Bayindir Khan believed him or not is hard to say. In short, Gazan set out for the enemy, and other Oghuz nobles followed him. They rescued the prisoners and crushed the enemy.

When Lady Burla heard of Gazan's words, she did not speak to her husband for exactly one year. "You sold me for your mother. You sold your son. You sold your people. You are a scoundrel son of a scoundrel!" She spoke these words in my presence; I heard them.

Gazan protested, "This was a war ruse. It is not a woman's concern!" however, despite how much he pleaded, it was fruitless. Gazan was forced to come to Gunortaj, to Bayindir Khan's court, and speak to him. After that, Bayindir Khan sent Lady Burla a command. Gilbash delivered his order: "A woman is a woman; she should not interfere in the military affairs of men. Gazan is our son, our son-in-law, and he will remain so forever. Burla, my daughter, sit where you should sit. Be silent where you should be silent. You must obey your husband!" This is what Gilbash said.

Lady Burla obeyed her father and forgave Gazan. From that day on, whenever any Oghuz nobleman swears by his mother's name, he remembers Gazan.

"I believe your oath. Now tell me all, Gazan," the Khan said. With that, he descended from his throne and stood before Gazan. Then he inspected him from head to toe and then looked deep into his eyes. "Tell me who helped the spy escape. He wasn't a bird, after all. Someone helped him, right? Who tricked the guard like a child and helped the spy escape? Tell me who, Gazan!" he demanded. When Gazan said nothing, the Khan shook his head. "Gilbash!" he called out and turned to go back to his throne.

Gilbash was strong. Without hesitation, he grabbed Gazan's neck from behind and squeezed so hard that Gazan lost consciousness and fell to the ground. Alone, Gazan had the heart of a chicken. Everyone in Oghuz knew that.

"Splash water on his face," Bayindir Khan ordered Gilbash.

Gilbash nodded and picked up the water pitcher from the table at the far side of the room. He hurried over to Gazan and poured water onto Gazan's head. The water splashed onto his face and soaked through his clothes to his skin. Moments later, Gazan shivered and came to again.

Bayindir Khan looked at his son-in-law. "Gazan, my son, what's wrong with you? Did you faint?" he asked.

"Nothing, my Khan, nothing at all. I don't know what happened to me. The world went black and I passed out," he replied. Narrowing his eyes, he looked at Gilbash. "Give me that water. I'm thirsty."

Gilbash gave Gazan the pitcher of water. Gazan drank greedily as though he had not had water in a thousand years. *Is he going to drink a river or what?* I mused to myself.

Bayindir Khan looked first at me and then at Gazan. "Go on writing, Gorgud, my son. I'll ask you once again, Gazan. A moment ago, you swore an oath. Speak the truth. Who helped the spy escape? You will tell me yourself or—"

"Aruz released him, my Khan!" Gazan blurted. "My Khan, it was Aruz!"

"Your uncle?" Bayindir Khan asked.

"Yes, my Khan, it was Uncle Aruz," Gazan replied.

"You mean, Old Horse-Mouthed Aruz?" the Khan asked again.

Bayindir Khan put it wonderfully. Old Aruz's mouth really did look like a horse's. Old Horse-Mouthed Aruz—what a name! I must remember it. To my amazement, a moment later, Gazan was using the nickname for Old Aruz. Gazan was already giving voice to the thoughts flashing across my mind. Maybe he can sense my thoughts and repeat them? I will put this to the test.

"Yes, my Khan, Old Horse-Mouthed Aruz released that spy," Gazan repeated. He glanced at me as though seeking my approval. I nodded my head several times, trying to give him a secret sign. *Yes, you are on the right track, Gazan. Continue like this and everything will be all right, God willing. You are on the right track,* I thought.

"I am telling the truth, my Khan, believe me. Aruz is the cause of all the misfortunes. I swear on my mother's name. If you do not believe me, ask Lady Burla," Gazan said more courageously. "Aruz is a disaster upon the Oghuz. You spoke the truth when you said Old Horse-Mouthed Aruz."

Gazan could barely resist giving me a sign. But God spared us, and we escaped this danger.

Bayindir Khan seated himself comfortably without saying a word and began gently stroking his beard. He kept silent for some time. We could see that he was lost in thought. His eyes were fixed as he gazed off, unblinking. Gilbash and I glanced at one another. Bayindir Khan was making his decision. Thoughts raced through my mind. *Can Gazan lead the Khan the way he wants him to go? What will happen if I'm suddenly asked about Old Aruz?* One thing was clear: Old Aruz had to be sacrificed. There was no going back. His being Gazan's maternal uncle would be further proof that the Khan's decision was unbiased.

No love was lost between Salur Gazan and Old Aruz, nephew and maternal uncle. Although they were almost the same age, Old Aruz had never wanted to be young. He had grown a beard and moustache ahead of time, and looked much older than young Gazan. I chose his name, Old Aruz. And now Bayindir Khan had added a new nickname, Old Horse-Mouthed Aruz. Perhaps, people would one day think that Gorgud, the scribe, invented this name. Bayindir Khan would not wish to be known as the giver of names. Although he did not look at me when he said the name "Old Horse-Mouthed Aruz," his voice implied that he was telling me the nickname. He was saying, "Remember this, Gorgud, my son."

The mutual hatred between nephew and uncle had an obvious and deep cause, but it also had a cause that was well hidden out of sight and mind—a forgotten cause. While Bayindir Khan was immersed in thought, I recalled that cause.

Times were hard in Oghuz. An unknown tribe came and camped on a spur of Mount Gazilig, cutting off the waters of the River Buzlusel, one of the tributaries of the mountain River Sellama. They liked the place so much that they decided to settle there. No one could understand their language or find out what they wanted.

I was sent to them. The Oghuz noblemen, assembled in council around Gazan, told me, "Tell them not to cut off our water. We will give them whatever they want." They also said, "This is Bayindir Khan's command. He said Gorgud should go to meet their leaders. We give our consent to whatever their terms may be." The noblemen were openly sending me to my death.

Their chief had one eye and was weak and sickly. His eye gave me a terrible look as though he wanted to devour me alive. I stood rooted to the spot. Almighty God, bring me home safely to Oghuz, I said in my heart, seeking shelter in the Stone of Light, and taking refuge in the skies and beseeching God.

"You must give us two men and one hundred sheep every day. Then we will unblock the river," said a man who knew our language, kneeling near the one-eyed chief. The chief squeaked something inaudible, his voice matching his appearance. The same interpreter shouted his words to me, "Or else after cutting off your water, we will cut off your air. We will lay waste the Oghuz! That is our last word."

"What do you need two men every day for?" I asked the interpreter.

"We will eat the sheep, and our chief will eat the men's hearts," the translator said, looking lovingly at One-Eye.

What horror! I thought. They eat people! With that, I bade leave to return.

"Go," they said. "But if early tomorrow you do not do as we requested, our understanding will be rendered worthless. You will have only yourself to blame."

I don't know how I got back to Oghuz. I went to Gazan and recounted everything. The nobles were troubled and thought long and hard.

Bayindir Khan suddenly stood up, went to the window, and looked out at the yard. "Gilbash!" he called out. Gilbash immediately went up to him, bowing. "Gilbash, another bird has gotten caught in the thorns; it is covered in blood. Go and take him out of the thorns. Let him fly away. Let him live," the Khan instructed. He thought for a moment before quietly continuing. "It doesn't matter that it is a bird. A bird, too, wants to live, to breathe, to spread its wings and soar up into the blue sky."

Gilbash rescued the bird from the thorns and let it go. When he came back to us, Bayindir Khan was looking at Gazan intently. "So, Gazan, you are accusing Aruz, are you?" he asked, pacing back and forth. "This is what you said. Why would Aruz have done this? I mean, the spy, why did Araz set him free? Why did he defy the nobles? Aruz is not stupid. When he takes hold of a task, he knows beforehand what he will do. So he must have had a secret purpose—"

"Father Khan…" Gazan sought permission to speak.

"He will not do anything without a purpose. What did you say?" Bayindir Khan asked impatiently.

"Father Khan, the spy was already his. By setting him free, Aruz actually released one of his own men. Am I not right?" Gazan asked.

Bayindir Khan fell silent again. Everything was going well. The spy was spying for the enemy; the spy was Old Aruz's man; and Old Aruz was well aware of his every move. Old Aruz directed his every move himself, so Old Aruz himself betrayed Oghuz. Everything was already clear. The investigation could be considered finished. *May God help us,* I thought.

If the Khan knew or realized who used the spy to inform Bayburd of Beyrak's wedding, what would happen then? This message came from Old Aruz, but who incited him to do it? Almighty God, come to our assistance…

"You are saying that Aruz set the spy free, aren't you?" Bayindir Khan asked Gazan slyly.

"Set him free, Khan! Set him free," Gazan said promptly, without thinking.

I suddenly realized that Bayindir Khan knew everything. He knew that Gazan had summoned a council of the noblemen and held a vote. He knew that no single person had set the spy free; the noblemen had all agreed that he was innocent and decided that he should be released. If Bayindir Khan knew this, then why was he seeking the person who freed the spy when no single person did?

Bayindir Khan broke the silence. "Can you tell me how Aruz behaved when the spy was caught?" At last, Bayindir Khan decided to ask Gazan the question he really wanted to know. "And why have you said nothing about the council of the nobles, Gazan? You did hold a council, didn't you? You have taken two decisions, after all. The first time you all shouted, 'Death!' Am I right?"

"You are right, my Lord," Gazan replied weakly. He had clearly decided to answer "yes" to all the Khan's questions. He continued. "I said it myself, my Lord. I was the first to say, 'Death and only death; blood and only blood. May this be a lesson for Oghuz. The path of a spy is the path of a traitor! He who betrays Oghuz betrays me and betrays Bayindir Khan, the Khan of Khans.'"

When the Khan remained silent, Gazan kept speaking. "I said, 'Can this be tolerated? Blood has to be shed. Revenge has to be taken. Only blood can wash away the deeds of the traitor. Death—only death—is his reward. Quarter him, chop him into pieces, hang him, slash him, crush and destroy him, and not only him, but also many other suspects in Oghuz!'"

Bayindir Khan raised his eyebrows, waiting for Gazan to go on. He was divulging valuable information.

"There is Wild Dondar, Alp Rustam, Bakil, and Aruz, my Khan. Outer Oghuz is full of enemies! They speak without deliberation and do whatever comes to their minds. They want us, Inner Oghuz, to be wiped from the face of the earth. Never! It will not happen!" Gazan cried. "We will destroy them, each of them, one by one! Gorgud...Gorgud—" Suddenly, he fell silent, as though he had fainted. But then he quickly turned toward me, his eyes wide. "Gorgud, isn't this what I think?" he beseeched me. "Speak, Gorgud! Tell our Khan!"

I raised my head but lowered it quickly again. *What can I say?* I wondered. To be honest, Gazan did not expect an answer from me. He had poured out his heart, and then fallen silent. *Did Gazan really say those words?* I didn't think he spoke only to gratify the Khan. For the first time, Gazan had uttered thoughts he had kept hidden for many long years. He spoke, sighed deeply, and then was still, waiting for whatever was to come. A moment ago he was like a dragon; now he was meek as a lamb.

Both the Khan and Gilbash were looking at Gazan as if they were seeing him for the first time. *Almighty God, you are great,* I thought. *Have mercy upon us; have mercy. I have not known Gazan well until now. Almighty God, forgive him. Forgive him for his sins, for he himself does not realize what he said—as though he wanted to divide the Oghuz. Forgive him. You alone are great, almighty God.*

> *In a while, Gazan's words were to come true. Bayindir Khan would order him to let his tent "be plundered by the nobles of both Inner and Outer Oghuz."[40] But the order would not be obeyed. The tent would indeed by plundered, but the nobles of Outer Oghuz would not be invited. This would further fan the flames of enmity.*

Bayindir Khan looked out at the courtyard again. Finally, he turned back to face us. "Gilbash, have them bring my grandson, Uruz, to me," he said. "You are now free. Go and rest. We will meet later."

We all bowed to the Khan and left the chamber.

---

[40] According to Oghuz tradition, the chief of the tribe would open up his tent to his fellow tribesmen every few years so that they could come and take whatever possessions they wished, except for the chief's wife. The chief's greatest blessing was his fellow tribesmen, and this ceremony of plunder proved it.

§ § § § § §

It was not easy to find young Uruz. He had gotten bored waiting in his grandfather's courtyard, and had gone out through the Red Gate at the far end of the yard toward Horse Square. Bayindir Khan was soon informed of the child's whereabouts. The Khan smiled beneath his moustache. "So he's gone out, has he? Didn't he want to see the slaves then?" he asked. "Never mind. When he comes back, have him come here. I want to see him. Do not let him leave without seeing me." He shook his head, amused. "Horse Square, eh? He thinks he is so grown up, that son of a scoundrel!" Bayindir Khan then let out a chuckle, rose slowly, and entered his inner chamber.

Gilbash and I went out to the yard. Gazan was not with us. Again, the sun was moving above the elm tree. The tree was already casting its carpet of deep green shade. Gilbash looked sideways at me. "It is good to heed good advice. If you have advice for me, let us sit, Gorgud," he said quietly. He had managed to ask a question and give a command in one sentence. Without waiting for my answer, he sat down, cross-legged, in the shade of the elm. "Come here. Come and sit down," he said. "Would you like something to drink or maybe something to eat? Are you hungry?"

I sat down across from him. "Yes, I am hungry," I replied. "I would like some food, but I do not want any wine. You need to have a clear head to stand all Bayindir Khan's questions. It would be shameful to be drunk!"

Gilbash smiled. "You are right. I will not drink wine, either. How about some grape juice?" he suggested. Without waiting for my answer, Gilbash nodded to two stewards, who had been standing nearby, watching for the least hint of an order from Gilbash.

The stewards ran up to us. "Yes, Lord!" they said, bowing.

"Fetch us what is freshly cooked. Bring pilaf, bread, and buttermilk, too," Gilbash replied. Then he looked at me. "What do you say to grape juice, Gorgud?"

"Yes, grape juice would be very good. Please have them bring it," I replied without thinking, not realizing that I was falling into a trap.

Gilbash nodded. "Go and bring everything I have ordered," he told the stewards. The servants turned and ran to the kitchen.

When it was just the two of us again, I looked at Gilbash and sighed. "Gazan must have gone to the Khan's inner chamber with him, huh?" I asked casually, hoping to find out what was going on.

"You are very attached to Gazan, I know," Gilbash said slyly, not addressing my comment.

"You, too, have spent much time with Gazan," I replied.

"Indeed, much time. I cannot deny it!"

"But today my mind is steeped in gloom. Misfortune must not befall Gazan, Gilbash," I said solemnly. "Gazan is the pillar of all Oghuz. You know that."

"Do you know how good grape juice is, Gorgud?" Gilbash asked, changing the subject. Again, he did not say whether Gazan had gone with Bayindir Khan into his inner chamber, or if he had been taken elsewhere. I was trying to discover Gazan's fate, but Gilbash was Gilbash; he carefully left both my questions unanswered. Clearly, he was trying to distract me by talking about grape juice.

This is a trap, I thought. *It's a trap for a hare. What did I do? I fell right into some kind of a trap!* I tried to remain calm and smiled politely. "Grape juice? Of course, I know! Grape water is the juice of fresh grapes."

Gilbash began laughing hard. "They will bring it in a minute, and you will drink it and see. Grapes, you say?" He shook his head, still laughing.

"I'll see. So what?" I asked, my voice rising. My patience was wearing thin.

"Don't get angry, Gorgud. Don't get angry. Grape juice is wine, isn't it? I mean, what is grape water after three months?" Gilbash grinned. "Think about it!"

The stewards carried in the food and water jugs. First, they spread out a large tablecloth, and then they laid out all the food. Bowing, they withdrew to their previous position, awaiting additional orders.

"Look, here's the grape water. Isn't it wine? The only difference is that this has been kept a few months in barrels—wooden barrels—and now it is being served. We have the same grapes, though, and the same grape water. Right?" He laughed again and began pouring wine into my cup.

I was upset. Scowling, I cursed myself for failing to spot the obvious trap.

"I told you not to be cross," said Gilbash, gently putting his hand on my shoulder. "We are brothers. Can you not take a joke? Drink, Gorgud. Drink and revive your spirits. Nothing will happen. Your head can stand the strongest wine. This wine isn't strong at all." He shook his head for emphasis. "Not at all."

So we ate and drank, gradually reviving our spirits. The sun cast its carpet over the Khan's courtyard, and then beyond the walls over Gunortaj, and eventually over all of Oghuz. The carpet moved slowly. It was no longer the shade of the elm; it was a different covering.

A horseman appeared at the Black Gate. He swiftly dismounted, and the stewards led his horse to the stables. He got into a discussion with one of the stewards, asking questions and getting answers in return. Then he slowly began to make his way toward us. We had already eaten our meal, and when the sun started to burn our necks, we drained the pitcher of grape juice and got up.

"Who can this be?" I asked, talking more to myself than to Gilbash.

"Don't you recognize Shirshamsaddin?" Gilbash asked, a smile flickering across his face. "I know him by the way he walks." Gilbash smiled at me, turning his gaze away from the Black Gate. Yes, it was Shirshamsaddin. For some reason, I hadn't recognized him.

Shirshamsaddin began to walk more quickly, almost running up to us. He bowed in greeting. I looked at his face, and his eyes were imploring me, as if to ask, "Please Gorgud, ask me the reason for my visit. Gilbash will avoid it. I don't know what will become of me..."

"Salam aleykum, Shirshamsaddin!" I greeted him, trying to forestall Gilbash. "Has anything happened? Are you here on business? Did you come yourself, or did the Khan summon you?"

"No, Gorgud, my father," Shirshamshaddin replied, letting out a small sigh of relief. "Nothing has happened, thank God. All is well in Oghuz. Bayindir Khan did not summon me. I felt I should pay a visit." He then turned to Gilbash and smiled. "My heart was anxious, and I followed my master, Gazan, here," he explained. "If you grant me permission, I will wait for him here."

"What are you talking about? Are we strangers?" Gilbash asked, looking confused. "You are welcome, my warrior! May you bring us gladness."

This is interesting behavior, I thought. To be honest, I didn't expect such courtesy from Gilbash.

Shirshamshaddin frowned, slightly embarrassed. "I haven't brought you anything; I came in such a rush. The idea suddenly came to me, and well, here I am. Wherever my master, Gazan, goes, I go, too!"

> *I couldn't help but laugh! Gilbash and I looked at each other. Shirshamsaddin was the most loyal of warriors. He was always at Gazan's side. Shirshamsaddin fulfilled the same role for Gazan as Gilbash did for Bayindir Khan. I wondered what Bayindir Khan would think when he heard that Shirshamsaddin had come. Shirshamsaddin was probably going to be summoned to the inquiry, anyway. He might be wild, but his suspicions were accurate. Shirshamsaddin is brave, but not the brightest warrior in Oghuz. God knows if he will spoil everything. However, his words betrayed him well. Gilbash had said, "May you bring us gladness," to which Shirshamshaddin had replied, "I haven't brought you anything; I came in such a rush." What can you do but burst out laughing?*

Gilbash began laughing to himself. Poor Shirshamsaddin anxiously looked from me to Gilbash and back at me, puzzled. I smiled. *God almighty, I have never seen this lad do or say anything clever, but maybe he is wrapping us around his little finger. Whatever will be, will be, almighty God, but may it end well,* I thought.

Hardly suppressing his laughter, Gilbash spoke up. "Shirshamsaddin, you were right to come here. The Khan had already told me to summon you here—but only after Gazan. We would have sent word to you. It is good that you have come yourself. My friend, do not worry that you were not able to bring anything. You can make up for it next time," he said. With that, he turned his back to Shirshamsaddin and nodded to the stewards. "Give Shirshamshaddin whatever he wants. Fill his belly; give him water and wine. Make him happy."

"Thank you for your kindness," Shirshamshaddin said quietly, nodding.

Paying no further heed to Shirshamsaddin, Gilbash touched my arm. "Let's go, Gorgud. The Khan is waiting for us. We must not be late," he said. With that, he set off without looking at me. I hesitated a moment. One thing was clear: When we had been eating pilaf and talking to Shirshamsaddin, I had noticed that Gilbash kept looking at the Khan's window. He was expecting an order; apparently, that order had come. "Let's go," Gilbash repeated. The words seemed to be for himself. The two of us then went to the Khan's chamber, leaving Shirshamshaddin behind.

When we entered, we saw that Bayindir Khan was waiting for us. "Take your seats," said Bayindir Khan.

We took our previous seats, heads bent. I sat near the window; Gilbash was in front of the window. *He has to be able to look out the window,* I thought. *He has four eyes. He sees everything and knows everything. Maybe he has eyes in the back of his head.* Thinking of eyes reminded me of One-Eye. *Pray God, this misfortune will not befall the Oghuz again.* I was beseeching God when Bayindir Khan's voice suddenly brought me back to reality. But before Bayindir Khan spoke, I recalled the following…

> *The text of* The Incomplete Manuscript *broke up here. Unfortunately, we will never know what it was that Dada Gorgud remembered.*

…"Gorgud, my son, and Gilbash, tell me what you think. What do you make of our recent conversation? Was Gazan telling the truth?" Bayindir Khan asked.

Gilbash and I glanced quickly at one another again. Gilbash nodded to me to start first. *Of course, I had to be the first to speak,* I thought. *The Khan spoke my name first.*

> *You scoundrel! Now I'll show you. Do you think you got the better of me with your grape juice?*

I cleared my throat before speaking. “My Khan, this is what I think: Gazan told the truth. He just failed to mention the council of the noblemen. He must have forgotten about it. He was worked up,” I said carefully. “The truth is—and hard though it is for me to say it, I will do so—misfortune will befall Oghuz. If it won’t happen today, then it will happen tomorrow, my Khan.”

“Really?” Bayindir Khan feigned amazement. “Speak, Gorgud, my son. Don’t hold anything back. Tell me what misfortune is hovering over our tribe. You say shocking, terrible things.”

However calm the Khan had tried to sound, I realized that he had been shaken by my words. Growing bolder, I said, “Don’t ask me, my Khan. Don’t ask me. Gazan pointed the finger at Aruz, didn’t he? Ask whomever you will, but do not ask me. You have seen this yourself. But mark my words: Inner and Outer Oghuz are not the Greater Oghuz that they once were. There is discord between them. It is hidden today, but it will appear tomorrow. May almighty God protect the Khan.”

“Carry on, Gorgud,” Bayindir Khan said, leaning back against a bolster and frowning at me intently. “Tell us what you are referring to. Please, carry on.”

When Bayindir Khan narrowed his eyes and looked intently at a speaker, it meant that he was engrossed in the subject, concentrating heart and mind on the conversation. Nothing could distract him. I had seen only a few occasions when the Khan narrowed his gaze like that. Now he had directed that same look at me.

I continued. “The heart of this story is buried deep, my Khan. It is a long conversation with many layers.”

“Gorgud, my son, have enemies swept into Oghuz? Have the rivers and streams overflowed? Has the earth trembled, and have the mountains come crashing down, revealing what lies beyond?” Bayindir Khan asked. “Gorgud, what is the matter? Are you in a hurry? We have no other matters to attend to. We have as much time as we need.” The Khan looked at Gilbash for a moment. “Aren’t I right, Gilbash?”

Gilbash remained silent. Instead, he looked at me, waiting to see how the conversation would unfold.

“Gorgud, you say this matter has many layers, so take off those layers, one by one. Strip the subject until it is naked. Our time is abundant,” Bayindir Khan said. He waited a few seconds before continuing. “I’ve heard that that fool, Shirshamsaddin, has come. He is impudent. Was he summoned?” Then he shook his head. “No. Never mind. You may not know, Gorgud my son, but the Oghuz have relaxed. They’ve relaxed a great deal. Everyone does just as they please. Shirshamsaddin wanted to come to the Khan’s court, so he came to Gunortaj. If he doesn't want to come tomorrow, then he won't. This is not right. It's not right at all."

I bent my head in silence. I wasn't sure what to say.

"It does not concern you. Why have you bent your head? It does not concern you!" Bayindir Khan said quickly. "We were talking about something else. What was I saying just now?" He thought a moment until he remembered. "Yes, we have no other matters to attend to. So you must begin from the very beginning. Take off every layer. Strip the subject until it is completely bare. I want to see the secret at the core. I will see what you know—and what you do not know."

Bayindir Khan paused. I sensed that he had not finished. With that, I looked back up at him and waited for him to speak again.

"Maybe you don't realize, Gorgud, but the day will come when you will need all these stories, incidents, dreams, and thoughts," he said. "So you must be alert. Be alert, but first of all you must be just. It is no easy matter to be just; you need to know this. Now, I am listening to you. What is at the heart of this discord? You said there is discord. I did not say that, did I, Gilbash?" He looked at Gilbash, slightly confused.

"This is what he said, my Khan. Gorgud said it himself," Gilbash replied.

"Then he must answer for his words," Bayindir Khan said, nodding.

Silence reigned for some time. No one attempted to break it. *Where will I start, God almighty? Should I say everything that I know? If Bayindir Khan flies into a rage with Inner Oghuz, what then? What if he sends Gilbash at the head of a punitive expedition?* I thought. *What if he mercilessly beats all the noblemen of Inner Oghuz, one by one, and the noblemen get together and resolve to take revenge on me? Almighty God, you alone can help me. If I hide something—if I do not talk about it and Bayindir Khan already knows what I have concealed—what then? He meant it when he said, "I will see what you know—and what you do not know." What can I do? To whom can I turn? It is good when I speak the truth. Almighty God, inspire my soul. Stone of Light, I sat in your shade. Almighty God, forgive my sins...*

Finally, I began to speak. As fast as a horse can run, so swiftly does a minstrel speak. But this is not true of every minstrel. I was a minstrel by God's command. Sometimes it seemed to me that I could bring messages from the unknown. *What will happen next? How will it happen? No one knows, but I do—I know,* I thought. I began to talk, and I talked for three days and three nights. During that entire duration, Bayindir Khan did not say a word; he never attempted to interrupt me.

Sometimes we ate, in silence, and then I would talk again. Bayindir Khan would sometimes slip into sleep, and Gilbash and I would lay our heads where we could and rest. However, every time Bayindir Khan stirred, Gilbash would quickly nudge me to wake up. I would then rub the sleep from my eyes and be ready to start talking again as soon as I saw Bayindir Khan open his eyes.

Three days and three nights passed. During this time, we didn't think about Salur Gazan, Shirshamsaddin, Uruz, or any of the other noblemen waiting their turn in Bayindir Khan's courtyard. I, Gorgud, spoke carefully, while Bayindir Khan, the Khan of Khans, listened to my words. What did I say? Why did I say it? Maybe I should not have revealed what I divulged to Bayindir Khan. All that I know is that God inspired my soul, and I poured out my heart. After those three days and three nights, half-living, half-breathing, and almost fainting, I said my last word and closed my mouth.

This section of The Incomplete Manuscript *had some stains, like the ones I found earlier. The manuscript is not torn but it is, nevertheless, illegible. Here, two or three pages written in Dada Gorgud's hand can be considered lost to us forever. I don't think that anyone damaged the manuscript deliberately; it wasn't like that. But all the accidents irrespective of size have a common denominator: destiny. I don't mean the destiny of the Oghuz, but the destiny of* The Incomplete Manuscript *itself—the destiny that produced our manuscript now in its present form. The question, "What is it?" had become cloaked in meaning for me now.*

The subsequent text should be considered a continuation of the tale told by Gorgud to Bayindir Khan for three days and three nights.

§ § § § § §

...once again, the nobles sent envoys to me, asking me to name the warrior. I went to them and asked, "You say that he has beheaded enemies and shown heroism, don't you?"

"Yes, Gorgud. He has beheaded enemies and shown heroism. He has rescued merchants from the clutches of the enemy," the nobles answered.

"You say this young man is brave-hearted and bold?" I asked again.

"He is brave-hearted and bold," they responded. "Also, he is strong."

I then turned to Baybura. "Lord Baybura, what have you been calling your son until now?" I asked curiously.

"I call my son Basam Bamsi," Baybura replied.

"Then let his name be Bamsi Beyrak—Bamsi, the Bold," I said.

The boy was standing before me. His face shone, but sorrow lay deep in his eyes. Suddenly, I felt a sense of foreboding. I looked hard at the boy, feeling no compassion. *He is not one of mine,* I thought. *His road will take him very far away. God knows. He is not mine. I wish him well.* Yellow snakes began to turn in my stomach.

After I had given the boy his name, I took him to one side, away from the onlookers, and took him to the heart of where his name came from. Baybura and the other nobles rejoiced, and Baybura put out a magnificent feast at his home. At one point during the feasting, however, my heart suddenly contracted. I quickly got up and went out of the tent into the field. It was a clear, moonlit night, and the air was fresh and a soft. A cool breeze blew down from sleeping Mount Gazilig. I filled my lungs with fresh air.

Just then, Beyrak appeared from nowhere, almost as if he had been following me. "Gorgud, I am yours to command," he said.

He was indeed courteous, but as I looked at him, I could feel a sharp pain in my spleen; the yellow snakes still turned in my stomach. There was a strange glow in the boy's face and eyes. My ears caught a whisper or a groan. I could not determine if the whisper came down from the sky, or if the groan rose up from the earth, but I could hear only one thing: "This boy will bring disaster upon Oghuz."

Beyrak continued to stand tall before me, his gray eyes reflecting obedience. As I gazed upon him, though, I saw that a volcano was seething deep within those eyes. He was looking at me from beneath his brows, curious to hear what I had to say. I frowned for a moment, but then my frowned disappeared before speaking. "Beyrak, my son, were you not frightened when you rescued the merchants from the ruthless enemy?" I asked.

"Why should I have been frightened, Gorgud? I was not afraid of anything," Beyrak responded boldly.

"Then tell me, how did you manage to overcome them? They were many and you were alone."

"Gorgud, I will tell only you. Those that you called enemies were my companions. I had sent them in advance to intimidate the merchants. Then I moved in and scattered them."

"How were you able to do it? Didn't you cut off their heads?" I asked. My surprise had no bounds.

"I did, Gorgud. I could do no other. I beheaded one of our men. His name was Yalanchi, the Liar's Son. He betrayed us. He wounded one of the merchants, seized his belongings, and hid them in the saddlebag," Beyrak replied. "And he hid them from me."

"Do you mean Yalanchi, the Liar's Son, or Yalinchig, the Naked?" I asked.

Beyrak shook his head. "No, Gorgud, it wasn't Yalinchig, the Naked. It was his twin brother, Palanchig, the Pack Saddle. I cut off his head right away."

My blood froze in my veins. I forced myself to ask, "Did anyone know about this? Your father, the Inner Oghuz nobles—anyone at all?"

"No, no one knows apart from one of my warriors, and I trust him," Beyrak said quietly. "Apart from him, only one man knows, and that is you, Gorgud."

I was stunned by Beyrak's words. *Is this how this scoundrel son of a scoundrel earned his name?* I wondered. It was hard to believe that one so young could be so cunning. "Then why did you reveal your secret to me?" I asked.

"You don't know, Gorgud, my father…" Beyrak replied.

At this spot, The Incomplete Manuscript *became hard to read again. But it did not seem too important to me to reconstruct the damaged section. I clearly understood two points from the text. Beyrak revealed this secret to Dada Gorgud, and he thought that Gorgud would not tell the secret to a third person. To be more accurate, he knew for certain that Gorgud would not breathe a word. This revealed to us another of Gorgud's functions, which we might miss when reading the final literary version of the Gorgud's epic.*

Everyone could go and reveal their secrets to Gorgud; he was the keeper of secrets. Every man in Oghuz knew that a secret told to Dada would be kept safe. Gorgud would keep a secret from everyone; no one would ever hear of it. But if one keeps a secret and tells no one about it, demons will follow that person every step of the way. In the end, everyone must answer for his or her deeds. We know about the existence of these beliefs in ancient tribes.

The best way was to confide one's secrets in Gorgud and let him deal with any accompanying demons. It follows, therefore, that the people of Ancient Oghuz avoided secrets as much as possible; they did not like secrets at all. In this regard, the number of secrets that Dada Gorgud kept determined his level of sacred powers. I think this was the first main point.

The second point lay much deeper. In my opinion, Beyrak resolved two issues at once. By confiding his secret in Gorgud—one of the most respected men in Oghuz—he hoped to make him his ally ahead of time. In fact, he wanted to turn Gorgud into his ally for future ventures that were still fermenting in his mind.

This hidden intention should not be dismissed because as Gorgud said earlier, "Whatever comes to your mind, you may see in this life." At least one of these suppositions, most probably the first, is confirmed in its right to exist. In a short while, Gorgud himself would hint at the heavy burden imposed by secrets by being a willing (or unwilling) keeper of secrets.

…"I gave you my secret. It is up to you to keep it, Gorgud," said Beyrak. Moments later, he fell silent.

What can I say? I thought. I was amazed. *That scoundrel son of a scoundrel just bound me up in his secret!* I knew I had to keep it whether I wanted it or not. Suddenly, it felt like terrible torture. In fact, to keep such a secret was even worse than torture…

> *It should be said here that the fate of keeping secrets did not fall to everyone in Oghuz. Yes, it is torture, but the path of respect and honor also passes through this torture. Who did not tell me their secrets? The dissatisfied, murderers, victims, mothers who knew the real fathers of their children, fathers who doubted the faithfulness of their wives, lovers, the loveless, the lonely, the beloved, mothers-in-law fed up with their daughters-in-law, fathers-in-law furious with their sons-in-law—I preserved all the secrets of Oghuz. I survived by entrusting them in turn to the Stone of Light. What would I have done without the Stone of Light?*

§ § § § §

…After talking to Beyrak, I turned back to the tent. The nobles were drinking and having a good time. They were all speaking at once; nobody was listening to anybody else. Meanwhile, I was lost in dark thoughts. I kept thinking about Beyrak. *I must ask the Stone of Light about this lad's future. Almighty God has marked out his path. No slave has ever spoken to me in that way. His future seems very dark. The Stone of Light,* I thought. *I must ask the Stone of Light.* I repeated these words under my breath several times.

My black mood did not escape the nobles. Lord Baybura did not take his eyes off me. He approached me, looking slightly concerned. "Gorgud, our father, why don't you try the wine? Don't you like it? Tell me what you would like, and it will be brought," he said. "You know, this is an auspicious day for me! You have named my son. I think you've given him a fine name. I want the day to be good for all the nobles." He quickly turned and got a few of the stewards' attention. "Don't just stand there, stewards! Please bring Gorgud some strong wine. Drink it if you want to, and if you don't…" his voice trailed off.

I was out of sorts. I could not digest what Beyrak had told me. If the nobles got me drunk on wine, I realized I would not be able to go to the Stone of Light. It would not be good to stay there with my thoughts. "The road is long, and the world is dark," I said. "I ask your leave, oh, nobles. Eat, drink, and be merry, but please grant me permission to go, Lord Baybura." Without waiting for a reply, I stood up and smiled, adding, "I congratulate you, Lord Baybura. May I come to your son's great wedding." Then I faced the noblemen and nodded. "May happiness dwell in your tents, noblemen. I wish you all good health. Now I must go."

Lord Baybura tried to persuade me to stay. In fact, he almost begged me. The nobles supported him. "Please stay," he pleaded.

"No, no," I replied, still smiling. I glanced over at Beyrak, who was the only one who was silent. His cold eyes watched me. With that, I waited no longer. I immediately left the tent, mounted my horse, and galloped away without a backward glance.

§ § § § § §

I don't know how I got to the mouth of the cave that night, but somehow, I managed to reach the Stone of Light. The moon was shining and the stars were twinkling; they added to each other's beauty. The Stone of Light glowed with its mysterious radiance. I placed my hand on the heart of the Stone of Light. "Stone of Light, today I have heard one more secret. Do you hear me?" I asked quietly.

The Stone of Light should have given a sign in response. The silence of night enveloped everything around me. The silence almost pierced my eardrums. I repeated my question. "Stone of Light, most beautiful of stones, wisest of stones, if you are awake and not asleep, talk to me. I was told another secret today. Shall I confide this secret in you, or shall I carry this secret to my grave?"

Again, silence reigned. *Is not silence itself a sign?* I wondered. *Of course, it is a sign. It is a sign that I should reveal the secret to the Stone of Light.* With that, I told the Stone of Light the story from beginning to end. Maintaining its silence, the Stone of Light listened to me as I spoke.

I didn't know the exact moment when I fell asleep that night, but I dreamed…

This dream cannot be written as it was; it cannot. Almighty God, help me to turn this into a worthy epic, Chronicles of the Oghuz. May the Oghuz weep bitterly. May Lord Baybura lament his son. May he cry out loud and choke on his sobs.

The dream revealed the truth to me. *Can I, an unworthy man, foresee Beyrak's future?* I wondered. No, the Stone of Light told me everything. First, it sent me to sleep. Mist seeped from the Stone of Light; slowly, a white curtain descended over everything, and the mist embraced me within itself. The Stone of Light's mist of sleep showed me the adventures of Beyrak.

I deeply respected the Stone of Light's wisdom. Were it not for the Stone of Light, how would I know what I knew? Who would I have been without the wisdom of the Stone of Light to guide me? I would be just plain Gorgud—Gorgud, like any other. Did not the Stone of Light take me to the bosom of God? This I what I dreamed…

§ § § § § §

...The Shah woke early that morning for some reason. First, he stretched luxuriantly, and then—and this was unlike him—he screwed up his eyes against the sun, which was shining through the velvet curtains shot with gold. He continued to toss and turn in his bed.

The Vizier[41] was waiting in the reception room in front of the court. Envoys were expected to arrive that day. They were to come from a distant land—from a city in the sea. The roads were long and dangerous. Only the Lord knew how they would get here.

After a while, the Head of the Shah's Guard came into the chamber, wondering where the Shah was. He and the Vizier exchanged looks. They were silent for a few moments. Finally, the Vizier spoke. "The Pivot of the Universe is still resting," he said lazily.

"The envoys should reach the palace soon," the Head of the Guard announced.

"And?" the Vizier interrupted, suddenly becoming more alert.

"Lele has given an instruction. It is urgent. Or—" the Head of the Guard began.

"Do as Lele has instructed! What are you doing talking to me?" the Vizier asked, growing impatient.

"I haven't said anything, Vizier. Why are you angry?" the Head of the Guard asked. He fell silent and did not say another word.

Safiyar, the chamberlain,[42] emerged from the inner chambers. Usually this meant that the Shah was about to enter the reception room—but not this time. The Shah's arrival was delayed. Safiyar went up to the Vizier and said something to him quietly. The Vizier then left the room without saying a word. The Head of the Guard beckoned Safiyar over to him.

"Where has the Vizier gone, my son?" he asked. "What did you say to him?"

Safiyar looked conspiratorially about him before speaking. "I told him about the envoys. The Shah instructed the Vizier to keep them waiting, to keep them occupied. The Pivot of the Universe is delayed. He also asked about you. I told him that you were here awaiting orders," he explained.

"Is that what you said? You did right. How is the Pivot of the Universe? God willing, he is in good humor," the Head of the Guard said with a small smile.

"He is well. Thank God, he is well," Safiyar replied. "I would sacrifice myself for him."

---

[41] The Vizier was the most senior figure in the government and chief aide to the Shah.

[42] The chamberlain was the head of the Shah's servants.

“Thank God,” the Head of the Guard nodded. “Now go and do your work.” With that, he dismissed the chamberlain. Safiyar walked out of the room.

At that very moment, Huseyn Bay Lele entered the room. The Head of the Guard stood up straight, like a taut string. Without looking up, Lele walked to the throne, stood for a moment, and then sat at the right foot of the throne, his head still lowered. He began turning his prayer beads. The Head of the Guard approached Lele and stood opposite him, blocking the light.

“Get out of the way! For the sake of the Shah of Chivalrous Men, don’t block God’s light!” Lele muttered. He didn’t bother to look up at the Head of the Guard.

“Lele, may I die at your feet,” the Head of the Guard responded. “I ask you, for the sake of the Shah of Chivalrous Men, to settle my problem today.”

“All right,” Lele said. “I have told you to be patient. It is time for the Shah to come now. Wait, no, go and do your work in God’s name. I will help you later. After all, I have given you my word.”

Safiyar reappeared in the throne room doorway. He quickly walked inside, looking all around the room. Then he turned toward the door, bowed, and held his pose.

The Shah ordered him into the throne room. The Vizier and courtiers entered from the other side, bowing. Lele jumped up. The Head of the Guard lay with his face on the ground. Lele immediately went up to the Shah and bowed to him courteously.

The Shah smiled. “So, you are back at last, Lele,” the Shah said, looking at him.

The Vizier stepped forward from the group of courtiers and approached the Shah. “My Shah, the envoys await your command,” he whispered.

“I know, I know. I will talk to you later, but first I will meet the envoys,” the Shah replied. He turned to Lele. “Tell me, have you settled the matter?” he asked.

Lele nodded. “I have, my Shah, I have. May I sacrifice myself for you? I have done as you instructed.”

“Good. Excellent,” the Shah said. He gave an approving tap to Lele’s shoulder and helped him to stand. “Get up. Get up now. Go into the inner garden and wait for me. I will come when I have finished with the envoys. Come this way.” As he took Lele aside, he leaned in toward Lele’s ear and whispered, “Is he here?”

“He is,” Lele whispered back. “May I sacrifice myself for you?”

“What does he look like? Is there a resemblance?” the Shah asked curiously.

“Very much so—like two peas in a pod. May I sacrifice myself for you?” Lele replied. “With a dark veil, no one will be able to tell the difference.”

"Good. Do as I have instructed. Go to the inner garden. I will receive the envoys, then—" the Shah stopped for a moment and frowned. "Wait. You are not coming to the meeting with the envoys?" he asked.

"I don't know. I have not been told to," Lele answered.

"Vizier!" the Shah shouted.

The Vizier emerged at the double behind the Shah. "Yes, my Perfect Councilor?" the Vizier replied, awaiting orders.

The Shah suddenly seemed to remember something and spoke no more. Silence fell. A few moments later, the Shah himself interrupted the silence. He looked at Lele. "Lele, you see this matter through. This is more important. I will come when I have finished. We will discuss the meeting with the envoys when we eat dinner together this evening."

Without further ado, the Shah turned and left the throne room. The Vizier, the Head of the Guard, and other courtiers followed the Shah. Lele paced up and down the throne room for a while, deep in thought. Eventually, he left, too, leaving the throne room empty.

> *This is how the second parallel tale in* The Incomplete Manuscript, *the tale about Shah Ismail Khata'i, begins. It breaks off here for the first time. The text of the manuscript returns to the previous narrative—as though nothing had happened—in exactly the same way the manuscript had shifted in time and subject without any explanation earlier.*

§ § § § § §

In my dream, I saw what looked like a cave. A bearded man was sitting in the cave. I looked a little more closely and saw that he looked like Beyrak. In fact, he *really* looked like him. This Beyrak sat in the upper part of the cave with various pilaffs, breads, and sherbets spread out before him. There was even wine. On one side, there were three or four girls sitting decorously. One beautiful girl sat close to Beyrak.

One of the girls was playing the saz.[43] Suddenly, another girl stood up, raised her arms above her head, and began to dance. Beyrak embraced the moon-faced beauty next to him. She leaned closer to him and smiled. "My brave warrior, why don't you sing a song?" she asked. "We will get to hear your voice. You are always listening. Open your arms wide, dance, and sing. Do you like the girls?"

"I like you most of all," Beyrak replied. "I love you very much."

"Really? What do you love about me? Aren't there many beautiful girls in your land? I heard you have beautiful girls. You have girls who ride horses

---

[43] A stringed instrument traditionally played by Turkic ozans or bards.

with the men and wield their swords. Is it true? Tell me! Don't hide your face from me, though. Never hide your face!" the moon-faced beauty replied.

Things gradually began to fall into place for me. Beyrak and the girls were probably in Bayburd Castle. Beyrak was a prisoner in that castle. I also knew that he had been blinded by his tears at being away from his home and family, and Oghuz, for sixteen years. Despite all of that, I saw Beyrak laughing and joking behind his bearded face.

"Are such things possible? Can one of them compare with you?" Beyrak asked. "I have found the culmination of all my desires in you. I love you."

"What about your fiancée, Banuchichak?" The infidel's daughter did not give up. Instead, she slipped out of Beyrak's embrace and turned to face him. "You had a fiancée, Banuchichak. What about her? Have you forgotten her?" she asked curiously.

"I did not love her as I love you. My father betrothed us to one another before we were born. I did not disobey my father. There is no one for me to forget, my beloved. There is only you," Beyrak said. "My eyes only see you, and my heart only loves you. I have forgotten everyone, but I will never forget you. Tell your father. Let him cut me in two. Only then will I forget you."

"Oh, my soul! You're the apple of my eye. Beyrak, Beyrak, my Beyrak!" the moon-faced beauty cried. "I love you. I have eyes for no one but you. My eyes are only for you, and my heart only loves you. I will tell my father and mother. I can bear it no longer. Only in the grave can I have another fiancé lie beside me. In life—you, only you..." With that proclamation, the moon-faced beauty stood up.

I wondered if the bearded man I saw in my dream was not Beyrak; I knew that I could see anything in a dream. I wondered if my mind had been wandering. The couple embraced each other lovingly. Their lips met; they kissed; and they sucked and bit one another, losing themselves in passion. Meanwhile, the other girls did not stop dancing. They took a pitcher of water, still dancing, and splashed it on the couple's faces. Beyrak and the moon-faced beauty pulled apart, but then quickly embraced again. This time, the girls stopped and watched the spectacle.

Suddenly, one of the guards came in from outside. "Come on! Be quick!" he warned with urgency in his voice. "Your father, Bayburd, is coming. Bayburd himself is coming!"

In that moment, I was absolutely sure that the bearded man was Beyrak; the moon-faced beauty was Bayburd's beloved daughter; and they had been conversing in Bayburd Castle.

Still sleeping, my mind then carried me to another place. I began to watch the calamity that befell Oghuz. I saw One-Eye. I saw people whose lips were parched and cracked with thirst. One-Eye's troops had cut off all Oghuz's roads, making it impossible to stay and impossible to leave. People were weak before the ruthless, godless army. Furthermore, I saw prisoners, slaves, female slaves, and the youth of Oghuz going to be sacrificed to One-Eye. I also saw the council of nobles meeting in the tent of Old Aruz.

Old Goja was angry. "Where are the warriors who say that all the world is mine? Where is Salur Gazan, pillar of the Oghuz? Where is his son, Uruz? Where is Beyrak, Ganturali, Shirshamsaddin, and Garabudag? Where is Father Garaguna?" he asked incredulously. "Nobles, tell me, is it the fate of Outer Oghuz to fight One-Eye alone?"

Baybejan, Wild Dondar, Wild Garjar, Aman, and Giyan Seljuk stood up, one by one, to speak fervently. It was not clear to me what they were saying. Then I saw the young men of Outer Oghuz pass by old men, who were begging for help, crying out, "Water! Water!" Giyan Seljuk, the elder son of Old Aruz, was leading the young men to battle against One-Eye.

Old Aruz was looking for someone in the group, but he couldn't seem to find the person. He approached someone standing nearby. "I couldn't see Basat. Where can he be?" he asked impatiently.

"My Lord, we have been seeking him since morning, but have not found him anywhere. Maybe he has returned to the forest," the man replied.

"Find him! Find him and tell him his father wants him. If he wishes, let him come. If he does not, may I see him in hell!" Old Aruz spat venomously.

Then I saw myself present at the council. Yes, it was me. Old Aruz had sent someone to find Basat, and then he turned and looked at me, shaking his head, as if to say, "God gave us only one son—and he is blind." But his tongue said something else. "Gorgud, my grief is great; you can see for yourself. Great God has given him power and strength, but his mind remains feeble. He has not grown up. What can I do?" he asked. "Maybe he will come and we can help him together. My heart is uneasy, though. Only he can defeat One-Eye. Giyan Seljuk is stout of heart and mind, but his strength is very weak." He sighed, adding, "If only he had the strength of Basat's arm, Gorgud."

"And what does Basat say?" I asked. "Is he refusing this fight?"

Old Aruz shrugged. "I don't know. He says that he does not want to shed a man's blood. I told him that he is an enemy. He said that he didn't care if he was an enemy or not; he didn't want to shed blood," Old Aruz replied. He shook his head in desperation. "Gorgud, my grief is great. If he comes, will you speak to him?"

"Let him come and we will see. He is young; he doesn't understand," I said. "We will make him understand. What a thing to say, huh? 'I never shed blood.'"

"Yes, that is what he said. Please explain to him, Gorgud," Old Aruz said. "Try to set him on the right path. I have sent my son, Giyan, light of my life, to a certain death. He was not born to fight. He was not born to face One-Eye." With that, Old Aruz sadly hung his head. Tears begin to flow down his cheeks.

I do not know how much time passed. Old Aruz's stewards had found Basat, and they pushed him into the room where we were. Basat said hello and was greeted in return, and then he lowered his gaze, waiting. Old Aruz nodded to the stewards to leave. "Basat, my son, where have you been?" he asked.

"Father, I was in my place in the forest," Basat replied.

I spoke up. "Where is that, Basat?" I asked.

Basat kept his head down. "There is a small glade in the forest. I was alone in the glade; there were only trees around me. Wolves, lynx, and bears walk freely in the forest. They are kind to me and I am kind to them. That glade is my place in the forest—near Goghan, the Lioness," he explained. "She loves me very much. Father knows that place."

I glanced at Old Aruz and he looked at me. All three of us were silent for a while. I thought back to years ago when Basat was still young. At that time, he did not have arms that were as thick as oaks, or a back as broad as a hill. He was not as tall as a tree. He had gone into the forest and disappeared in that very glade; no one could find him. Old Aruz was deeply saddened and wept for his son. That's when he called for me and I came. "Gorgud, help me find my son. May God guide you," he said. "Please tell me where my son is!"

I had received inspiration after Old Aruz's request. I closed my eyes, and my heart flew to the Stone of Light. Suddenly, I knew where Basat was. "Old Aruz, your son is in the forest," I told him. "There is a glade in the forest—a glade among hornbeams, limes, and oaks. There is also a lioness, Goghan; her den is there. That is where your son is."

Old Aruz's stewards went to the place I had told Old Aruz about. Luckily for them, the lioness was not in her den. They found the boy and brought him back as fast as they could.

Once Basat had returned, I looked at him and said, "Son, you are a man. Your place is with your father and mother in your home. You have your tribe, and you will be the pride and pillar of the Oghuz one day. Do not walk in the forest among the wolves and birds, and in the dens of lions." Apparently, my words had no influence on Basat at all. Later, I heard that he would often run away from people and go back to the lioness' den in the forest. But since everyone knew where Basat would run off too now, they would find him quickly and bring him back to his father. Sometimes he would come back by himself.

Old Aruz broke the silence by plunging into sobs. He called the women and children into the room, and they began to wail and cry, too. Basat stood before them, without stirring, still as a stone. I looked at Basat's figure and imagined his fight with One-Eye. I asked the Stone of Light what the outcome would be, and Basat was clearly the victor.

Finally, Old Aruz composed himself and fell silent. He looked at his son and then looked at me. His eyes begged me to persuade him. I cleared my throat. "My son, Basat, you can see how things are. You had an older brother, Giyan Seljuk; he went to fight One-Eye. No brave warriors remain in Oghuz," I said slowly. "What do you say, Basat? Will you just keep on eating and sleeping, or will you take up arms, mount your white stallion, and go and gouge out the only eye of the one-eyed ogre? He is the enemy, Basat—Oghuz's enemy and your father's enemy. Brave warriors have fought enemies and become heroes."

A long silence followed. Then Basat asked, "What is an enemy, Gorgud?"

I was confused by his question; I didn't know what to say. But the answer came spinning to me from the Stone of Light itself. "Basat, if we reach an enemy first, we kill them," I said carefully. "But if they reach us first, they kill us. That is an enemy, Basat."

"Is it good for a slave of God to shed the blood of an enemy, Gorgud?" Basat then asked.

"Yes, it is, Basat. An enemy is created so that his blood can be shed. Look, what do you do when you catch a wild wolf in the forest?" I asked.

Basat thought for a moment. "Is not the wolf that you call wild a breathing, living animal created by almighty God?" he asked. "I do not disturb them and they do not disturb me. Even Goghan, the lioness, will not harm me. She loves me; she licks me with her tongue."

"And what would you do if someone wanted to shed your blood?" I asked.

"I would not harm anyone wanting to shed my blood. I would think that they did not understand," Basat said.

Old Aruz could not restrain himself anymore. "And if someone wants to shed your brother's blood—to end his life—will you forgive them?" he cried.

"No, I could not forgive that!" Basat replied. He looked hard at his father. "Who has Giyan wronged that they want to kill him?"

"My son, Basat, Giyan could not bear what had befallen Oghuz. He could not bear to see women, children, and the elderly made homeless, wandering in search of water," Old Aruz said. "He went to fight One-Eye. You tell him, Gorgud!"

I looked down. "Yes, he went, my Lord," I said quietly. I raised my head and saw that Old Aruz's words had finally made his son anxious. He looked fixedly into the distance and could not find words to express himself. I continued. "What do you say, Basat? Everyone knows—and I know, too—that only you can defeat One-Eye. It is not a job for Giyan Seljuk."

"My son, what do you say?" Old Aruz asked, almost begging Basat.

"If one hair should fall from Giyan's head, then I will deal with One-Eye," Basat answered at last. Both Old Aruz and I understood that this was his final decision.

§ § § § § §

News came fast. Giyan Seljuk had fallen at the hand of the one-eyed ogre. His gall bladder had been pierced, and he had spilled his blood on the battlefield. The fleeing troops saw the tragedy with their own eyes; they said his gall was pierced and that he had given up his life. The earth and sky spun down onto Old Aruz's head. He fell to the ground, tears pouring, and he cried and howled out in pain.

Women and children came at the sound of his cries. When they learned about what had happened, they wailed, too. Meanwhile, Basat looked off into the distance, emotionless. Suddenly, however, he began to change before our very eyes. His eyes blazed red. His body stiffened. His arms swelled. As time progressed, he literally began to grow taller. Soon, he unexpectedly leaped into the air. I thought his head would reach the clouds! He leaped, did a somersault in the air, and landed on the back of his stallion, Tekel, who was standing beneath the balcony. Tekel reared up as if he had been waiting for that exact moment.

With that, both horse and rider took off in a cloud of dust. Old Aruz did not even have a chance to wipe his tears. He and I stood in amazement, watching the clouds of dust slowly disappear into the distance.

...Then I saw Bakil in my dream. My Khan, it was you who sent him to the Georgian Marches. Bakil was visibly downcast. I do not know whether he concerned our affair or not, but his quarrel with Gazan and their falling out had saddened him. I saw in my dream that...

> *The account of Gorgud's dream is suddenly cut here. However, the damaged pages are not important for an understanding of the overall content. For me, these missing sentences do not hamper a full understanding of Bakil's story at all.*

...In my dream, I went to the Georgia Marches, to Bakil's country, and stood outside his home. I saw a woman sitting on a rock outside the tent, crying. It was Bakil's wife. Her name was Surmalija Cheshme. "Why are you crying?" I asked her. "Why are you grieving, my daughter, Surmalija Cheshme?"

Surmalija Cheshme raised her head. She looked at me, unseeing at first, and then she finally recognized me. "Gorgud, is it you?" she asked anxiously. "I am crying for my young son, Imran."

"What has happened to your son?" I asked.

Surmalija Cheshme sighed. "Gorgud, do not ask. Yellow snakes are turning in my stomach. A scene played before my eyes. You know about yourself, but you do not know about us. Do you know that the troops of Gara Takur came from Georgia and attacked us? Bakil is ill in his bed. He went hunting and broke his leg," she said.

"Go on…" I urged.

"My young son, Imran, went in his father's stead to fight Gara Takur. I begged him not to go! But he went into battle, anyway. He went to fight at his tender age. I know what will happen. Soon, he will be a victim. The sword of the infidel enemy is poised in the air; my son's head is bent; and that sword will cut his head off!" she cried. "Can you see it, too, Gorgud? Help me! Please come to my aid. May my dark head be sacrificed for you? Can you help me? It is all my fault. I am so wretched, so unhappy—"

"Where is Bakil?" I interrupted her.

"Where should he be? Bakil is at home. He is bedridden. I told you he broke his leg hunting," Surmalija Cheshme replied. "May Gazan's home be destroyed, Gorgud! He has brought these misfortunes upon us."

"What does Gazan have to do with this?" I asked, surprised.

"Please return my son to me, Gorgud," Surmalija Cheshme cried. "Then I will tell you everything. Otherwise, I will curse you all." She continued. "Gorgud, fetch me my little Imran. If you don't, I will beseech God to send you not one, but one thousand sworn enemies! Bakil thought we should move to the outer reaches of the bloody Abkhaz[44] land. By moving camp there, he wants to get far away from his homeland and family. Gazan is to blame. Don't you know about this, Gorgud? Weren't you on that hunt? Gazan invited Bakil on the hunt. Did you not see the quarrel that flared between Bakil and Gazan? Gorgud, you are a man of mercy. I beg you, please pray to God that the infidel does not strike my son. He wants to strike him. Look, look at the vision!"

I began to watch the vision as though in a separate dream. I saw Bakil's young son, Imran, on his knees before Gara Takur. I saw the boy's head lowered and Takur's sword raised up in the air. Compassion flooded my veins, and I turned my heart to the Stone of Light. "Oh, Stone of Light! Oh, wisest of stones, beloved stone! Be true to yourself. Frustrate the infidel's intentions. Do not let him kill the boy. Give the boy a stay of execution. Freeze the vision…"

I saw what I had said took place. At that moment, the vision froze. Only Gara Takur's eyes darted back and forth in amazement; his arms and legs

---

[44] An area on the east coast of the Black Sea, now known as Abkhazia, which is mentioned in the epic, *The Book of Dada Gorgud.*

were frozen rigid. His sword hung, unmoving, above the boy's head. I looked at Surmalija Cheshme. "You asked for help. Look! God reached out his hands to help you. Look, look at the vision! Don't you see that everything is frozen? Great God has not refused mercy to you and your son," I said enthusiastically. "Now, tell me, where is Bakil? What is this enemy? What is this quarrel? How could you curse Gazan? Tell me calmly. Your young son is suffering."

At first, Surmalija Cheshme could not tear her eyes from the vision. She, too, seemed to see what I saw. Then she fell at my feet and embraced them. "Gorgud, you have been sent here by almighty God! May those who do not believe in you be cursed!" she cried. Then she looked up at me, looking nervous. "Listen to me, Gorgud. I have sinned. I told people that Bakil's leg was broken. Oh, my tongue! I could not hold my tongue. I told the servant. How was I to know?"

"A serving wench may wear smart clothes, but she will not be a lady. Just remember that," I said.

"I don't know, Gorgud. I don't know who the servant told. I'm not sure who she passed the news on to. Eventually, Gara Takur found out about it and said, 'Let's go and plunder Bakil's tents and land. He has done us much harm since he came here!'"

"And Bakil is in bed?" I asked, thoughtfully.

Surmalija Cheshme nodded. "Yes, Bakil is in bed. He said, 'Let my son, Imran, attack the enemy in my stead.' This is what happened!" she replied. "What are we doing talking here? Please come inside. Bakil will be glad to see you."

"How will he see me, Surmalija Cheshme?" I asked. "This is just a dream. He will not come into my dream."

"He would if you wanted him to. Why wouldn't he? Gorgud, do it, please! Bakil will tell you why he fell out with Gazan," Surmalija Cheshme said urgently. "You will be able to hear the whole story and then recount it to Bayindir Khan. You will understand why I cursed Gazan."

Since when have we entered one another's dreams? I wondered. *We cannot do it.* Many questions raced through my mind. *Why did this woman curse Gazan? What is Gazan's role in Bakil breaking his leg and Gara Takur's armed attack on the marches of Oghuz?*

Ultimately, I agreed to follow Surmalija Cheshme into her home. She quickly took me to Bakil's bedchamber. I saw Bakil in bed, his face swollen and his leg wrapped in bandages. He was groaning from pain. "Bakil, what has happened to you, my warrior?" I asked.

I loved Bakil very much, and I suddenly remembered when Georgia sent cudgels instead of tribute, and whomever the Khan had asked grimaced and would not come near. Only Bakil said, "If the Khan orders me, I will go and defend the marches of Oghuz." He did end up going and defending the marches. He showed much valor, and at that time, no bad tidings came from the Georgian Marches to Oghuz. I loved Bakil for his loyalty to the Khan and for his loyalty to Oghuz.

Now I was moved to see him in such a bad state—to see him grinding his teeth from pain. I quickly took some grass from my bag. It was grass that grew around the Stone of Light, and it was different from other grass. If you chewed it, all your pains disappeared. You would also see one thousand phantoms, and you would leave your body, fly into the blue sky, and then eventually return to your body. I put some of this grass into Bakil's mouth. "Chew it, Bakil," I instructed.

Bakil looked at me, his gaze weak. I don't know whether he knew me or not, and I saw him struggle to chew. As he chewed, his strength gradually began to return and his eyes lit up. Moments later, Bakil laughed. "Gorgud, is that you?" he asked incredulously.

"Yes, it's me, Bakil."

"What have you given me?"

"Grass. Chew it and your pain will fly away."

"It has already flown away, Gorgud," Bakil's eyes twinkled. Suddenly, however, he frowned at me. "What are you doing here, Gorgud?" he asked. Then he shifted in his bed and looked at his wife. "Surmalija Cheshme, tell the servants that Gorgud has come," he ordered. "Ask them to prepare some food."

"It is not the time for food, my Lord," Surmalija Cheshme replied, lowering her gaze.

"Why? What has happened? Is there news? Where is young Imran?"

"Young Imran—" Surmalija Cheshme almost started to weep again. Her voice trembled.

Bakil sensed that something was wrong and began struggling to get up. I placed my hand on his shoulder. "Bakil, don't get up! Don't hurry to eat," I said quickly.

Bakil relaxed but only a bit. "Gorgud, this leg of mine was throbbing and throbbing," he replied. "Where has the pain flown to?"

"It is the grass, Bakil, the grass that you have been chewing. It has driven away your pain."

Suddenly, Bayindir Khan stopped me at this moment to question me about the special grass. I told the Khan all that I knew about it. "It is medicine for pain," I said. "It drives away consciousness. You begin to see yourself from outside. Your soul leaves your body and rises up into the endless sky. There, it flies and flies until it finally returns to your body." Bayindir Khan ordered me to bring him some of the grass. He did not say what he needed it for, though, and I did not ask.

Bakil slowly came to. His eyes filled with light. He did not stop laughing loudly, surprising himself. Suddenly, he looked around and asked, "What has happened to young Imran? He set out against the enemy. Has he not returned?"

"He has not," Surmalija Cheshme answered quietly. She kept her head down.

"What has happened to him?" Bakil asked one more time, turning to me.

"Bakil, your young son was about to be killed by Gara Takur, but almighty God did not permit it. How old is he for you to send him against Takur?" I asked, shaking my head. "You were not right to send him." I had spoken what I knew was in Surmalija Cheshme's heart.

Bakil sighed. "What was I to do? Do you know what Gazan told me? You don't know. You weren't on the hunt," he said defensively. Then he looked at his wife. "Please leave us alone. Let me talk to Gorgud privately." With that, Surmalija Cheshme shot me a look of sorrow and went out.

"Do you know what happened on that hunt?" Bakil began as soon as his wife had left the room. Anger rang in Bakil's voice. He repeated his question, "Have you heard what Gazan got up to on the hunt? Do you know how Beyrak swore at me?"

"No, I haven't heard. Tell me," I said calmly. "Tell me."

"The time will come when you will listen to me, Gorgud, but not now. Now we must save young Imran. I must catch up with Gara Takur. Then I will tell you all about it," Bakil said with a look of desperation on his face. He then tried to get up from his bed, but he did not have the strength to stand and fell back down, breathing heavily. "My leg is broken, Gorgud. I don't know how, but Gara Takur knows about it. Help me. Please help my young son."

"Your wife told me. You must not do anything. I will deal with this," I said quietly.

"How? How will you deal with it? You don't know Gara Takur!" Bakil blurted. "It is my fault. I sent my son, still wet behind the ears, against Gara Takur. It is my fault…" The poor man began to sob.

What am I going to do? I wondered. Again, I had no choice but to cast myself on the mercy of the Stone of Light. Without waking from my dream, I began to say the Prayer of Salvation so fervently that I could hardly stand. I was about to fall, but just managed to stay upright by holding on to Bakil's bed. I prayed from my heart: *Oh, Stone of Light, do not withhold your light from me, your slave. The sins of this father and mother are great, but this boy has no sin. Take pity on his tender years. Send your light onto Gara Takur's raised sword so that it might dazzle the infidel and the boy can escape, I beseech you.*

The Stone of Light did as I asked. It sent a shaft of light to Takur's sword. The sword blazed with light, and this light fell into the eyes of the infidel, blinding him. At this moment, I, too, moved quickly and unlocked the frozen vision. Takur pressed his hands to his eyes, dropping his sword. Young Imran grabbed the sword, shot to his feet, and held the sword against the infidel's throat. His strength grew tenfold. Gara Takur fell at his feet.

"Do you see, Bakil? The boy has defeated Takur. Now he is cutting off his head!" I exclaiming, showing Bakil the vision, too.

Bakil, who a moment ago had been weeping, now laughed out loud, clapping his hands. "Come now!" he cried. "Make ready the celebration. Imran is returning a victor!"

Surmalija Cheshme quickly entered the room again. As soon as she saw the vision, she wanted to fall down at my feet. I held her arms and would not let her do so. She could not keep silent, though. "Gorgud, may whomever does not believe in you die! You are our father. Your might has accomplished this, Gorgud. God gave inspiration to your soul. May you enjoy good health, and may your road be open! May your words be balm to those who hear them! May you be our constant support!" she rejoiced. Then she added, "Tell the nobleman; tell him: Will it go well or ill for the traitor to the Khan?"

Suddenly, I felt a stone in my stomach. My heart could not bear it, and I promised myself that I would get to the bottom of Bakil's story. If need be, I would also tell the Khan. The Khan would know what to do. Bakil then spoke to me…

> *According to the version in the epic, Bakil's anger with Gazan over the hunt had hidden causes. Gorgud was wrong when he thought that the conversation with Bakil would not concern the main story. He wrote: "…Bakil's story is long and complex. I do not know whether this story affects our affair or not; only you know, my Khan." In fact, this hunt has special significance in determining who freed the spy from the dungeon and helped him flee the country.*

…Bakil told me that news had come from Salur Gazan. The messenger had been Fair Gonur, the old shepherd. Bakil told him to go to the pen and choose any sheep he wanted for kebabs and take them back to Gazan. The fair shepherd selected the sheep and took them away to Inner Oghuz.

Time passed, and one day, Bayindir Khan summoned Bakil. Arshin Direk had captured Old Gazilig and cast him into a dark prison at Duzmurd Castle. Whoever went to rescue him returned empty-handed. Bakil told everyone who went there that Duzmurd would not be easy. Duzmurd had high walls and strong guards defending the fortress. Alas, no one took heed of Bakil's words. Aman even assembled hired troops, but they returned empty-handed, too. Old Gazilig could have been locked up in the seventh heaven. Bayindir Khan wanted to take counsel with Bakil about Duzmurd Castle.

Old Gazilig's son, Yeynek, sought leave to release his father from torment in Duzmurd Castle. The Khan gave him leave. Word was sent to Bakil that he must tell Bayindir Khan about Duzmurd—about the surrounding countryside, roads, and tracks. I wondered how that all went.

"I went to Gunortaj Palace for the grave visit. I had traveled much in those places, but nonetheless, I sent spies and heard again and again about every path and every blade of grass. Then I went to Bayindir Khan and told him what I knew," Bakil explained. "I ended with the words, 'Hired troops cannot take Duzmurd Castle. Love for Oghuz must burn in the heart of every soldier who goes near Duzmurd.'"

Bakil said that the Khan had listened to him with great care and favor. Then he summoned Old Gazilig's son, Yeynek, and ordered him to prepare forthwith and assemble the men of Oghuz to undertake the perilous mission. Gazan had, of course, also been present at the council. As the men all left the Khan's chamber, Gazan had turned to Bakil with a suggestion. "Let's go hunting. True, we have yet to see the deer or gazelle that you promised to bring, but never mind, we respect you," he said. "You are our guest here. Hunting before an attack has its own flavor."

Bakil paused for a moment and looked at me. "Gorgud, you know how I can shoot, don't you? My arrow can pin the front leg of a gazelle to its ear!" he bragged. "I have shot many gazelles in this way and then set them free. Many hunters in Oghuz have sent me gazelles that they have caught using my technique, saying that they belong to me."

I nodded and grinned. I knew that Bakil was an excellent hunter.

When Bakil was satisfied with my acknowledgment of his impressive skills, he continued. "Now, listen to me. Gazan invited me to go hunting with him, and I accepted gladly. There were many men on the hunt, including Shirshamsaddin, Gazan's brother, Garaguna, Gara Chakir, and his son, Girggunug. You know that wherever the father goes, the son goes, too. Beyrak was also there," Bakil said. "Gara Chakir shot an arrow, and Gazan told him that he had displayed the skill of a true warrior. Girgunug then shot an arrow, and Gazan praised him, too. When I shot an arrow, Gorgud, the arrow sliced through the air, piercing the animal right through and coming out the other side. When Gazan saw this, what do you think he said?"

"What did he say?" I asked.

"Gazan said, 'This is not the skill of a skillful man; this is the skill of the horse,'" Bakil scoffed. "His words meant nothing to me. I told Gazan, 'My shooting is renowned throughout Oghuz. You must know this.'"

"And what did Gazan reply?" I asked.

"He said, 'If the horse does not work, then man cannot display skill. Your horse is clever. The skill belongs to the horse,'" Bakil replied.

"And then what happened?" I asked.

"The nobles tried to test me again. Beyrak was especially zealous, saying that Gazan was right; the horse was the skilled one," Bakil said. "'So it's not my doing?' I asked them. Beyrak said, 'No.' Gorgud, my eyes filled with tears!"

"What did you say after that?" I asked.

"I told the nobles, 'I will shoot this arrow with my eyes closed. I will hit the animal!' I said," Bakil replied.

The nobles burst out laughing. Then Beyrak had looked at Bakil and said, "You have gone rusty out in the Georgian Marches, Bakil." Suddenly, the nobles fell silent.

"Beyrak," Bakil had said. "I am bearing the full load; you are bearing a few pounds. Come, I will shoot an arrow with you, and I will show you who has the skill—the man or the horse."

Furious, Beyrak stepped closer to Bakil. "Are you mocking me?" he asked.

Bakil hadn't answered Beyrak. Instead, he turned to Gazan and said, "My Lord, put him in his place. May he know his limits…"

Bakil then looked at me. "Gazan clearly liked Beyrak's courage. Although he said nothing, I realized that he had known of Beyrak's intent," he said. "Then Beyrak moved closer to Gazan; he was furious—*really* furious. Turning to me, he cried, 'Or what? Go on. Tell me!'"

"What did you do?" I wondered.

"Again, I paid no heed to Beyrak. I looked at Gazan and said, 'Gazan, call off your dog. Did he really say that to me? He should know his place.'"

Beyrak began to get angrier and angrier. "Me know my place?" he had asked incredulously. "Bakil, you have been away from Oghuz too long. It has been so long since you've seen another man that you don't know what you have become. You have achieved nothing. And I should know my place? You should know your own place, or I will cut off your head, Bakil!"

Beyrak then placed his hand on his sword. Bakil restrained his wrath. Looking once more at Gazan, Bakil shook his head. "Gazan, my Lord, I am telling you for the last time," he said slowly. "I will not answer for my actions."

Gazan did not allow the clash to deepen. "Nobles, stop this quarrel. Enough. Be quiet, both of you. Finish the argument now," he said. "We came here to enjoy ourselves. Have you forgotten?"

"Did you just call me a dog?" Beyrak demanded.

"Is there another dog here, but you?" Bakil asked. "Of course, I did."

Beyrak then raised his sword. "Dog yourself, carrion crow! Come out and fight!"

As Bakil moved to draw his sword, Gazan glared at Beyrak. "Didn't I tell you to finish the quarrel here? Didn't I? Shirshamsaddin, take him away!" he growled. Shirshamsadin immediately put his arms around Beyrak and led him to a fast-flowing stream nearby. Then Gazan focused his attention on Bakil. "And you, Bakil, listen to what I have to say. The fame of my bow has traveled as far as Trebizond. Although you are a brave man, you cannot compare with me. Do you understand? Know your place! I'll tell you once more: It is down to your horse that you can pin the leg of a gazelle to its ear. It is down to the skill of your horse!"

"Is that right?" Bakil had asked Gazan, beside himself.

"Yes, that is right," Gazan had said matter-of-factly. "What do you say, noblemen? Isn't that right?" He looked around at the nobles, waiting for their reply.

The nobles agreed with Gazan, their heads bowed. "Yes, that is right," they said in unison.

"You have dragged my name through the mud before the nobles, Gazan," Bakil said gravely. "I no longer know you, and you don't know me."

With that, Bakil had turned his horse around, summoned his warriors, and they left for home. Bakil admitted to thinking many dark thoughts on that journey. He thought long and hard and eventually came to a final decision. Gazan would not let his challenge pass. Without batting an eyelid, he had denigrated Bakil's skills. The nobles had defended Gazan, too.

Bakil looked at me, recalling the events that had unfolded. "Of course, if Gazan wanted, he could've lowered me in Bayindir Khan's esteem, too. Or he would gallop into my home country and raid my lands. What won't Beyrak do?" he asked with a shrug. "He will do anything. What should've I done? How could I do it? These thoughts occupied me until I reached home…"

I remained quiet, waiting for Bakil to continue.

He said that the foremen came to meet him and took his horse. Seeing his heavy heart, they said nothing. Indeed by the next day, everyone would know about the incident. Bakil's warriors had been quiet on the journey; they, too, had been downcast at Bakil's break with Gazan and his quarrel with Beyrak. Furthermore, fear of Bayindir Khan hung over them. *What if Bayindir Khan should hear from Gazan and vent his fury on us?* they wondered. *What would we do?*

Bakil went inside his home. As soon as Surmalija Cheshme saw his countenance, she rushed over to him. "What has happened, my Lord? You left so joyful and have returned so sad," she said.

"Gazan disgraced me before the nobles. We went hunting and shot gazelles and deer. He did not like me. He said my skill was just the horse's," Bakil replied.

"Did he? What of it? Don't people across Oghuz send you gazelles and goats with their hooves pinned to their ears, which they say is your mark?" Surmalija Cheshme asked incredulously. "Gazan can say what he likes. He is only talking to himself."

"No! Gazan has offended me, and I must settle scores with Beyrak," Bakil shot back.

"What has Beyrak done now?" Surmalija Cheshme asked anxiously.

"He is responsible for everything. I put up with a great deal, my lady. Beyrak drew his sword against me! The nobles separated us. Do you know what I thought?" Bakil asked. "I thought, 'We must leave this place before Gazan and Beyrak unite and attack my land and family.' I have become an enemy of Oghuz. May God overlook my sin."

Surmalija Cheshme began to shake her head. "Don't do it, my brave Lord! Don't do it! Things do not go well for the man who goes against his Khan. Stand upright; cast away this downheartedness. Why are you looking at me so sadly?" she replied. "Go hunting. Forget these bad thoughts. Gather the warriors. What is wrong with our mountains that you go hunting in other mountains with Gazan?"

When Bakil didn't immediately answer, Surmalija Cheshme continued. "Do you know what would happen without you? Without you, Oghuz would not have one day of peace, my Lord. Is it easy work to defend these marches from Gara Takur? Why has not a single one of them come to defend the marches?" she asked. "You are here. You live and breathe here, and that is enough for our enemies to keep away. Isn't it? Isn't this what your spies say? Arise, arise, my brave Lord. I will tell them not to unsaddle your horse. Go hunting. I want gazelle meat. Bring me game, my brave Bakil..."

Bakil looked me in the eyes. "My wife had distracted me, but then it dawned on me: Gazan is not Bayindir Khan. I thought, 'Of course! I will go to Bayindir Khan and tell him the story.' I knew that Bayindir Khan would punish Beyrak; the real punishment was for Beyrak. Beyrak's sin was greater than Gazan's. He knew how to ingratiate himself. It's a skill he learned in Bayburd," he said. "My lady was right, though. I needed to go hunting. I wasn't thinking straight. I was angry, and an angry mind cannot be clever."

With that, even though Bakil had just returned from Oghuz, he assembled his knights, sergeants, and warriors, and then mounted his horse. There were high mountains and steep cliffs in his lands. There were endless gazelles in those mountains. Surmalija Cheshme had been right; Bakil hadn't shot an arrow at the gazelles of his own mountains for a long time.

He had looked at his assembled men. "Come, take your provisions! Take your arms, my warriors! Come, let's go hunting to the black mountains..."

As soon as Bakil spoke those words, I woke quickly from my dream. Opening my eyes, I found myself back at the Stone of Light.

§ § § § § §

The Shah did not have the patience to talk at length to the ambassadors. He and Huseyn Bay Lele were the only two who knew the reason. Looking at the Shah, the Vizier, though not fully informed, was able to divine a reason for his behavior. The Shah had certainly been disquieted after his conversation with Lele. He did not seem to wish to hear what the ambassadors had to say, even though he had been impatiently awaiting their arrival from faraway places.

"My Shah, I would sacrifice myself for you. He asks if we also intend to send envoys to visit them?" the Vizier whispered into the Shah's ear.

Suddenly, the Shah moved his head aside. "Why not? It is not a bad idea. God willing, we now have such intent," he said.

The ambassadors consisted of four men. One of them knew Turkish, and he was interpreting for them. "Your Excellency, did you say how long you were on your journey?" The Shah asked the ambassador another question without waiting for the interpreter.

"More than a year, Your Majesty."

"One year. Since you have made such a long journey, each of you has earned a gift. You say that your capital is surrounded by water?" The Shah asked, his voice more disbelieving than mocking. "Well, so—" Again, not waiting for the interpreter, he stood up to say his last word. When everyone saw him move, they immediately jumped from their seats. "You have traveled a long way and now you are tired," the Shah said. He turned and looked at the Vizier. "Vizier, see that the guests are looked after and served well. In a day or two, we will continue our conversation, God willing."

The Shah impatiently left the throne room without looking up. The Vizier and ambassadors bowed and held their positions as though frozen. Then the Vizier stayed with the ambassadors and tried to continue the conversation, but he was restless. While the ambassadors spoke about their capital; about the places and countries they had traveled through; and about races and nations they had heard of but not seen, the Vizier paid attention to each word, inscribing them in his brain and on paper.

If His Majesty asks something, what will I answer? he wondered. His interest was really with the Shah and Lele, so he was more inattentive than ever and often interrupted the ambassadors to ask them about what he had already heard. The ambassadors continued their conversation, feeling more at ease and giving detailed, lengthy answers to each question from the gray-haired, pensive official.

"You say that if our men go to your country, they will have to pass through Ottoman territory. Is there no other way?" the Vizier asked again, thoughtfully.

The head ambassador, a pale-faced Byzantine Greek, pondered the question as he understood it for a few seconds. Shortly after, he opened a map and started to discuss something with another ambassador. He then turned to the Vizier and gave his reply.

The interpreter translated his words: "Your Excellency, I have sought long and hard, but the shortest route passes through Ottoman territory. There are other routes, too—several of them—but they are very long and not as safe. A sea crossing would be required and there are brigands on this route," he said. "If the Shah grants his permission, we can plan another route in our minds and then draw it on the map. If we have to pass through Ottoman territory, then so be it. The Ottomans will never know."

"Of course, we will discuss it in more detail with our Perfect Councilor, God willing. So, according to your map, the Ottomans are located right between our countries. It is very interesting," the Vizier said. Then he looked at the ambassadors. "Is it true that your capital is in the sea?"

Looking at one another, the ambassadors confirmed that information for the thousandth time. The Vizier made some more notes for himself and then kindly invited the guests to dine. Everyone expressed their consent and stood up. With that, the Vizier went out of the throne room, followed by the ambassadors and other courtiers. The throne room was left empty once again.

§ § § § § §

The Shah hurried across the garden to his secret rest chamber. Lele sensed the Shah's approach from his breathing. He opened the door and closed it quickly after the Shah. The Shah asked Lele a question with his eyes. Lele bowed, and the Shah went straight to his bedchamber. A young man was waiting anxiously near the window. As soon as he saw the Shah, he prostrated himself. The Shah took off his veil, went up to the young man, and began to examine him closely. Lele came in and stood a little distance from the Shah. He crossed his hands over his chest, awaiting orders.

"Stand up so that I can look at you. Come into the light," the Shah said to the young man. He began to study his face. "Bravo! The Lord has created nothing more beautiful." After some time, he paused in his contemplation, moved away, sat on a Byzantine stool near his couch, and turned to Lele. "Lele, tell me, where did you find him? Well done to you, too, I might add. You have earned a thousand bravos!"

Without drawing a breath, Lele began to speak. "May I sacrifice myself for you, my Perfect Councilor? As soon as I received your order, I understood that this was a very grave matter of state. May God keep you; your wisdom is beyond question. I began to journey from village to village; I could not ask anyone, as I would have been divulging the secret," he said. "So, step by step, I journeyed through the land. There were several boys. When the nose matched, the chin did not; when the chin matched, the ears did not. At last, I could not find a better likeness than the boy you see before you. If he meets with your approval—"

"Very much!" the Shah exclaimed. "He very much meets my approval. What is his name?"

Lele let out a small sigh of relief. "His name is Khizir, my Shah," he said, shooting the boy a warning glance, as though he himself might have wanted to answer the Shah.

"Have you told him about the matter?" the Shah asked.

"Yes, I have. May I sacrifice myself for you? He is ready for any order."

"Very good," the Shah nodded. "His first task is to go with you tomorrow and be seen in public at the dawn prayers."

"Very well, my Shah. But do you yourself not plan to go walking in the city tomorrow morning?" Lele asked. "You wanted to go to the bazaar."

"I will go to the city with the Vizier. But do not breathe a word to him about this! You know yourself. Our main purpose is to make the people—the courtiers, everyone from children to adults—believe that I was in two places at the same time. It's all settled!" the Shah reminded Lele. "Prepare him well. Teach him my gait and manners. I think it is too early to do without the veil, though. What do you say?"

"Yes, it is too early to do without the veil. May I sacrifice myself for you? We must not hurry in this matter," Lele replied. "Everything will gradually fall into place."

The Shah looked closely at Khizir again, as though he wanted to find a hidden mark or line on his face. Unable to find one, he stood up, satisfied. "Good, I am going," he said. Then he looked around the room. "The place where he sleeps must be far from prying eyes. This place will be good. Have a bed prepared for him in a corner of the room. Also, Lele, teach him how to play shatranj."[45]

"Very good, my Shah. I shall teach him. He—" Lele suddenly stopped midsentence.

"Well, he what?" the Shah asked curiously.

"He..." Lele hesitated. He didn't know if he was right to speak or not, but the arrow had already been shot. "He can write poetry."

"He can write poetry?" the Shah asked, surprised.

"Yes, he can, my Shah."

The Shah did not ask anything more. He glanced at the boy again and left the room without further ado. Lele accompanied him to the door, and then went back to Khizir. He sat on a carpet, his legs crossed. He then nodded to Khizir, who came and took a seat opposite him. Both were silent. They sat quietly for some time.

§ § § § § §

With the passage of time, Khizir began to resemble His Majesty more and more. Lele allowed him to walk more often among the people in the guise of the Shah. He would sit in the throne room, his gold-ringed fingers stroking the gold fringes of his veil, and even though his entourage—all the courtiers—would have their heads bowed in silence, they would look at the movement of his fingers and give thanks and praise for the Shah, which was actually Khizir.

Khizer stood, sat, and even turned his head to one side like the Shah. He also raised his hand abruptly to call attention without bending his spine, just like the Shah. Lele had also already taught him how to play shatranj. Sometimes Lele would order the guards to leave the rose garden, and then he would prepare a place for the Shah and Khizir to play shatranj together. The Shah loved his rose garden very much. In his spare time, he would visit the garden and ask Khizir to tell him about his village home.

Khizir came from a mountain village a long way from the capital. His father was alive and he had sisters. His mother was dead, though; a mountain stream had carried her away. His older sister, Zarnisa, did all the housework. His father had already grown old. He had not gone into the Shah's service. Once, when the centurions were recruiting from village to village, he joined the Red Caps for the Shah's campaign in Dagestan,[46] but when they came back, he left them. He sowed and harvested and went to Ardabil or Tabriz to sell his produce, and then he would return, managing as best as he could to feed his hungry family. The other sister, Parnisa, was little. Khizir felt sorry for her because she was growing up motherless.

---

[45] An old name for chess.

[46] The Red Caps, or Qizilbashi, were a militant movement that supported Safavid Shiism and helped Shah Ismail come to power. The Red Caps were made up of predominantly Azerbaijani Turkic tribes.

A whole line about the Shah is illegible here, and the next page is missing altogether. There is no link whatsoever between the previous passage and the next one. Getting ahead of our story, I can say only that we will not get any more detailed information about Khizir's family. But what was the significance of beginning to give information about the family? Did the unbelievable metamorphosis in Khizir's fate later in the story affect his father and sisters? It is impossible to say for certain. This is one of the vanished secrets of The Incomplete Manuscript.

§ § § § § §

"How can you write a poem every day? There must be a secret here," the Shah asked, giving Khizir a quizzical look. Khizir was concentrating so much on the game that, although he heard the words of the Pivot of the Universe, he did not take them in. Lele jumped up to cuff Khizir, but the Shah would not let him. "Never mind, let him think," the Shah mused. "He's facing a difficult move." Suddenly, the Shah looked over at one of the rose bushes. "Lele, look over there," he said, pointing.

When Lele looked in the direction that the Shah was pointing, he saw that a small bird had gotten caught in the rose bushes again. He looked back at the Shah. "Go and release him. Let him fly," the Shah said. Then he turned to look at Khizir. "Think as much you like, but you have no way out of this situation. Your king is in a bad position, lad. He cannot move. You have no choice but to surrender." Without waiting for an answer, the Shah then clapped his hands on his knees and stood up.

Lele ran over to the bird, freed it, and carried the rescued bird back over to the Shah. The Shah shook his head at Lele. "For the sake of the Shah of Chivalrous Men, do not torment that poor bird!" he exclaimed. "Let him go. Let him fly!" Lele immediately opened his hands to the sky and released the bird. It circled once overhead, and then flew away.

The Shah turned his attention back to the boy. "You still haven't said how you write these poems. I cannot remember what you said yesterday, but I liked it very much," he said.

Khizir's eyes shone, and a happy smile covered his face. "May I sacrifice myself for you? Your Majesty is my inspiration," he replied. "It has entered my soul."

"Bravo to your teacher!" the Shah said. He looked at Lele again. "What about you, Lele? Do you like the poems or not?"

Lele nodded. "I like them very much. May I sacrifice myself for you?"

The Shah smiled in satisfaction, but then suddenly became serious. He stood up and covered his face with his veil. This was a signal that he was leaving. The next day would be hard. He had summoned a military council.

Recently, the Shah had thought of nothing but the Uzbek ruler, Sheybani Khan. He did not know why, but he could not bear him. Even from afar, he hated Sheybani. He had ordered preparations for a military campaign. Only the Lord of the Universe knew what would happen and how it would happen…

§ § § § § §

After taking my medicine, Bakil's leg was gradually getting better. He did not want me to leave so soon. But a dream is a dream; it does not depend on one's wishes at all. I finished my chat with Bakil, bade him farewell, and went out. Moments later, I saw Surmalija Cheshma sitting in the spot where I had seen her a short while ago. *Is she waiting for me?* I wondered. Intrigued, I approached her. "What is wrong, Surmalija Cheshma? What do you want of me now?" I asked. "Your boy has been saved and returned to you, thank God. What do you want?"

> *In my heart, I also thanked the Stone of Light. I could do no other for reasons that are known to you, my Khan.*

Gazing at me sorrowfully, Lady Surmalija Cheshma began to talk. "I wish you good health, Gorgud, my father. May God prolong your days, watching over our dark heads. May the world's debt to you grow and ours with it. But Gorgud, my father, please listen to me. Lord Bakil may have told you the true cause of what has befallen us. He came home and said, 'I have quarreled with Oghuz. I have become an enemy. I will gather my goods and chattels and move camp from here.'"

"How did you respond?" I asked.

"I said to Bakil, 'You have quarreled with Gazan, so stay at odds with him. You have gotten angry with Beyrak, so remain angry. But do not quarrel with our monarch, Bayindir Khan, the Khan of Khans, my Lord. Do not become an enemy to our ruler! If you become an enemy, misfortune will befall you.' And it did. He says we will move camp to Georgia. What kind of talk is this?" Surmalija Cheshma asked.

She continued. "He said, 'Know that I have become an enemy to the Oghuz.' What is he saying? Whether you become an enemy or not, it is enough that the idea, inspired by Satan, has come into your head. Then what happened? Didn't the enemy's troops, led by Gara Takur, descend on your people like a cloud? I sent my young son to fight the enemy. He was about to be killed by the tyrant, Takur. I can tell you that nothing goes well for the man who has become an enemy to his ruler!"

I could tell that Surmalija Cheshma had much more to say. I listened patiently as she went on.

"What would have happened if almighty God had not sent you, Gorgud, to save us from this misfortune? Gorgud, my father, I say to you—and if not to you, then to God—bring Bakil onto the right path. It is for Bayindir Khan himself to decide whether or not to punish Gazan and Beyrak. What has changed now? For years, Bakil has defended the borders of the Oghuz; he has protected them night and day. No bird has flown over Oghuz land. Enemies came and were defeated, and fled crying. What has happened to Bakil now? Why do Gazan and Beyrak want to gladden the hearts of our enemies? Will Oghuz gain peace by breaking Bakil and cooling relations with him?" she asked, beginning to sob.

I listened while Surmalija Cheshme worked herself up into an even greater rage. When she was finally done speaking, I looked at her and smiled sympathetically. "Surmalija Cheshma, my daughter, if you are right, I entrust Bakil to you for safekeeping. Do not let him become an infidel enemy. Now he is in bed. Let him eat and sleep and enjoy his days. Of course, I will convey your words to our Bayindir Khan. I will also speak to Gazan," I said. "There is no substance to this matter. With God's help, you will smooth out this quarrel and put an end to it. But tell me one thing: How did the enemy know that Bakil was ill and unable to lead his troops? Is there a spy in your camp, too?"

Surmalija Cheshme remained silent for a long time. Then she sighed and began to speak. "Father Gorgud, you would like to know whose fault it was? The fault was mine," she muttered. "Yes, the sin was mine; it is a long story. The conflict between Beyrak and Bakil has not grown from nothing. You remember, Gorgud, how Bakil took me away on the back of his horse? Don't you remember? Maybe you don't know the story. At the time, Beyrak was sniffing around our tent. There was still time before his wedding…"

"Go on…" I urged.

"Before the wedding, Beyrak went to hunt maidens in Outer Oghuz. He saw me—and he wanted me. At that time, Alp Rustam had turned his mouth from me. I have no secrets from you, you know. Alp Rustam and I loved each other. When night fell and the moon cast its light on the glade behind our tent, he would arrive first, and then I would slip into the shadow of his embrace. That is how we loved one another," Surmalija Cheshma explained.

She continued. "When Shokhlu Malik plundered Gazan's home, my father was one of those who went to Gazan's aid. He went into battle alongside Old Aruz. My father was killed. He never returned. Whom could Alp Rustam ask for my hand in marriage? We carried on as we were, saying, 'Tomorrow, tomorrow we'll sort things out,'" she said. "I didn't know where Bakil appeared. Alp Rustam's nephews pointed me out to him; they discussed and arranged everything. They had an aim, Gorgud. They wanted Alp Rustam to tie the knot with their sister."

"The brothers kidnapped me and cast me before Bakil. Alp Rustam knew nothing of it. As soon as Bakil saw me, the sap rose within him. He threw me onto his chestnut-maned stallion and galloped away. When I opened my eyes, I was already in Bakil's home. All Alp Rustam could do was vent his wrath upon his two nephews; he hacked them to pieces. Oh, those days, those moon-lit nights…" she said, her voice trailing off.

As Surmalija Cheshme spoke, she remembered the past and was clearly moved. She spun the vision of the past before my eyes, too. "Beyrak placed his eyes on me, Gorgud. The eyes are bad; they are faithless. Years later, Beyrak wants to avenge the hurt on Bakil. Don't let him! Alp Rustam was wretched, disgraced in Inner Oghuz; he became crazed and killed his two nephews. Can a candle burn in the home of a murderer of his two nephews? The fault was mine, Gorgud. May God forgive us of our sins," she said quietly.

"As far as Bakil's leg goes, well, I sent him out hunting," she continued. "I told him to go and revive his low spirits. He went and broke his leg while hunting. He told me—only me—and now I am beating my brow! If only this had not come to pass. You keep asking me about a spy. I was the spy, Gorgud, but I did not know it. I had told the serving wench that Bakil had fallen off his horse and broken his leg."

"You did?" I asked, waiting for more of an explanation.

"Yes. The serving wench asked, 'What happened, my dear lady? Why has the color drained from Bakil's face?' I replied, 'Do not speak of this, but my Lord has broken his leg. He is in bed and cannot get up. No one must know of this. No news of it must reach Gara Takur!'" She sighed, recalling the conversation. "The serving wench told another wench, and she told one of the man servants, and he blurted the news to the slaves. What came from thirty-two teeth spread to everyone! This is how the news got out, Gorgud. If Bakil knew, would he not flay me alive? You are seeking the culprit. I am afraid that I am the culprit. It's me…"

As I listened to Surmalija Cheshme's words, what had befallen Bakil gradually became clear to me from all sides. I had long pondered the cause of the quarrel between Bakil and Beyrak, and the cause of Alp Rustam's misery, and at last, I had found two important truths. I recounted these two truths to the Stone of Light. The Stone of Light listened to me in silence, which I took as a sign that it accepted my words. The first truth was that nothing should be told to a serving wench. Whatever you do, a serving wench is not a lady. You can treat her tenderly or adorn her beautifully. You can dress the serving wench in fine clothes, but she will not be a lady. My second truth was that…

The Incomplete Manuscript *is torn here. Gorgud's revelation of the second truth is left until later. But the careful reader can see the context that gave birth to one of Gorgud's well-known sayings found in the introduction to the epic: "You can dress the serving wench in fine clothes, but she will not be a lady."*

§ § § § § §

"My Khan, this time my dream took me to Gazan's tent. Shirshamsaddin came into my dream, but whatever I do, I cannot recall that dream. May you forgive me, God willing. All I know is that Shirshamsaddin is so closely connected to Gazan that if Gazan told him to die, he would die for him. If he told him to live, he would live for him. So if you see Gazan or Shirshamsaddin about the spy, there will be no difference between them," I said. "During the council's discussion about the spy, Shirshamsaddin would immediately agree with every opinion that came from Gazan's lips."

Bayindir Khan gave me a sign to stop talking. I fell silent immediately. "Gorgud, this Shirshamsaddin you talk about is a feather-brained man. He does not know what to do. He acts first and thinks later. He has no plans. I remember once that he came to me without any reason. He does not know what he is saying; he does not think. Could he have anything to do with the spy?" he asked.

"I don't think so at all, my Khan," I said, but the louse in my hair had run down to my feet. "Neither more nor less than any others."

Bayindir Khan was lost in thought again, knitting his brow. "Carry on with your tale," he said after some time. "We will leave the conversation about Shirshamsaddin until later. You carry on. Or have you finished what you wanted to say?"

In fact I had gotten lost. I was struggling to bring together all that I had said and all that I had seen in my dreams. Bayindir Khan understood this and did not insist.

Bayindir Khan continued. "All that you have said is an ill omen for Oghuz. But it is no more than an omen. Do you understand what I mean, my son?"

"Yes, majestic Khan," I replied. "I understand."

"Then let us draw some conclusions," The Khan said quietly.

"Yes, it is the time for conclusions, my Khan," I nodded. I could feel cold sweat trickling down my back.

Bayindir Khan rose and began to pace the room. Although my head was bowed, I concentrated on Gilbash and could see that he was following Bayindir Khan's every move, awaiting a word from him. He also understood that the affair was approaching its end. Before starting to speak, Bayindir Khan cast a glance in my direction to see if I was writing or not. I was adjusting my pen, and when I had finished, I was ready to put my pen to my paper.

Walking to and fro, Bayindir Khan calmly began to speak. "Of course, there is trouble in Oghuz. It is no longer the Oghuz of old. The spy affair has opened my eyes to many things—Gazan and Aruz, Aruz and Beyrak, and Beyrak and Bakil. Inner Oghuz is displeased with Outer Oghuz, and Outer Oghuz is displeased with Inner Oghuz. And then there is the spy. Old Gazilig sets out on a raid. His friends flee, abandoning him to the enemy. Giyan Seljuk goes to One-Eye, breathes his last breath on the battlefield, and then his friends leave him to the mercy of fate. Gazan might speak disrespectfully; Bakil might take offense and go to Georgia, leaving the borders open as the skies—and then the spy," he recapped. "Shirshamshaddin comes to my palace without permission. The honorable nobles do not heed my orders and avoid going to the Georgian Marches, and the last hope is Bakil. The question must be asked: Am I Bayindir Khan, son of Gamghan, or not? No, it is better not to live than to live like this. If this is how Oghuz has changed, it is better to die."

The Khan paused a moment to let me catch up with my writing. "Old Aruz comes and goes. He speaks openly about his heart's desire to become the Noble of Nobles. He cries, 'Were it not for my son, Basat, One-Eye would have crushed Oghuz. Where was Gazan? Where was Garaguna? Where was Beyrak?' We are fed up with his endless talk about Basat. Basat took revenge on One-Eye for his brother, Aruz's son, Giyan Seljuk, and now the whole of Oghuz must be grateful," he said.

I wrote as fast as I could, keeping silent and making sure not to miss a single word.

The Khan continued. "Beyrak is cunning. He earns his name. He makes Gazan trust him and chooses imprisonment in Bayburd Castle rather than going into battle against One-Eye. This is how it was; I know better than anyone. A man from Bayburd told me this. And then there is the spy. What should I do? Of course, someone is stirring the pot, and of course, the hand of whomever is stirring the pot can be seen in the spy affair. You can be certain that whomever is stirring the pot of Oghuz is the man who freed the spy," he said. Then he looked at me. "What do you think?"

Bayindir Khan finished his speech, and then fell silent. I felt that he wanted to say something else, but was holding back, leaving some matters until later. There was no decision. There were slopes; there were steep inclines; but there was no peak. The Khan had to make a just decision on every matter; therefore, he was keeping his counsel. But he was still thinking. Maybe other men would be summoned to the investigation, too. With the help of almighty God, all would be well in Oghuz.

"It's certainly Gazan, but we cannot reveal this. Gazan is our son-in-law. I do not need a man who wears his guilt on his face. I need a man who wears his guilt in his soul. Have you understood me, Gorgud?" Bayindir Khan asked. Without waiting for an answer, he slowly walked out of his chamber. Left in the Khan's chamber were just myself...

The text breaks off here, but nevertheless, I think it's possible to complete the last sentence with "...and Gilbash." This ending fits what has gone before and completes the picture. But you cannot miss something strange in the content of the manuscript. Gorgud's attempts by means of his dreams, or maybe under the guise of his dreams, to tell Bayindir Khan what he knows lend the tale a different harmony, a different color. Maybe this prompts a reply to the question of who the real "spy" is. We can feel this nicety in the words of Bayindir Khan when he says, "You can be certain that whomever is stirring the pot of the Oghuz is the man who freed the spy."

Maybe Bayindir Khan is trying to combine two lines in this way. By positing the idea—"The man who wants to cause turmoil by setting the Inner Oghuz against the Outer Oghuz and the man who freed the spy are one and the same"—perhaps, the Khan wanted to covertly hint at a specific person. Dark clouds are beginning to gather over that person. As the Khan expected, Gorgud sensed what he wanted, and now another issue had risen, namely, that everyone who would be questioned in the investigation should be able to name the same person. As we have already seen, the first person to read this name on the face of Gorgud was Gazan himself.

...the Khan, Gilbash, and I were left alone again in the Khan's chamber. After a rest, the Khan looked as cheerful as before. He looked at us and smiled. "Shall we start? Let's start. I have listened carefully to you, Gorgud. This is my conclusion: All is not as I would like it to be in Oghuz. There is conflict and the nobles' growing feud will destroy Oghuz from within. Is this not what you wanted to say, Gorgud?" he asked.

I bowed my head. "Yes, my Khan, this is what I wanted to say," I said softly.

"Excellent, excellent," Bayindir Khan replied, continuing to look at me. "But we do not want to be distracted from the matter in hand. Let's get back to the spy. Then it will not be difficult to come to a decision. Am I right?"

It was clear that Bayindir Khan had already taken his decision. However, his soul would not rest if he did not finish the discussion about the spy. What were we to do? We could only carry out the wishes of the Khan and to accept the fate, the destiny, that God on High had ordained for us.

Both Gilbash and I agreed with Bayindir Khan. Then the Khan turned to Gilbash. "I want to see Shirshamsaddin. Summon him. You said he was somewhere here. He has probably been whispering to Gazan. Summon him," he ordered.

Gilbash bowed and went out. I began to arrange my pen and papers. The Khan watched me for a few moments. Then he spoke. "Do you know, Gorgud, my son, that whatever we do and whatever we do not do has one purpose, and that is to find the scoundrel in our midst?" he asked. "Who is the spy and who isn't the spy is a separate matter. Who is causing turmoil in Oghuz? You know, that is the main question. You think that by saying, 'Basat! Basat!' all will be put right? Look, Gorgud, if you say, 'halva,' will you taste sweetness in your mouth? Why are you silent? Speak."

For some time, I did not know what answer to give Bayindir Khan. My courage had flown away. However, seeing that Bayindir Khan insisted on an answer, I said, "Majestic Khan, if you say, 'halva,' your mouth will not taste sweetness. If you say, 'halva-halva,' your mouth will still not taste sweetness. But—"

"But what? Tell me," Bayindir Khan interrupted, interested in what I had to say.

"If you say, 'halva,' many times, your mouth *may* taste sweetness, my Khan," I said.

Bayindir Khan bit his lip, deep in thought. He did not utter another word. Moments later, Gilbash entered the Khan's chamber, followed by Shirshamsaddin.

I thought, If the Khan knows that Gazan has a hand in this affair, and knowing that, does not want to punish him, then it means that everything is following a pre-arranged path. Old Aruz is the only person who is guilty, and that suits everyone. He wants to bring real disaster upon Oghuz. Who knows how great his involvement really was in the spy affair? From the beginning, Gazan took a step on the right path by mentioning Old Aruz's name. Shirshamsaddin will do the same, God willing. May almighty God be his inspiration...

As soon as Shirshamsaddin was in the Khan's chamber, he prostrated himself and did not rise. Bayindir Khan cast him a glance of indifference and then looked at Gilbash. "Get him up," he ordered. "Get him up and bring him closer. Let him sit down."

It was blindingly obvious that the conversation with Shirshamsaddin was a cause of displeasure to Bayindir Khan. But Shirshamsaddin was not aware of it at all. Without waiting for Gilbash, Shirshamsaddin rose to his knees, crawled toward Bayindir Khan, and sat in front of him. Bayindir Khan looked down at him. "Shirshamsaddin, open your ears and listen to me carefully. I have just one question for you; there is no need for lengthy discourse. If you do not tell the truth, do not be offended at the punishment I shall mete out. Tell me, Shirshamsaddin, who helped the spy to escape from Oghuz?"

"Yes, magnificent Khan, your command is right. You are always right. May your high mountains reach up into the heavens, my Khan," Shirshamsaddin began. "May almighty God help you. May your life-giving waters flow eternally…"

> *"The high mountains," he says. "Your life-giving waters," he says.* Son of a scoundrel! Where did he find these words? *I wondered. They have nothing to do with the matter in hand, but they are very fine.*

Shirshamsaddin's lips ground out the words like a millstone. "Khan, please listen to me. These words have been piercing my heart for a long time. I have long wanted to see your dear face. Hear my voice, Khan of Khans. Do you remember how you assembled troops in the valley of Darasham, and together we set off for the fortress of Aghja?[47] You took me with you on the campaign, do you remember? I swear by almighty God that no one told me, 'Attack the enemy. Attack!'" he said. "How could I think that I would attack your enemy without your permission? No. Such a thing did not come to pass. Almighty God knows that I do not know how it came to pass; I do not know. Maybe someone has told you baseless words about me. Do not believe them, magnificent Khan."

Bayindir Khan sat, unmoved. He knew there was no way out. Shirshamsaddin would not come to the point until he had emptied his heart. The Khan had to be patient and listen. Wise men have always ruled the world, and Bayindir Khan showed his wisdom by allowing Shirshamsaddin to unburden his heart and by forcing himself to listen.

But Shirshamsaddin did not want to stop. He had finally unburdened his heart, but he still carried on. "I am ready to die for you, my Khan. I shall be in your service all my life and will never say that I am tired! Morning and evening, I shall pray to almighty God for you; I shall not falter for a moment. Would I attack your enemy without your permission? God forbid! Never! Not at all! Do not believe it, Khan…"

---

[47] Darasham is a placename in *The Book of Dada Gorgud*. The author has used it in his own way.

At last, Bayindir Khan realized that it was hopeless. Shirshamsaddin would go on and on like the large intestine. With his previous anger spent, the Khan gently stopped Shirshamsaddin. "Shirshamsaddin, stop for a moment. Rest; otherwise, you will kill yourself, my brave man. I am an old man. I do not have time to listen to you until morning. You have spoken and I have heard. You have sworn and I believe you. Not one more word about it, my scoundrel son of a scoundrel" he said. "What is done is done. Do you understand me?"

Without raising his head, Shirshamsaddin answered, "Yes, my Khan. I understand you. Why would I not? Am I someone who does not understand?"

"No, of course not. You are one of the wisest of men and one who best understands. Let us get to the heart of the matter together. Shall we get to the heart of the matter, my brave man?" Bayindir Khan asked. He wanted to give Shirshamsaddin a little encouragement. "What do you say?"

"Whatever you say, I say, too, my Khan," Shirshamsaddin replied quietly. "I say nothing else and never will."

"Then I will repeat my question. Are you ready? Yes? Good. Tell me, my warrior: Who helped the spy escape from Oghuz? Tell me," the Khan demanded.

Shirshamsaddin saw that there was no way to avoid answering the question. "It was Aruz, my majestic Khan. It was Aruz. If you wish, hang me. If you wish, cut me in two—"

"You say it was Aruz, do you? So how did Aruz do it? Was it not *you* who had been guarding the spy, you scoundrel?" Bayindir Khan interrupted. He had hit the bull's eye.

Shirshamsaddin was thoroughly confounded. He stole me a glance, as if to ask, "What should I do?" Who was I to say anything? Bayindir Khan had asked a good question. Who was guarding the prisoner in the pit? It had been Shirshamsaddin. Who had escaped from the pit? The spy! What did Aruz have to do with it? Bayindir Khan had not yet asked the main question; he had not asked about the council. It was clear that everyone who took part in the council was party to the escape.

The affair was thickening. If it went on like this, Shirshamsaddin could spoil everything. Come what may, Bayindir Khan would confuse him and get to the truth. It was for him to decide who was right and who was wrong. *Can we equal the Khan in wisdom?* I wondered. *Can we equal the Khan in skill? Are our senses as great as the Khan's?* Bayindir Khan wanted to know the truth.

"Tell me how it was! Start from the very beginning. You threw the spy into the pit and locked him in. I know that you met a lady by the name of Boghazja Fatma that night; I know that you met," Bayindir Khan fumed. "What did you talk about?"

[insert note a]

This was the first time that Bayindir Khan had uttered Boghazja Fatma's name. Shirshamsaddin had had an effect on him. Bayindir Khan knew about Boghazja Fatma, but did not breathe a word about her. So why was he holding the investigation? Did Bayindir Khan know everything already? If so, then all that was left for us was to make our way to the torture chamber in the corner of the courtyard.

[end note a]

The color drained from Shirshamshaddin's face until he was as pale as the new paper before me—a gift to Bayindir Khan from Trebizond.[48] I thought he would breathe his last breath in that moment. But he maintained his composure. The words of that scoundrel son of a scoundrel made the louse in my head run down to my feet and cold sweat trickle down my spine.

"My Khan, take pity on me and let Gorgud speak," Shirshamshaddin muttered. "Gorgud knows everything."

Silence fell. Bayindir Khan did not speak for some time. Finally, he glared at the man before him. "You scoundrel! I am asking *you.* Are you trying to avoid your guilt? 'Let Gorgud speak.' He has already spoken! Now it's your turn!" he replied.

> *That is just what Bayindir Khan said, "Gorgud has already spoken." And with these words, he broke Shirshamsaddin. Almighty God, they would have broken anyone. How can the wretch know what I said? In pursuit of his quarry, Bayindir Khan had set a trap that amazed us all.*

Shirshamsaddin was still crouched down. Although he raised his head, he could not look Bayindir Khan in the face. He would have stayed in this pose, saying nothing, had Gilbash not crawled to him, nudged him hard, and hissed, "Do as the Khan has ordered—or else! Do not tire the patience of the Khan."

Bayindir Khan's patience really was about to snap. He was on the verge of summoning the flagellators from the torture chamber. I had heard the screams and groans rising up to the sky from the Khan's torture chamber. It was notorious. The flagellators were not the worst; other torturers would take pincers from the fire and plunge them in your mouth.

Shirshamsaddin kept silent. He looked as though he would never answer.

"Flog the meat from his bones! Take him to the torture chamber. Give him to the flagellators!" Bayindir Khan shouted, unable to endure the silence any longer.

---

[48] Now known as Trabzon, Trebizond is an ancient town on northeast Turkey's Black Sea Coast.

Shirshamsaddin blacked out. Just as Gilbash was about to drag him from the room, a thought occurred to the Khan. His heart softened. "Stop for a moment, Gilbash," he said. "The scoundrel son of a scoundrel drove me to my wits' end. Throw water on his face. Bring him to his senses."

God Almighty, when he opens his mouth, what will he say? Yes, of course. Of course, Shirshamsaddin was our weakest link! Bayindir Khan would never speak like that, even to Bakil. He would not send him to the torture chamber. Shirshamsaddin had really infuriated him.

The water brought Shirshamsaddin to his senses. Without waiting to be told, he splashed water in his eyes and washed his face. Then he started to speak. While he spoke, I wrote as fast as I could. Every now and then, I would look up at Bayindir Khan and see that he was listening intently. Sometimes a smile would creep across his lips. *What is in his heart at this moment?* I wondered. *Only God knows!*

"Majestic Bayindir Khan, I swear I am one of your few truly devoted slaves in the whole of Oghuz. I may sometimes have sinned; I may sometimes have trespassed; but for the love of God, believe me, Khan. I knew not what I was doing! Would I, without waiting for the Khan's command..." his voice trailed off as he tried to arrange his thoughts. "The moon shone that night. No, before that moonlit night, some events occurred that were, I believe, directly linked to the spy. Salur Gazan, pillar of our nobles and the whole of Oghuz—long may he remain so—gave his tent, his goods, and chattels for plunder. Inner Oghuz came to plunder, Khan, but this time Outer Oghuz did not come."

"Go on..." the Khan said.

Shirshamsaddin went on to explain in detail what had happened while the Khan listened intently. Meanwhile, I continued writing.

Gazan had asked Shirshamsaddin, "Why haven't they come to the plunder? Do you know anything about it?"

"No," Shirshamsaddin had replied. "I have no idea. But my Lord, have you forgotten? You yourself did not invite them. You said, 'Let the Outer Oghuz keep away.'"

"Really?" Gazan had frowned.

"Yes, really," Shirshamsaddin had answered.

Gazan then looked Shirshamsaddin in the face again and asked, "Shirshamsaddin, do you think that not inviting Outer Oghuz to the plunder will create discord or not? Will my uncle, Old Aruz, be angry with me and take offense? What do you think?"

Shirshamsaddin replied, "Gazan, you know yourself that you know nothing of Outer Oghuz. The fires of discord burn in Outer Oghuz. You should have invited them to the plunder, my Lord. They have already given their word, my Lord."

"You are right," Gazan agreed. "May this transgression pass us by." Then he quickly looked left and right. When he was sure that Shirshamsaddin was the only man listening, he added, "Lady Burla did not allow it. She said that if I invited her uncle and the Outer Oghuz nobles, she would go to her father."

Shirshamsaddin paused from telling his story and looked up at the Khan. "She would go to you, majestic Khan. Yes, Gazan told me this, but I beg that this may remain between us only. That same day, Beyrak burst in to see Gazan. I felt a sense of foreboding. I did not want to let him in to see Gazan, but my Lord had summoned him. I alone already knew what they would speak of—and what they would not speak of, my Khan," he said. "You will ask how I knew; I will answer your question. My Khan, I swear to you that I must mention one more matter here. Just one day before the plunder of Gazan's home, Beyrak and Lady Burla had a secret meeting. I did not tell Gazan. I thought there was nothing in it, so why stir dark suspicions in his heart? But now I think that this meeting had something to do with what was to happen next."

"What happened?" Bayindir Khan asked.

"Lady Burla and Beyrak met at night on the banks of the Uzun Pinar in the garden behind Gazan's tent. What passed between them and what did not, I know not, nor do I want to. It was not my business! However, I was hiding behind a mulberry tree. I could not see anything—it was pitch dark—but I did catch some words. They were talking quietly," Shirshamsaddin explained.

"What did they say?" the Khan asked.

Shirshamsaddin recalled the conversation as best as he could remember.

"Tomorrow, go to Gazan and tell him that there is a spy in Oghuz. The time is ripe," Lady Burla had said.

"But what if Gazan asks why I have kept silent about all of this?" Beyrak had asked.

"Say, 'I thought long and hard and saw that Outer Oghuz did not come to the plunder today,'" Lady Burla replied. "Say, 'I thought this could not be a coincidence.'"

"So Outer Oghuz will not come to the plunder tomorrow?" Beyrak then asked cheerfully.

"How could they come?" Lady Burla asked. "I have arranged everything so well that Aruz and his son, Basat, will not be able to free themselves of this net for one thousand years."

"Of course, they will not, Lady Burla. It will be very difficult for them to get out of the net you have cast; therefore—" Beyrak began.

"Stop there! Tell Gazan that the spy is Aruz's son, Basat," Lady Burla had commanded.

"No, Lady Burla, this cannot be. Gazan will not believe me. Basat, a spy? He will ask, 'Why have you left it until today? Not only have you brought news of a spy, you have told me who it is.' We must be more cunning," Beyrak said.

"Then what shall I do?" Lady Burla wondered.

"Do not worry. Someone else will tell Gazan who the spy is," Beyrak said confidently. "I will sort it out."

"Very well, brave Beyrak," Lady Burla had replied. "May your roads be clear. Do not tarry now. Go!"

"May we meet again, magnificent Lady Burla," Beyrak then said. With that, he had climbed over the fence.

Shirshamsaddin looked at Bayindir Khan. "He came in secret, my Khan," he said quietly. "And in secret, he left. Now I knew that Beyrak was in Salur Gazan's presence, and reporting to him the affair of the spy. Beyrak could not have been long with Gazan when Gazan summoned me, too."

Shirshamsaddin then went on to recap the conversation he had shared with Gazan while Beyrak was nearby.

"Shirshamsaddin, do you know what tidings Beyrak has brought?" Gazan had asked.

"I know not, my Lord," Shirshamsaddin had replied. "He did not tell me." (However, Shirshamsaddin did indeed know.)

Gazan continued. "There is a spy in Oghuz, Shirshamsaddin. You should be aware of this. Where have your eyes been looking? Why were you not aware of this spy affair? Beyrak had to tell me this in your stead!" he had said irritatedly. "You eat my meat, and this is how you serve me? All Oghuz is talking about the spy. You were ignorant of this and so was I!"

"Maybe it is a trick, my Lord?" Shirshamsaddin had suggested. "The enemy may be spreading tidings of the spy to provoke us. Maybe they have set a trap to create turmoil in Oghuz..."

"Don't be such a fool," Gazan had replied, clearly angry. "Beyrak says that when he was in captivity in Bayburd, Bayburd had a maiden daughter. She had been suckled on pure milk. Together, they—" Gazan paused for a moment. He smiled and looked over at Beyrak. "Yes, Beyrak, what happened?" he asked sarcastically. "Are you ashamed?" Without waiting for an answer, Gazan looked back at Shirshamsaddin. "The maiden told him about the spy. I also think—"

"What do you think, my Lord?" Shirshamsaddin had asked eagerly.

"I think that I went hunting; I had organized a great hunt," Gazan had replied carefully. "Do you remember? The infidel's spy was ready and reported what he knew. While I was away, the infidel troops raided Oghuz. They laid waste our land and took my people captive, didn't they? I am asking you, Shirshamsaddin. Didn't they?"

"You spoke true, my Lord," Shirshamsaddin had answered. "They did."

Gazan continued. "Besides, before Beyrak's wedding—before he took to his marriage bed—the spy did his work again. News reached Bayburd. They came and captured Beyrak, a nobleman, on the eve of his wedding!" he had exclaimed. "Never before have I encountered such churlishness! Was this so or not?"

Beyrak lowered his head and was silent.

"It was so, my Lord," Shirshamsaddin had replied. "They were deeds of great evil. You remained a prisoner of Bayburd for sixteen years. It was a disgrace, my Lord."

"And there is more. Bakil went hunting, and he fell and broke his leg. The spy informed Gara Takur, and Gara Takur's army attacked the marches of Oghuz. It had been the spy again," Gazan had said. "Do you understand what I am saying, Shirshamsaddin?"

"I understand, my Lord," Shirshamsaddin had nodded. "I understand. How could I not?"

Just then, Beyrak had interrupted. "My master, Gazan, do not let Bayindir Khan know about the infidel. If he knows, his wrath will be terrible," he warned.

"Against whom?" Gazan had asked uneasily.

"Against the infidel, my Lord," Beyrak had replied, quickly covering his tracks.

Shirshamsaddin paused in his recap and looked at the Khan to make sure he was still listening. He was. "I saw, my Khan, that Beyrak was very cunning. He wanted to fill Gazan's heart with doubts and fears," he said quietly.

The Khan only nodded. He looked at me to make sure I was still writing and then nodded at Shirshamsaddin to continue. Shirshamsaddin took a deep breath and began where he had left off.

"My Lord, if Bayindir Khan is angry, then he will be angry with us!" Shirshamsaddin had said. "He will ask why we have not yet punished the infidel."

Gazan had looked at him, thinking. "You are right. If the Khan is angry, he will be angry with us. And why have we not yet arrested this infidel son of an infidel—I mean, the spy? Why have we not cast him into a dark dungeon and given him a taste of his own blood?" he had asked. "Answer me, Shirshamsaddin!"

Both Shirshamsaddin and Beyrak had stayed silent. What could they say? Gazan waited a few moments. Finally, he answered his own question. "We don't know who this spy is," he then blurted. "Shirshamsaddin, do you know who he is?"

"No, my Lord, I don't," Shirshamsaddin had answered quickly.

"And you, Beyrak, do you know?" Gazan then asked.

"I do not," Bayrak had replied.

"And when you were in Bayburd, did that girl—I mean, the infidel's daughter—tell you anything about the spy?" Gazan then asked.

"No, she didn't. She only said that we had a spy in Oghuz," Beyrak had answered.

Gazan became lost in thought. After a few minutes, he spoke again. "What am I to do, nobles? How am I to find out who the spy is?" he had asked.

"Might the spy be from Outer Oghuz, my Lord?" Beyrak had asked carefully.

Gazan had frowned at Beyrak's comment. "You say Outer Oghuz. Are you thinking of Aruz again? No, my friend, Aruz can think only of Basat. Can you make a spy out of Aruz? Aruz, a spy?" he had asked. He shook his head. "No, not him."

"Then…" Beyrak had begun cautiously.

"Then what?" Gazan had asked, clearly losing patience. "For the love of God, hurry up! The sun has already passed its noontide peak. The nobles will have already begun the plunder. Afterward, they will say, 'Gazan himself did not join us! He did not show us the scent of his goods and riches.' Shirshamsaddin, has Lady Burla left the tent?"

"She has left, my Lord. My lady has gone to the glade in the forest where the Buzlusel flows down from the cliffs. The ladies-in-waiting are with her," Shirshamsaddin had replied.

"Good. The further she goes, the better," Gazan had stated. He then looked at Beyrak. "Beyrak, you wanted to say something?"

Beyrak hesitated. "Nothing, my Lord. Maybe—"

"I've got it!" Gazan had suddenly interrupted, seemingly pleased with himself. "Let's call Gorgud. He always says that God gives inspiration to his heart. He says he can bring tidings from the future. We have not put him to the test at all. The future has its place. What need do we have of it? We don't need the future! Let him give us tidings from the past. Let him say who the spy is. Am I right, nobles?"

> *Look at the scoundrel! He wants to sow the seeds of doubt about me. No matter, we will see…*

"You are quite right, Gazan," Beyrak and Shirshamsaddin had answered together.

"Then, Shirshamsaddin, go and find Gorgud as quickly as you can," Gazan replied. "Have him come to me."

Shirshamsaddin had winced. "Lord Gazan, it is no easy task to find Gorgud. And this is urgent. It will take time," he warned.

Gazan shook his head. "We don't have time. Then what shall we do?" he had wondered. Suddenly, he had an idea. "This is what we'll do! Go to the plunder and tell the nobles that they should go ahead without me. Let them take whatever they want. Tell them that my goods and riches are a blessing to Oghuz." Then he had looked at Beyrak. "You go, too," he had instructed. When Beyrak and Shirshamsaddin didn't immediately take off, Gazan frowned. "Why are you standing here? Go to the plunder and choose the most beautiful goods!" he had urged.

"Me?" Beyrak's eyes had filled with sorrow. "You mean me, my Lord? My eye does not seek out your riches; I do not covet even a straw. You should know that I need nothing."

Shirshamsaddin had been dumbfounded by Beyrak's comment. It meant that Shirshamsaddin *did* have his eye on Gazan's riches. "Gazan, my master, I have need of nothing from this tent," he had said quickly. "Your love is wealth enough for me."

"Very well," Gazan had said slowly. "Do I not know you? Must you present yourselves to me?"

Shirshamsaddin had not been sure if Gazan was joking or speaking straight from the heart. Neither Beyrak nor Shirshamsaddin said a word. Gazan looked at the two men. Finally, his eyes focused on Shirshamsaddin. "Shirshamsaddin, you go and convey my words to the nobles. Then go to my bedchamber, take the casket that you will find near the candlestick, and bring it to me."

Shirshamsaddin did as he was told. When he reached Gazan's home where the nobles were gathered outside, he conveyed Gazan's words to them. "Nobles, Gazan has sent you a message," he had said. "He says that whatever he has today belongs to you—to Oghuz. Let the plunder begin!"

At that moment, one of the nobles, Tarsuzamish, had come forward. "We are not beginning the plunder," he said.

Shirshamsaddin was confused. "Why do you not begin, Tarsuzamish, my brother?" he had asked.

"Outer Oghuz has not yet come. How can we begin without them?" Tarsuzamish had replied.

Since Shirshamsaddin had been aware of the affair, he revealed the heart of the matter to the nobles without consulting Gazan first. "Nobles, Outer Oghuz will not take part in the plunder this time," he had said. "Only the nobles of

Inner Oghuz will take part. Please, come inside. Please, Tarsuzamish, this way…"

The nobles had looked at one another, unsure what to do. Then they slowly began to move forward. One after the other, they began to enter the tent. In a short while, they began to plunder, and oh, how they plundered! They carried goods out with their hands; they carried goods out with their teeth. While all of that was going on, Shirshamsaddin then slipped into Gazan's bedchamber without delay. No one had managed to enter the room yet. Shirshamsaddin found the candlestick—an antique gold candlestick, a souvenir of the raid on Trebizond—and he wanted to hide it from the plunderers, but then he thought of Gazan's wrath and averted his gaze.

He took the casket near the candlestick and brought it back to Gazan. Gazan and Beyrak were talking; Beyrak was speaking and Gazan was listening carefully. When Beyrak saw Shirshamsaddin, he immediately fell silent. Gazan also frowned, but seeing the casket in Shirshamsaddin's hand, he remembered that he himself had sent him to fetch it. He took the casket from Shirshamsaddin, opened it, and took out the one long hair that was inside.

"What is this hair casket, Gazan, my Lord?" Beyrak had asked, confused.

"This is the hair casket that Gorgud gave me when I was freed from Shoklu Malik's captivity. He said, 'Take it, Gazan. It contains a single hair of mine—a magic hair. When you are in trouble, light this hair, and you will see me near you,'" Gazan had replied.

"Is it really magic?" Beyrak had asked.

"Of course, it is magic!" Gazan had exclaimed. "Now we'll see what kind of hair this is. We'll find out if it's magic or not." Gazan then turned to Shirshamsaddin. He pointed at a nearby torch on the wall. "Give me that torch," he instructed. With that, Shirshamsaddin carefully handed Gazan the flaming torch. Gazan then held the torch to the hair, and it began to burn.

Yes, the scoundrel son of a scoundrel was telling the truth. When Gazan lit my hair, my whole head was on fire! But I had given him my word and had to appear before him.

Shirshamsaddin had closed his eyes. When he had opened them, he saw that I was in the room with them. He didn't know where I came from or how I got there. At that moment, Shirshamsaddin then looked at Bayindir Khan. "If you wish, my Khan, ask him and he will tell you himself. I didn't know and neither did Gazan or Beyrak. We were all dumbfounded," Shirshamsaddin added.

Just try not being dumbfounded, scoundrel!

Suddenly, Shirshamsaddin's eyes widened. "No, my Khan, I've made a mistake!" he said quickly. "Before Gorgud arrived—before the hair was lit—Gazan asked me about the plunder. The plunder had taken place. It was *after* the nobles had finished the plunder that Gazan had lit Gorgud's hair. Yes, of course, the plunder was already over. The nobles had taken whatever caught their fancy from Gazan's home. They were all satisfied."

"Okay, so then what happened?" the Khan asked, unmoving. Shirshamsaddin glanced at me briefly before continuing his story.

Gazan had asked, "Have the nobles gone?"

Shirshamsaddin had replied, "They have, my Lord."

Gazan then asked, "Did they go away satisfied?"

"Yes, they went away satisfied, my Lord. They were highly satisfied. And why would they not be satisfied? They took whatever caught their fancy! May God be satisfied with you," Shirshamsaddin had said. "I want you to know, my Lord, that I took nothing..."

Gazan had looked at Shirshamsaddin long and hard, but said nothing. Then Shirshamsaddin spoke again. "Beyrak has not gone. He is here. Do you wish me to call him or tell him to go home?" he had asked.

"No, tell Beyrak to come here. You come, too," Gazan had replied. "We will get to the bottom of this spy affair."

With that, Shirshamsaddin went out and called Beyrak, and the two men went to Gazan together. That's when Gazan decided to light Gorgud's hair. When Shirshamsaddin, Gazan, and Beyrak opened their eyes, I was sitting cross-legged in the middle of the room.

Gazan had stammered, "Gorgud, is it you? Have you really come?"

"You called me, didn't you?" I asked. "Or did you not believe me?"

Gazan then said, "I...I have seen many miracles. But the like of this, I have never seen!"

Shirshamsaddin began stammering as well. "I...I...I..." was all he could manage to say. Meanwhile, Beyrak looked like he was about to pass out.

Collecting himself, Gazan then greeted me with respect. "Gorgud, you are welcome. May you always be with us!" he had said. With that, he sat down opposite me, his legs crossed. "You know, Gorgud, that we need you. If we did not, I would not have troubled you."

"Tell me, Gazan, tell me what has happened," I had said. But then I looked at Shirshamsaddin and Beyrak. "Who are they?" I wondered.

Shirshamsaddin paused again to glance at me and clarify. "Gorgud may not have recognized us at first, my Khan," he said. "We were standing in the half-light." The Khan only nodded, indicating for Shirshamsaddin to continue with his version of the story. Shirshamsaddin gulped and started again.

He said that he had quickly spoken up. "My Lord, I will go out and come back later," Shirshamsaddin had said quietly.

Beyrak had nodded. "My Lord, should we wait outside?" he asked.

Gazan then looked at me, wondering if the two men should stay or go. I had shrugged. "No, why? Let them stay. They were standing in the dark; I did not recognize them at first. Shirshamsaddin, is that you? Beyrak? Come here! I am ready, Gazan," I replied.

Shirshamsaddin and Beyrak immediately moved closer and sat to one side. Gazan then began to speak. "Do you know why I called you, Gorgud?" he had asked.

"I know, Gazan, I know," I said quietly. "There is a spy in Oghuz…"

Gazan was surprised. Turning to Shirshamsaddin, he gave him a hard look. "Gorgud knew about it? Everyone knew but me! Was it so hard? Never mind; it can wait. But do you see, Shirshamsaddin? Your deeds…" he had sighed with frustration. Then he shook his head, trying to concentrate. He looked at me again. "What do you say, Gorgud? I say they are bitter tidings."

"Yes, Lord, bitter tidings," I had replied. "Bitter, indeed."

"Gorgud, what are we to do now? Whom should we suspect? Whom should we arrest and cast into a pit?" Gazan had asked. "If we cannot arrest the spy, you know that Bayindir Khan shall vent his wrath upon us!"

"'I know," I had nodded. "He shall."

"Speak, Gorgud!" Gazan had urged. "God gives inspiration to your heart. You bring tidings from the future. You say what will be and what will not be. Tell us, who is the spy?"

"Do not ask, Gazan," I had said solemnly. "Do not ask at all."

"Why should I not ask?" Gazan had asked, confused. "Can I not ask?"

Again, I had said, "Do not ask, Gazan. You will repent later…"

Gazan quickly became furious. "I will not! I will not repent! Just tell me his name. I will bring such misfortune on that infidel son of an infidel that I will tell my black slaves to flog him until his soul leaves his body!" he had shouted. "Bayindir Khan's torture chamber will be a pleasant meadow in comparison!"

Shirshamsaddin stopped telling his version of the story. He glanced at me again and then at the Khan. "This is what was said, my Khan. I am telling you what Gazan said and how he said it. I am telling you what I heard. I want you to know that I am not adding a single word," he said quietly. He then turned and looked sideways at me. "Is that not so, Gorgud?"

In that moment, a small bird caught in a rose bush in the Khan's garden was more fortunate than I was. If only I could take his place, almighty God, *I thought.* After this, I do not know how I will look the Khan in the face again…

I was silent. Bayindir Khan didn't take his eyes off of Shirshamsaddin, indicating for him to continue until he was entirely done. Without needing a verbal prompt, Shirshamsaddin continued dutifully.

I had said, "I tell you again, Gazan, do not ask me who the spy is." Clearly, I was trying to avoid telling Gazan news of the spy.

Shirshamsaddin then quickly added, "Gazan was desperate, my Khan. How else could he plead with Gorgud? The affair was growing…"

Shirshamsaddin said, "The affair was growing…" This means that Gorgud already knew who the spy was; he could just tell Gazan. However, if Gorgud, in some mysterious fashion, did know the identity of the spy, he would also know who helped the spy escape from prison. This is simple logic. Then what is all the investigation for? All Bayindir Khan would have had to do is ask Gorgud about it from the start. Gorgud would have been obliged to tell the Khan the truth, whether he wanted to or not.

If we look closely, we can see that no, that is not all the Khan had to do. Bayindir Khan's real, secret purpose was different.

Shirshamsaddin continued. "My Khan, eventually Gorgud cast the stone from his lap. He told us who the spy was. He had said, 'You know Boghazja Fatma.[49] The spy is her only son. Nobles, hear this, but do not repent…' After the spy was announced, Gazan had leaped up joyfully. We also breathed more easily. But Beyrak's countenance clouded over; I don't think he had expected that answer from Gorgud. As I have already told you, my Khan, Beyrak had his own intentions regarding the spy…"

§ § § § § §

Huseyn Bay Lele kept Khizir in a secret hideout, far from prying eyes. The Khan liked to rest in a chamber in the corner of a small garden behind the throne room, and this was Khizir's hiding place. Only three men could enter this room—the Shah himself, Lele, and Khizir. No one else could see him. Sometimes in the evening, when there was not a soul in the garden, Lele allowed Khizir to leave the chamber and go out into the arbor. Alone, he would wander the perimeter of the garden, breathing in the scent of the flowers and talking to them.

---

[49] Boghaz, an ancient Turkic word that is still used in some dialects in Azerbaijan, is used to refer to a pregnant animal.

He had chosen a pen name for himself—Khatai—and he would sign his pen name at the end of each of his poems. The Shah never tired of listening to the poems, and Lele was glad that the Shah's bird had perched on Khizir; he had become accustomed to him. Sometimes the Shah and Khizir would play shatranj together. Over time, Khizir mastered the rules of the game. During the games, however, no one else but Lele was present, of course. Lele himself would wait on the pair.

Lele had observed that although the Shah and Khizir looked very similar, they were complete opposites. Khatai was as gentle, good-natured, and peaceful as the Shah was shrewd, courageous, indulgent of no one's fault, and imperious in his position as Shah. Khatai had a special love for the Shah. His voice was soft; his heart was gentle; and his manners were delicate. *He is one of life's unfortunates,* Lele sometimes thought. The unfortunate's only consolation was that since he came to the palace, life had gotten better for his father and sister under Lele's protection. Lele had not breathed a word to Khizir's family about Khizir—it was a state secret—but he sent gifts to them on behalf of the boy. He also followed their problems and resolved them whenever he could. For this, Khizir nurtured boundless love in his heart for Lele.

Until the battle of Chaldiran,[50] palace life passed very gently for Khizir. However, after the wrongful battle, which so displeased God, his life was suddenly turned upside-down. There was a village called Chaldiran, and it was there that the battle between the Ottoman Sultan Selim and the Shah began. The Shah led the battle himself. He divided his commanders into flanks and gave orders to attack or withdraw as needed. His tent was pitched on top of a hill. No one could approach the tent when orders were being given. Servants would hear the Shah's voice from the tent, and heralds would deliver the orders. Khizir was also inside the tent, dressed like the Shah, but wearing a cloak on top. He watched the Shah closely all the time, paid careful attention to every word and order of the Shah, and sometimes watched the battle through a special hole in one side of the tent.

At one point, Lele had disappeared in the heat of the battle. He had fallen from his horse, and enemies descended upon him like black crows. Khizir's heart filled with blood; he could not watch, as if this would change anything. He immediately turned to the Shah and petitioned him. "My Shah, grant me leave to fight one battle for you! Let me go, my Shah. Should I be watching from a tent? I cannot bear it here," he cried. "By God, my heart will break…"

The Shah was silent; he was in his own world. Khizir did not know if he had heard him or not. Suddenly, the Head of the Guard rushed up to the tent.

---

[50] Chaldiran battlefield lies in what is now West Azerbaijan Province in Iran. The battle between the Safavid and Ottoman empires took place in August 1514.

The Shah brought himself back to reality and went forth to meet him. The Head of the Guard began to speak. "My Shah, may I sacrifice myself to you? The left flank...the left flank is giving way, my Shah!"

"Quickly, tell Khalil Sultan Zulgadar to help the left flank!" the Shah ordered.

The Head of the Guard prostrated himself. "May I sacrifice myself to you, Perfect Councilor?" he began.

"What is it? Tell me! Make haste!" the Shah cried.

"Zulgadar has turned traitor. Zulgadar has run away, my Shah," the Head of the Guard reported.

The Shah was shocked by his news. "Run away? The scoundrel! A traitor spawns a traitor. Go and find Ustajli Abdulla and send him immediately to the left flank. Go! Do not tarry!" he replied.

Another guard galloped up to the tent. In a single move, he leaped from his horse and fell at the Shah's feet. He brought more bad tidings. "My Shah, the right flank has broken!" he announced.

The Shah was shocked rigid. He lost all hope. "Well, go! All of you go! Just leave the guards here. Have them come to the front of the tent," he said. Then he thought for a moment. " No, wait for me. Just a moment," he said, changing his mind. "I am coming."

The Shah then entered the tent. Khizir was already awaiting orders. "Where is your veil? Put on your veil!" the Shah ordered Khizir. Khizir obeyed his command and put on the veil. It was as though a large mirror stood in the room, and one man began to converse with himself in the mirror.

"Listen to me. There is little time left. Don't interrupt me, lad. Listen—listen carefully. A little while ago, when I left the tent, I fell among the enemy. I was about to be taken captive. My horse stumbled and threw me off, and I lay trapped beneath the horse. My leg was hurt. The enemy surrounded me. You know Sultanali Mirza Afshar. Do you remember how he cried, 'I am the Shah! I am the Shah!' and leaped into the fray?" the Shah asked. "The enemy released me and captured him. Listen to me carefully. If Sultanali is freed from the hand of the enemy, give him a great reward. He rescued you. But punish Zulgadar, God willing. You have just heard what he did."

Khizir was confounded. *What is the Perfect Councilor saying?* he wondered. He did not understand him at all. When the Shah paused for breath, Khizir threw himself at the Shah's feet. "My Shah, may I sacrifice myself for you? What are you saying? How did Sultanali Afshar rescue me? How am I to punish Zulgadar?" he asked with panic in his voice.

The Shah grabbed Khizir by the shoulders and pulled him up. "Get up, lad," he ordered. Then he spoke more gently to the boy. "Get up, my Shah. This battle is already over. I am going, but you are staying," he said. "Please, take your veil—" Khizir tore off his veil. Deeply moved, the Shah looked at him and smiled. "Thanks be to the Lord of the Universe. Put it on. Nobody must see your handsome face."

Voices from outside began to fill the tent. "My Sage, my Perfect Councilor, the flanks! The flanks are lost. Make haste, my Shah. May I sacrifice myself for you? The enemy is near! It is time to leave...Can you hear? They are calling!"

The Shah put his head outside the tent. "For the sake of the Shah of Chivalrous Men, I am coming!" he cried. "I am coming." Then he turned back to Khizir. His voice changed; gentleness had returned to it. "Are you ready? Now you are to enter the battlefield alone. Neither Lele nor I exist. No one knows of Khizir. Understand that the Shah cannot die—never," the Shah said. "I have to die. Moreover, I must seek revenge. Now look, I am plunging into the very heat of battle. May God help me or Selim. Listen to me. You go outside in front of the tent. The guards are waiting for you. I myself am going." The Shah went to the back of the tent and lifted up a piece of wood in the wall of the tent. "Look, do you see Selim's standard and pavilion? That is where I am going."

Khizir was frightened. "My Shah, I...I cannot, my Shah!" he said quietly.

"You can. You can do it very well. This battle will pass. In a little while, the sun will rise again. Morning will break. The land will be yours. Do not cry, lad. I am leaving you such a great land. It is a secret from all. No one will know. You are turning into me. In times to come, the essence will be you; however, the outside, the zahir,[51] will be me. I will exist. Are you ready?" the Shah asked.

"Whom are we deceiving, my Shah?" Khizir asked softly, his head lowered.

"Look into my eyes, my Shah," the Shah replied. "*No one.* Truly, we are deceiving no one. For the sake of the Shah of Chivalrous Men, what has happened to you? Why do tears well in your eyes? Control yourself! This is like a game of shatranj. Or are you afraid?"

"I am afraid, my Shah. Maybe Lele—" Khizir began.

The Shah shook his head. "No, do not be afraid. Lele is no more. Lele has given himself into the clutches of death. May his place be in paradise," he said firmly.

A cannon ball fell near the tent and exploded. The horses shied, and screams rose up to the sky. The Shah looked back at Khizir and smiled. "You

---

[51] In Sufi thought, zahir is the external, visible cover, concealing the essence (batin) within.

are already free, poet. Did you ever imagine this? Go! Your guards are waiting for you. It is time to escape. The army is broken, but I—" he said.

"My Shah, my Perfect Councilor!" Khizir cried, begging the Shah to reconsider his plans.

"Do not interrupt me! I could not keep such a vast land from disaster. But I have to do it. I am going. You know, my Shah, a voice came down to me from the sky this morning. A little while ago, I heard that voice a second time. 'What are you doing there, lad?' the voice said. 'You have accomplished your task.' It was the voice of the Shah of Chivalrous Men. 'Come here,' he said. 'They are waiting for you here. Everyone loves you here.' That is why I cannot be stopped," the Shah explained. "Go out, my Shah. Go out of the tent. You will hear no more of me. My corpse will not be found. You live! Live long, Shah Ismayil!" The Shah almost whispered his final words. He removed the piece of wood at the back of the tent, lowered his head, and went out. But before disappearing altogether, he turned and looked once more at Khizir. "I want you to know this: My name was Shah Ismayil, but myself, I am not Shah Ismayil."

Khizir stood shocked in the middle of the tent. Chaotic noises outside were growing louder, but nobody dared to enter the tent. Finally, courage came to Khizir. He straightened his posture and, just like the Shah, strode toward the door of the tent. As he was about to leave the tent, however, he froze. Then he turned and looked back at the hole, but the back of the tent was covered; the piece of wood was in its place. There was no way back. Calling for help to the Lord of the Universe, for the sake of the Shah of Chivalrous Men, Khizir stepped out of the tent, leaving it empty.

§ § § § § §

..."Did you hear? Shirshamsaddin!" Gazan had thundered as he never had before. "What are you doing, sitting there? Get up! Fly fleet as an arrow. Find that scoundrel. Seize him and bring him to me!"

With that, Shirshamsaddin and Beyrak had flown out of the room. But when Shirshamsaddin looked again, he could not see Beyrak anywhere. Shirshamsaddin knew that Boghazja had a tent at the mouth of the vale, and so he had gone as fast as he could to that tent. When he finally reached it, he banged on the door. No answer came from within. Eventually, he picked up a stone and kept banging on the door. Again, no answer came. Then he heard some voices coming from within, but he could not make them out. Shirshamsaddin looked at Bayindir Khan as he recalled his story. "Someone was talking to Boghazja Fatma, my Khan," he noted.

Time passed, and the door was still not opened to Shirshamsaddin. He waited there. Then Shirshamsaddin turned to those behind him, who were out of breath and only just catching up, and said, "'Go through Oghuz with a fine-toothed comb. Find Boghazja Fatma's son and bring him to me. Go now! Make haste!"

Shirshamsaddin's men went out and eventually found Boghazja Fatma's son. As soon as they brought him to Shirshamsaddin, Shirshamsaddin put a rope around the boy's neck. Then he had slowly dragged him to Gazan. Gazan met the men at the White Gate.

Shirshamsaddin paused a moment, looking up at the Khan. "I looked and Beyrak was there, but Gorgud was not," he said.

Bayindir Khan only nodded, staying silent. With that confirmation, Shirshamsaddin continued telling the story.

He had cast the wretched spy at Gazan's feet. "This is the scoundrel!" he had said. "Look, my Lord Gazan. The spy is at your feet."

Gazan had clapped his hands together and burst out laughing. Clasping his hands behind his back, he then began to walk around the wretch. "How old is he? He's still wet behind the ears! But just look at what he's done!" he had said incredulously. "Now tell me, you scoundrel, when did you start spying?" he then asked, his expression growing dark. "Who were you conspiring with when I was hunting? How did you set our foes against Oghuz? Who is your accomplice? Tell me!" With that, Gazan had kicked the boy.

The spy had writhed around on the ground, groaning, and then he fell silent; he did not utter a single word.

"Take him and cast him into the pit!" Gazan then ordered. "Let him come to his senses in there. Then he'll tell us the truth!"

The pit was Gazan's dungeon. It contained dug-in floors, and each floor held one prisoner. Anyone who was sent to the dungeon would break down utterly. It had many floors. Furthermore, the stench was an assault on the nose. Shirshamsaddin explained how Gazan's men would roll a millstone to the entrance, and then they would push the stone aside and pour down water and leftover scraps of food. Whatever the prisoners could catch as the slop went down was theirs. Rats and rice ruled the bottom of the pit, and sometimes they would attack the prisoners. The screams and moans often bored through the enormous stone.

Shirshamsaddin and his men had lowered the scoundrel into the pit, just as Gazan had instructed them to do. Still, the spy had made no sound. The servants rolled the millstone back into its place at the entrance to the pit, and Shirshamsaddin went back to Gazan. As soon as Shirshamsaddin saw Gazan, he noticed that Beyrak had been speaking to Gazan; however, he wasn't sure exactly what. As soon as Beyrak saw Shirshamsaddin approach, he stopped talking.

Gazan had turned around and looked at Shirshamsaddin. "Have you thrown that scoundrel into the pit?" he asked without emotion.

"We have, my Lord. There was room on the fifth floor. We threw him there. If he makes the slightest movement, he will fall right to the bottom of the pit and end up among the rubbish and insects," Shirshamsaddin had replied. "He cannot breathe. Never mind, though; the pit will bring him to his senses."

Gazan had nodded approvingly. "You did right, nobles," he said. "But do not let that infidel son of an infidel die. He may still have something to tell us. Let him give us information. Two days are enough. Then get him out, but before you bring him to me, Shirshamsaddin, splash him with water to get rid of at least some of the dirt and stench. Clean him up."

"It will be done, Gazan, my master," Shirshamsaddin had answered courteously.

After that brief exchange, Gazan invited Beyrak inside, and the two of them went into Gazan's council chamber. Shirshamsaddin had not been invited inside with Beyrak. He admitted that he did not know what they talked about, noting, "All I know is that Beyrak parted from Gazan well into the night when the moon had already floated away to the other side of the stars."

Bayindir Khan nodded again and glanced at me to make sure I was still writing every detail down. I was. With that, he asked Shirshamsaddin to continue. He did.

It was morning. Gazan had not yet woken. Lady Burla had wanted to see Shirshamsaddin, and so he met up with her. As soon as she saw Shirshamsaddin, she began asking questions. "Shirshamsaddin, Gorgud was here yesterday. Can you tell me the reason for his visit?" she had asked.

"My Lady, Gazan summoned Gorgud and he came," Shirshamsaddin had replied. "My Lord had a question for him; he asked and received a reply."

"What did Gazan ask, Shirshamsaddin?" Lady Burla had then wondered.

Shirshamsaddin had hesitated. "My Lady, ask him this question yourself," he had said. "Ask yourself."

Lady Burla shook her head. "I am asking you. Will you not tell me?" she pressed.

"And I am telling you that it is a secret. I cannot tell you without asking Gazan," Shirshamsaddin had said firmly.

"Shirshamsaddin, my old fellow, does Gazan have secrets from me?" Lady Burla insisted.

Shirshamsaddin paused in his story and looked up at Bayindir Khan. "I thought to myself, 'Men discovered this world by their intellect. What secret is there here? Soon the whole of Oghuz will know about the spy. Yesterday, we raised such a commotion when we threw him in the pit. The female servants, the stewards, and the cooks—everyone saw it. Why am I standing here and not telling the lady what I know? I don't know. Maybe the relations between the lady and Beyrak had made me so disobedient that…'" his voice trailed off and he looked down at the floor, thinking. A moment later, he looked back up at the Khan. "At last, I made up my mind to tell Lady Burla what I knew," he said matter-of-factly.

"Go on…" the Khan said quietly, intrigued.

Shirshamsaddin had said, "I will tell you, my Lady, but only you. First Beyrak came. Maybe you realized that, too? Beyrak brought the news about the spy. My Lord flew into a rage. He wanted Gorgud and Gorgud came, too. My Lord asked him who the spy was and Gorgud told him."

"Who was the spy?" Lady Burla had blurted as if she knew nothing about it. In that moment, Shirshamsaddin had wondered if she was playing a game with him. She then asked, "Did you catch him and bring him to my Lord? Who was that scoundrel son of a scoundrel?"

"My Lady, the spy was Boghazja Fatma's only son," Shirshamsaddin had replied.

"Ah, Boghazja Fatma's son, you say?" Lady Burla had gasped. "When Gazan went hunting…before Beyrak entered his bride's chamber…when Bakil broke his leg hunting, it was Boghazja Fatma's son! Oh, the scoundrel! Oh, the knave!"

Shirshamsaddin had nodded. "Yes, my Lady, it was so. They were his works. I threw him in the pit. Gazan thought that he would come to his senses in there."

"Really? He will come to his senses, for the love of God. But, Shirshamsaddin…" Lady Burla's voice had trailed off.

"Yes, my Lady?" Shirshamsaddin had asked.

"Shirshamsaddin, as my eyes do not drink water, I cannot believe that the spy is Boghazja Fatma's son," she had said slowly. "What do you say?"

"Me? What do I say? I say what Gazan says. This is what Gorgud said, too, my Lady," Shirshamsaddin had answered.

"And what about Beyrak? Did he say who the spy was?" Lady Burla then questioned.

Shirshamsaddin shook his head. "He did not, my Lady. He did not say."

"He didn't say? Very well. Go now," Lady Burla then said. "It is time for my Lord to wake up. He may be in a good mood this morning, God help me. Then he won't make a fuss."

"We will see, my Lady," Shirshamsaddin had replied. With that, he went out into the yard and to the edge of the pit. Once at the pit, Shirshamsaddin had heard faint moans beneath the stone.

Shirshamsaddin looked up at the Khan again. "I thought, 'God willing, he will survive these two days. He cannot breathe his last in one day. The Lord said two days, and he was right. Men of courage have not been able to endure three days in this pit and have breathed their last. With God's help, he will survive,'" he said quietly.

After briefly visiting the pit, Shirshamsaddin then went to find Gazan. Gazan had already taken his seat in the council chamber. Shirshamsaddin also entered the chamber. He courteously greeted Gazan, who greeted him in return. Without looking at Shirshamsaddin, Gazan then continued the conversation he had been having with himself. "You toil night and day, Gazan. You are battered by hardship, and this is the response you get! There is a spy alongside me? Are my wife, my son, and my family captive to this enemy?" he muttered. "If it be thus, then I will show you my power. You will know who Gazan is. I am alone…alone. Had I an informant in Inner Oghuz, would you have spied under my nose? The men upon whom I relied ate and slept. They slept so much that their sides ached; they stood so long that their spines wasted away."

> *Look at this scoundrel! He may well have invented this story! "They slept so much that their sides ached; they stood so long that their spines wasted away." Gazan would never say that. These words belong to* The Chronicles of the Oghuz.

Gazan had continued. "These are my defenders; the battlefield is vast and I am alone. Can you clap with one hand?" Gazan had then turned to Shirshamsaddin. "I am asking you, Shirshamsaddin. Didn't you hear? Can you clap with one hand?"

Shirshamsaddin had said the first thing that entered his mind. "You might, my Lord. Why not?" he blurted.

Gazan gave him a reproachful frown. "So how do you clap with one hand?" he had asked.

"One hand, my Lord, can produce the sound of silence," Shirshamsaddin had answered.

Gazan's jaw dropped and he gaped at Shirshamsaddin. He was silent for some time and did not return to the subject.

> *"One hand can produce the sound of silence." Oh, Shirshamsaddin…I glanced at the Khan and saw that he was all ears for this scoundrel. Gazan may have been astounded at this answer, or maybe he failed to grasp its meaning.*

"What news do you have of the prisoner in the pit?" Gazan had then asked softly.

"He has not uttered a word," Shirshamsaddin had reported. "Nothing but moans and groans have reached my ears."

Gazan then nodded, deep in though. "We will wait," he said.

"We will wait," Shirshamsaddin repeated.

A short while later, two men arrived from Inner Oghuz. They were Sari Gulmash, son of Elin Goja, and Donabilmaz Dolak Uran, son of Aylik Goja. They had quarreled during the plunder and wanted Lord Gazan to settle their dispute. Donabilmaz Dolak Uran had been in front as they plundered Gazan's tent and dropped a silver whip, which Sari Gulmash had picked up and wanted to keep for himself. Gazan contemplated this matter for some time. Finally, he asked, "Who has the whip now?"

"I do, my Lord," Sari Gulmash had replied. He glanced over at Donabilmaz Dolak Uran. "His hands were so full that he kept dropping things as he went. I picked one thing for myself. Did I do wrong?"

"You may keep it," Gazan then said. Then he had turned to Shirshamsaddin. "You had a silver whip, Shirshamsaddin. Where is it?"

"The stable boy has it," Shirshamsaddin had answered, feeling embarrassed.

"Give it to Donabilmaz Dolak Uran," Gazan ordered.

Shirshamsaddin had nodded. "Very well, my Lord," he said. "Let's go." With that, he left the council chamber with the two men, silently cursing them, and steered them back to the main White Gate. When the three men had reached the gate, Shirshamsaddin looked at Donabilmaz Dolak Uran. "Perhaps, tomorrow or the day after tomorrow, you may come and collect the silver whip from me," he then said.

"Thank you, Shirshamsaddin," the two men had replied in unison. "We wish you well." They left the courtyard, quietly saying prayers.

Shirshamsaddin was about to return to Gazan when he saw a figure clothed in black suddenly approaching. He could not make out the person's face and was unsure if the person was a serving wench or a lady. Finally, the shrouded individual stood in front of Shirshamsaddin.

"Shirshamsaddin, my brave Lord. Is it you?" the person then asked. The voice clearly belonged to a woman, but Shirshamsaddin still did not know who she was.

"Yes, it is. But who are you?" he had asked slowly.

"'You don't recognize me? I must talk to you. Listen to me. Hear my voice, my brave Lord! I have come to seek your patronage. Do not send me back a broken-hearted wretch," the mysterious woman had answered, sounding incredibly upset.

"Come, come!" Shirshamsaddin had said at once. Then he politely offered her food and something to drink. He even offered her clothing. "Who are you? Tell me. Who are your people in Oghuz? I did not recognize you," he then said. "Why are your crying? Please tell me…"

The woman began to cry even louder. After a few minutes, her crying slowed and she sighed. Then she finally stopped crying altogether. "Shirshamsaddin, do you really not recognize me, my Lord?" the woman then asked again.

"I would not have asked had I recognized you. Who are you?" Shirshamsaddin had asked, losing patience. He knew that Gazan may have already been looking for him.

"It is I, my Lord," the woman then announced. She slowly uncovered her face.

In that moment, Shirshamsaddin stopped telling his story and looked at Bayindir Khan. "Being struck by lightning would have been better than what I saw," he noted. "It was Boghazja Fatma herself." The Khan said nothing and kept a straight face. With that, Shirshamsaddin continued.

"Is it you? How dare you come here? Go back to where you came from! You have no business here. If my Lord wants to see you, then I will send you word," Shirshamsaddin had hissed. "If you wish to see your son, you will need to speak with Gazan. I cannot say whether he will want see you or not, though!"

Shirshamsaddin was about to return to the courtyard when the poor woman fell to the ground and embraced his feet. "Stop! Don't go!" Boghazja Fatma had begged. "I will say two words, and then you can go…"

"Calm down, Boghazja Fatma," Shirshamsaddin had whispered. "Calm down! You need to control yourself. You also really need to go."

"Know, my brave Lord, that you are not aware of my predicament. Listen to my voice," Boghazja Fatma then said. "Listen to my words!"

Shirshamsaddin interrupted his own story again. "She was about to cry again, my Khan," he said. "It would have been better if my leg had been broken. It would have been better if I had managed to run away with my broken leg as long as it meant not listening to her. But I did listen, my Khan, and I will tell you exactly what she told me…" his voice trailed off. With that, he continued to recall what had happened.

"Shirshamsaddin, my brave Lord, do you not remember me? You know only yourself. How can you know me? I will remind you. Do you remember, my brave Lord, what happened many years ago? Can you see that story? Can you see yourself in that vision?" Boghazja Fatma had asked.

As Boghazja Fatma spoke, Shirshamsaddin began to watch what she was saying before his very eyes. Events unfolded, one after the other. She continued to tell her story. "Can you see? Look closely. Look, there we are together! There is Baragchug. Do you remember that day? Tell me! Do not be shamed, my brave man, my lion…"

As soon as Shirshamsaddin had heard the word, "lion," it was as though a sword had been plunged into his heart. She had been the only person to ever call him that. Suddenly, Shirshamsaddin remembered everything at that moment. It was impossible to forget her; it didn't matter how much he had wanted to. Still, Shirshamsaddin collected myself and managed to remain calm. But he could not tear his eyes from the vision.

Boghazja Fatma continued. "Look, look into your memory. You were a brave warrior. You were upright as a reed. Your arms were strong as stones, hard as cliffs. Your fervent eyes were dark as the starless sky. Your slender fingers were white as marble, and your body was nimble. You were young, my lion. Do you remember that moonlit night?" she had asked quietly.

"Your dog's name was Baragchug, wasn't it?" Shirshamsaddin then asked, unaware of the words that were flowing freely out of his mouth. "There was a gully at the back of your tent, wasn't there?"

Boghazja Fatma smiled and nodded her head. "Yes, our dog's name was Baragchug," she had replied. "Yes, there was a gully at the back of our tent."

Shirshamsaddin continued. "That moonlit night, I crossed the gully and knocked softly on your gate. That dog barked so loudly, and you came to see what was going on. You were a beautiful girl then..." his voice had trailed off, remembering.

"He barked because he wanted to see you. Baragchug never barked like that for anyone else! Gone are those days, my Lord. They are gone, never to return," Boghazja Fatma said with a sigh. She looked away. "What did I want to say?" Then she looked directly at him. "Help me, my brave Lord. Only you can help me, only you, because—"

"What help, old woman? What are you saying?" Shirshamsaddin had interrupted. His voice was suddenly cold as he wondered what he could have in common with the mother of a spy.

"Because, my lion, a token remained to remind me of those long-lost days. Do you know what happened that night?" Boghazja Fatma asked slowly. "That night, you entrusted me with a deposit. I have never revealed this secret to you. Now I will."

Shirshamsaddin was perplexed. He did not understand what secret Boghazja Fatma was talking about. "What secret are you talking about, old woman?" he blurted. "Have you taken leave of your senses?"

"No," Boghazja answered with sadness in her voice. "I have not taken leave of my senses, my brave Lord. I am talking about the secret whose arms and legs you have bound, and whom you have cast into that dank pit—our son!"

Shirshamsaddin couldn't believe what he had heard. "Not our son, but *yours*..." he clarified, his voice trailing off.

"No, my lion. He is ours. I am speaking the truth; he is your son, my Lord—our son. This is my secret," Boghazja Fatma had revealed. "Thanks be to God that I could reveal it to you. Now you know me. This boy is my reminder—my token of that night. Help, my lion, spare our son!"

Boghazja Fatma had disclosed her huge secret without pausing for breath. Once it was unleashed, she started to sob all over again. "My child, my poor son, who has never seen his father's face. My innocent child…" she had cried.

Shirshamsaddin suddenly felt like he had no power to speak. He had been dumbfounded. Again, he collected himself and managed to utter a few words. "How—how?" he had stammered. "You have just shrunken this great world for me! My son is the spy? You have brought shame upon me in this world! My son is this spy? I would shed his blood with my sword. I would tear out his heart, rip it out, and break it into pieces. Now this is my son, you say? You should not have told me this news, Boghazja Fatma. You should not have brought the black waves that engulf me!"

Despite Shirshamsaddin's anger and confusion, Boghazja Fatma continued to cry for their son. She hoped that Shirshamsaddin would find it in his heart to pity the boy and help set him free, especially after hearing that the boy was his own flesh and blood.

Shirshamsaddin then continued. "Almighty God, only you can show me the way! Only you can help me!" he had sighed. Then he glared at Boghazja Fatma. "Get up; stand on your feet! You cannot stay here like this. You have said what you wanted. Go now and let me think. Almighty God, to whom can I confide my sorrow? Only you can tell me, God on high! Tell your slave. What am I to do now? Where can I go?"

"Gorgud! Go to Gorgud!" Boghazja Fatma then blurted. "He will show you the right way, brave Lord. Spare your son! You must know that God cannot forgive this sin." Having said her final word, Boghazja then slowly walked away.

All of us in the Khan's chamber, including Bayindir Khan, were listening, open-mouthed, to Shirshamsaddin's incredible words. Only the saz[52] *was missing. I had even forgotten to write it down! The Khan was downcast; he looked full of sorrow. Shirshamsaddin was a true minstrel. Almighty God, how you inspired him, I do not know. I stared at him and saw that he had not learned those words by heart. He had spoken them spontaneously.*

"…I looked again and saw Boghazja Fatma come out of Gazan's tent. She looked around, surreptitiously, and then she covered her face with a shawl and

[52] A plucked stringed instrument, traditionally played by Turkic ozans or bards.

went through the gate. I did not see Gazan until the next morning. He had withdrawn into his chambers and did not come out," Shirshamsaddin recalled to Bayindir Khan.

"Okay, so then what happened next?" the Khan asked. He looked at me once more to make sure I was still writing everything down. As soon as he looked back at Shirshamsaddin, Shirshamsaddin began to continue with his story.

The next morning, Gazan had suddenly convened an advisory council. Bakil, Aruz, Beyrak, and Shirshamsaddin had shown up for it. Once everyone was accounted for, Gazan began the council. He seemed out of sorts, but Shirshamsaddin had thought it was because of the plundering. He wondered how Gazan would respond if Old Aruz stood up and started to rebuke him. However, Old Aruz did not say a word. Instead, he sat there quietly with a scowl on his face.

"Nobles, this is the state of affairs," Gazan had begun. "A spy has been found in Oghuz. You know Boghazja Fatma's son; it is her son. But he is a young lad, wet behind the ears. It is up to you to decide what we should do."

Old Aruz spoke first. Without looking at anyone, he asked, "Who brought the news about the spy? Let him speak. We would like to know, too."

At first, Gazan did not want to say that it was Beyrak who brought the news. "Does it matter? It is clear who the spy is. Gorgud said his name. There is no more to be said about it," he had replied dryly.

"No, there is. Beyrak brought the news, did he?" Old Aruz asked, stepping forward.

Beyrak could not hold back. "Yes, I brought the news!" he shouted defensively. "What of it?"

"Are you shouting at me?" Old Aruz asked angrily.

Gazan tried to ease the tension. "Nobles, calm down! This is not what we are here for. This is no place for quarreling," he scolded the men. "What shall we do with this boy? This is why I summoned you. Are we going to kill him, or are we going to release him? He is very young. What are we going to do with him?"

Ultimately, the nobles would have the final word on the matter. Shirshamsaddin had planned on saying his piece at the end, with the help of God. He noted to the Khan that Old Aruz had calmed down first, which was unexpected. Beyrak also fell silent.

Bakil was the first to speak. "We cannot act without considering it first, nobles. We would be stirring up conflict in Oghuz," he said.

Old Aruz supported him. "Bakil is right. We must be correct if we are not to bring reproach upon ourselves," he had advised.

Seeing that the time was right, Shirshamsaddin then also spoke. "Nobles, this spy has not said a word. He has not admitted his guilt. God knows if he is guilty or not. It seems to me that this boy's guilt is in doubt," he said carefully.

"He is not guilty," Old Aruz said matter-of-factly, taking Shirshamsaddin's side.

Bakil nodded. "Not guilty," he declared, also taking Shirshamsaddin's side.

Gazan listened carefully to every speaker. Before giving his final word, however, he looked at Beyrak. "And what do you say?" he had asked.

Beyrak had shrugged. "Whatever you say, I say, too," he replied.

Gazan then sighed and calmly completed his speech. "So be it. May it be as you have spoken. If the boy is not guilty, he is not guilty. I am of the same opinion as you, nobles," he had said. "Shirshamsaddin, go and release him from the pit. Hose him down; clean him up; and give him to his mother. Let him go."

The nobles then stood up, pleased with the final decision. Suddenly, a look of hesitation covered Beyrak's face. The men all looked at him, waiting. "Nobles, they should both vanish from Oghuz for good lest anyone say that the Oghuz nobles have gone soft in the heart," he had said. The nobles looked at one another, but no one said anything.

Shirshamsaddin stopped his story and looked up at Bayindir Khan. He gave a small shrug. "This is how the council finished, my Khan. We all went out into the yard. I carefully dragged the spy out of the pit, pulling the rope with my own hands. The nobles came and stood at my side. The poor wretch had no strength left. After he had been dragged from the pit, he could not stand and lay prostrate on the ground. A stench pervaded the surrounding area. While he was lying on the ground, Gazan ordered the serving wenches to fetch water and give him a good wash. Then Gazan gave another order, and the servants fetched new clothes from the tent, dressed him, and seated him to one side. They also brought him food. The boy kept his head bowed and ate and drank in silence. In fact, he filled his stomach without uttering a word."

Shirshamsaddin continued. "But, my Khan, when he glanced upward, a stone struck my heart. His eyes were the eyes of Old Gaflat, my father. When I studied his face carefully, I began to detect many other similarities. Yet when I turned around, I saw that all the nobles, including Gazan, were staring at him in the same manner. I did not understand anything," he said. "Some time passed, and Boghazja Fatma turned up. Without looking at any of us or uttering a word, she wiped the tears from her eyes, embraced her son, and helped him up. Leaning on one another, they slowly then left the yard. After that, all the nobles mounted their horses and galloped out of the yard without saying a word."

Bayindir Khan continued looking at Shirshamsaddin, which made Shirshamsaddin feel slightly uneasy. "I swear to you, my Khan, I have not seen either the boy or his mother since!" he blurted. "They vanished into the blue yonder. I do not deny that I searched for them. I asked if people had seen them, but no one said they had. Since then, sometimes in the evening, I find myself sobbing because of my son. Yes, my Khan, this is how it is. May God give inspiration to your soul. If I have sinned, forgive me for the love of God."

When he had finally finished telling the story, Shirshamsaddin fell silent and bowed his head. Bayindir Khan remained in his place, still deep in thought. I put down my pen and rubbed my fingers. After sitting for a short while, Bayindir Khan then rose and left the chamber without saying a word to any of us. We were saddened by Bayindir Khan's sorrowful countenance.

In the Khan's absence, night had fallen on the Khan's courtyard. No one had the strength to say, or write, or listen to anything more. Shirshamsaddin, Gilbash, and I eventually rose and went out into the yard. Gilbash asked the servants to show us to our separate quarters. I passed the night half-sleeping, half-waking. In the morning, I awoke with the first rooster and bark of the dog. Then I dressed and waited for Gilbash.

The text breaks off here. The continuation shows, though, that the missing text is neither long, nor of significance.

§ § § § § §

The sun was already shining bright into every corner of the Khan's courtyard at Gunortaj Palace. The voices of servants and serving wenches mingled with the chirping of birds, mooing of cows, lowing of buffalo, bleating of sheep on their way to pasture, and whinnying of horses from the stables. Fires were being lit across the yard, while a steward was using a piece of green cloth to extinguish the torches that had burned all night along the walls.

As I went out into the yard, one horseman rode into the Khan's yard through the Black Gate, followed by three or four more horsemen. They dismounted, and the grooms then led the horses to the stables. Gilbash greeted the horseman who had ridden in front, and as soon as he saw me, he led the man in my direction. *Who is that man?* I wondered. When I saw that it was Bakil who was approaching me, I realized what was going on. *Today must be his turn.*

As he reached me, he greeted me courteously and was greeted in return. Food had already been laid out for us on a cloth under the elm tree, and we sat down. We ate and drank, and when our bellies were finally full, Gilbash turned to me. "Shall we go?" he asked casually.

"Is the Khan still asleep?" I asked in return.

"He has risen. Come, you come, too, Bakil," Gilbash replied.

Gilbash led the way, and together we went into Bayindir Khan's chamber again. Bayindir Khan was sitting in his place. He bore no sign of the previous night's tiredness. "Come, Bakil, come over here," he said to Bakil with a polite smile. "Sit down. Welcome!"

I also bowed to Bayindir Khan before going over and sitting where I had left my pen and paper the night before. Bakil was a courteous and scholarly man. He greeted Bayindir Khan with reverence, bowed deeply, and took his seat where the Khan had shown him. Gilbash went behind Bakil and sat down, his legs crossed.

Once everyone was settled, Bayindir Khan focused his attention on Bakil. "Bakil, do you know why I have summoned you?" he asked.

"No, I do not know, majestic Bayindir Khan. The reason is good, God willing. The borders of our country are quiet, and there is no cause for the Khan to be alarmed. Maybe the Khan has news? Command me as you will, Khan. I am your willing slave," Bakil replied.

"No, Bakil, no bad tidings have come. I want you to know that I am very pleased with you. I have no worries about the Georgian Marches, thanks to you. I have summoned you for another reason. I will listen to you. You will talk to me, and I will listen to you," Bayindir Khan said.

"Very well, my Khan. Whatever you wish to ask, I am ready to answer," Bakil smiled. He was still in the dark about the affair and felt very comfortable.

This is what Bakil told me long after these events: At first, he thought that the Khan had heard about the dispute that arose between he and Gazan while they were hunting. He was emboldened by my presence because I had come to him in a dream that night and told him that I supported him in the dispute. Almighty God, you are on high. Since when have we been entering one another's dreams? Since when have we seen the same dreams? The world is confused. If you set us against one another before we die, what will our end be?

"Bakil, I have been informed that you were at the council with Gazan. You imprisoned an Oghuz spy, and then released him. Why did you do so?" Bayindir Khan asked. "This spy's guilt is obvious; his deeds are known. The harm he has caused Oghuz is there to see. What was the reason? Tell me. Why did you consider him innocent and voted for his release, not his death?"

Bakil finally understood why he had been urgently summoned to the Khan in the middle of the night. He kept calm, but at the same time was rather worried. What could he say? I knew more or less what he would say, but I did not know how he would say it. Bayindir Khan had great faith in Bakil. The Khan knew full well that Bakil would tell him the truth, so he could follow a straight path in his interrogation, rather than use cunning. He asked his question directly.

It is true, if you pay attention, that Bayindir Khan posed direct questions to Bakil and did not "play games" with him as he had with Shirshamsaddin and Gazan. The Khan valued Bakil for his bravery and flawless service on the borders with Georgia. Additionally, he already knew about Bakil's grudge. Gorgud had already conveyed to the Khan all the details of the argument with Gazan during the hunt. Bakil was an invaluable witness for the Khan (if the Khan was going to make any accusations against Gazan). Even Beyrak himself could have gotten his fingers burned because of Bakil's story.

Bakil was a courageous man; he was willing to tell Bayindir Khan what had happened without any trickery. "Bayindir Khan, I would like to tell you that before going to Gazan's council, I had already thought how to rescue that poor wretch," he admitted. "Are you surprised? Do not be surprised. Let me tell you what happened and what did not. I was sitting at home the day before the council. I heard a voice outside…"

With that, he started telling what had happened from his perspective. I began writing as quickly as I could.

"Bakil, Bakil!" a woman's voice cried out. "I'm not going anywhere until I've seen Bakil!"

At first, Bakil thought he was hearing things. But when he had turned around to see a steward running up to him, he realized that the cries and moans had been real. "What is it?" Bakil had asked the servant.

"My Lord, a woman has collapsed at the gate and is lying there, sobbing!" the servant said, out of breath. "She says she will not get up until she sees you."

"Who is she? What is her name? What does she want?' Bakil asked.

The servant had shrugged. "She won't tell us anything. She insists on being taken to you. What shall we do?" the servant asked.

God, who can it be at this time of night? Bakil had wondered. He then looked at the servant. "I am coming. Wait…" As they started heading toward the gate, various thoughts crossed Bakil's mind: *Can news have come from Oghuz? Can news have come from Georgia? Has some daughter of a scoundrel been driven from a caravan? But no caravan has passed through in the last few days…*

When they reached the gate, Bakil had immediately noticed someone covered in dark clothing. He could not tell if it was a man or a woman. He and the servant stepped closer, and then the servant spoke. "Here is my Lord," the servant had said cautiously. "Say what you have come to say."

The shrouded individual removed the shawl, revealing a woman. She was then about to lie at Bakil's feet when he stopped her. "What do you have to say? I am Bakil. Tell me," he had said quietly.

"'Listen to my words. Hear what I have to say, Bakil. You really have not recognized me? Look at my face; look carefully," the woman had replied. "Do you recognize me now?" She raised her head and showed Bakil her face.

He suddenly did recognize the woman. It was Boghazja Fatma.

I looked at Bayindir Khan. Bayindir Khan was fidgeting in his place, but he was very interested. He did not interrupt Bakil and continued to listen in silence.

"Do you not recognize me, brave Bakil?" she asked again.

"'I know you. I recognize you," Bakil had said softly. "But what has brought you here? Please get up." Boghazja Fatma would not get up. She cried even more. *Now she will bring everyone out of the tent,* Bakil thought to himself, slightly alarmed. "Why are you weeping Why are you groaning? Tell me your sorrows. If you do not tell me, what can I do then?" he asked.

"Bakil, you are a man of courage. You would never abandon poor Boghazja Fatma in her time of trouble! Do you know what has happened? My only son has been arrested and called a spy. A rope bound his white hands behind his back. They have thrown my boy into the dungeon of dungeons in Gazan's yard!" Boghazja Fatma had cried. "They have buried him alive in that pit. Help me, my brave Lord. You are my only hope!"

"Was your son a spy?" Bakil then asked.

"No, of course not, Bakil! May I die for your lips, Bakil? May I die for your tongue? He is the most obedient of sons. My son is not a spy. My son is a helpless slave of God," Boghazja Fatma said defensively. "Gazan and Beyrak have tricked him, Bakil. Beyrak brought news of the spy to Gazan. Gazan said, 'Go, catch him! Bring him back and let him know the taste of blood!"

"What does this have to do with me? Why have you come to me?" Bakil then asked Boghazja Fatma.

"Bakil, have you forgotten me? I was a beautiful girl once. There was a gully behind our tent. Our dog's name was Baragchug. You were the only person that the dog did not bark at. Have you forgotten those days when you used to come to us, brave Bakil? Have you forgotten those nights?" she asked.

Bakil paused in his story for a moment. He looked up at Bayindir Khan. "Memories flooded my brain, my Khan. I remembered the days of my youth. I shut my eyes for a moment, but quickly pulled myself together," he admitted. "I had remembered, but I told her to say what she had to say." He continued explaining what had happened.

"Bakil, you are the father of my son. You left me your keepsake, Bakil. I have revealed my secret to no one; I have kept my secret in my heart for many long years," Boghazja Fatma had revealed. "Now they want to destroy our child. Now they want to crush our son. Do not let them! Go to Bayindir Khan, the Khan of Khans. Tell him everything. Our son is not a spy, Bakil. I have told you the truth."

Bakil had been shocked by the news. In fact, he was suddenly frozen where he stood and could not move. His mouth became dry. After a few moments of silence, he finally found his words again. "'Is it Beyrak who first talked of the spy affair?" he asked.

Boghazja Fatma nodded. "Yes, it was Beyrak, Bakil. Beyrak was in Bayburd for sixteen years. What does he know about Oghuz? Beyrak has destroyed my house!" she blurted angrily.

"He is alive. I am alive. Go, Boghazja Fatma. Go home and do not worry. I am not Bakil if I do not take revenge on Beyrak. Beyrak will have to answer for this!" Bakil had muttered.

Boghazja Fatma continued. "Don't let them destroy our child. You are my hope, my refuge. Bakil, only you can save our son…" her voice trailed off.

Bakil looked at Bayindir Khan again. "My Khan, I turned her into a wayfarer. She stood up, left the yard, became a black shape on the horizon, and disappeared. Then I went back indoors," he said. "The day before, I had been informed about the council. I did not linger long. I told the stewards to saddle the horses as I gathered my warriors. Soon after, we had galloped off. We would reach Inner Oghuz when the first rooster crowed the next day."

Once Bakil had reached Inner Oghuz, he had met Gazan, Old Aruz, Beyrak, and Shirshamsaddin. The five men gathered in the council chamber. Once they were all situated, Gazan began his speech. "Nobles, I have summoned you to a council meeting. This is the state of affairs: There is a spy in Oghuz. I was informed of it but did not believe it at first. Then I reflected for a while; I searched my memory," he had begun. "When I was away hunting, the spy had gone and done his work. When Beyrak was about to enter his marriage bower, the spy did his work again. Bakil went hunting and broke his leg, didn't he? Again, the spy did his work!"

"Who is this spy whom you talk about, Lord Gazan?" Bakil had asked.

Old Aruz could not restrain himself any longer. "Who brought the news about the spy?" he had demanded.

Gazan looked at Bakil and then at Old Aruz. Bakil had thought that Gazan spoke very reluctantly when he answered. "Beyrak did; Beyrak talked of the spy. But Gorgud came, too. The spy is Boghazja Fatma's young son. Gorgud told us that. We have caught the boy and thrown him in the pit. But he is very young; he's still wet behind the ears. He does not look like a spy at all. He does not talk. In fact, he does not say a word. Is this correct, Shirshamsaddin?" Gazan asked. He turned to look at Shirshamsaddin.

"Yes, my Lord. This is so," Shirshamsaddin had replied.

"Now, nobles, it is your turn to speak. What should we do? Let us discuss it. What do you say?" Gazan then asked. He fell silent, waiting for the nobles to discuss the matter.

Old Aruz had spoken first. "Beyrak brought the news, did he?" he asked.

"I did! Do you have anything to say about it?" Beyrak had snarled at Old Aruz.

"Are you snarling at me?" Old Aruz asked, visibly angry.

"Yes, I'm snarling at you!" Beyrak then replied, stepping forward.

Gazan grew impatient with their behavior. "Nobles, be quiet! This is not the time for quarreling. Let us settle the affairs of the spy. Leave tomorrow's affairs until tomorrow. Listen to me. What do you think? Is he guilty or innocent? Should we kill this wretch or release him? He is a poor lad…" his voice had trailed off.

Both Old Aruz and Beyrak calmed down. Old Aruz then spoke again. "He is not guilty at all. I say he is innocent. Let us release him."

"He is not guilty," Bakil had quickly agreed. "Let us release him."

Shirshamsaddin then repeated what the other two men had said. Only Beyrak did not say anything. When he continued to remain silent, Gazan had turned and looked at him. "And what do you say?" he asked.

"Whatever you say, I say, too," Beyrak had said.

Gazan nodded. Then he looked at each noble. "Since you say he is not guilty, I also say he is not guilty. Shirshamsaddin, go and open that stinking pit and free that poor boy. Give him to his mother and let her take him home," he had ordered.

"No, my Lord!" Beyrak had raged. "No, he should leave Oghuz, never to return. He should vanish completely, lest there be any idle talk!"

Even before the council, Bakil knew that Gazan had had no desire to punish Boghazja Fatma's son. If he had wanted to, he would never have summoned the nobles to the council. He would have chopped him in two, and that would have been the end of it. Bakil knew that Gazan and Beyrak both wanted to release the boy, and they did it through the council.

Bakil looked at Bayindir Khan. "But it is good that it was so," he added. "Otherwise, I would have had to settle scores with Beyrak at the council for his impudence on the hunt. I had made up my mind on my way there."

Once it had been decided that the boy would go free, Shirshamsaddin and two men went to the pit and rolled the millstone to one side. Bakil had also gone to watch with his own eyes and to set his mind at rest. Gazan and Old Aruz went, too. The boy was bound to a thick rope, and they dragged him out on it. Once he was out of the pit, he had been was washed and given food and something to drink.

Bakil stopped describing what he had seen; clearly, he had been deeply affected, especially after hearing Boghazja Fatma's news. He waited a moment before speaking. "I looked at his face, my Khan, and he was like my son, Imran," Bakil said quietly. "He had his eyes, his countenance. Compassion boiled in my veins when he looked at me. Then his mother, Boghazja Fatma, turned up. She held him under one arm, and without saying a word—without looking at anyone—she and the boy slowly went out of the gate and were gone. I have not seen them since."

Bakil stopped talking. I stopped writing. I was covered in a cold sweat again. I did not dare look at Bayindir Khan. The Khan was also silent. I thought to myself, *If the Khan had known that this was how it was, would he have started this investigation?* I couldn't find an answer to my question.

Bayindir Khan then asked Bakil something that I had not expected him to ask. "Bakil, you say that you have a score to settle with Beyrak. He insulted you on a hunt. What hunt was this? I would like to know. Tell me..." he said.

> *Bakil stiffened like a bow, took aim, and shot his arrow. If only it had gone straight at the target, almighty God.*

"Bayindir Khan, Khan of Khans, do you remember the tribute sent by the infidels in Georgia? They sent a horse, a sword, and a staff. You were worried. Every year, we would receive gold and coins and would divide them among the nobles and the warriors. 'To whom can we give these?' you asked. Gorgud stepped forward and said, 'My Khan, do not worry. Let us give all three things to one warrior.'"

Bakil continued. "None of the Oghuz nobles would accept this tribute. Whoever you looked at drew in his horns. You looked at me and asked, 'What do you have to say?' I thought in my heart, 'If my Khan's words fall to the ground, may my head fall to the ground, too.' I was happy to move my people far away to the Georgian Marches. I stood at the entry to Georgia. I stood guard for Oghuz—"

"I remember, Bakil. I have not forgotten this. Why are you asking me this? I told you to tell me about the hunt," Bayindir Khan interrupted Bakil with the utmost courtesy.

"Understood, my Khan. I will tell you about the hunt. But first, I have something else to say. I served on the border; I rarely went to Oghuz. I discharged my task properly. I knew all the castles both near and far from Outer Oghuz and traveled the roads, paths, rivers, streams, and through all the settlements. I drew plans for you, my Khan, in case there was ever a raid. In a word, my Khan, whatever your heart may desire from the Georgian Marches, we are ready to bring it," Bakil said quickly.

"Thank you, Bakil," Bayindir Khan said. "Thank you for your trouble. I know your worth."

"Yes, Khan, you give me my due. But, majestic Khan, not everyone has been like you. Many were jealous of your regard for me," Bakil replied.

"Who was? Tell me more. I am all ears," Bayindir Khan said, curious.

Bakil started to tell Bayindir Khan the story he had once told me in his dream. The first time I listened, but this time, at a sign from the Khan, I was ready to write it down. We all waited for Bakil to start speaking.

One day, Bakil had been at home, giving orders to his assembled warriors, when a courier suddenly arrived. "Bayindir Khan wishes to see you," the courier had said. Without hesitating, Bakil had moved fast. He had his horse quickly saddled and set off on the long road. He ended up reaching Oghuz in one day. Once he arrived, he went straight to the Khan. The Khan had asked Bakil about Duzmurd Castle.

Bakil had given the Khan plenty of detailed, accurate information about the roads and paths to Duzmurd Castle. He also told him about the castle's people and its soldiers. One of the leaders, Arshin Dirak Takir, had used to send nonsensical orders to Bayindir Khan. Bakil knew that at that time there had been enmity between Duzmurd Castle and Outer Oghuz. There had been raids and attacks. Outer Oghuz had invaded Duzmurd Castle and vice versa.

The Khan's Vizier, Old Gazilig, was held prisoner in Duzmurd. Long years had passed, but no one had managed to free him from captivity. Aman had even gathered his hired soldiers, laid traps, and drawn plans, but he had not been able to rescue Old Gazilig. Now it was his young son, Yeynak's, turn. He was to rescue his grandfather, the Khan had decided. The Khan had asked him in Balik's presence, "Yeynak, will you go and bring back your grandfather?"

"Not with hired soldiers, but with the your permission, my Khan, I shall go with the warriors of Oghuz," Yeynak had replied.

When he heard this, Bayindir Khan immediately ordered that a great army be prepared. "Yeynak, go and get ready," he said.

As Bakil was leaving Bayindir Khan, one of Gazan's men had been waiting for him. "My Lord, Gazan wants to see you. He wants you to come to Inner Oghuz," he said.

Gazan, the Noble of Nobles, wishes to see me? Bakil had wondered. A short while before that, Gazan had also sent his shepherd to Bakil. Bakil had separated a flock of sheep and told the shepherd to drive them to Gazan, so that he could enjoy kebabs. *Now Gazan wants to honor me,* Bakil thought. With that, he rode to Inner Oghuz to appear before Gazan.

Upon seeing Gazan, Bakil had conveyed his greetings and was greeted in return. Gazan then invited Bakil to go hunting, saying, "Bakil, you are a long way away. We hardly see you! I am going hunting early tomorrow with the nobles. Will you come with us? Our deer and gazelles cannot compare with yours in number, but this is our hunt. I would like to invite you. What do you say?"

"Thank you, Gazan," Bakil had said graciously. "Thank you!"

So Bakil had completed his preparations by the next day. Early the next morning, he and his warriors joined Gazan. The men reached the foot of the Red Mountain and pitched their tents. Of the nobles, Garaguna, Gara Chakur, Girggunug's son, Shirshamsaddin, and Beyrak were all there.

The nobles rode their horses and ate and drank strong wine. Later, they raced on horseback, and Bakil's chestnut stallion outran the rest. Bakil also shot an arrow that pierced the ear of a deer and pinned it to its leg. This was his seal, his sign, as most people knew. In Barda and Ganja, Bakil would go hunting and pierce the ear of his quarry and pin it to its leg. He would look at the animals he hunted. If they were thin, then he would let them go. If they were not, then he would eat them. Whenever a noble shot an animal, pinning its ear, the noble would say, "This is Bakil's seal!" and then he would send it to Bakil. Garaguna had sent him a deer killed in that way. Wild Dondar had sent him one, and Old Aruz had sent him one, too.

While on Gazan's hunt, Bakil's horse had outrun all the nobles' horses. Once again, Bakil had been able to pierce the ear of an animal that was running past him while on his galloping horse. He pinned the animal's ear to its leg. The nobles gathered around the quarry. Gazan then came riding up, too. "What is going on? Why have you gathered here?" Gazan had asked, slightly confused.

"Bakil has pinned the ear of a deer to its legs again from his horse!" the nobles had exclaimed.

Gazan dismounted. He took a good look at the quarry, and then he turned and smiled at the nobles. "Is this the skill of horse or man?" he had asked.

"This is the skill of man," the nobles replied.

"No, this is the skill of the horse. If the horse does not do his job, a brave man cannot boast," Gazan had corrected them.

Bakil sighed. "My Lord, be fair. I was not boasting. I shot this arrow, and I drew this bow," he had said.

Beyrak shrugged, joining in on the conversation. "They told you it was the horse's skill," he had stated. "Didn't they, Bakil?"

Bakil paused in his story and looked at Bayindir Khan. "My Khan, I have never liked Beyrak—and I know why. Few men know this, but I shall tell you. For shame, he had his eye on my bride. He had been hanging around Surmalija Cheshma's tent. Before his wedding, he went chasing girls in Outer Oghuz, and he watched their tent. At that time, I drove him away from the tent, and did it with Alp Rustam. That is another story, my Khan," he explained, shaking his head. "I just want to say that Beyrak never forgot that insult, which is why he had spoken out on that hunt."

Bayindir Khan remained silent. I continued writing. Then Bakil picked up where he had briefly left off.

"Gazan was right, nobles," Beyrak had challenged. "Of course, it is the horse's skill!"

Bakil knew he was a skilled hunter, though, and he wasn't ready to back down so easily, especially not in front of the nobles. "I shall shoot the arrow with my eyes closed and hit the quarry," he had confidently replied.

The nobles laughed. Beyrak laughed loudest of all. "You've gone rusty out in the Georgian Marches, Bakil!" he had sneered.

"Beyrak," Bakil had warned. "You have gone too far. I am bearing the full load; you are bearing a few pounds."

> *That wasn't bad. "I am bearing the full load; you are bearing a few pounds." That must be included in* The Chronicles of the Oghuz. *Beyrak was both courteous and curt.*

Bakil had continued. "Come, if you wish, I will shoot an arrow with you, and I will show you who has the skill—the man or the horse," he said calmly.

"Are you mocking me?" Beyrak then asked.

Bakil knew that the whole ordeal had been Gazan's doing; Beyrak had always been his favorite. This was Gazan's affair, not Beyrak's. So Bakil then turned to Gazan and, mustering restraint, said, "Gazan, tell your favorite to know his place, or—s"

Beyrak had then looked at Gazan. Gazan did not utter a word. He shrugged his shoulders. This time, Beyrak became furious. He moved toward Bakil with anger in his eyes. "Or *what?* Tell me! Let's see!" he shouted.

Bakil clenched his teeth together and tried to keep his composure. *Bayindir Khan shall not be dishonored. Dishonoring Gazan is tantamount to dishonoring Bayindir Khan,* he had thought. *I will continue this hunt and try to mind my own business...*

However, Beyrak seemed to have other ideas. Beyrak stepped forward again. "Bakil, don't you know what I can do to you?" he cried. "Who do you think you are? Are you threatening me?"

Again, Bakil chose to not answer Beyrak. He did not want to disgrace himself while in Inner Oghuz. With that, he slowly turned to Gazan, but could not suppress his anger any longer. "Gazan," he had said through gritted teeth.

"Tell this dog of yours to be quiet and sit in its place. Did you hear what he said to me? Is it not you who invited me hunting? What does he want of me?"

Suddenly, Beyrak was even more furious. "Did you just call me a *dog?* You are a lone wolf. You howl a long way from Oghuz. How long is it since you have seen a brave man's face or heard a brave man's words?" he had taunted. "I'm a dog, am I? I'll kill you, Bakil!" He drew out his sword, waiting.

Bakil immediately withdrew his sword as well. He then looked sideways at Gazan, who looked almost awestruck by what was unfolding. "Gazan, my Lord, I will not answer for my actions!" Bakil said in a serious tone. "I am telling you for the last time—"

Gazan did not let the affair get out of hand. Without looking at anyone, he said, "Nobles, stop! Stop this talk. What is this? Have we come hunting or to play word games?"

"Did he call me a dog? He is a dog himself!" Beyrak had continued. "He is a carrion crow. I'll kill him. Let me go, nobles!"

Gara Chakur and Garaguna had grabbed Beyrak's arms and needed to stop him by force. Gazan then intervened. He had turned to Beyrak. "This matter is finished. Didn't I tell you to stop this talk?" he asked with disgust in his voice. Then he beckoned to Shirshamsaddin, who put his arms around Beyrak and led him down to the spring. After that, he calmed down.

Moments later, Gazan then turned to Bakil. "Bakil, I shall tell you this, and remember it well: No one can match where my arrow falls. No one has ridden where I have ridden. Everyone knows who I am. Don't you know that I am Salur Gazan, Noble of Nobles?" he asked authoritatively. "Therefore, I tell you, know your place. Know your limits. This skill is not yours, but your horse's. May this be the end of the matter." With that, he mounted his horse and galloped away.

After Gazan's little speech, the hunt had fallen apart altogether. The nobles mounted their horses and rode away. Bakil, too, in great pain, set out from the Red Mountain with his warriors, heading straight for the Georgian Marches. While on the road, he had thought a lot to himself. *Gazan humiliated me before the nobles and the warriors. But who is Beyrak to have words with me—to fight verbally with me? Of course, someone must have taught him. I, Bakil, toil for Oghuz, knowing neither day nor night, I have moved my family and tribe to protect the borders of Oghuz! Beyrak was raving nonsense before my warriors...*

His angry thoughts had continued the whole way home. *The day will come when I will show you who you are, Beyrak. May you sacrifice yourself for the white beard of the Khan of Khans. But who knows, would Gazan have gone that far without Bayindir Khan being informed? Maybe they met and talked and planned the hunt as a game? Or maybe this affair was quite different?*

Did they want to humiliate me on purpose? May Beyrak have a grudge against the Khan, against Oghuz. May he not collect tribute on time. May he lose heart in his work. May his heart and soul grow cold toward Oghuz. May he withdraw from the Georgian Marches. May the Khan vent his wrath upon him...

When Bakil finally reached his home, everybody immediately saw his dark mood. Still, Bakil remained silent. A short while passed, and he was asked the same question over and over: "What has happened? You left so joyful and have returned so sad." After so many questions and concerned faces, Bakil finally broke his silence. He revealed all that had happened and how it had happened. He explained all about the hunting trip that had gone wrong, and he explained how he was told that his hunting skills were impressive only because of his horse's skills. He also discussed the animosity that had been displayed by Beyrak.

"What did Beyrak say?" Bakil's wife, Surmalija Cheshme, had asked.

"What could he say? He talked nonsense, and then he wanted to draw his sword!" Bakil had replied. "But the nobles stopped him."

"'What a scoundrel son of a scoundrel!" Surmalija Cheshme sighed. "Did you give him what he deserves?"

"How could I not? The feud is old; he cannot forget it," Bakil had said. "However, I will take my revenge..."

Surmalija Cheshme had frowned anxiously. "What can you do to him? Gazan is Bayindir Khan's son-in-law, and Beyrak is his favorite. Whom do we have, my Lord? Do not be troubled."

"I have earned my keep with my sword and with my loyalty. What has Beyrak done? He idled away sixteen years in Bayburd, and now he can do whatever he likes? No!" Bakil had exclaimed.

"Of course not, my Lord. You are Bakil, and don't forget it. Were it not for you, Oghuz would not enjoy a single day of peace. Were it not for you, the forts stretched along the Black Sea would open their gates and crush Oghuz!" Surmalija Cheshme had tried to comfort him. "Do not think about it, or is there—"

"Yes, the matter cannot end like this. I have rebelled against Gazan; this is clear. I am moving to Georgia. Let the whole of Oghuz search for Bakil. Let the Khan of Khans question Gazan once," Bakil had said bitterly. "If he does not question him once, let him question him twice. Let him ask, 'What has happened to Bakil? Where is he? Why does he not come to Oghuz?' Then let Gazan and Beyrak answer before Bayindir Khan! Let's see what they will answer. Get ready, my Lady. We are moving tomorrow."

"My Lord, an angry mind cannot be clever. Do not rebel against Oghuz. What is the difference between rebelling against Oghuz and rebelling against the Khan? It is clear that things do not go well for the man who goes against his Khan," Surmalija Cheshme had replied. "What is wrong with our Mount Gazilig that you should go hunting at the Red Mountain? Do not let the sweat cool on your horse. Gather your companions. Go hunting, my Lord, and be of good cheer. May your eyes be glad, and may you banish dark thoughts from your mind!"

Bakil hesitated. "No, I shall not go," he had muttered.

"'My Lord, my heart's fancy is to eat game. You cannot disappoint me, can you? Won't you go?" Surmalija Cheshme had reproached him.

"In that case, I will go," Bakil then said.

Bakil glanced at me and then at the Khan. "With that, I gathered all my warriors and hunters and set out into our snowy mountains. What happened next and what did not happen is another story, and the Khan knows everything full well," he said quietly. "Gara Takur's army charged against us, my young son—and Gorgud came to our aid…"

> The Incomplete Manuscript *breaks off here, but the text is quickly restored again. Most likely, the omitted passages describe the clash between Imran and the infidel. A little earlier, the reader saw the "vision" of this incident in the language of Gorgud as recorded in* The Incomplete Manuscript.

"A little while longer, and my son would have been killed at the hand of the infidel; the borders of Oghuz would have been broken; our people would have been captured while I was ill and confined to my bed. Now, my Khan, I ask why? Of course, because of Beyrak and because of Gazan! Yes, my Khan, I have been insulted by Beyrak. He can be Beyrak, but I am Bakil," Bakil said confidently. After he had said this, Bakil fell silent.

> *A steward suddenly edged open the door and put his head around it. Having gained Bayindir Khan's permission with a nod, Gilbash rose and went out. He returned quickly and spoke softly to the Khan. Bayindir Khan shifted in his place. "Let them wait," he said. "We are about to finish. It is enough for today." Gilbash then went out.*

"Bakil, I have listened to you carefully. Now you listen to me," Bayindir Khan said slowly. "I had reports of what happened to you. I know and you know that there is now injustice in Oghuz. Be patient, Bakil. I know you and I know Beyrak. Do not lose hope. You will have justice. He will have justice, too. Now go and rest. I will need you later in relation to this matter. Stay nearby."

Bayindir Khan rose. We stood up, too. Bakil stepped forward and kissed Bayindir Khan's hand. Bayindir Khan embraced and kissed his face. Bakil then left the room backward, bowing.

When it was just Bayindir Khan and I left in the room, the Khan stretched a little, and then looked at me. "Gorgud, my son, do you know who has come?" he asked.

"No, splendid Khan," I replied. "I don't know."

"My daughter, Lady Burla, has come. Banuchichak has come with her."

"Really? And she came, too?"

"Really. Yes, she came, too. What do you say to that? Shall we spend time with them, or shall we complete the investigation?" Bayindir Khan asked. "The end of the investigation is still some way off."

"Why have the ladies come, my Khan? Did you summon them yourself because of this affair, or have they come themselves to embrace you?" I asked.

"How can I know? Either way, we can put their visit to good use. What do you think? Should we involve them in our inquiry, too? A man confides in his wife. Gazan may tell Lady Burla his secret, and Beyrak may tell Banuchichak," the Khan said casually.

I knew that there was a reason for the women's visit. Bayindir Khan had, of course, already thought whether or not to interrogate them. Realizing this, I said, "It would not be bad if we could ask them a few questions. There are still matters to clear up."

The Khan nodded. "You are right. Go and ask them to come in," he said. Then he went and stood at the window.

I went out and could not find Gilbash, so I called a servant and told him Bayindir Khan's order. "Very well," the servant said. He turned to go retrieve the women.

A little while later, Lady Burla and Banuchichak approached the Khan's chamber together. They both greeted me courteously, and I greeted them in return. Lady Burla then smiled at me. "How is the Khan, my father? He is in good health, God willing," she said.

I nodded and smiled back. "All is well, Lady Burla. Do not worry yourself." Banuchichak looked at me but did not say a word, nor did I ask her anything.

"Will you come in with us?" Lady Burla then asked.

I hesitated. "I don't know. If the Khan thinks it is necessary, he will summon me," I replied.

I was not sure when Gilbash had gone into Bayindir Khan's chamber. All I know is that he came out and looked at the three of us. "Daughters, both of you, and you, too, Gorgud, are to go in now. The Khan awaits you," he said.

The ladies walked toward the chamber first, and I quietly followed them. When we got to the entryway, Lady Burla and I continued walking into the chamber. Banuchichak waited in the wing.

Bayindir Khan was standing where I had left him alone—at the window. He turned to see his daughter as she walked in and reddened. "My daughter, Lady Burla, is it you? Burla, the tall; Burla of the long hair; Burla of the black eyes; Burla of the pistachio mouth; here you are!"

"Father, I have come to kiss your hands," Lady Burla smiled. She went up to her father, kneeled down, and gently kissed his hands.

Her father kissed her on her cheek. "Daughter, how are you? What are you doing? Sit down. Sit here." Bayindir Khan took his own seat and instructed Lady Burla to sit opposite from him. "Have you come alone? My daughter, didn't I tell you to bring Banuchichak? Have you told her how much we miss her? We do, you know."

Lady Burla smiled and gave a sign to Banuchichak, who had still been waiting quietly at the open door. "She has not come. She said that you offended her, my father," she mused.

"Did she really?" Bayindir Khan asked, surprised.

"Did I?" Banuchichak flushed in the doorway. "I have never said such a thing!"

"She is offended, is she?" The Khan asked, obviously enjoying the little charade. "So I have hurt her feelings? Let it be. My daughter, our time has past; we have grown old. What could we do? She has grounds for offense."

"Why do you say you are old? I wish old age upon your enemies!" Banuchichak replied. Then she walked up to Bayindir Khan, kneeled before him, and embraced his feet. "May those who have betrayed you grow old. May the gall bladder split of those who do not love you. Are you well, Khan of Khans?"

"Really? Who is this girl, Burla? I do not know her at all!" Bayindir Khan exclaimed, stroking Banuchichak's head and cheek.

"She is herself, my Khan. Weren't you talking about Banuchichak? I know her as Banuchichak," Lady Burla smiled.

"Really? Is it you, Banuchichak? Are you well? Are you in good health, daughter? If you are going, when will you come back? Is it one year or ten years since you left? I have forgotten your very countenance. Let me have a good look at you," the Khan said. "What has happened to you? You have grown thin! Your face has grown pale. Come, come and sit here. Now tell me, should we send you an invitation in the future? How long has it been since we've seen one another and talked? We grow old, yes, and still you dislike us."

Banuchichak twirled down onto the carpet where Bayindir Khan had indicated, crossed her legs, and then smacked her knees with her hands. "You are not old, my Khan. It has not been a year since you have seen my face; it has not even been a month. How quickly you miss me! So you say I have grown thin and pale? We have one Khan of Khans. This is what happens when I do not see him. Do not ask me anything, Khan of Khans. Also, we saw new serving wenches in the yard; one is prettier than the other. Do they not keep you from growing old?" she joked.

Bayindir Khan laughed out loud. His face—so melancholy just a moment ago—shone bright. I had been forgotten. But as I was sitting to one side, watching the conversation unfold with a joyful heart, the Khan then motioned me over to them. "Gorgud, come and take your place. There is work to do," he smiled. He seemed to have sensed what was in my heart.

I bowed my head and went and took my place. Gilbash went and took his seat, too. Bayindir Khan then turned to the ladies. "Daughters, whom shall I talk about? I shall talk to you about the ruler of Trebizond. His envoy has come. You know our Ganturali? He complained about him. It is a long story. But the ruler of Trebizond chose the most marvelous silks and the most beautiful lace of Trebizond, and then he sent them. We shall have our talk, and then Gilbash will take you to see them. You will be able to choose whatever you like. What do you say to that?" he asked.

"Thank you, Father Khan!" Lady Burla exclaimed. "May your riches never end."

"Thank you, Khan of Khans. You have no compare in the whole of Oghuz—in this mortal coil, you know," Banuchichak said.

I have not forgotten this phrase: "You have no compare in this mortal coil." Mortal coil. Just look at the woman's words.

"I know, I know. You should know it, too," Bayindir Khan said.

"Do we not know? We all know this," Banuchichak could not stop herself. Then Banuchichak looked at me very carefully, too. She was interested in what I was writing.

Noticing this, Bayindir Khan said, "Good, daughters, we can talk about this later." Then he looked at me. "Gorgud, my son, cross out what you have written up until now. Record what will be said from now on. Did you hear what I said?"

"I heard, majestic Khan. I shall do it," I said. I was about to obey his orders...

The manuscript is cut off here, and we will never know why Gorgud failed to comply with the Khan's orders, and why the conversation between the Khan and his daughters found its way into the manuscript. An interesting conversation has, therefore, been included in the manuscript for reasons unknown to the reader.

"Let us begin," Bayindir Khan said. "Lady Burla, Banuchichak, I will ask you some questions. You must give only correct answers. Agreed? This is the matter: Did you know that there was a spy in Oghuz? Or did you hear nothing about it?"

The two young women looked at each other. Lady Burla spoke first. "How could we not have heard, Father Khan?" she asked. Then she looked back at Banuchichak. "Didn't you hear, girl?"

She nodded. "Yes, we heard, my Khan," Banuchichak replied.

"Good," Bayindir Khan said, pleased with the answer. "So you heard, too. Of course, you could not fail to have heard. Gazan went hunting; didn't he, my daughter, Burla? The spy did his work, and his family was taken prisoner. What about Beyrak? A day before his wedding, the spy brought news again, and they stole such a brave man, such a lion. For sixteen years, you wept bitter tears, my daughter, Banuchichak, and you nearly wed another man. Do you remember? You could not forget…" His voice had trailed off for a moment as he silently recalled the events that led up to where they were. Then he continued. "Okay, let's return to the matter in hand. The spy did his work while Oghuz slept, unaware."

"Yes, Father Khan, you are right. The spy has cost us dearly. Uruz was almost lost," Lady Burla moaned.

"So, you are right, daughter. Now, girls, tell me: Who was this spy? How did Gazan catch him? How did Shirshamsaddin put him in the pit? Was it so?" Bayindir Khan asked carefully.

"It was so, Father Khan. It was so," Lady Burla said immediately. "You know everything very well. It was so."

"If this is how it was," Bayindir Khan said, narrowing his eyes at Lady Burla. "Then how did the spy disappear? Did he fly into the sky? Did he burrow into the ground? Did he turn into a bird and fly away? Where did the spy go? Will you tell me, my daughter, Burla?" Bayindir Khan's voice was stern.

Lady Burla understood from the Khan's seriousness that he wanted accurate information from her. But she did not lose her composure and, as though she had been ready to reply to the question, she straightened her back and looked directly at her father. "Father Khan, listen to me; I will tell you. You did well to call us. I have the right information," she began. "Yes, the spy was caught. You should know that the spy was Boghazja Fatma's son. He was thrown in the pit. I wish you could have seen how Gazan shouted at the top of his voice. 'I'll kill that scoundrel son of a scoundrel!' he had said. 'I'll chop him in pieces!' he yelled. 'I'll divide him up among everyone!' he raged. But what happened?"

"But what happened? I'm interested, too, Lady Burla. What indeed happened?" Bayindir Khan asked, flushed with surprise.

"None of this happened, Father Khan," Lady Burla said. "The nobles came to the council—Bakil, Shirshamsaddin, Aruz, and Beyrak. And do you know what Gazan told me after the meeting? 'My Lady,' he said. 'It was laughable. The nobles decided that the spy was innocent! I was left on my own, and so I could not do anything about the matter.'"

"Is that so?" Bayindir Khan asked.

Lady Burla nodded. "Just before the council, Boghazja Fatma came, Father. I do not know what she said to Gazan. Know this, Father Khan: Gazan will only talk only to you. He cannot hide anything from you," she replied. "Whatever Boghazja Fatma said made Gazan suddenly change. A moment ago, he had been shouting; now he was quiet. He had been furious with me, and now he had the spy pulled out of the pit and given to his mother. The slaves nearly strewed the road with flowers and told him to go. That was the end of the spy."

"Majestic Khan," Banuchichak began, looking at me and my pen and paper. "If you want to know the truth, the spy was not Boghazja Fatma's son at all."

"Really? Then who was the spy?" Bayindir Khan asked.

"The spy was Aruz's doing, my Khan. Lady Burla, you start," Banuchichak replied.

Lady Burla nodded. "It was really so, Khan. Banuchichak is telling the truth. The spy was Aruz's affair."

"Look, look, you are bringing up Aruz again! What does this have to do with Aruz? Why would Aruz spy in Oghuz? What would he profit?" the Khan asked, growing frustrated.

"I shall tell you," Lady Burla said matter-of-factly. "He would profit by becoming the Noble of Nobles. You would strip Gazan of the position and give it to him. The infidels would have come and raked through our land. Aruz would have said, 'Gazan was not strong, but I am strong. Didn't my son, Basat, defeat One-Eye? The title Noble of Nobles should be mine!' Aruz cannot sleep at night because of this desire, Father Khan. You know it all full well yourself."

Bayindir Khan thought for a moment. He didn't say anything as he let his daughter's words sink in.

"Lady Burla is right, my Khan," Banuchichak added. "'Basat vanquished One-Eye; Basat did this; Basat did that.' That Basat has brought disaster upon our heads, and Aruz keeps talking about him. He keeps his eye on the title of Noble of Nobles."

I remembered something. Old Aruz was not the only person to sing Basat's praises in Oghuz. After Basat vanquished One-Eye, old and young, girls and boys, all kept repeating his name. Lady Burla wasn't married to Gazan then. She talked about Basat, and before Banuchichak allowed Beyrak to become close to her, Basat's name could be heard on her lips, too. Who didn't admire Basat?

After Basat had vanquished One-Eye, all the girls in the whole of Oghuz gave Basat their hearts. Bayindir Khan knew his daughter well and scolded her. "When she mentions his name, she drools like a calf. Do not mention his name again, my girl! I would not give a lame goat to this backwoodsman, and you can tell Aruz that. I wonder if my girls are trying to get their own back on Basat and Aruz now," he had said.

"Do you think so, too?" Bayindir Khan asked Banuchichak pensively.

"Yes, magnificent Khan. I think so, too," Banuchichak replied.

"It was Beyrak that brought Gazan news of the spy, wasn't it?" Bayindir Khan asked again.

"This is what Gazan told me," Lady Burla replied.

"Do you remember that day?" the Khan asked.

"Yes, Father Khan, I remember it. It was the day our tent was plundered. All the Inner Oghuz nobles came," Lady Burla recalled.

"Outer Oghuz didn't come, did they?" the Khan asked.

"Gazan did not invite Outer Oghuz to the plunder," Lady Burla answered in a low voice, her head bowed.

"Which of you saw Beyrak the day before the plunder?" Bayindir Khan frowned, looking at Lady Burla.

"I did not see him," Banuchichak said quickly. "'I am going to the banks of the Pinar with a friend,' he had said. 'There will be a feast.' This is what he told me."

"I—I didn't see him, either, Father Khan," Lady Burla stammered, flushing bright red. "What of it?"

Did Shirshamsaddin say the opposite of what Lady Burla just said? Though I could not see it, I sensed that Bayindir Khan did not like Lady Burla's answer. The Khan had real faith in Shirshamsaddin. He did not say a word about Lady Burla's lie.

"You didn't see him then?" Bayindir Khan asked. He was talking more to himself. "Then answer my question, daughters. Why did Beyrak raise the matter of the spy right then, during the plunder? What ideas do you have?"

"I have no idea," Banuchichak said. "He mentions it now and then. What difference does it make?"

"I cannot think of anything, either," Lady Burla said.

"Has Beyrak never mentioned to you the conversation in Bayburd Castle about the spy?" Bayindir Khan asked Banuchichak. "You are his wife, after all."

"No, he has not mentioned it. Beyrak keeps his own counsel, glorious Khan. He never says an idle word. He bides his time," Banuchichak replied.

"So," Bayindir Khan said. "Now I shall ask you my last question, daughters. How did it come to pass that, at the council, the nobles all supported—what was that old woman's name? Boghazja Fatma, yes—how did they all support her son and pronounce him innocent?"

Lady Burla looked at Banuchichak; Banuchichak looked at Lady Burla. Both bowed their heads and thought quietly for a few moments. Bayindir Khan sat quietly, too, interested to hear what they would say. He looked at me and smiled. I remained quiet, ready to write.

"Father Khan, I have thought about this and...I don't know," Lady Burla finally replied.

"What do you say?" Bayindir Khan then asked Banuchichak slowly.

"Glorious Khan, it's all because of that Boghazja Fatma. Whatever she said or did not say made the nobles change their minds," Banuchichak said simply.

"So what did she say?" Bayindir Khan asked.

"I don't know what she said! I don't want to lie," Banuchichak said. "But, Khan, someone is giving her instruction; that much is obvious. That woman is not intelligent, and no man would look at her face..."

Again, I felt my blood freeze in my veins.

"Daughters, that is enough. You have tired me out. Gilbash, get up and take these girls and show them the goods from Trebizond. They may choose whatever they like. As for you, Banuchichak, do not disappear like crumbs of bread among the hungry. Do you hear me, girl? Don't wait for me to send for you. Come whenever your heart desires," the Khan said, smiling. He turned to Lady Burla. "Lady Burla, my daughter, tell Uruz to choose a racehorse for himself. Gilbash!"

Lady Burla and Banuchichak kissed the Khan's hand. The Khan embraced them, kissed them on the cheek, and they left. Gilbash left with them. After they had gone, Bayindir Khan paced the room for quite some time. He was thinking. Eventually, he turned and looked at me, still pacing. "Gorgud, my son, this affair is growing day by day. It is getting very complicated. So much time has passed, and the end is still not in sight. But the girl did well to finger Boghazja Fatma's collar; she said that Boghazja Fatma had instructed the nobles. If this Boghazja Fatma had been more intelligent, who instructed her to play this trick on the nobles?" Bayindir Khan smiled again.

"Long live the Khan! Hasn't the investigation come to its end? The spy is no longer in our midst, and the nobles have all confessed their guilt. What is left?" I asked. I wanted to change the direction of the conversation.

"There is something left, Gorgud. Yes, there is something. We don't yet know who instructed Boghazja Fatma. There is another question left, too, which I will tell you later. Now tell me, though, who shall we hear first—Aruz or Gazan?" the Khan asked. "Where is Gilbash? Gilbash, where are you? Come here!"

Although Gilbash had gone out of the room, he heard the Khan's voice came running into the room as fast as he could. "Yes, Khan, I am at your service. I was choosing a horse for Uruz..." his voice trailed off.

"Later, later. First, Gilbash, tell me who is here and who is not," Bayindir Khan said.

"They have all come; they are all in separate rooms. However, Old Aruz is not expected until tomorrow. Gazan is here. Bakil is here. Beyrak has come; he is with Gazan. Shirshamsaddin is here, too. Uruz rides to the horse field every morning. He has a ride; he gallops. One of our thoroughbred horses has foaled, and the foal is now grown. I will give it to the boy. Who is left?" Gilbash recapped.

His eyes lit up as he remembered more. "Oh, the girls chose some fine goods. They did not stay and, saying prayers for the Khan, left for Inner Oghuz. Banuchichak left with Lady Burla. My Khan, I will tell you, there is one more matter..." he said, his voice trailing off. He hesitated for a moment and looked at me, and then at Bayindir Khan again. The Khan nodded for him to continue and he did. "Old Gazilig said to me, 'Gilbash, tell the Khan to send me away on a mission. Council follows council, and I am not there. I don't want gossip in Oghuz.'"

Bayindir Khan thought for a moment. "Old Gazilig speaks the truth. Tell him to prepare gifts. He should choose horses swift as falcons and the strongest camels; remember the booty from the last caravan? I am talking about the gold flagons. He should take them and set off for Trebizond with a couple of nobles, servants, and warriors. He must convey my greetings to the king. He should tell him that we boxed Ganturali's ears. Then Gilbash—you must tell him yourself—Old Gazilig should present the gifts, eat and drink, enjoy his time there, and then come back," the Khan ordered.

He waited a few seconds to let Gilbash process the information and then continued. "We will have finished our work by then. He must leave tomorrow, though. Understood? Besides, he must tell the king what happened at Duzmurd Castle. Duzmurd is close to Trebizond. The king will be interested. Now go and tell him what I have told you. Then summon Gazan to me. We'll take a look at him." The Khan paused again and looked at me. "What do you have to say, Gorgud, my son? Are you tired? Do you have the strength left to continue? It's not easy to write and correct a manuscript. I know you…"

What response could I give to a command from Bayindir Khan other than "yes"? I thought. "No, Glorious Khan, I'm not tired at all. Is it possible to have enough of your words? I am ready," I said. But all I could think about was how I missed the Stone of Light. I wished I could rest against the stone and fall asleep. *I would like to talk to the Stone of Light…*

Bayindir Khan studied me carefully. Finally, he turned to Gilbash. "Go and do what I have told you, and then bring Gazan," he instructed.

Gilbash left and the Khan became silent. Suddenly, he looked sideways at me. "Gorgud, your words say one thing, but your eyes say another. Are you aware of this?" he blurted.

"No, glorious Khan," I replied. "I am not aware of it. What do my eyes say?"

"Nothing. I will tell you what I have to say later—at the end. We understand each other, don't we?" the Khan asked mysteriously.

"You give the order, Khan, and as much as you tell me to understand, that much shall I understand," I replied.

"Very good. Now let's see what Gazan has to tell us! Come in, Gazan, come and take your seat here," the Khan called out.

Gazan entered immediately. He gave a courteous greeting, bowed, and came and sat opposite me. Bayindir Khan smiled at him. "Were you comfortable? Was your bedding soft? Were you well served?" he asked curiously. "How are you spending your time?"

Gazan nodded. "I wish the Khan good health. Everything is very good. Do not worry at all!" he replied.

Gilbash came in at that moment. He exchanged looks with Bayindir Khan and took his seat, too. "Gazan," Bayindir Khan slowly began his speech. "Last time, you spoke and I listened. You swore and I believed you. I have one last question for you. Answer this question and I shall tell you my decision."

"As you please, Khan. What is the question?" Gazan asked, shifting in his seat.

"Gazan, tell me what you and Boghazja Fatma talked about. Boghazja Fatma came to you. What did you tell her when the two of you were alone?" Bayindir Khan asked without beating around the bush.

Gazan bent his head and fell silent. Bayindir Khan was also silent, his cup of patience full to overflowing. The silence lasted a fair while. At last, Gazan broke the silence. "Father Khan, I shall tell you everything just as it was. You draw your own conclusions at the end. If I have any guilt, the neck of my dark head is before you, finer than a hair's breadth. Strike it, my Khan."

"Speak, Gazan, speak," Bayindir Khan said calmly. "I am listening to you."

Gazan cleared his throat and began to speak…

§ § § § § §

It was evening, and Shirshamsaddin had just put the spy into the pit. A servant then went and told Gazan that a woman had come and wanted to see him; however, she would not give her name.

Before Gazan continued telling his version of the story to Bayindir Khan, he stopped to clarify something. "I had had a conversation with Lady Burla earlier," he said. "Lady Burla had come to me and said, 'Why have you imprisoned this poor woman's young son? You know that the spy is one of Aruz's men!'"

"How did you respond?" the Khan asked.

"I said, 'No, my Lady," Gazan replied. "'Aruz has nothing to do with this affair. The spy is Boghazja's son.'" The Khan nodded and Gazan continued with his story. I resumed my writing.

"No," Lady Burla had said. "This concerns Aruz."

"This concerns Boghazja Fatma," Gazan had said, shaking his head. "Mother and son united and did this work together."

"Look," Lady Burla then sighed. "You keep talking about Boghazja Fatma! Can it be that you are remembering your youth?"

Again, Gazan stopped his story and looked at the Khan. "I did not know how to reply, my Khan. I know that Lady Burla has been here and told you the whole story, but she may not have told you how everything *really* was," he said slowly. "Now I shall tell you how it really was, Father Khan…"

Bayindir Khan smiled. "Tell me how it was, Gazan," he replied. "You tell me how it really was."

Gazan had immediately wanted to pass over the matter. Still, he knew that Lady Burla had no problem saying whatever entered her mind. He had looked at her, shaking his head. "What are you talking about? Is this you? How many times does a man have to explain a conversation?" he asked. "We finished this conversation twenty or twenty-five years ago. We finished it! Are you out of your mind?"

"I am not out of my mind. It's you who is out of his mind, Gazan. I'll tell you again: Her son is not the spy. The spy is one of your Uncle Aruz's men. What's the matter? Don't you like what I've said? Are you trying to cover up for him because he's your uncle?" Lady Burla had asked.

Gazan became furious. "What are you saying?" he had demanded. "Am I to get up, take my black whip, and give you a taste of your own blood? Listen to this, my Lady. Gorgud came and said who the spy was. It was not my doing!"

Lady Burla took a step back. She frowned. “When did Gorgud come?” she had asked. “Why didn’t I see him?”

Gazan thought Lady Burla needed additional proof. “Shirshamsaddin!” he suddenly called out. “Shirshamsaddin, come here and speak. She doesn’t believe me!” When Shirshamsaddin didn’t immediately come, Gazan then looked irritatedly at Lady Burla. “Should Shirshamsaddin come?”

“No, there’s no need,” she had muttered. She relaxed a little after that. A few moments later, she spoke again. “Oh, Gazan,” she said. “Boghazja Fatma is a poor, helpless woman. She has grown old alone. She has just one son, and he is fatherless, I tell you.”

“No!” Gazan shouted, realizing what Lady Burla wanted to say next. “It has nothing to do with me, I can tell you. The nobles will come. There will be a council. Whatever they say, I will do.”

With that subject dropped, the couple began to talk about the plunder. Gazan had asked, “Have you forgotten that it was you who would not let me invite my Uncle Aruz to the plunder?”

Lady Burla had then looked him in the eyes. “If you invite your Uncle Aruz, I will go to the Khan and say that you have strayed from the true path. I will say you swore at me and make my life impossible!”

After she had spoken, Gazan decided that he would not invite Old Aruz to the plunder. However, when the other nobles from Outer Oghuz heard that he would not be invited, they decided not to come, either. Gazan had been upset with what Lady Burla had threatened him with. “You bound my hands and feet!” he argued. “You told me not to invite Aruz.”

“I did well; I did the right thing. Now you listen to me, Gazan. Your Uncle Aruz has long since had his eye on your red throne—on becoming Noble of Nobles. Don’t you know that? Your Uncle Aruz has his eye on your army, too. Haven’t you noticed? If you don’t know, then listen: Your Uncle Aruz went to my father, the Khan. He talked to my father about you,” Lady Burla had said slowly. “‘Who rescued Oghuz from One-Eye? My son, Basat, did! Give me my due, Bayindir Khan,’ he said. I did not tell you this before, but I am telling you now, my Lord. Your Uncle Aruz wanted to make Basat the Noble of Nobles of the whole of Oghuz!”

Gazan had frowned; he had not known or heard any of what Lady Burla was saying before. “What did the Khan say?” he had asked

“What could my father have said?” Lady Burla had shrugged. “He has grown old. He is no longer strong. What do you want of him, my father, the Khan?”

“Bayindir Khan will never grow old. He will never lose his strength!” Gazan had said matter-of-factly. “Never say this again or—”

Bayindir Khan interrupted Gazan's story. "She said I'd grown old, did she?" said he asked quietly, nodding to himself.

"Yes, Father Khan, that is what she said," Gazan replied. "What are you upset about, though? Do women have brains?"

The Khan grinned a little and urged Gazan to continue with this story.

"Oh, Gazan! If I did not love you deeply, would I have spoken those words? Aruz is busy trying to incite the Oghuz nobles against you!" Lady Burla had cried. "You must know this, my Lord. This affair will not end without a fight; mark my words."

"What of it? If Aruz wants a fight, he shall have a fight!" Gazan had said. "He will have to deal with me, Salur Gazan. The time has come for Inner Oghuz to be purged. I will deal first with the enemy within. Whoever it may be, we will see…"

At that moment, a servant approached the couple. "Lord Gazan, a woman has come to the gate. She wants to see you, but she won't say her name. What shall we do?" he had asked.

"Invite her in. Let's see what she has to say," Gazan had quickly replied with hopes of ending the conversation he had been having with Lady Burla.

Before the servant could turn around and retrieve the mysterious woman, Lady Burla told him to wait. "Hold on. Why won't she give her name?" she had demanded. "Go and tell her that if she won't give her name, she can't come in."

"My Lady, don't—don't do this. Let us handle our own affairs," Gazan had responded quietly. When Lady Burla glared at Gazan, he gave up. He looked at the servant. "Very well, then. Tell her that if she does not give her name, the Lord will not receive her inside," he sighed.

The servant then disappeared to go find out the woman's name. Meanwhile, Gazan turned back to his wife. "My Lady, go inside. We have our own affairs to attend to," he said.

Of course, Lady Burla did not go. She had stayed where she was until the servant came back. When the servant finally returned, he looked at Gazan, "My Lord, the old woman is Boghazja Fatma," he had said. "She said she has a private matter to discuss with you."

In that moment, Lady Burla had turned into a raging torrent. "What? *What?*" she cried. "Boghazja Fatma alone with you? No!"

"Come now," Gazan had said, trying to calm his wife. "What could she have to say of any importance? What do we have in common? I have no secrets from anyone. She must have come to lament her son's fate. Tell her to come another time. Tomorrow—"

"Tomorrow?" Lady Burla blurted, shaking her head. "No, wait." She looked at the poor servant. "Have her come right now. Whatever there is to say can be said in my presence. Do you hear me, Gazan? She must speak in my presence, or else…"

"Bah!" Gazan had said flippantly. "Or else what?"

"Or else I will go to my father, the Khan!" Lady Burla had threatened again.

"Very well, my Lady, fortune of my life, queen of my home. What is wrong with you?" Gazan had asked, trying to calm his wife down.

"I will go to my father, the Khan!" Lady Burla repeated angrily. "Whatever Boghazja Fatma has to say, she can say it now!"

Gazan stopped telling his story and took a deep breath. "'I will go to my father, the Khan!'" he said to Bayindir Khan, imitating his wife. "This is how she always threatens me, my Khan. If I open my mouth—if I say just one word—she immediately says, 'I will go to my father, the Khan!' If I want to do something else, again she says, 'I will go to my father, the Khan!' She frightens me with your name, my Khan; mark my words. What can I do?" he asked, sounding stressed. "You are up above. You know how deeply I love you even without Burla. Who was I? I was a raw young boy. Didn't you make me Noble of Nobles? Didn't you give me an army? Are you not my backbone, my support? I'll get back to the subject…"

After Gazan vented a little, he went right back into his story where he had left off. I continued writing.

"No, have her come tomorrow," Gazan then said. This time, however, he hadn't flinched.

Lady Burla had had enough. She suddenly started sobbing. "I—I will not stay here a moment longer! The two of you say what you have to say and sniff each other out. Reminisce about your bygone days. You, Gazan, have thrown what was between us to the black winds!" she cried. "You have sold me for—for less than a black goat! You are Lord Gazan, but I am Lady Burla—Lady Burla, daughter of Bayindir Khan!" With that, she stormed out of the room, fuming.

Gazan then turned and vented his rage on the servant. "What? Are you frozen in that spot? Scoundrel son of a scoundrel, couldn't you have given me the message in private? Fetch that snake-bitten Boghazja Fatma! Go and fetch her, the infidel daughter of an infidel!" he spat. The servant quickly left, completely perplexed.

What does Boghazja Fatma want from me? Gazan then began to wonder. *Doesn't she know the fate that awaits her son, the spy? Doesn't she know that there is no mercy in Oghuz for spies—and never can be? She knows. Then why does she want to talk to me? She would not have come to bargain. She won't say the reason. Or is she going to make me change my mind with her tears? Let her come. Let her come, and we will see what she has to say…*

Soon, Boghazja Fatma came through the gate. She approached Gazan and immediately fell at his feet in desperation. She sobbed and groaned, but she could not move Gazan's heart. He waited in silence for the flood of tears to finally dry up. When she had stopped crying, Gazan had looked down at her. "What do you want, woman? Why have you come?" he asked angrily.

"'My master, Gazan, I have come to die at your feet. I have come to cast myself on your mercy. Your broad skirts—" Boghazja Fatma began.

Gazan had interrupted her. "Old woman, cut short your long speech! Don't you know what your son has done? Your son has been spying in Oghuz! What mercy are you talking about? My only son, Uruz, was almost killed by the enemy while my aged mother fell into enemy hands. My wife, Lady Burla, and that scoundrel, King Shoklu..."

Gazan then paused in his story. He glanced at me and my writing hand, and then focused on the Khan again. "In short, my Khan, I really scolded that woman," he said, almost sounding proud about it.

"Go on..." Bayindir Khan said quietly. He gazed at Gazan, eagerly waiting for him to continue.

"Every moment has its secret," Gazan had said to Boghazja Fatma. "And this is not the moment for mercy. Could you not foresee what would befall your son? The scoundrel son of a scoundrel has brought misfortune upon Oghuz!"

The poor woman then opened her eyes wide, swollen from crying. She had looked into Gazan's eyes, pleading. "I did not foresee it, my Lord; I could not, my Lord. But, Gazan, my only hope—my only refuge—is you."

"I am? What are you talking about, old woman?" Gazan had snorted. "Do you realize what you have said? I am your hope?" He began to laugh.

"You are, Gazan. You said yourself that every moment has its secret. Well, I have a secret, too. I have kept this secret inside for twenty-two straight years. I have hidden it from everyone," Boghazja Fatma said quietly.

"This does not concern me," Gazan had replied.

"This *does* concern you, Gazan. I am telling you now that this concerns you. My son—"

Gazan had rolled his eyes. "Your son, what?" he asked.

"My son is not a spy," Boghazja Fatma said firmly.

"Bah! Your son is not a spy. Then who was the spy? Me?" Gazan then asked sarcastically.

"Gazan, have you forgotten me?" Boghazja Fatma then asked sadly.

"Be quiet!" Gazan warned. He looked around to see if anyone was watching them.

"Gazan, you have forgotten me. I was a beautiful girl—" she began.

"Be quiet, for the love of God!" Gazan then snarled.

Boghazja Fatma continued. "Now I have grown old. There was a gully behind our tent. Have you forgotten the black dog in our yard? His name was Baragchug. You were the only person he didn't bark at, if you remember—"

"Hold your tongue! For the love of God, hold your tongue! Why are you saying all this? Why have you come?" Gazan had asked, growing more agitated by the second. "What does it matter if I have or have not forgotten? So what? Your son is a spy, Boghazja Fatma, a spy! Cry and moan if you want, but—"

"He is your son, Gazan," Boghazja Fatma announced in a low voice.

"Your son is a spy and he will be punished!" Gazan had ranted. Suddenly, however, Boghazja Fatma's words sank in. "Wait, *what?* What nonsense are you talking about, old woman? Stop it!"

"He is your son," Boghazja Fatma repeated.

> *I looked up at Bayindir Khan and saw that he was struggling not to laugh. Oh, Boghazja Fatma, what a clever one you were! He was probably thinking,* May almighty God protect us from the outcome! *Of course, the matter would not end like this; there would be an outcome, for sure. Would Bayindir Khan be really angry then or not? Only God would know...*

"Mine, eh? Why should the boy be mine?" Gazan then asked quietly. "Wasn't your name Boghazja Fatma of the Forty Lovers?"

"A mother knows who her son's father is, Gazan," Boghazja Fatma said calmly.

> *Did Boghazja Fatma really say that to Gazan or not? I don't know. But Gazan was right to say, "A mother knows who her son's father is." If a mother doesn't know, then who does?*

"Prove it!" Gazan then challenged. With that, he went to check the door and slammed it shut.

"Gazan, I kept this secret for many long years. I kept the secret from everyone. The time has now come. Now I am telling you. Do not take vengeance on our son, Gazan. Don't do it!" Boghazja Fatma had begged.

Gazan had persisted. Black doubts gnawed at his heart. "Why didn't you tell me this before?" he had asked.

"What would have been the point? Whether I said something or not, what difference would it have made?" Boghazja Fatma asked with a shrug. "He wasn't the courageous athlete; the stocky boy that you would want at your side; that you would instruct and teach; that you would take hunting and raiding. He is quiet and meek; if you don't ask, he doesn't answer. He speaks only when spoken to. Look carefully at his face and eyes, my Lord Gazan. You will see yourself. You will remember your youth…"

Gazan stopped his story. "My Khan, I was slowly coming to believe this woman! I admit it, my Khan. I was with this woman several times when I was young. I began to think, 'I may well have a son! Why would she lie? And what should I do now?' I was very confused, my Khan," he admitted, adding, "I wondered what my guilt had been. What misfortune had befallen me? What was the dagger thrust into my heart?"

"What happened next, my Lord?" Bayindir Khan asked curiously. Gazan took a deep breath and continued telling the story from his perspective.

"'Go, Boghazja Fatma, go!" he had ordered. "The nobles will meet tomorrow for a council. I will see what I can do. But look, do not tell anyone about this secret. No one must know what you have revealed to me just now. Now go!"

Boghazja Fatma had nodded. "Very well," she said. "Thank you." With that, she turned and walked away.

Gazan shrugged. He looked up at the Khan. "I was upset, my Khan, but then I remembered Gorgud's words."

I perked up. Gazan and I made eye contact. I nodded at him.

Gazan continued. "Gorgud, you said, 'Don't regret it later, Gazan.' You were wrong to raise the spy affair." Then he turned back to look at Bayindir Khan, looking tired and defeated. "Yes, my Khan, we fell into Beyrak's net. Many thoughts entered my mind. 'How will I get out of this at tomorrow's council of nobles? How will I exonerate Beyrak? Whatever I may say, Bakil—and Aruz will be there, too—will oppose me. What will I do?' I was left alone with these thoughts after my conversation with Boghazja Fatma, and I will officially finish my speech here. Am I guilty or not, great Khan? If you say that I am, my blood is yours to take." Gazan stopped talking and bowed his head.

Silence fell in the room; however, Bayindir Khan was in high spirits. He clapped his hands and burst out laughing. "This Boghazja Fatma that you just spoke about—what a clever woman she was! She went to see each of the nobles, spoke to them before the council, and told them the same thing: 'The boy is yours!'" he exclaimed.

Gazan's mouth fell open. He had no idea what was going on. Slowly, however, he was beginning to put together all the pieces.

The Khan continued. "Look, Aruz is coming tomorrow, and I can tell you that he will say exactly the same thing. You will see tomorrow!" he laughed. "What was that line you said, Gazan? Oh, yes: A mother knows who her son's father is. Gorgud, my son, you remember this line. One day, you will need it! Oh, Boghazja Fatma…" his voice trailed off as he continued chuckling. Then he looked at Gazan, me, and even Gilbash. "Aruz will come and you will see!" he added, pointing at each one of us.

Although Gazan still did not really understand what was going on, he felt relieved. He eased up a bit as the Khan joked and laughed. Suddenly, though, the Khan became serious again. He looked at Gazan. "Gazan, do you know your real guilt? Your real guilt is not that you freed the Oghuz spy; he has gone, vanished, no more. Your real guilt, Gazan, is something I will tell you later," he said. "I will talk to Aruz tomorrow, and then I will let you all know my decision. Now go, all of you. Such bearded, grown men…"

As I stood up and stretched a bit, the Khan looked at me intently through narrowed eyes. "Gorgud, my son, Boghazja Fatma was clever to twist so many men around her little finger," he said. "Wasn't she?"

I could not bear that gaze and bent my head, not saying a word. I felt my face get hot and flush red as a beetroot. Gazan looked at Bayindir Khan, and then he, too, focused his gaze on me. However, he was not bold enough to say a word, either.

§ § § § § §

For several days, Huseyn Bay Lele had gone to the Shah's throne room, but Rahim, Head of the Guard, had not allowed him to enter. However, even though Rahim would not allow Lele into the throne room, he was not against him sitting and waiting in a corner of the courtyard. He would even perform small services for Lele, occasionally bringing him water from inside. Sometimes they would sit together and discuss the affairs of the day over a glass of tea.

The servants would spread out a large carpet and cushions for them under the elm tree. They would sit and watch the comings and goings and reminisce about the old days, sometimes discussing people whom they recognized. Rahim listened carefully to Lele; he enjoyed his conversation and was not yet weary of it. He truly wanted to help the distinguished man—to help him sort out his affairs—but the Vizier stood in the way. Rahim could not make a single move without the Vizier's direction or approval.

One day, Rahim approached the Vizier to tell him about Lele. "Master Vizier, there is a man who comes to the court every morning. He says, 'I wish to see the Shah,' sits down and waits until dusk, and then leaves. He has come from the Ottoman lands, but he is from hereabouts by origin."

"Oh?" the Vizier asked.

Rahim continued. "Yes, he knows many things. He tells very strange stories about the youth of the Shah, Lord of the Age. May I sacrifice myself for him? He knows all the nobles. He knows the army. He tells tales of interesting events on his travels…"

"What is his name?" the Vizier asked, attempting to sound interested. "Who is his family?"

"His name is Huseyn Bay," Rahim replied. "I don't know his last name or who his family is."

"Why does he say he wishes to see the Pivot of the Universe?" the Vizir asked.

"He says that he will tell him himself. He says he has important news. But he does not say from whom," Rahim replied.

"Go and find out whom the news is from. If you find out, tell me. It is now time for the evening prayer. The Shah has returned from his expedition, God willing, so you go, too, and do your work," the Vizier ordered, not taking the Head of the Guard's words too seriously. With that, he put an end to the conversation.

Lele went to the Shah's courtyard again the next day. Again, Rahim greeted him and barred his way, suggesting that he sit and wait beneath the elm tree. However, Lele seemed a little impatient this time, and Rahim quickly sensed this. After they had been sitting and chatting for a little while, Lele stopped talking and looked sideways at Rahim. "Head of the Guard, tell me the truth," he said. "The Vizier does not allow me to enter into the presence of the Shah, isn't that so?"

Rahim had not expected the direct question and was rather confused at first. He sipped his tea before answering. "No, what are you thinking of? Master Vizier would very much like to arrange this meeting, but the Shah is away. He is on an expedition. It is not possible. And besides—" he said carefully.

"And besides what?" Lele interrupted.

"Nothing. You have said your first name—that is true—but you have not said who your people are. It won't be easy to present you to the Shah without knowing who you really are," Rahim explained. "What do you say?"

Lele thought for a while. *If I open up to him now—if I tell him who I was from beginning to end—how can I know that old fox, the Vizier, would tell the Shah the truth? He would never want me to re-emerge like this—to suddenly reappear out of nowhere. He must have a cozy position now. But what shall I do? If I don't tell him, then how can I see the Shah, for whom I would sacrifice myself? By God, I am desperate. I am caught between two fires.*

"Well?" Rahim asked again, bringing Lele out of his own mind.

"But couldn't the Vizier tell the Shah that a poor wretch has come from a distant land to serve him and would like to say a few words to him?" Lele asked.

Rahim hesitated. "I don't know if he could say so or not. It's not my job, you see," he replied. "He might say so and he might not."

"Say that I have escaped from Turkish captivity. Say that I was taken prisoner at the Battle of Chaldiran, and now I have returned," Lele then said.

"I am not sure, by God. Did you really fight at Chaldiran?" Rahim asked, amazed.

Smiling at Rahim's obvious amazement, Lele grinned and nodded. "Yes, I did fight; I did do battle. You must have been a child then!" he exclaimed.

"Yes, I was a child. My master—I'm talking about my father—was a guard. He died at Chaldiran," Rahim said.

"There has been no battle like Chaldiran," Lele sighed.

"Tell me a little about it, for God's sake. I have asked many people about that fight; they all tell it in their own way," Rahim said. "Who was the commander of your detachment?"

Lele smiled again. His face and eyes lit up. Rahim was sure to make him open up and tell him everything. He just did not know if the young man was playing a trick on him. "Did Master Vizier ask you to talk to me?" he asked cautiously.

"No, not at all! Not for the faith of the Perfect Councilor. I wanted to talk to you myself," Rahim said. "You know, I don't remember my father at all. I mean, I have forgotten his face. But his voice still echoes in my ears…" The boy's eyes filled with tears.

Lele looked into the boy's eyes and trusted him. At the same time, his heart was so full that he was looking for a pretext to unburden it. He began the conversation tentatively. "You want to know about Chaldiran, you say? Yes, this was the day that God turned his face from us. Have you ever seen an elephant?" Lele asked.

"No, I haven't."

"I first saw one ten years ago at Chaldiran. The Ottomans had bound cannons to the elephants' legs and lined them up. We had to laugh when we saw them. Try as we might, we could not break their ranks," Lele said, remembering the past. "It was a terrible battle; the battlefield was strewn with human heads. You asked whose detachment I was in. I shall not give you the answer now. You will find out yourself later. Now tell me the name of your father."

"He was Sergeant Gurbanali," Rahim said proudly.

"Yes, Sergeant Gurbanali…" Lele said, his voice trailing off. He looked at the boy intently and paused for thought. At that moment, an image of a handsome standard-bearer came to his mind. "Your family is from Mughan, isn't it?" he then asked.

Rahim was stunned; his hair stood on end. "It is, my Lord. It is! Did you know my father?" The boy's eyes shone and he was breathing rapidly.

"I saw your father's death with my own eyes. He was a standard-bearer. He fell from his horse; an arrow had pierced his chest. Whatever anyone may say, don't believe them," Lele said matter-of-factly. "Even after he had breathed his last breath, they could not take the standard from his grasp, you know. The flag remained upright in the hand of your dead father."

Suddenly, Lele's eyes began to smart. *I must not break down,* he though. *I must not! What has happened to me?* He quickly reached for his glass of tea, but he did not drink. Instead, he held the glass tightly and was soon lost in thought once more.

Rahim bent his head. He was even afraid to breathe. He was afraid that if he uttered a word, he might distract this enigmatic man, so full of secret adventures, who had at last begun to talk. He could almost hear his own heart beating in his ears and temples.

Lele began to speak some of the words that were forever etched in his mind. Rahim only listened, completely mesmerized by the legend who sat in front of him...

"Advance! Charge, charge! Don't hang back. He for whom I would sacrifice myself has gone into the heat of the battle!" a guard shouted.

"For the sake of the Shah of Chivalrous Men, don't hang back; I shall follow him for whom I would sacrifice myself. God, God..."

"I am the Shah! I am the Shah!" Sultanali Bey Afshar had cried as he attempted to advance. The Ottomans had fallen upon him, though, and he had a very narrow escape.

"Malbashoghlu, come onto the battlefield! Come out and show us what you're made of! Make way, make way..." The Shah had then cut that strong man in two with a single stroke of his sword! He didn't even have the chance to gasp before he had spread his hands and fell to the ground.

"Lele! Lele! He came to the rescue with his detachment. Don't withdraw! Over here, over here! Lele, attack! Destroy them, for the sake of the Shah of Chivalrous Men! Advance! Come on, Red Caps, come and surround them. Be brave...be brave!"

"Lele, I—I—"

"Get up, boy! Get on your feet; you won't die. Not with this wound..."

"Where is the Shah? Rescue him! Rescue the Shah! The right flank is broken. Let him know. Blow the horn! Move back! Go slowly, step by step; don't break the lines. Where are you going? Come back to the line, you varmint!"

...Lele tore his eyes away from a distant point that only he could see and finished his speech. "See, Captain Rahim, this was Chaldiran. Ten years have passed, but these voices still echo in my ears."

Rahim began to talk to himself, his eyes closed, as though he were asleep. "I still hear my father's voice. 'My Shah, my Shah, on the path of the Perfect Councilor, the right flank has broken! My Shah, the right flank has scattered.

My Shah, hurry, the left flank—the left flank is destroyed. It is time to leave. Come, come here!'"

Then they both fell silent. The only sound in the courtyard came from the wind rustling the dense leaves of the elm tree. A bee buzzed across the yard. Then silence fell all around. Slowly, the two men came around. Rahim stayed in his place, his head bent. Lele brushed away the bee that was attacking his face.

Rahim did not dare look Lele in the face; he had already realized who he was. Even though he had heard about Huseyn Bay Lele from stories and legends, he had only just recognized him. "Lele, may I sacrifice myself to you? For the sake of the Shah of Chivalrous Men, forgive me. Pardon my sins," he whispered.

"Who are you with, Captain Rahim?" Lele asked.

"Lele, I am yours," Rahim replied. Finally, he lifted his head, looked Lele in the face, and quickly lowered his head again. He then stood up, ready for orders. "Lele, it is you. Hide yourself no longer, for God's sake. I did not know you at first. Everyone thought you were dead. Forgive me, for God's sake!"

Lele was silent for a few moments. "I have been thinking of myself as dead until now, you know," he admitted. Then he could contain himself no longer. "You asked which detachment I was in," he added.

"I made an error," Rahim said quickly.

"I was in the Shah's detachment, boy," Lele said sadly. "The Shah's."

The sun reached its zenith. Now Rahim no longer disturbed Lele. He did not hurry him or say, "That's enough for today. Go and rest and come back tomorrow." He stood aside and gazed at him from a distance, lovingly and respectfully. However, in his head he was wondering what he would say to the Vizier. *So, suppose I tell the Vizier who he is. I have to tell him, right? Once the Vizier knows who he is, won't he kill him? And he may even give this task to me...* This thought froze Rahim's heart.

Lele summoned Rahim with a nod of his head. Rahim immediately went up to Lele, but he did not sit down. Lele looked at the young man. "Captain, I would like to discuss one matter with you. Do you have any objection?" he asked.

"You are welcome, Lele," Rahim replied.

"I have completed my journey after six long months of covering my tracks. I was an Ottoman prisoner for ten years, but what I have suffered these six months far outweighs the suffering of those ten years. I can see that this palace and this court have changed a great deal. I have not seen a single familiar face. I have not recognized a single guard or steward," he said calmly. "As for the Vizier, he is difficult to know. This is how he was even in those days when—"

Rahim's eyes widened. Lele did not finish his sentence. Instead, he changed the subject. "As for me, you can see yourself. I do not want to reveal my secret yet. All I ask of the Shah of Chivalrous Men is to lay my head at the feet of the Perfect Councilor. May I sacrifice myself for him and die? Tell me, what must I do to achieve this?" Once he had put this question to Rahim, Lele fell silent. Then he fixed his eyes on an unknown point far in the distance and waited for an answer from the captain.

"Lele, you know the Vizier much better than I do. What can I say? God is merciful. With your permission, I will tell the Vizier all about you. Let's see what he says this time," he said.

"We have no other way out?" Lele asked.

Rahim frowned. "I cannot see any other way out. I will not be here when the Shah returns from his expedition. I take over as the palace's night sentry. When the Shah is here, you have to be at least a block of houses away from the palace. Things have changed," he said quietly.

"I can see that you are telling the truth. Things are both different and the same, you know. Actually, it was me who made this law. When the Shah came, the guards in the yard had to be changed. Who knows whom they met during this period, whom they talked to?" he replied. "Oh, such is the world. It does not change..."

"It does not change, Lele. You are right," Rahim nodded.

Then should I heap ashes of shame onto my head? Lele thought to himself.

Rahim continued. "With your permission, I will go and talk to the Vizier and tell him the truth. In the name of God, there is no other way," he said. "There is no other way."

"You are probably right. Go and talk to him. Tell him that I am sure to find a way of talking to the Shah, and then—no, don't say that. It might look as though I am threatening him. Tell him that Huseyn Bay Lele says he has brought a message from Lady Bahruza. Have you got it? Don't forget. Tell him this exactly. Yes, tell him I have brought a message from Lady Bahruza," Lele instructed.

"I shall do what you have told me," Rahim assured him.

§ § § § § §

The Vizier still could not believe his ears. "So, he told you himself that he was indeed Huseyn Bay Lele? Did he actually say so, or are you just making an assumption?" he asked a second time.

"He said it himself, Master Vizier. I guessed at first, but then he confirmed it himself," Rahim said excitedly.

He confirmed it himself. Oh, Lele, God has many miracles, but none as amazing as this. There are witnesses who saw him die on the battlefield. They even told the Shah! the Vizier thought incredulously. He looked at Rahim again. "He said he brought a message from Bahruza?" he asked slowly.

"Yes, Master Vizier, this is what he said," Rahim replied.

"Then, then...why?" the Vizier asked, utterly confused. He did not continue.

Rahim did not say another word. The Vizier stared at him as though waiting for more information, but the captain remained silent, wondering how the Vizier would react to the news.

The Vizier began to nod slowly to himself. "This is what we will do then. Tell him that the Vizier did not believe you. Say that I even got very angry when Bahruza's name was mentioned. That is good. But tell him that the Vizier wants to meet him in person. Bring him to me in the throne room tomorrow," he instructed. "Now listen to me carefully, Captain Rahim. If anyone hears about this conversation—if anyone hears that Lele has come or that he is still alive—you will be killed. This is a state secret. Tell him yourself. Do not reveal the secret to anyone."

"I understand, Master Vizier," Rahim said quietly.

The Vizier rubbed his hands together as he thought about what to do. "We don't know yet if this really is Lele or not. We cannot believe him just because he says he is. As soon as I see him, everything will become clear to me. Now go and tell him what I have told you," he concluded.

Rahim bowed and left the Vizier's chamber. Long into the night, the Vizier stared into the candle flame, deep in thought. Finally, he blew out the candle and was about to lie down on his bed when a final thought entered his mind: *It is not worth thinking about. Of course, Lele died at Chaldiran. This man is not Lele, God willing.*

§ § § § § §

When Lele followed Captain Rahim into the chamber, the Vizier recognized him at once. The way he walked was enough for the Vizier to recognize him. He was about to jump up from the bolster, where he had been reclining, when he saw Rahim and quickly pulled himself together. He looked away from pair and remained still, as though turning thoughts over in his mind.

Lele stood looking at him; God knows what he was thinking. The Vizier eventually regained his composure and nodded to Rahim to leave the chamber. Rahim bowed and started to walk out. Suddenly, however, the Vizier called out to him. "Stand guard outside. Don't let anyone in. Come when I call you," he said. With that, Rahim went out without saying a word.

The Vizier remained seated, unsure of how to proceed with the meeting. There was no more doubt in his mind; he knew Huseyn Bay Lele was standing before him. Lele had been the Shah's favorite confidant. Nothing could be done in the palace without his knowledge. The mention of his name would strike fear into the hearts of the courtiers and other viziers. Many sought a hiding place when his voice resounded. But now he had fallen out of sight and mind. Everyone thought he had died at the Battle of Chaldiran. Yet he was standing large as life before the Vizier, looking at him with hidden mockery.

Wanting to act as though he did not recognize him, the Vizier spoke casually. "You are the person who calls himself Huseyn Bay Lele?" he asked, not looking at his guest.

Silence followed. Lele did not say a word.

"Why don't you speak?" the Vizier demanded. "We know that Lele is dead. Who are you? Why are you here?" The Vizier asked, raising his voice.

"Yes, I am he who is called Huseyn Bay Lele. Did you really not recognize me?" Lele spoke confidently.

"You do...*look* like Huseyn Bay Lele," the Vizier said slowly, looking at Lele only for a moment and then looking away. He got up and stood opposite Lele. Finally, he looked directly into Lele's eyes. They stared at one for quite some time.

"Vizier, I can see that you either did not recognize me or did not want to recognize me," Lele said. "Allow me to refresh your memory. You were a young boy. At that time, he for whom I would sacrifice myself had journeyed to Shirvan. Your father came to the palace to see me. He was one of the secretaries of Hasan, the Tall. In your house, in the Girkhlar District in Ardabil—"

The Vizier could bear it no longer. He stepped forward, wanting to embrace Lele, but something held him back. He stood and gazed admiringly at him from a distance. "Lele, Lele, yes, it is really you! I sensed it. I sensed that you had not died. Thank God. Sit down, Lele. Come here, come here, and sit down!" the Vizier exclaimed. Then he looked toward the entryway. "Captain Rahim!"

Rahim hurried in. "Yes, my Lord?" he asked.

"Captain, tell them to bring fruit, tea, and sherbet. Hurry up. Hurry!" the Vizier ordered.

"Yes, sir!" Rahim replied. He understood what was going on from the Vizier's mood. Although he raised his hand to his eyes, he could not conceal his joy. Bowing, he left the room again to fetch what the Vizier wanted.

"So, Lele, for the sake of the Shah of Chivalrous Men, tell me what happened to you," the Vizier began. "Everybody thought you had been killed, but what happened? Where were you? Where have you come from?" He gently helped Lele sit against a bolster.

"My story is a long story," Lele sighed, making himself comfortable. "How I, an unfortunate wretch, got out of the battle alive, I still don't know. When I came to, however, I found myself among the captives. The Sultan distributed the prisoners in Tabriz[53] and gave me to a man from Trebizond called Abdulla Bey Momin," he began. "At first, I suffered greatly; I had no one to tend to my wounds. Later, they found out who I was and I did not suffer so much anymore. Doctors treated my wounds, but they kept watch over me for ten years."

"What did you do all that time?" the Vizier asked.

"I took care of Abdulla Bey Momin's secretarial work and sorted out his library. A year or so ago, he died. They detained me no longer. They let me go because he had willed it so. They set me free and told me to go wherever I wished, and so I went," Lele replied. "I should have died at the Battle of Chaldiran, Master Vizier. Why I did not die, I don't know…"

A few minutes later, a servant brought fruit and juice into the chamber. He arranged them on the table and left. Then the Vizier took the sherbet and poured it first into Lele's goblet and then into his own. He smiled at Lele, saying, "Please, drink."

Lele was already lost in thought, as though his dreams had taken him far away. Still, he took the sherbet and sipped it. Then he finished his speech. "Now, with your help, I would like to come before him for whom I would sacrifice myself, lay my head at his feet, and seek his forgiveness for my sins," Lele explained. "If he decided to shed my blood, believe me, there would be no man happier in this world."

The Vizier listened carefully to Lele, occasionally nodding or saying, "Yes, yes, God willing." But then he asked, "Lele, why should he shed your blood? You should know that Zulgadar became a traitor. However, you were not a traitor. Your courage is renowned. If you only knew how the Shah longed for you. If you only knew how the bitterness of Chaldiran hurt his body and damaged his soul—and the separation from Lady Bahruza. We tried so hard, Lele. We sent many messages to the Ottomans, but only in vain. You say you have brought word from her, according to Captain Rahim. Isn't that right?"

Lele bit his lip, realizing that the main reason why the Vizier met him was that he claimed to have brought word from Lady Bahruza. *Let it be so,* he thought. *May there be no hindrance to my meeting the Shah. All matters are now in my hands.* He needed to make something up. "Yes, Master Vizier," he said. "I have varied tidings. We shall discuss them together during our meeting with the Shah, God willing."

---

[53] Tabriz is the modern-day capital of Iran's East Azerbaijan Province.

"Of course, Lele," the Vizier agreed hastily. "Our Shah is on an expedition, though. He shall return either today or tomorrow. As soon as he returns, I shall tell him about you myself, God willing."

"Then—" Lele began.

"Yes, yes, come to the court!" the Vizier exclaimed, interrupting. "I will give orders that they serve you well."

"Thank you," Lele said quietly. He understood that the Vizier did not intend to prolong the conversation. With that, he smiled courteously and stood up. The Vizier stood, too, and accompanied him to the door.

When Lele went out, Rahim was standing on the other side of the door, waiting for orders. The Vizier looked at him and nodded. "Captain, see our guest out and then come here. Give instructions that whenever he comes to the court, he should be served. Be quick and come back here," he instructed.

"Yes, sir," Rahim replied. Then he accompanied Lele across the courtyard and into the street. Before the two parted, he turned to Lele. "Shall you come tomorrow, Lele?" he asked.

"I will come," Lele replied.

When Rahim returned to the Vizier's chamber, he saw that the Vizier was downcast and his blood was black as pitch. The Vizier greeted him coldly. "Close the door firmly behind you," he said. "Come and sit down."

Rahim closed the door carefully. Then he went and crouched before the Vizier, awaiting orders once more. The Vizier began slowly turning his prayer beads, one by one. Clearly, he was in no hurry to speak. At last…

The manuscript becomes difficult to read in this section. It is hard to say what awaited Lele in the palace. Why he so longed to meet the Shah may best be explained by the example of a moth that strikes itself against a flame. Poets say this is the power of love. Who knows? What role does the Vizier play in this? Certainly, it is not hard to see that the Vizier would not be pleased at Lele's return to the palace or at his possible reinstatement to the pinnacle of power. But Lele reminded the Vizier of his father with good reason.

The Vizier was very much in Lele's debt for some reason, and the slightest mention by Lele was enough for the Vizier to "recognize" him in their face-to-face meeting. Subsequent events lift the curtain of secrecy on one very interesting point. When he tells the Shah about Lele, the Vizier implies that he, too, knows the Shah's secret.

§ § § § §

The Shah was still looking out of the window at the orchard, his back to the Vizier. The Vizier was silent, thinking. He did not know what to do or how to advise the Shah. The Shah asked him again, "Well, why are you silent? Now what shall we do with Lele?" he demanded quietly. The Shah's voice rang with an unusual harshness. The harshness had nothing to do with Lele, but with the Vizier and his ineptitude.

Sensing this, the Vizier sighed helplessly. "What could I do, Pivot of the Universe? He deceived me by mentioning Bahruza's name," he attempted to defend himself.

"Well, let's stop talking about Bahruza. Take action. Or, if he comes and finds me out—" the Shah began.

The Vizier interrupted. "He cannot find anything out. How could he? Maybe—"

The Shah interrupted the Vizier's thoughts. "No, Vizier. I am deeply in his debt, you know. This is not the action I mean. I mean—"

"I will think of something, Perfect Councilor," the Vizier said quietly, bowing his head.

"Lele, Lele…" the Shah said, his voice trailing off. "I cannot believe that he is alive! People had seen him slip from his horse with their own eyes. They saw the enemy fall upon him. How could this happen? I remember how he taught me to play shatranj. 'Look at the board,' he would say. 'Find an empty square and move your forces there. Start the attack from there.'" The Shah's eyes suddenly filled with tears as he remembered the past. It was as though he were ashamed of himself.

Sensing this, the Vizier spoke up. "He will not say anything to me. I realize this now. He will talk to you, though," he said. "So let him come and let us see if he really has brought news. If he tells a lie, permit me, you for whom I would sacrifice myself, to find a way."

"We will meet him sooner or later; you are right," the Shah said. "But do I need the news he says he brings from Bahruza? Maybe you need this news?"

"In any case, my Shah, it would be right for the people—for the palace—to believe that you are concerned about her," The Vizier advised.

"When will you bring him here?"

"I told him that you are on an expedition. I said he should come later. If you wish, he could come today…"

"Today," the Shah said decisively, nodding. "Let it be done today."

"But not in private," the Vizier said quietly. "He may misunderstand. You must not meet him alone."

The Shah nodded. "Good, let's go. It's time for prayers, God willing. Come after prayers. If I meet him on my own or not, what difference does it make?" he asked curiously. Without waiting for an answer, he left the chamber as the Vizier followed. All the while, the Shah was uneasy in his heart.

That morning, Lady Tajli would not let the Shah into the throne room; maybe that was the source of his unease. He remembered his conversation with Lady Tajli, and again, it wrung his heart. When she had come into his bedchamber, the sun had already reached its place in the sky. Although he was awake, the Shah remained in bed. He had been in no hurry to rise. Lady Tajli had gone up to the bed and said, "Get up, my Shah. Get up. See where the sun is! Have a bite of breakfast, and then you can go back to sleep..."

"Lady Tajli, is it you?" the Shah had asked, stretching in bed and gazing sleepily at his beloved wife.

"Yes, it is I, my dear, for whom I would sacrifice myself," she had smiled. "Are you getting up or not? Get up now. Have breakfast and then do whatever you want. Should I tell them to serve breakfast here?"

"No, wait a moment. Why are you acting like this so early in the morning," the Shah asked. "Is something wrong?"

"Nothing," Lady Tajli replied quietly, shrugging.

"Tell me, anyway," the Shah said. He leaned against a pillow, his sleep gone completely. He felt that Lady Tajli was not her usual self; she was like someone who had something to say. She also appeared downcast. "What's wrong with you?" the Shah asked.

In fact, the Shah himself had slept badly the previous night. His dreams had flashed before his eyes. While he had been asleep, his pupils darted here and there, as though he were watching a vision. Several times, he woke up in fear, got up from his bed, and drank some water. Then he had tried to fall back asleep to no avail.

"What has happened to you, my Lady?" the Shah asked again, his concern growing.

"My Shah, for whom I would sacrifice myself, last night I had a bad dream—a *bad* dream," Lady Tajli admitted.

The Shah's interest grew stronger. *Women are usually sensitive,* he thought. Then he said, "Tell me your dream. What did you see?"

Lady Tajli's eyes gazed at a spot on the floor as she began to relive the nightmare she had experienced. She remained silent.

The Shah grew impatient. "I am talking to you, Lady Tajli!" he said. "What's wrong?"

Lady Tajli looked away for a moment, collecting her thoughts. Finally, she looked at her husband. "I dreamed that you had forsaken me, my Lord," she said, her voice trembling. "You had gone far away and left me alone. Your voice could be heard from the seventh heaven, calling me up. You asked me, 'What are you doing there? Why are you still there? Come here! Do you know how beautiful it is here? Everyone who loves you is here.' I asked, 'Why did you forsake me, my beloved for whom I would sacrifice myself?' You answered, 'For the sake of the Shah of Chivalrous Men, leave them there. Whatever are you doing there? Our place is here, close to the Shah of Chivalrous Men. Come, come…' At that very moment, I suddenly woke up. Please don't go anywhere today! Stay here before my eyes. If you permit me, I will serve you myself!"

This is what he said, too: "Everyone who loves you is here," the Shah thought. *Now he is calling Tajli there.* The Shah almost shuddered as these thoughts passed through his mind.

Lady Tajli did not notice it. She was too busy trying to forget the dreams she had experienced. "God forbid—God forbid for the sake of the Shah of Chivalrous Men," she whispered. "Do not take your grace from us, for the sake of your unity!"

"What else did you dream?" the Shah then asked.

"I also dreamed that you kept running away from me. No one could stop you. You kept on running, my Shah," Lady Tajli replied sadly. "You were both with me and not with me; both mine and not mine. My heart nearly burst."

"Then what? Then what did you dream?" the Shah asked anxiously, trying to conceal his concern.

"May God protect us," Lady Tajli answered. "I dreamed no more. Don't go; don't go to the court today! Work will not run away. The state will not collapse. Won't you recite poetry to me today? Let's have a poetry council today…"

The Shah shook his head. "Now is not the time for poetry. There is important work to be done. Of course, I have to go," he said irritably.

"My Shah, light of my eye, the blackest thoughts have entered my heart. Something is hanging over you! Look at your complexion. Hunting—you talk about hunting very much. Do not go on this hunt—this expedition. I will not let you go anywhere. Don't go anywhere. Don't go anywhere today, please!" Lady Tajli begged. "You are the defender of the faith, the defender of the state."

The Shah did not respond. He began dressing himself.

Lady Tajli continued, feeling more desperate by the second. "Very well, my Shah," she said. "I dreamed something else! I saw jet-black clouds cover the moon. I saw jet-black ravens spread their wings and fly up, up in the sky. It was a bad dream—a bad dream. Don't go anywhere today. Don't go. Please don't go!" With that, she burst into tears.

The Shah did not give a thought to his wife's emotional pleas. He continued getting ready for the day. "Get out of the way. Of course, I must go," he said. "We shall see one another in the evening, God willing. When I come back in the evening, I shall read you the poetry I have just written. How does that sound, my Lady?"

"Read it now, please!" Lady Tajli begged him, tears pouring down her cheeks.

"No, wait until the evening. I will read it when I come back," the Shah said dryly.

Lady Tajli clasped the Shah's knees and fell down before him. "I won't let you go. You may kill me, but I won't let you go!" she shouted.

"Get out of the way!" the Shah demanded. He freed his legs from his wife's arms and moved toward the door. Then he turned to face Lady Tajil one more time before leaving. "What did you say? 'Everyone who loves you is there?' Yes, of course. Everyone who loves me is there, God willing." As he said this, he went out the door, carrying Lady Tajli's sobs with him all the way to the throne room.

§ § § § § §

When I reached the Stone of Light, the night was well advanced. The moon had almost completed its path across the sky. My heart was trying to get out of my mouth; I was so out of breath. I had galloped straight to the Stone of Light, without stopping, after Bayindir Khan had granted me permission to leave. Gilbash had a fast horse from the stable for me. It had flown as swift as a falcon.

"Stone of Light, fairest of stones, wisest of stones," I said. "I do not know how many days I have been apart from you, but I cannot bear this parting. I have no idea what tomorrow will bring. Only almighty God knows. Maybe Bayindir Khan's wrath will fall upon me. When he knows the story, what else can he do but be angry? You alone know that what I did was for Oghuz. I did it for the future of Oghuz. Give inspiration to the Khan's soul, Stone of Light. Give mercy to his veins. May he not take his love from us, thanks be to almighty God!"

I embraced the Stone of Light, sank to the ground, and stayed there. A good while passed, and finally, my eyes filled with sleep. I was so weary that I don't know when I fell asleep.

Gorgud's story breaks off again here, but maybe it does not really break off. The remainder of the text does not allow us to assume that there are any gaps. Or, to be more accurate, there may or may not be gaps. If any part is missing, then it is the part concerning Gorgud's thoughts; it has nothing to do with the main subject or layer of information in the manuscript. However, we can say that though the rest of the story is not a natural continuation of the preceding text, it is a logical continuation.

Strange lines began to be discernible in the illegible pages. When you study them carefully, those lines look like odd pictures—almost in the same way that when you look at clouds, you begin to see strange animals. One of the sketches drew my attention more than the others.

The lines were turning into a silhouette. But I could not make out whose it was. For some reason, the young Orientalist appeared before my eyes and lingered for a long time. Then when I opened my eyes, I had lost that sketch.

In the morning, before I entered the Khan's courtyard, I could see the commotion from afar. Horsemen were dismounting; some riders were washing their hands and faces; some were sitting on the grass; others were drinking water and eating yogurt brought by the serving girls. I understood. Old Aruz had come. He had not come alone, however; he had come with a large group of warriors. Of the Outer Oghuz nobles, I saw Aman, Wild Dondar, Wild Gachar, Alp Rustam, and many others, too.

I caught up with them, dismounted, greeted them politely, and was greeted in return. When Old Aruz came up to me, he took my hand and drew me to one side. "How are you, Gorgud?" he asked. Then he dropped his voice to a whisper. "Do you know why the Khan has summoned us? Is there a raid?"

"Aruz, there is no question of a raid. Maybe the Khan has something to ask you. He will ask you. Why have they all come?" I asked, gesturing toward the nobles.

Gilbash was watching us from the side. He was probably afraid that I would speak out of turn. Moments later, he came up to us. I wondered if he had caught my last words. "You are all welcome!" he said. "Gorgud, this is no trouble for us at all." He looked at Old Aruz. "Aruz, tell the nobles that they should take their ease after traveling so far. They must be hungry…" With that, the nobles went with Gilbash to the wooden trestles on the other side of the yard where food and drink were served.

During the meal, Gilbash turned to Old Aruz and me. "We should go to the Khan now," he said in a hushed voice so as not to be overheard by the others. "Let us not interrupt the nobles' meal. They should not notice anything."

Old Aruz, Gilbash, and I went into the middle of the yard and set off for the Khan's chambers. When we were almost there, Gilbash looked sideways at us. "You wait here while I give the Khan some news," he instructed. Gilbash then entered the chamber. Old Aruz and I stood at the door.

Old Aruz sighed. "Gorgud, I have a bad feeling about this," he said quietly.

"What is up with you? Has the Khan never summoned you before? Has he never asked you questions or discussed matters with you?" I asked with a smile. "It's nothing. Don't waste your time gathering dark thoughts, Aruz."

Luckily, Gilbash came back out at that moment and invited us into the chamber. Once inside, I almost did not recognize Bayindir Khan. I stared at him, utterly confused, thinking, *Almighty God, was this yesterday's Bayindir Khan?* The Khan was dressed in golden robes as he sat on his high throne. His eyes shone brightly, and he was upright and proud. It seemed as if he had become younger than us over night!

Old Aruz immediately dropped to his knees. He crawled toward Bayindir Khan. Bayindir Khan carefully studied Old Aruz's face, following his every move. I bowed, moved swiftly to my place, and sat. Old Aruz then reached Bayindir Khan but did not stand. "Your Majesty Bayindir Khan, Khan of Khans, pillar of all Oghuz," he began. "You called me and I came. Whatever orders—whatever commands you have—all the nobles of Outer Oghuz and I are ready to wield our swords unto death on your behalf," he said quietly. He bowed his head again and waited for Bayindir Khan to speak.

"Aruz, you are welcome," the Khan said. "May you bring us gladness. The nobles are welcome, too."

"The nobles have come to kiss your hand, my Khan," Old Aruz said.

"May they enjoy good health. Take my greetings to them. Let them eat; let them drink; let them enjoy their time," the Khan replied, nodding. Then he asked, "Aruz, do you know why I have summoned you?"

"No, I don't know. They did not say, my Khan," Old Aruz answered.

"There was an affair in Oghuz. The news reached me. Nothing about this affair pleases me. It partly concerns you, too. I have a question for you, so I summoned you now," the Khan explained.

"What is this affair, my Khan?" Old Aruz asked.

"You will find out now; do not hurry. Come, come over here," Bayindir Khan pointed out his place to him. "Sit down there." He turned and looked at Gilbash for a moment. "Gilbash, have they made the nobles comfortable?" he asked.

Gilbash nodded. "They have, my Khan. They are eating and drinking."

"Good. Sit down, Gilbash. Take your seat, too," Bayindir Khan said.

Gilbash went behind Old Aruz and kneeled down. Old Aruz sat in front of him, his legs crossed. Casting a glance at me, Bayindir Khan resumed his speech. "Now, Aruz, listen to me. News was brought to me. 'There was a spy in Oghuz,' they said. Can you believe it? A spy in Oghuz! They were right. Gazan went hunting; meanwhile, the spy did his work. Bakil broke his leg; again, the spy did his work. Beyrak was imprisoned; this was the spy's doing. The whole of Oghuz gave its response to the work of this spy. We should have punished him severely. But what happened? The spy was revealed and caught. He was kept in Gazan's dungeon. Then all of the nobles assembled at a council. But what did you do? 'Not guilty,' you said. You released the spy and he went. Is this how it was, Aruz?" the Khan asked, showing no emotion.

Old Aruz remained silent. I could not tell if he felt nervous or not at the accusations being thrown at him.

The Khan continued. "Tell me! This spy should have been hacked to pieces for all Oghuz to see. He should have been broken into bits so that no other man in Oghuz would take this path! But you did not do that. Now I would like to listen to you," he said. "You had said, 'Give him to his mother. Let him go.' Am I right? Did this episode happen differently? What do you have to say, Aruz?"

Old Aruz was clever. Apparently, he had anticipated what the Khan would say. When Bayindir Khan had finished his speech, Old Aruz began a speech of his own. "Bayindir Khan, this spy story is a long one. I will tell you why I had said that the spy was not guilty. However, I will also tell you that this spy affair was a trick by Gazan and Beyrak. I was the real target," he said. "I received news from Inner Oghuz: 'Gazan is saying that there is a spy, and the strings of this spy are being pulled by Aruz. We think you should know.'"

Old Aruz continued. "My Khan, I have reached this age. You know that no man would contradict me in Outer Oghuz. I have been on all the campaigns. You sent me on military expeditions and I went. During Gazan's imprisonment, I turned Outer Oghuz upside-down. I gathered a big army, went to Gara Malik, and scattered his outposts. Would I keep a spy and spy on the whole of Oghuz like that?" he asked, shaking his head. "This is ridiculous, and I don't want to weary you with it. I shall talk to you about another matter, though. Gazan has become my enemy, you know."

"Go on..." Bayindir Khan said.

"Even though I am his maternal uncle, he ignores me, my Khan. He does not acknowledge my sons and—as if this were not enough—he does not want to listen to the other Outer Oghuz nobles. It is a long story, my Khan, and every man in Oghuz already knows it," Old Aruz said matter-of-factly. "I am against anything Gazan says. And who is Beyrak? I don't know him at all! He took one of our girls as a wife—you know, Baybejan's daughter, Banuchichak—but whether Gazan is right or wrong, Beyrak will never turn his back on him. Beyrak was the one who told Gazan the story of the spy. They pondered long; they puzzled hard: 'What will we do? How will we bring down Aruz in Bayindir Khan's eyes? Let's link him to the spy! The Khan will believe it. He will be furious with Aruz, and we will set Outer Oghuz against Inner Oghuz!'"

Bayindir Khan looked at me to see if I was writing or not. Seeing that I was writing, he raised his hand to interrupt Old Aruz. "Aruz!" he said loudly. "You said that your story with Gazan was a different story. What is this story? You have caught my interest..."

Old Aruz made himself comfortable and looked at me. For the first time, he realized that I was writing, but he did not say anything. Instead, he turned swiftly to Bayindir Khan. "Bayindir Khan, I don't know the real reason myself. What is my fault? What is my guilt? I would like someone to tell me. But with your permission, I will tell you what I know," he said. "You can draw your own conclusions after that."

"Please, Aruz, you are welcome," Bayindir Khan encouraged him.

Old Aruz began from the very beginning—Gazan's childhood, his youth, and his marriage. Then Bayindir Khan gave Old Aruz a piece of advice, saying, "There is no need for all these words. They do not concern the spy." Then the Khan had looked at me. "Gorgud, keep only what is necessary and erase the rest." I did what Bayindir Khan had said. For this reason, Old Aruz's story remained incomplete.

"Bayindir Khan, do you know why Gazan bears me ill will?" Old Aruz asked.

"No, I don't know," Bayindir Khan replied.

"The reason is Basat's defeat of One-Eye," he said. "Mark my words."

"Really?" Bayindir Khan asked. He acted so surprised that even I believed he knew nothing about it.

"Yes. Believe me. The reason is Basat, my son. Did Basat do anything bad? You will say no. Didn't Basat rescue the whole of Oghuz from the hand of its bitterest enemy?" Old Aruz asked.

"He did, Aruz, we know," the Khan replied, nodding. "But get back to the subject."

"I am right in the middle of the subject, my Khan. Listen to me, and then everything will become clear to you," Old Aruz said. "What the spy affair is about, why Gazan and Beyrak have turned their backs on Outer Oghuz—I will tell you all of it."

I realized that Old Aruz's story would not do without Basat, so I kept my patience. I looked and saw that Bayindir Khan was also struggling to keep his patience, but we both listened to Old Aruz's story, anyway.

"My Khan, you know that One-Eye and his monstrous host came and blocked the River Sellama, which flows through Outer Oghuz. There was no counting the number of his horde. Whence they came, no one knew. Their tongues were not like our tongues; their religions were not like ours," Old Aruz began. "First, I wanted to find out why they had come; I chose Alp Rustam and his warriors and they went. I had also told them, 'Look, see how many they are. Find out what their rules of battle are. Figure out what they have for weaponry and ammunition.' In short, they went. Alp Rustam returned and told me, 'My Lord, they are a monstrous tribe, the likes of which I have never seen before...'"

I was curious to know where Old Aruz's story would go. More importantly, I wondered how Bayindir Khan would react at the end. I listened intently and wrote everything down.

"Did you meet their leader?" Old Aruz had asked.

"We met, my Lord. He summoned us. He was very interested in us and asked me many questions," Alp Rustam had replied.

"What do they want? Are they going to stay here long?" Old Aruz then asked.

"My Lord, the troops want to cut off the River Sellama. They have gathered large stones and broken rocks on the riverbank. They are waiting for the sign," Alp Rustam said. "Lord Aruz, they will cut off our water…"

"Can it be true? Is this how they will fight? Is this how a noble warrior fights?" Old Aruz had asked. After hearing that information, he quickly convened a council of the nobles. He had invited Gorgud, too, and he came.

Old Aruz had opened the council. "Nobles, this is how matters stand. One-Eye has gathered a great host and has come to settle in our lands. They have passed through the upper reaches of the River Sellama at the foot of Mount Gazilig, through Outer Oghuz and Gunortaj, and pitched their tents on the caravan road to Inner Oghuz," he began. "We sent an envoy, Alp Rustam, to find out what they wanted, but they did not speak of their intent. Their language is not ours, nor is their religion. What is clear, though, is that they will bring misfortune upon the Oghuz. Now, nobles, what shall we do?"

The nobles were curious to know what Alp Rustam had learned. Old Aruz informed them. "Alp Rustam says they plan to dam the Sellama in another place. If this happens, our only hope rests with almighty God. What do you say? Shall we raise an army and troops and go into battle against One-Eye, or shall we have to answer our old men, women, and children when they ask, 'What are you good for?'" he asked.

"War! We want war!" the nobles had cried out in unison. "You lead us against One-Eye. Old Aruz, you are our pillar!"

The council had not even adjourned yet when a servant then brought bad news. "A tributary of the Sellama has been cut off," the servant reported.

All the nobles became enraged. But then Aman spoke up. "We must send word to Bayindir Khan and Inner Oghuz!" he said. "This war is not the war of Outer Oghuz alone. We are not the only people who drink this river's waters. Today we have been left without water; tomorrow it will be the turn of Inner Oghuz!" The other nobles had agreed with Aman. With that, couriers were sent to Bayindir Khan and to Gazan. Old Aruz and the nobles then went their separate ways in order to prepare for battle.

Early the next morning, the Outer Oghuz nobles raised a great army. Warriors had been stationed at the head, and armed and unarmed servants had been put on the flanks. The Outer Oghuz army climbed along the Sellama's dry riverbed toward One-Eye's camp. The army advanced along the tributary until it reached Buzlusel. Suddenly, at a bend in the riverbed, the cunning enemy unblocked the river.

Torrents poured down on the Outer Oghuz army, and the warriors could not get out of the riverbed fast enough. The water swept everyone away back to Outer Oghuz. By chance, one of One-Eye's scouts had spotted the army and alerted One-Eye. The torrents claimed the lives of some and crippled others, dashing them against the cliffs. Without losing one soldier, One-Eye had managed to drive back the Outer Oghuz troops.

The following morning, another army had gathered, ready to try and take on One-Eye again. This time, the army chose a different route. Outer Oghuz wanted to approach One-Eye from the rear. It turned off the caravan road and crossed the slopes of Mount Gazilig. Unfortunately, One-Eye's army anticipated the Outer Oghuz troops again and stopped the troops in the same place as the day before.

Battle began. Old Aruz claimed that he had never seen the likes of a battle like the one they fought in that day. Arrows did not kill One-Eye's army. Swords did not slay them. They wore armor. Even their horses had armor across their chests. Ultimately, it had been a dreadful battle.

Old Aruz paused and looked up at the Khan. "Heads were strewn across the battlefield," he said quietly before picking up where he had left off.

I must remember this. One of Old Aruz's expressions was razor sharp: "Heads were strewn across the battlefield."

Outer Oghuz had been defeated once again. The army had no other option but to retreat, leaving the dead on the battlefield. After Outer Oghuz had failed to conquer One-Eye the second time, the nobles had approached Old Aruz again, asking what they should do next.

"Has word come from Bayindir Khan or Gazan yet?" Aman had asked.

"It has not," Old Aruz had said.

Baybejan Malik then spoke up. "We should send someone to tell them what has happened! Let the Khan of Khans take action," he had said with urgency in his voice. "The sorrow that today lies upon Outer Oghuz will tomorrow fall upon Inner Oghuz, and then on the whole of Oghuz."

Baybejan Malik had taken no part in the battle against One-Eye. He had been busy preparing for his daughter's wedding. He was to give Banuchichak to Beyrak in marriage. They had been planning on entering their marriage bed any day.

"Lord, first bring your sons and join the army, lest Bayindir Khan question the troops that we sent into battle," Old Aruz had replied to Baybejan Malik.

"Aruz, it would be no bad thing if your son, Basat, were to join the troops, too," Baybejan Malik then said.

"You are right. Tomorrow my son will join the troops," Old Aruz agreed.

The next day, Old Aruz had ordered the nobles to assemble once again. However, bad news had come the night before. Without Outer Oghuz's knowledge, Gazan and the Inner Oghuz nobles had faced One-Eye's forces near the bend in the river, above the caravan road. They had joined battle and were defeated.

After the battle, the nobles had been scattered; some fled to Inner Oghuz while others sought out shelter in Outer Oghuz. Old Aruz never saw Gazan that night, but he had seen his brother, Garaguna. Old Aruz then brought him home to help care for him. Garaguna had suffered a slight wound on his arm, and the servants brought ointment and dressed it.

"Garaguna, were you so sure of your strength that you joined battle without us?" Old Aruz had angrily asked Gazan's brother. "Scoundrel! Didn't I tell you that we should fight One-Eye together?"

"Gazan said, 'I will hunt down One-Eye's army. What need do I have of Outer Oghuz? Let the spoils be ours!'" Garaguna muttered. "He gathered the nobles, and we had galloped off without further ado."

"Were you ambushed?" Old Aruz asked.

"Yes, we were ambushed. Many of us were laid low. Aruz, have you ever seen such an army?" Garaguna then asked incredulously.

"No, I haven't," Old Aruz had replied.

"Nor have I! What shall we do now?" Garaguna wondered.

"We need to find Gazan. We shall go to Bayindir Khan together," Old Aruz had said.

"May it be as you say," Garaguna had replied.

Gazan had already gone back to Inner Oghuz and was resting. When Old Aruz and Garaguna arrived at his home, one of Gazan's servants let him know they were there. "Your Uncle Aruz and Garaguna have come," the servant had told him.

He came out to greet the pair, stricken by grief. His face was dark, and his eyes darted back and forth. He had looked at Old Aruz, his eyes wide. "Aruz, have you ever fought in such a battle?" he asked. "You fought at Trebizond; shoulder-to-shoulder we wielded our swords. But have you seen such an army as what we just witnessed in your entire life?"

"I have not," Old Aruz had said briskly. "But why did you go into battle alone? I had sent word to you! I had said we should go into battle together. What happened?"

"How was I to know? Have any of you seen One-Eye?" Gazan then asked.

"Alp Rustam has. We sent him as an envoy," Old Aruz said.

"How many of them were there?" Gazan asked, interested.

"I swear to God, I don't know. They say he is a mighty giant who can spin a millstone in each hand," Old Aruz had replied.

"Really?" Gazan had gasped.

"Yes, really!" Old Aruz exclaimed.

"Then what shall we do?" Gazan had asked curiously.

"What can we do? We must go to Greater Oghuz. Mount your horse; let's go to Bayindir Khan now. He is the only man who can help us!" Old Aruz had replied.

Old Aruz stopped for a moment and looked at the Khan. Then he looked at me and then at the Khan again. "My Khan, do you remember that Gazan and I came to see you? We had a long discussion. Then you called Gorgud and Gorgud came. This is what you said to him, my Khan: 'Gorgud, go to One-Eye. Tell him that Oghuz wants to agree to terms with him. Let him spell out his terms.'"

The Khan nodded. "Yes, I remember that conversation," he said.

Old Aruz continued. "Then you told the nobles: 'Nobles, quietly prepare for battle. But whatever ideas you may have, do not act yet. We must be prudent. Let us wait awhile. Let us muster our forces. Let us find out One-Eye's terms. Meanwhile, I will send envoys to Trebizond and Georgia to reach an understanding with them. Oghuz cannot tackle this alone. Gorgud must go and come back. We shall gather once again, and only then shall we take our final decision."

"I remember," the Khan said, nodding again.

"We returned to our homes. Gorgud went with me. The nobles assembled again, and we told them what you had said. They approved the your action and turned their attention toward Gorgud," Old Aruz recalled. "'Farewell, come back safe and sound, Gorgud!' they said. 'Whatever they want, we will give them, but they must let our water flow. Old men, women, and children are crying out for water!'"

"With this, we sent Gorgud as an envoy to One-Eye. This was the second envoy that we sent to One-Eye, my Khan. The first was Alp Rustam, as I told you. Gorgud did not take long; he soon returned. He came and brought bad news. They set terms, my Khan, that none of us had ever heard before. 'Every day, give us a flock of sheep and two men so that our chief, One-Eye, can eat their hearts,' they said. My Khan, they *ate people!*"

Old Aruz had paused for emphasis. The Khan remained quiet. I waited for Old Aruz to continue speaking so that I could keep writing.

"We thought and talked long and hard. What was our way out? What could we do? Look, giving sheep wasn't too difficult, but One-Eye wanted to eat two people a day. That would be much more difficult! Again, we thought and talked long and hard. We held a council and decided that every household must give one person. Those who had a slave or prisoner would give them; those who did not would give a son or daughter. My Khan, the wailing of Oghuz rose up into the sky!" Old Aruz explained.

He continued. "A short time passed, and all the households eventually gave their share. But when their turn came around again, the people began to shy away. We faced our angry and terrified people on one side and One-Eye's troops on the other—and the troops could appear from nowhere in the blink of an eye," he said. "At this time, my son, Giyan Seljuk, could bear it no longer. He gathered a band of people and attacked One-Eye's camp at night. My gray-eyed son perished, though. He breathed his last breath on the battlefield…"

Bayindir Khan interrupted. "I'm sorry for your loss, Aruz," he said quietly. Old Aruz nodded, acknowledging the Khan's sympathy. Then he continued along with his version of the story.

I had gone to him. "Let's talk to Basat. I know—I sense—that only Basat can vanquish One-Eye," I had said to Old Aruz.

"Very well, but how?" Old Aruz had asked. "I don't know where Basat is. He won't come out of the forest! He has a place in the forest, you know. He goes there; he is close to the wolves. He calls Gogan, the lioness, his mother."

"So what? We'll find him somehow and bring him here," I had replied. "I'll speak to him."

With that, Old Aruz and I had sent Old Aruz's servants and warriors off in every direction with the goal to find Basat and bring him back to Old Aruz. Time passed, and eventually Basat had been found. The servants and warriors had brought him back to his father.

"Father, did you call me?" Basat had asked, confused.

Old Aruz had nodded. "Yes, I called you, my son. Do you know what has happened?"

"I don't know, Father. They didn't tell me," Basat had replied.

That is when I had spoken up. "Basat, an enemy has come and caught Oghuz unawares. Our army fought them and lost. Our renowned warriors perished at the hand of this enemy. He is exacting a terrible tribute. They wanted to eat two human hearts a day. Everyone has given a son or daughter," I had said solemnly. "What do you say? I have seen this enemy. Their leader is called One-Eye; he is a one-eyed ogre. But he is nothing compared to you. Only you can overcome him—"

"I won't go," Basat said, shaking his head.

"Why not?" Old Aruz and I had asked.

The matter was then considered in great detail, and Basat finally set his terms. At that time, Giyan Seljuk had just set out to fight. Old Aruz and I had managed to persuade Basat by using Giyan Seljuk's name and saying that he was already attempting to defeat the one-eyed ogre himself.

"If Giyan Seljuk loses a hair on his head, then I shall do battle," Basat had pledged.

After Giyan Seljuk perished on the battlefield, Basat immediately changed, donned his armor, gathered his band, and set out, just as he had pledged. For three days and three nights, no word came from Basat and his band of warriors. We had to send out a scout, and we had also sent out a spy, but they did not return. Finally, Old Aruz and I could bear it no longer. With two or three warriors, we prayed to almighty God and set out in Basat's footsteps.

We journeyed and reached the bend in the River Sellama, gushing down Mount Gazilig. It was noontime, and we did not hear any voices anywhere. Had we come at another time, we would have fallen into an enemy ambush. But in that moment, it was like days of yore in Oghuz. Birdsong was the only sound we had heard. We went on a little further. Over the crown of the hill, we came across One-Eye's camp. Not a living soul breathed. We tied our horses together and hid in a quiet spot. After a short while, we had stealthily climbed to the top of the hill and looked at the enemy camp.

We saw that the nomads had moved on, but they had left behind their tents. Tents were rent asunder; cooking fires were doused; smoke hung in the air. A cluster of people were moving the stones that blocked the River Sellama and piling them up on the riverbank.

Old Aruz had looked at me. "Gorgud, who are these people?" he had whispered.

"Old Aruz, glad tidings, those are our people," I had replied. "Basat has at last vanquished One-Eye! These people are unblocking the Oghuz waters."

"Then where is Basat?" Old Aruz had asked anxiously.

"Haven't you seen your son? Look, see the tree over there? Your son is stretched out. He's asleep in its shade," I responded, pointing toward a huge tree.

Old Aruz paused for a moment. He smiled at me, remembering when he saw his son for the first time after that battle. Then he looked at Bayindir Khan. "My Khan, I looked once more and saw that indeed Basat was resting in the shade of a huge elm. I roared with laughter. Then I shouted out to my son, and we all rushed down the hill to the tree. Basat saw us, rose, greeted us, and was greeted in return. He said, 'Father, I have beheaded One-Eye! I have avenged the blood of my brother, Giyan Seljuk. Are you pleased with me?'"

The Khan grinned, imagining the scene in his own mind. He remained quiet.

Old Aruz continued. "I said, 'Come, come here, my son! Let me kiss you.' Then I clasped Basat to my chest, kissed him and kissed him, but did not bite."

"I kissed him and kissed him, but did not bite." Yes, this is what he said. But he did not say that he wept or that he shed bitter tears, crying, "Giyan Seljuk!" We walked around that place until evening, seeking any sign of Giyan Seljuk, but we found nothing.

Once we had found Basat safe and sound, I had said to him, "Let's talk, brave warrior. How did you vanquish One-Eye? What happened to his troops?"

"“Don't ask, Gorgud. One-Eye was ugly; he was not a sturdy warrior," Basat had replied. "But there was sorcery. One-Eye was a sorcerer. Did you feel this?"

"Really? What form did this sorcery take?" I had asked, interested.

"I saw it in different forms. First, when I reached the bend in the river, I knew that we were being followed, but I gave no sign. Attackers came down from the crown of the hill, surrounded us, and wanted to destroy us. 'Stop!' I said. 'I have not come to fight; I have been sent as a present to One-Eye,'" Basat had explained. "They thought a good while before finally taking my warriors and me to the camp. 'I have terms for One-Eye,' I said. 'Let me meet him.' One-Eye came. He was feeble and weak, and he had a shrill voice. His hands were short, and a small wooden sword hung from his girdle, which dragged along the ground. At his side was an interpreter, who translated what One-Eye said to me and vice versa."

One-Eye had started to clap his hands excitedly and laugh. "Just look! A lovely lamb has come to us from Oghuz!" he had exclaimed. Then he studied Basat's face and body carefully. After a few moments, he pointed at Basat's chest and said, "My eye has seen this boy, and my heart loves him. Ask whatever you will of me. They told me you have something to say."

"I...I would like to draw swords with you," Basat had announced. "If you defeat me, you can eat me. If I defeat you, though, you will take your troops and army and leave these parts, never to return!"

"You against me? Don't you know me? Haven't you felt my strength?" One-Eye had asked. He then roared with laughter. His attendants had laughed, too.

"If you want, I'll prove to you that your strength is no match for mine," Basat had said confidently.

"Many of your people have come and perished here. I approve of your courage. Didn't I say that when my eye saw you, my heart loved you? I'll do battle with you, but I have a condition, too. If I beat you, I won't kill you. I'll make you my servant. You'll be my servant. What do you say?" One-Eye had asked.

Beyrak had nodded. "I say yes," he then replied.

"Prepare the battlegrounds!" One-Eye then announced to his attendants.

The battlegrounds had been inside their camp. One-Eye's attendants took Basat and his men there, where they drew a line around the men in the sand. One-Eye had then pointed directly at Basat. "Strip this warrior! Let him be naked as the day he was born," he ordered. Seconds later, his attendants had stripped Basat naked. However, then they gave him a shepherd's cloak and his sword.

Next, One-Eye entered the battlegrounds. Shouts of "Live long!" rose into the air in unison. Basat had thought to himself, *What strength does this weakling have that such big troops obey his every word?* At the same time, he began asking God for help as he, too, slowly entered the battlegrounds. Once inside, he had immediately raised his sword and wanted to attack One-Eye, but his arms and legs froze.

One-Eye hadn't even been looking at him. He was strolling to and fro on the battleground, chatting to the onlookers, laughing, and making them laugh. *Almighty God, what's wrong with me? Why have I frozen? Why is my sword still? Why does this small man not even look at me?* Basat had wondered, trying not to panic.

Suddenly, he saw One-Eye right in front of him. He almost thrust his small wooden sword into Basat's eyes. In that moment, Basat's senses had returned. He swung into action and leaped aside. With that, One-Eye playfully started to stroll about the battlegrounds again. Then Basat's eyes settled on a pair of eyes at the top of the camp. The two eyes were watching him from the charnel house that the newcomers had set up just below the brow of the hill. The eyes bored into Basat. At first, he did not know them, but then he did. It was his mother, Gogan, the lioness. She had found him!

"Strength came to me, and I wanted to attack One-Eye. However, he had suddenly disappeared," Basat had explained. "Father, who did I see instead?"

"Who?" Old Aruz and I had asked together.

Basat had looked at Old Aruz incredulously. "Father, I saw you!" he had exclaimed. "It was you. You were standing before me! One-Eye had turned into you in the blink of an eye. I had trouble holding back my sword and nearly killed you."

At that moment, the battlegrounds crowd had burst out laughing again. Basat had been both confused and furious. "What are you doing here, Father?" he had asked.

"My son, I came to help you..." Old Aruz had replied in One-Eye's shrill voice.

But Basat had been smart enough to know that his father was not standing before him. One-Eye had cast a spell on him. He began to walk around the circle, fixing his eyes on One-Eye. Suddenly, One-Eye had spun around and was either pulled into the earth or flew into the sky; he was no longer there. His soldiers had been beating their swords and lances against their shields, shouting in strange voices. Basat quickly became deaf from the noise and shouting.

Yet again, Basat then felt that two eyes were boring into him. This time, though, they were sending him a sign. *Don't hurry,* a thought had entered his mind. *Don't hurry at all. If he is to be killed, he will be killed only with his short sword. Wait for the right moment.*

Suddenly, Basat had heard breathing behind him. He spun around and saw the Khan's daughter, Lady Burla, standing there. Instinctively, he had courteously bowed his head and asked, "Lady Burla, how did you get here? The battlegrounds are no place for a lady! Come over here, lest you be hurt or hit. I'll look for One-Eye. Have you seen him?"

As soon as Basat had spoken, the soldiers roared with laughter again. Lady Burla then skipped around the circle, belly-dancing for some of the soldiers. *Almighty God, why is Lady Burla doing this?* Basat had wondered, completely shocked.

That's when he had suddenly heard One-Eye's shrill voice coming from Lady Burla's mouth. "Come to me, boy! When you cast your eyes upon me, you loved me with all your heart. I have given my soul to you. What's wrong? Make haste! Seek my hand from my father. Send an envoy to my father, the Khan, or I shall enter the bed of another and make you burn with jealousy. Come, quench my desire and I shall quench yours..."

One-Eye continued, still disguised as Lady Burla. "Basat, Basat, bravest of the brave, apple of my eye, love of my heart, what are you waiting for? Go to my father, the Khan, and ask for my hand. Make me your wife. I'll be the mistress of your tent; I'll be the woman of your bed; I'll kiss you thrice and bite once; I'll bite you thrice and kiss you once. Come to me, boy! What's wrong with you?'

When One-Eye spoke as Lady Burla, Basat had immediately lost his head. He shouted angrily and fell upon One-Eye, trying to seize him, but he couldn't ever catch him. Seconds later, One-Eye changed back into himself. Again, he started to pace the battlegrounds like a victor.

Words had then entered Basat's mind again from the charnel house. *Don't hurry! Don't hurry at all. Let him use up all his strength. Let him finish it. Let the magic leave him; only then should you pounce. But now, don't hurry. Listen to me. Look into my eyes. When the time comes, I shall give you the order to strike...* With only a look, Gogan, the lioness, had sent an important message to Basat, heartening him.

When Basat turned his attention to One-Eye again, he had transformed into me. I had been sitting cross-legged on the ground, playing something that looked like a saz; however, it didn't make a sound. The troops didn't like what they say. They yelled and clamored. One-Eye gave them a sign with his hand to wait. Then, without warning, he quickly jumped up into the air, turned a somersault, and morphed into an ugly, monstrous, naked Cyclops.

As soon as he landed on the ground, however, the cyclops on top of his head had fallen to the ground and stayed there. One-Eye immediately got to his knees and began feeling the ground around him. Meanwhile, the troops continued their clamor. One-Eye's beloved short sword had fallen when he somersaulted. That's when Gogan, the lioness, had sent Basat the sign: *Go, boy, your time has come! Pick up the sword. Don't let go of it!* With that, Basat quickly threw himself upon the sword and took it in his grasp. It was a clumsy sword made of wood.

"One-Eye had shuffled his enormous bulk, back and forth, over the battlegrounds. His shrill voice could scarcely be heard. This time, however, no sounds came from the troops. When he turned the somersault in the air, One-Eye had finally let go of his magic," Basat had explained. "He wanted to get it back, but no matter how hard he tried, he could not do so. I began to walk all around him, keeping his sword in my hand. I waited for a sign from Gogan, the lioness: 'The sign finally came: Run, boy, the time has come! Cut off his wicked head with the wooden sword!'"

"Then what happened?" Old Aruz had asked, completely mesmerized by his son's recap of what had happened.

"I ran, Father, and struck One-Eye's neck with the sword. It went in like a knife through butter and came out the other side. His head lay on one side, his carcass on another. The troops screamed and then fell silent," Basat had replied, remembering the dramatic events. "I grabbed One-Eye's head, raised it to the sky, and then walked around the battlegrounds. I had avenged my brother, Giyan Seljuk! But, Father, when I raised my head, I saw that—"

"You saw what, my son?" Old Aruz had whispered, his blood freezing in his veins. I had turned white.

Basat continued. "Father, don't be afraid at all. I saw that One-Eye's troops were no longer there. The battlegrounds were suddenly deserted—their camp, their tents; you can see for yourself," he had said quietly. "I don't know whether they were ever really there or not."

We had looked all around us. Indeed, there was no trace of One-Eye or his troops. I was at a loss for words. "What happened to One-Eye's body, Basat?" I had asked, trying to make sense of everything.

"Gogan, the lioness, took it," Basat had replied. "But this is his sword." He had pointed at a small wooden sword that was lying on the ground. We had looked at the sword for a few moments, and as we continued to look at it, the sword suddenly grew smaller. A few moments later, we couldn't see it any more; the sword had completely disappeared.

Basat looked at Old Aruz. "What shall we do now, Father?" he then asked, looking tired. "Shall we go home? May Giyan Seljuk's spirit be glad..."

Old Aruz nodded and placed his arm around his son's shoulders. "Let's go, my son, my Lion," he had replied proudly. "We'll celebrate this day."

Old Aruz let out a long sigh, remembering how proud he had been of his son in that moment. Then he looked at Bayindir Khan. "The warriors and servants had finished clearing the river. The River Sellama raced and roared again down toward Oghuz. The river's water reached Oghuz before us, my Khan," he said, ending his speech. "When we arrived in Oghuz, everyone—young and old, women and children—had gathered to gaze joyfully at the water."

Of course, I told Bayindir Khan about this incident at the time. I also reported to the Khan Basat's wish and Aruz's request. The wish-request was that Aruz wanted Bayindir Khan's daughter, Lady Burla, for his son, Basat. "Basat saved Oghuz from misfortune. It must hold a great wedding for Lady Burla and Basat!" I knew that Basat really was Lady Burla's heart's desire. Bayindir Khan did not agree. He said, "Is it my daughter's fate that she should marry a man raised in the forest—in the lioness' den? It is impossible. Gazan, son of Salur, asked for my daughter's hand. I have given my daughter to him."

Aruz was sore disappointed. Basat returned to the forest and did not come out. At Gazan's wedding, they were reconciled. When Gazan was chosen as Noble of Nobles, Inner Oghuz and Outer Oghuz came together again. I thought, I hope that Old Aruz does not raise the matter of the wedding again, lest there be unpleasantness. How good it is that Old Aruz has not said anything about Bayindir Khan's objection to the wedding. God willing, he will not say anything in the future, either...

Bayindir Khan had already heard Old Aruz's tale of One-Eye several times. But this time, he had been very interested, hardly interrupting Old Aruz with a word or a sign at all. Morning had become afternoon while Old Aruz had been talking. Finally, Bayindir Khan looked into the yard a good while. Then he turned to Gilbash and nodded. "Gilbash, that is enough for now. The three of you may go and rest. Eat and drink, and I shall see Aruz in the evening. I have something to ask him. After he has given his answer, give him gifts and see him out. He will be able to go home. Send many gifts, too, for the Outer

Oghuz nobles," the Khan said. "Go, nobles, you are tired. Rest and come back later." With this, Bayindir Khan rose and left the room for his inner chamber.

Gilbash, Old Aruz, and I also left the Khan's chamber. We headed out into the yard and toward the elm tree. But as soon as we heard the voices of the nobles from the wooden trestle tables at the other side of the yard, we quickly went to join their feasting.

The nobles of Inner Oghuz had mingled with the nobles of Outer Oghuz. Servants and slaves were bringing different dishes to them, one after the other. When we joined them, Shirshamsaddin had everyone's attention. We watched him, wondering what was going on.

"He'll eat it!" some of the nobles said.

"He won't!" other nobles disagreed.

Gilbash stepped forward, looking around. "What's this?" he asked. "What's going on, nobles?"

Shirshamsaddin's mouth was full. Only his eyes darted back and forth. He did not answer. Wild Dondar, an Outer Oghuz noble, spoke up. "Aman and Gazan have made a wager. Aman said that Shirshamsaddin cannot eat a whole sheep on his own. Gazan said that if the sheep is divided into four parts, he cannot eat it. But if it is divided into six parts, then he can," he explained, smiling. "Now the sheep has been divided into six parts and roasted over the fire. Will he eat it or not? What do you think?"

Gilbash burst out laughing. "He'll eat it," he mused. "He'll eat it. When Shirshamsaddin was younger, he ate a whole calf! Why shouldn't he be able to eat a sheep now?" He glanced at me and grinned. "Eh, Gorgud?"

Shirshamsaddin was growing weaker, though, as his stomach was already quite full. Cold sweat poured from his brows to his face, and from his face into his armor and onto his chest. He crammed the food into his mouth with both hands, trying to remain focused on his task. Then he looked at Gazan. Between mouthfuls, he managed to say, "My Lord Gazan, for your glory, I…I'll eat this sheep!"

The nobles carried on with their merry feasting. We ate our rice and meat, rose from the table, and went to the shade of the elm tree. Gazan and his son, Uruz, came over to us. Uruz greeted us courteously, and we greeted him in return. All the nobles smiled and nodded, noting, "He's a good lad." Uruz didn't stay with us long, though. He went toward the buttery to where the servants were. I watched from a distance. Uruz stopped a serving wench, spoke to her for a long while, and then the two of them stole away to the far side of the buttery behind a pile of freshly chopped logs. They disappeared from view. *Good for him,* I thought. *He has grown up!*

"What did the Khan say to you, Aruz? Won't you tell us?" Gazan then asked Old Aruz.

"Nothing," Old Aruz replied quickly. "He asked what's going on in Outer Oghuz. He also asked, 'What did you do? Why did Gazan not invite you to the plunder of his tent?'"

"And what did you say?" Gazan asked curiously.

"'I don't know,' I said," Old Aruz replied with a shrug. "'Gazan does what Gazan wants. He doesn't listen to anybody,' I said. 'He sets Inner Oghuz against Outer Oghuz,' I said."

Gazan frowned. "Really?" he asked, taken aback.

"Yes, really," Old Aruz was clearly challenging him.

Gilbash felt the tension and quickly stood up. "Nobles, nobles, stop," he interrupted. "Don't you want some wine?" Without waiting for an answer, he called over two servants, who were standing nearby, awaiting orders. When they approached, Gilbash said, "Go and fetch wine. Fetch the wine that came from Trebizond." The servants bowed and left quickly.

Gilbash looked sideways at me. "Grape water," he chuckled. "Eh, Gorgud?" I laughed, too. When I saw that Gazan and Old Aruz were interested in our inside joke, I told them the story about Gilbash's so-called grape water.

"Good for Gilbash!" they smiled.

The servants came back and poured us goblets of blood-like wine. Once every man had a glass in his hand, Old Aruz sighed and looked at Gilbash. "Gilbash, won't you tell us what Bayindir Khan is really up to?" he asked. He took a large sip of his wine and then turned his attention to me. "And Gorgud, what are you writing, anyway?"

I took a sip of my wine before responding. "The Khan ordered me to write down all the words that come from people's mouths," I said simply.

"Really?" Old Aruz was surprised.

"Yes, really," I said.

Old Aruz looked at Gazan. "I have never seen such a thing in all my life. Have you?" he asked.

"No, I haven't," Gazan replied, shaking his head.

Gilbash looked around and frowned. "Nobles, drink up your wine, and then let's go. We must not keep the Khan waiting!" he said urgently.

"It's time to go, nobles," Old Aruz replied, rising from the ground.

Gazan watched us go. Again, Gilbash, Old Aruz, and I went into Bayindir Khan's chamber. The Khan was already sitting in his place. He motioned us in and told us to sit, too. We went to our previous places and sat cross-legged. Bayindir Khan then stroked his beard a good while. Finally, he spoke. "Aruz, I listened to you speak earlier," he began. "I just have one question left for you; answer it."

"Of course, my Khan," Old Aruz replied quietly. He shifted uneasily where he sat.

"Aruz, before the council with Gazan, you met a woman known as Boghazja Fatma. What did she say to you?" the Khan asked. "And what did you say to her? Will you tell us?"

Old Aruz was taken aback. He looked down at the floor for a few seconds, thinking how he should respond. "Bayindir Khan, this was a conversation between a woman and me," he said slowly. "It has nothing to do with our matter."

"You mean you won't tell us?" the Khan asked, surprised.

"I won't, my Khan," Old Aruz replied.

"Do you want me to tell you?" Bayindir Khan raised his voice.

"You-you know yourself?" Old Aruz stammered.

"Boghazja Fatma came to you, sobbing. She begged you. 'Have pity on my only son!' she said. 'He is an orphan, an orphan who has a father.' 'What does this have to do with me?' you asked. 'Your son is guilty; that's why he must be punished.' Then Boghazja Fatma fell to her knees, embraced your feet, cried bitterly, and said, 'Aruz, don't you know? This boy is *your* son! He is a keepsake from our youth. There was a gully behind our tent. Do you remember it? Our dog's name was Baragchug. Have you forgotten? Only I don't remember, Aruz—did that dog bark at you or not? It barked at some people and not at others.' You were dumbfounded. 'Don't do this!' you said. Then Boghazja Fatma said, 'Gazan did not invite you to the plunder; he does not respect you. He will scold you before the nobles. Gazan will say that your son must die. Don't allow this, my brave Aruz…' Am I right?"

> *While Bayindir Khan was talking, Old Aruz's countenance darkened; his world contracted. He tugged at his beard. Bayindir Khan had spoken true. The Khan already knew that Boghazja Fatma had told Old Aruz the same story she had told the other nobles. I knew this, too. I myself had told Boghazja Fatma this; I had shown her the way. And now the Khan knew this, too…May almighty God help me.*

"You should not say these words to me. Did Boghazja Fatma come to you, my Khan?" Old Aruz asked. "Did the old woman betray me?"

"You are angry, Aruz. If you are angry, then you are wrong; mark my words. Oghuz's affairs cannot be resolved in this way," Bayindir Khan answered. "The spy, whoever he may be, must be punished. Let this be a lesson for Oghuz."

Old Aruz swallowed his wrath. "It all happened as you said, my Khan. What could I do? Mercy coursed through my veins. I thought he was my son. 'God had taken Giyan Seljuk and given me this boy,' I thought. Much misfortune had befallen me, Khan. One son perished at the hand of One-Eye; another son, you know, will not come out of the forest. We bring him out, but he always returns to the forest! His eyes are in the forest!" he muttered. "Then there is Gazan. Was I to blame for the spy episode? Who raised the matter of the spy? Wasn't it Beyrak? When One-Eye attacked Oghuz; when he cut off water for the old people and children; when the women were crying bitter tears as every household gave a son or a daughter as food for One-Eye; Khan, I ask you, where was Beyrak?"

Bayindir Khan remained silent. He watched Old Aruz move around where he sat. I continued writing.

Old Aruz continued. "If you want, I can tell you. Beyrak made the nobles of Bayburd imprison him. Mark my words! In order not to fight One-Eye, Beyrak was taken prisoner in Bayburd. Now no one asks Beyrak how he knew about the spy! Khan, your justice is great. You do not commit injustice. You are the Khan of Khans, the son of Gamghan. Who is Beyrak that Gazan clasps him to his chest like a lamb? Both of them—Beyrak and Gazan—envy my son!" he cried. Then he fell silent and bowed his head.

Bayindir Khan was thoughtful. He gazed at Old Aruz for a good while. "Where did you hear this from?" he asked. "Do you have a spy in Bayburd?"

"I don't have a spy in Bayburd. A caravan came from Bayburd and journeyed long through Outer Oghuz around the foot of Mount Gazilig," Old Aruz explained. "We attacked and captured them. The head of the caravan told me."

The Khan looked at Gilbash and frowned. "Gilbash, did I have word of that caravan?" he asked.

"No, Khan," Gilbash said quietly.

"Did my share of the spoils come?" the Khan asked.

"No, it didn't, Khan," Gilbash answered once again.

"It didn't..." Bayindir Khan said to himself.

Bayindir Khan did not delve deep into this matter and did not reproach Old Aruz. In truth, it was considered a crime in Oghuz to carry out a raid without Bayindir Khan's permission, and then, having carried out the raid, not to bring back spoils. The Khan had one aim in asking Gilbash about the caravan and getting an answer: He wanted to close Old Aruz's mouth. I thought that the Khan, of course, knew about the caravan a long time ago.

Old Aruz moved to get up. Gilbash quickly stood up, too. Then Old Aruz frowned at Gilbash and looked at Bayindir Khan. He did not say a word and stayed in his place. Paying no attention, Bayindir Khan continued. "Won't you tell us, Aruz, if you have not forgotten. You came to me after Basat defeated One-Eye and sought the title Noble of Nobles for your son. I said, 'No.' During a hunt, you raised this matter again and said in the presence of the Outer

Oghuz nobles, 'Now Bayindir Khan has not given his blessing to my son becoming the Noble of Nobles. The time will come when I will take this by force. You...'"

The *manuscript breaks off. This break draws a permanent veil over a very valuable moment. The story had actually reached its culmination in Bayindir Khan's question to Old Aruz. Did Old Aruz really say this or not? We shall never know. The Khan's patience is enviable. Only at the end of the manuscript, when the Khan reveals his secret intention, can we truly appreciate this patience.*

The mute, reproachful face of the young Orientalist appeared before me once more.

...was hunting, what did this hunt bring to Oghuz? We all witnessed this. The enemy came, combed through our land, and left. Our daughters and brides, and our children and old people were taken prisoner. His own mother was taken prisoner. His wife was taken prisoner. His son was taken prisoner. All of this happened because he left Oghuz open to the enemy. I had a lot to say before the hunt. Leave watchmen, if you do nothing else. 'No,' he said. 'Don't interfere.' I said, 'Gazan, this trip is a long one. You will go right into Georgia. Who will you appoint head of the army?' My Khan, what could he say?"

"What did he say?" Bayindir Khan asked.

"'I won't appoint you,'" he said. "'I'll appoint my son, Uruz.'" My Khan, Gazan is unjust; he is wrong. Had he appointed me head of the army, misfortune would not have befallen Oghuz. His son is young. He has never faced the enemy; he has never drawn his sword. He appointed his son. Gazan has no time for me. Gazan has strayed from the right path, Bayindir Khan. He completely disregards me. Let it be. If they call him Gazan, they call me Aruz. The day will come when we shall settle scores. All the Outer Oghuz nobles will support me, you know..." Old Aruz's voice trailed off.

"Will Beyrak support you, too?" Bayindir Khan asked, frowning.

"Who is Beyrak? Beyrak is not one of us. Beyrak is from Inner Oghuz. His father, Baybura—"

"Didn't Beyrak marry one of your girls? Isn't Lord Baybejan Outer Oghuz's standard-bearer?" the Khan asked.

Old Aruz thought awhile. "It is so, Bayindir Khan. You are right. Beyrak can be considered one of us, too," he finally said. "But he will not support us. He will support Gazan, and he will humiliate us. He will call me a spy and start a fight while we're hunting. He will quarrel with Bakil."

"Aruz, you shouldn't show me such a day for Oghuz. Oghuz has become divided, but I did not know it. Aruz, you are a brave man, a valiant warrior,"

Bayindir Khan said. "Have you lost your mind? Is your head spinning? Have you joined the children?"

After Bayindir Khan had spoken, I saw that he was really downcast, lost in thought. Old Aruz also kept silent, but then he muttered to himself, "This was all Gazan's doing. It is his fault. Gazan is guilty! Almighty God, have mercy on us, for the sake of your greatness."

Bayindir Khan did not say a word. He sat with his hands over his eyes. With a gesture of his hand, he then let us go. Gilbash, Old Aruz, and I went out into the Khan's yard again. Without bidding us farewell, Old Aruz found his servant. "Call everyone together," he ordered. "Tell them we are leaving."

The Outer Oghuz nobles all mounted their horses. Following Old Aruz's example, they did not say a word. They rode out through the Black Gate and galloped away from Gunortaj Palace, disappearing from view in clouds of dust. Bayindir Khan had offended Old Aruz, and the Khan had not stopped Old Aruz from leaving. He did not respect him.

Almighty God, protect Oghuz from dark days, I thought. *Amen.*

§ § § § § §

The Shah had not yet reached the throne room, but chants of praise rose into the sky, completely drowning out the cries of Lady Tajli that still rang in the Shah's ear. He dismounted in the palace courtyard and stroked his horse's mane. The Shah then stood and looked around the courtyard for a few moments as his horse was led away. People were being kept waiting outside the yard; it was impossible to let everyone in.

The Vizier came up to the Shah, bowing. "Please, come this way. May I sacrifice myself for you?" he greeted him.

The Shah looked over the Vizier's bowed head toward the elm tree in the yard. He noticed that someone was standing there. A thread seemed to snap in his heart, and without saying another word, he turned and went into the palace. The guards quickly closed the door. After that, no one entered the palace, except for two servants and the Vizier. They all had to stand respectfully in the courtyard, awaiting orders from the Perfect Councilor.

The Shah sat upon his throne. He turned his large emerald prayer beads, thinking. Then he summoned the Vizier with a look. "I saw him. He was standing under the elm tree. He must come to me, for the sake of the Shah of Chivalrous Men," he said softly. "Let us not prolong this affair."

"Will you wear your veil, Perfect Councilor?" the Vizier asked, also speaking softly.

"No, I won't. It will be fine," the Shah replied. "Have him come in at once." But then the Shah had second thoughts. He hesitated and then quickly said, "Very well, I'll wear my veil." With that, he took the veil from behind his throne and put it on.

The Vizier bowed and went out. The guards were lined up in rows in the doorway that led out to the yard. The Vizier looked for Captain Rahim among all of them. Sensing that the Vizier was looking for him, Rahim stepped forward and the Vizier went up to him. "Captain, is that man here?" the Vizier asked quietly.

"He is here, Master Vizier," Rahim answered.

"Go and bring him before the Shah without any fuss. I don't want to hear any talk about this," the Vizier ordered. "Do you understand?"

"Yes, sir!" Rahim responded. He went briskly into the yard toward the elm tree.

Lele stood, his heart troubled. When the Shah had passed within five or six feet of him, it seemed to him that the Shah saw him, but did not acknowledge him. *Of course, he saw and recognized me,* he thought. *But he acted as though he did not recognize me. The Vizier may have said something, God willing! When he turned away from me, my heart was in my mouth. It almost broke into pieces. Why did he do this? Although, what else could he have done before so many people? He was hardly going to call me and embrace me. But if he had asked me, 'Why didn't you die at Chaldiran?' or 'How did you survive?' then that would have been too much for me. I would die as a sacrifice. Let him give orders to the executioner as long as he does not ask me these questions. For the sake of the Perfect Councilor, Pivot of the Universe, you alone can help me.*

When Lele saw Rahim coming toward him, his heart began to beat as fast as a bird's. Lele could tell from the young captain's face that the Shah had summoned him. He began to collect his thoughts.

When Rahim reached Lele, he nodded politely at him. "Let's go, Lele," he said. "Come on."

Lele silently got up and followed Rahim. They walked up to the Vizier, who was waiting for them at the entrance to the court. The Vizier looked closely again at Lele from head to toe. Then he leaned in toward Rahim's ear. "Stand at the door yourself," he whispered. "Don't allow anyone in. Only come in if I call you."

"Yes, sir," Rahim answered, bowing in acknowledgement.

The Vizier turned to Lele. "Lele, we shall grant your wish. Our Shah, our Perfect Councilor, wishes to see you. Please, come inside," he said without emotion.

The Vizier and Lele went inside. Rahim closed the door tight from the other side. Bowing, the Vizier approached the throne where the Shah was sitting. "May I sacrifice myself for you? Huseyn Bay Lele, whom I told you about, has come and awaits your pleasure," he announced.

The Shah gazed at a double candlestick on the table in the middle of his throne room, lost in thought; he did not utter a word. The room fell silent. The Vizier turned to look at Lele. Lele remained quietly at the door. A good while passed before the Vizier turned to the Shah again. "My Perfect Councilor, Huseyn Bay Lele is in your presence," he repeated.

At last, the Shah moved his eyes from their fixed point and looked toward Lele. "Come closer," he said. "Come, Lele."

Lele kneeled and crawled on his hands and knees to the Shah. "My Sage, my Perfect Councilor, may I sacrifice myself for you? My Sage, my Perfect Councilor, may I sacrifice myself for you?" Lele uttered only these words. When he reached the Shah's throne, he bowed his head and remained frozen. Again and again, he said in his heart the words he expected to hear from the Shah: *Why didn't you die at Chaldiran, Lele? Why didn't you die at Chaldiran, Lele? Why didn't you...*

When the Shah saw Lele prostrate before him, he immediately ordered Lele to stand up. "Arise, arise, Lele!" he commanded.

Lele did not rise. Instead, he began to beat his head on the floor. At this moment, the Shah himself rose. He went over to Lele, placed both hands on his shoulders, which were heaving from sobs, and lifted him up. The Shah and Lele stood opposite one another, but Lele kept his head bowed.

The Shah's voice rang out like copper. "Arise, arise, Lele," he spoke. "That's better! You did well to come out of that battle alive. The Perfect Councilor for whom we would sacrifice ourselves must have heard our prayers, thanks be to God."

At first, Lele did not comprehend any of the Shah's words. He staggered and almost passed out. The Vizier stood to one side, amazed. He was watching them secretly, a dutiful smile upon his face. *How the Shah had greeted Lele!* he thought. Lele was already back at the palace—back in his position of authority. However, the damage caused by Lele's return was not beyond repair. Praising the Shah's action in his heart, the Vizier repeated the Shah's last words, "Thanks be to God; thanks be to the Creator."

Lele nearly died. In a single moment, the darkness that cloaked his eyes turned bright as the sun, showing him that the whole world—life, torment and trouble, struggle and strife, war and peace, kindness and tenderness, love and hate—was empty and hollow. Everything turned upside-down. In that moment, a great secret was suddenly bathed in light, made manifest to him, and he understood.

"I want you to know how glad you have made me, Lele. I want you to know how good it is that you did not die, but survived," the Shah said. "Come closer. Sit here. Where did the wind carry you? Where did you disappear to? Where have you come from? Tell me, tell me! For the love of the Shah of Chivalrous Men, do not be silent."

Finally, Lele came around. "How good it is that you did not die, but survived," he whispered hoarsely, as though to himself. "What?" Then, after keeping his head bowed for a long time, he suddenly had the courage to raise his head and look carefully into the face of the Shah. He almost pierced the veil that covered the Shah's face with his gaze. Lele gasped and his eyes widened, but his gasp was so small that even the Vizier, who was close by, did not hear it. "You—you are not the Shah. You are not the Shah; you are the boy!" he whispered.

The Shah's face changed. His hands shook; he could hardly say the word, "Quiet!" He immediately turned to the Vizier. "Vizier, don't stay here. Go outside!" he ordered. "Go away!"

"My Shah—" The Vizier hesitated.

"No, go out. For the sake of the Shah of Chivalrous Men, leave us!" the Shah cried. "Go out now. I must talk to Lele in private."

The Vizier walked backward out of the throne room. The Shah and Lele were left in the room. The Shah was struggling for breath and could scarcely speak. "Lele, what's wrong with you? We are doing nothing wrong. We welcomed you. Are you feeling quite yourself? Come and sit down," he said to him.

Lele did not move. "You are not the Shah," he said quietly. Then he became wholly convinced of his statement. "Of course, you are not the Shah!"

"Lele, don't do this..." the Shah said sadly.

Lele broke down. "What happened to my Perfect Councilor, to him for whom I would sacrifice myself?" he asked. "What happened to him?" Struggling to suppress his sobs, he tried to regain his composure. "What did you do to the Shah, damned poet? I recognized you. I knew you!"

"You say you recognized me?" the Shah asked, his voice stronger now. "Then why do we need this veil?" With that, the Shah took off his veil and cast it aside. "How is that now? You can recognize me better without the veil." Looking at Lele, the Shah began to turn his face left and right.

"I would recognize you veiled, too. Yes, of course, it is you, damned poet. I would recognize you by your voice alone. You can never deceive me!" Lele mumbled.

"Quiet!" The Shah demanded, growing angry. "Know your place! Those days are gone. Now I am the Shah. Understand that! You know, just one order from me, just one sign from my finger, just one look is enough to have you..." his voice trailed off.

Lele raised his head and drew himself up straight. He quieted down.

The Shah did not finish what he was saying; his heart could not bear it. The Shah then kneeled before Lele. “Lele, I swear by God’s name—I swear on the grave of the Shah of Chivalrous Men—I am blameless in this matter. He obliged me himself—”

“What did you do to the Shah, God damn you?” Lele interrupted. “Tell me!”

“Whatever the Shah did, he did himself,” the Shah hissed back. “Lele, you should know—”

Lele interrupted the Shah again. “Don’t preach empty words, boy. What has happened to the Shah? Is he alive or—tell me straight, tyrant! Do you hear me?” he asked through gritted teeth.

The Shah rose. Without looking at Lele, he went and sat at the foot of the throne. He spoke as though into empty space. “Do you remember Chaldiran, Lele?” he asked.

Lele’s blood almost froze in his veins. “Why do you ask? Can Chaldiran be forgotten?”

“Do you remember what you said to me before the battle started? ‘Put on the Shah’s battle dress,’ you told me.”

“What of it?”

“I put it on. Now listen to me; you wanted this. You listen yourself. Do you remember? You attacked. The Shah sent you to the right flank. He himself was in the tent with me, but he could not stay in one place. He came and went. Sometimes he went into the heat of battle, quenched his thirst, and then he would return to the tent. Do you remember how once, when he plunged into the battle, he cut Malbashoghlu in two? He struck his sword through the head of the giant like a sharpened razor through butter! You were on the attack,” the Shah recalled. “There was a small hole in one corner of the tent. I opened up the hole and watched the battle through it. You had given me strict orders not to stick even my nose out of the tent; you said to stay there. This time, when the Shah returned to the tent, I could see that blood was flowing from beneath his armor. He for whom I would sacrifice myself was wounded. I have not breathed a word of this to anyone. This is what you wanted yourself, Lele; this is not my doing!”

“Go on…” Lele said, waiting to hear more. With that, the Shah recapped what had happened that fateful day.

Khizir had flung himself upon the Shah. “My Shah, you are bleeding! May it be just a slight wound,” he said nervously.

“I cannot feel anything!” the Shah had replied. He moved the boy aside and began inspecting his body with his hands. Then he thrust one of his hands beneath his armor and removed it. His whole hand had been covered in blood.

He and Khizir exchanged glances. "It's nothing," The Shah had said, trying to dismiss all the blood.

Khizir shook his head. "No, let's open your armor. Let's dress your wound!" he had exclaimed.

"No, don't," the Shah said. "We'll tend to it later. It seems to have stopped. Nothing happened. Fear not, young man. The breath of the Shah of Chivalrous Men is with me. Nothing can happen to me..."

"My Shah, he for whom I would sacrifice myself, let me go. Let me be your shadow in the battle," Khizir had begged. "Let me fight in your place, Perfect Councilor! Am I only to watch from the tent?"

"It is impossible. Don't go out of here," the Shah had replied. Suddenly, there had been a loud noise. The Shah turned his head toward the direction of it. "What is that noise? What has happened?" he demanded. The noise had come from the mouth of the tent. With that, the Shah went out to see what was going on. Meanwhile, Khizir could hear everything from inside.

The Head of the Guard had galloped up with news for the Shah. "My Shah, he for whom I would sacrifice myself, the left flank is giving way!" he had said.

"What?" the Shah had asked, very angry. 'Make haste! Find Khalil Sultan Zulgadar. Tell him to go to the left flank."

"My Sage, my Perfect Councilor, he for whom I would sacrifice myself—" the Head of the Guard hesitated.

"What is it?" the Shah demanded. "Make haste! What has happened?"

"My Shah, Zulgadar has turned traitor. Zulgadar has fled!" the Head of the Guard announced.

"Fled? A traitor! His father was a traitor, too. Don't stand there! Go and find Ustajlu Abdulla Khan. Tell him to go to the left flank. Make haste!" the Shah had then ordered.

In that moment, another messenger had galloped up in haste. "My Shah, my Shah, the right flank! The right flank has given way, he for whom I would sacrifice myself! What shall we do?"

"The right flank?" the Shah had repeated incredulously. He turned to the Head of the Guard. "Make haste and go to the right flank yourself. Summon all the guards. Go! I shall come myself now. But first, send a messenger to Abdulla Khan..."

The men mounted their horses and galloped off. The Shah then turned and entered the tent again. He had started pacing back and forth in agitation. He was turning something over in his mind. Suddenly, he had stopped pacing and focused on Khizir. "Come closer!" he demanded.

Khizir moved closer to the Shah. Then he fell to his knees and felt that the Shah was about to say something of the utmost importance. Looking Khizir in the face, he carefully and solicitously said, "Listen to me carefully. Do not forget what I am about to say…"

"Yes, sir," Khizir had replied.

"Don't interrupt. Just listen to me."

Khizir held his breath as he listened to the Shah's last orders. The Shah's voice contained such sorrow that Khizir had a difficult time controlling his own emotions. "A short while ago, during the attack, my horse shied and threw me down. The infidel soldiers fell upon me. You know Sultanali Mirza Afshar. He charged at them, sword in hand, crying, "I am the Shah! I am the Shah!" Then he drove them back so that I could catch my breath and get to my feet," the Shah said. "If he escapes the clutches of the enemy, give him a generous gift. He saved you. As for Zulgadar, you have just heard what he has done. If he falls into your hands, punish him yourself."

Khizir couldn't bear what the Shah was saying to him. He was confounded. He wondered what the Shah had meant when he said, "He saved you." He also didn't know what he meant when he said, "Punish Zulgudar yourself." With that, Khizir began to panic. "My Sage, my Perfect Councilor, I don't understand a thing! You will settle these matters yourself after the battle, God willing!" he cried. "Thanks be to God!"

The Shah had then lost his temper. "Don't interrupt me! Listen to me. Keep this in your ear like an earring. There is little time left. This battle is already over, you can see. Yes, yes, the battle is over. The Shah of Chivalrous Men has turned his face away from me," he said firmly. "I must have committed a great sin. We have a little time now. Take off your outer garments…"

Khizir had been wearing an ordinary cloak, but beneath that cloak had been the same garments that the Shah was wearing. Khizir took off the cloak and cast it aside. Then he had silently waited for additional orders.

The Shah looked at Khizir once again. He smiled. "You really do look like me. Now, are you ready for this game? I can see, yes, I can see that you are ready. This battle is already over. Tomorrow the country will be yours!" he said, offering Khizir a small pep talk. "Don't interrupt me, my Shah. I am giving you such a big country, but it has been wounded. Now it is for you to take care of it. Do you understand?"

Khizir had been doing his best not to hyperventilate. "Whom are we deceiving, my Shah?" he quickly asked.

"We are not deceiving anyone. The inside has no meaning; the outside is what really matters.[54] Remember this," the Shah had replied.

"But I—I am afraid!" Khizir had blurted.

---

[54] In Sufi thought, zahir is the external, visible cover, concealing the essence (batin) within.

"Fear not. Fear nothing. You will not have time to be truly afraid," the Shah had replied. "One day, your life, too, will come to an end."

Voices could be heard outside again. One of the guards had come up to the door of the tent. "My Shah, you for whom I would sacrifice myself, come! Your troops have been defeated. We are waiting for you. It is time to leave..."

"I am coming, boy! For God's sake, have a moment's patience!" the Shah had shouted outside. Then he had turned back to Khizir. "Look, I could not keep this large country from calamity. I am leaving. Do not ask me why. You know, I heard a voice speaking to me from the heavens. 'Everyone who loves you is here,' the voice said. It was the voice of the Shah of Chivalrous Men. 'But why did you not help me here?' I asked resentfully. 'Boy, what have you seen there? You, whose work there is already finished, come here! They are waiting for you here. Everyone who loves you is here!'" he had said. "I cannot stay. Do not look for me. If God grants, I shall join the heat of battle and no trace of me will remain here. Fear not, they will not know my dead body."

"But Lele? What about Lele?" Khizir had clung to Lele as his last hope.

"You can be sure of this: Lele has perished. He is lost; he is gone; he has given himself up unto death. May his place be in paradise, God willing," the Shah had said quietly.

Lele listened to the young Shah with baited breath. When the Shah reached this moment in his tale, Lele began to shed tears. "No, you for whom I would sacrifice myself, no, my Perfect Councilor!" he weeped. "I did not die. I did not die a coward's death! God, kill me. Finish me off, God! For the sake of your unity, kill me, kill—"

Khizir continued his tale without listening to Lele. He wanted him to know what had really happened.

"Lele has died," the Shah had said. "No one will know you. Go! Go to the guards. Make haste and go from here. Go to the mountains, do you hear? They are waiting for you. Make haste! You know everything as well as I. Go now."

Agitated voices were raised outside the tent. Cannon balls had already begun to fall near the tent. The noise was deafening. At that moment, the Shah looked deep into Khizir's eyes for the last time. There was an opening in the back corner of the tent that had been covered with a wooden board. The Shah quickly pulled out the wooden board and went out. A moment later, he had disappeared completely into that black hole.

Suddenly, a guard burst into the tent. Without a word, he had put his arms around Khizir and, by force, led him from the tent. At first, the light had dazzled the new Shah; he had to put up his hand to protect his eyes. Then he had withdrawn his hand, lowered his head, and looked at no one. The horses had been standing ready, hoofing the ground. They had mounted. Suddenly, it was as if Khizir had forgotten everything, and he felt as if he had always been the

Shah. He looked left and right. Then he looked sideways at the worried guard. "Where is Mahammad Khan Ustajlu? Where is Dev Sultan Rumlu? Call the bugler! Rally everyone for the attack!" he had ordered.

"My Shah, it is late. The time for attack has passed," the guard had replied. Desperation was all over his face. "Let's gallop away from here. Everyone has withdrawn. We are the only ones left. It will be too late, you for whom I would sacrifice myself!" Paying Khizir no more heed, the guard then whipped his horse hard and the horses flew; there were ten or fifteen guards behind them. They immediately broke into a gallop, too.

Khizir wiped the sweat from his face. He had been kneeling at the foot of the throne and rose, his anxiety spent. He went up to Lele. "Lele, I swear by almighty God—by the spirit of my Perfect Councilor—that what I just said is the truth. I want you to know that I have not one grain of guilt in this matter," he said. "I swear on the spirit of my Perfect Councilor."

Lele was frozen where he sat. He neither made a move nor said a word.

"Lele," the Shah said cautiously. "Lele, do you hear me? Look, I was saying that I swear on the spirit of my Perfect Councilor—"

A scream tore from Lele's chest. "May the spirit of your Perfect Councilor punish you, boy! Ten years! Ten years ago exactly, he for whom I would sacrifice myself went to the other world. All these years, it was my longing for him that kept me alive. You have been the Shah for ten years!" he cried. "If only God had killed me on the road when I found you in your wretched village and brought you to the palace. It is I who created you! Look at the Shah. Are you really the Shah? You are a knave who should have died long ago. You—" Suddenly, Lele drew out a small dagger, hidden beneath his belt, and plunged it into the Shah's heart. "Die, knave! Take your due. I have not sinned, you say. I am sin enough for you!" Fire raged in Lele's eyes.

The Shah staggered but managed to stay on his feet for a few moments. Letting out a painful sigh, he clutched his chest and slowly kneeled. With his thoughts quickly leaving his mind, he spoke his last words: "Lady Tajli, you spoke true. Your dream has come true. I should have…" Then he fell onto the carpet and surrendered his spirit.

Lele looked in disgust at the Shah's body for a while. Then he turned and began to study the throne room. The door remained closed. Without losing time, Lele strode confidently to the side of the throne and tore down a carpet that had been hanging on the wall. He pushed hard at a point on the wall, known only to him. First, the wall came toward him. Lele stepped back, and the wall tilted to one side, revealing the entrance to a secret passage. A ladder led down inside the wall. Without hesitation, Lele entered the passage. Before going down the ladder, he then set a mechanism in motion to make the wall return to its previous position. The throne room was suddenly empty, except for the body of the unfortunate replacement Shah.

§ § § § § §

The Vizier opened the door and hesitantly peeped inside. When he saw what lay within, he slammed the door shut, stunned. A moment later, the Vizier dared to open the door again. He walked in and cast himself upon the body of the Shah. "My Shah, my Shah! Who has dared to—what has happened to you, my Perfect Councilor?" he cried. He turned the body over, saw the dagger plunged into the Shah's chest, and his horrified eyes nearly left their sockets. He did not utter another word. Instead, he began to look carefully all around him.

The Vizier rose and went up to the carpet cast upon the floor. Still shocked, he stood there, looking hard at the bare wall. He wanted to touch the wall with his hands, but he did not. He went and opened the door and called Captain Rahim inside. "Come, come and see what has happened!" he ordered. "We have lost the Shah!"

Rahim's knees trembled. He stepped forward, unsure what he would see inside the throne room. As soon as he saw the body, he lost his wits and began to stammer. "I—I—I..." he said, unable to form an actual sentence. Then he immediately kneeled and remained motionless before the body.

The Vizier had begun to pace the room. He started turning the prayer beads in his hands. "In the name of God, the merciful, the compassionate..." he recited. Then he stopped abruptly and glared at Rahim. "Has anyone else come into this room?" he demanded. "Didn't I tell you not to allow anyone into the room. Who was here?"

"Here?" Rahim gulped. Although Rahim had come to his senses, he could hardly speak. "No one else came into the room!" he cried. "But the Shah was not alone, you—"

"In the name of God, the merciful, the compassionate," the Vizier said loudly and started to pace back and forth again.

Rahim continued. "There was someone with the Shah, Master Vizier; Huseyn Bay Lele was with him! But where has he gone?" he asked. He began to look around the large room.

"What? Have you lost your mind, boy? Is there anyone here besides us? There is one door and the window is barred with iron. Who is Huseyn Bay Lele?" he asked. "Yes, yes, there was such a man. At one time, he was the confidant of the Shah. He was of noble stock. You have heard of Chaldiran. Lele perished at Chaldiran; he became a martyr. For quite some time, he had been the Head of the Guard. The Shah trusted him. He had authority. He was courageous. How have thoughts of Lele entered your head, Captain Rahim? There seems to be something strange about you…"

The captain was absolutely confounded by the Vizier's response. He had no idea what to say. *What is the Vizier saying?* he wondered. *What is he talking about?* He rose. "By God, I don't know what has happened. I don't know anything. Vizier, I swear by the one God, believe me, Master Vizier, I am telling the truth. Something was happening in this room. I could hear voices! I couldn't understand anything, so I went into the yard and called you. The voices were strange. It even sounded like my father's voice. He was crying out in alarm," Rahim replied, talking quickly. "'My Shah, my Shah!' he cried. 'The right flank!' Of course, it was my father's voice. But…maybe I imagined this voice. My father died at Chaldiran. He was a standard-bearer. What did he have to do with the right flank?"

The Vizier was not listening to the captain. He was lost in his own thoughts. Eventually, however, he took heed of the trembling captain. "Very well! Go now; go out. No one should stay with a corpse for a long time," he said quietly. "This is what we will do. Go and summon everyone. Gather them in the courtyard. Only open this window first." He pointed to the window. The window was shut tight; its frame was made of iron. "Break it!" the Vizier said. "Break the frame, for the sake of the Shah of Chivalrous Men!"

Rahim applied his strength and broke the frame at the bottom. He cast aside one corner and the window opened, filling the room with bright sunlight. Then he looked at the Vizier, awaiting additional instructions. "Now what, Master Vizier?" he asked.

The Vizier looked out the window and turned to face the captain. "Make haste! Gather everyone outside the window. I will tell them the news myself," he said. But then he hesitated and shook his head. "No, stop. Come here…" his voice trailed off.

The Vizier took the captain up to the body. With one swift yank, he pulled the dagger from Khizir's chest, wiped the blood off on the carpet, and handed the dagger to Rahim. "Go and hide this. Do not let anyone see it," the Vizier said quietly. Then he began to rearrange the garments on the Shah's body. "Everyone must think that the Shah died of illness. No one can ever raise a hand against the Shah; he cannot be killed," he muttered under his breath. "He was ill; he breathed his last breath. No one was here—no one. Do you understand, boy? No one was here."

Rahim nodded, his eyes wide. He did not say a word.

"Now go! Go and do as I have commanded you. Gather everyone before the window. Everyone, everyone should come—sheikhs, followers, guards, dervishes, everyone," the Vizier said. "Don't stand here. Go!"

Rahim stood frozen to the spot. Then suddenly, as though the ice had melted, he gave a sob and ran out of the room. The Vizier shook his head after him and resumed his work. He covered up the wound as best he could and laid out the body so that it looked at rest on the carpet. Finally, he rose, looked around the room once again, and whispered to himself, "God, grant that he may rest in peace. In the name of God, the merciful, the compassionate..." Then he slowly approached the window.

Anxious shouts and worried cries were soon coming from the yard: "My Sage, my Perfect Councilor, you for whom I would sacrifice myself, alas...You for whom I would sacrifice myself, what has happened? What has befallen you, my Shah?" the people cried. The cries quickly gained in strength and rose up into the sky.

The nobles had all gathered around Captain Rahim. In a moment, the square in front of the window had filled with people. At first, the Vizier covered his ears for a while against the voices from outside. Then he said, "Oh, God!" and put his head out of the window. He raised his hand and the hubbub stopped instantly, save for muffled sobs. Everyone waited to hear what the Vizier had to say. Only the sounds of weeping rose into the heavens.

The Vizier began his speech. "People, our house has fallen. Our fate is bitter; our hearth is ruined. We are in mourning! Our country laments! Our Sage, our Perfect Councilor, he for whom we would sacrifice ourselves, our great ruler, Shah Ismayil Ibn Heydar ibn Juneyd Safavi, today—on the twenty-seventh day of the month of Rajab in the year of Hijri 930[55]—has suddenly left us. He has abandoned this frail world," he said loudly. "He has entered the protection of the Shah of Chivalrous Men and has been welcomed into paradise. His deeds will live forever. May the one true God grant him resplendent peace." When the Vizier finished his speech, he did not know how a cry of grief escaped his chest. Tears streamed down his face and into his beard, and he suddenly found himself sobbing bitterly.

Wailing and lamentation enveloped the courtyard. Some fainted; others beat their chests. The whole city was gathered together. People were on top of one another. Black and green and red and black flags fluttered in the air above the turbans of the Red Caps. The anxiety, sorrow, and sadness of the people grew as the news set in.

Here, at this sad moment, the text about Shah Ismayil breaks off for the last time and ends. In reality, the subject can also be considered finished. Nobody can ever say for certain whether what is

[55] It is 930, according to the Islamic calendar, which begins when the Prophet Mohammed moved from Mecca to Medina. It is 1524, according to the Gregorian calendar.

described here truly happened or is simply the product of the imagination. There is a major difference between the Shah Ismayil who perished at Chaldiran and the Shah Ismayil who ruled for ten years after Chaldiran. That difference is the difference between Shah Ismayil himself and his lookalike, Khizir—that's all. I would like to believe in the version of The Incomplete Manuscript, *in, let's say, its truth. This is an event that happened in at least one parallel world. But who can say for certain that this is not how events occurred in our world?*

Darkness had already fallen. I stood and turned on the light. There seemed to be no one left in the Manuscripts Institute. However hard I tried to read the end of The Incomplete Manuscript, *I could not make myself do it. Instead, I gazed at the yellowed pages for quite some time before finally standing up and walking out of the building.*

§ § § § § §

Old Aruz took his band and left; the Khan's yard was suddenly deserted. Gilbash and Gazan went and sat under the elm tree. I also went up to them. Gazan looked at Gilbash. "Gilbash, did you see that Aruz took offense at what Bayindir Khan said?" he asked. Then he glanced at me. "Isn't that so, Gorgud?"

Gilbash nodded. "He has taken offense," he replied. "But, you know, he has taken offense at himself."

"Who else should he take offense at, if not himself?" Gazan grumbled. "Neither heaven nor earth could contain his arrogance. We are all supposed to be in his debt. This bonfire did not smoke properly; things will turn out ill. What do you think, Gilbash?"

Gilbash shrugged. "We shall wait and see. God does not like braggarts," he said. "And neither do we."

I liked Gilbash's phrase: "God does not like braggarts, and neither do we." Gilbash speaks rarely, but when he does, his words have great meaning.

"Let me go and see the Khan, nobles, and find if he has any instructions," Gilbash then said, rising. "Wait for me here." With that, he left for the Khan's chambers.

Gazan and I sat cross-legged on the carpet beneath the elm tree. Two servants appeared a few minutes later. "We are at your service. What would you like?" they asked.

"Is your belly hungry, Gorgud?" Gazan asked me.

"No," I answered.

"I don't want to eat, either. Shall we drink some buttermilk?" Gazan then asked.

I nodded. "Yes, let's drink some," I replied.

Gazan nodded to the servants. They bowed and left. Then Gazan looked at me and smiled. "Shirshamsaddin is sleeping where he fell. After all, he did eat a whole sheep. You know, the sheep was divided into six parts, which is why he could eat it. If it had been split into four, he wouldn't have managed it. Now he is paying the price," he mused. "He's not as young as he was."

I chuckled, agreeing with him.

Suddenly, Gazan changed the subject. "Maybe the Khan has finally gotten tired. Do you think we'll go back to the matter this evening?" he asked.

"I don't know. Anything could happen. I am very tired myself," I said.

Gazan looked at me, screwing up his eyes. "Gorgud, tell me, for the love of God, did Aruz greatly blacken my name?" he asked. "Did he stab my shadow with his sword?"

"He spoke much ill. He wielded his sword," I said.

"I knew in my heart that he stabbed my shadow. He stabbed me, yes; what's the difference? He is Aruz, the traitor, and I am Gazan," Gazan muttered. "What do you say, Gorgud? Shall we gather together the old women and the ladies of Inner Oghuz at the Black Gate? Should we let them put forward a proposal about me to Bayindir Khan? Would the Khan like that, or—?"

"No, of course, the Khan wouldn't like it," I interrupted. "Do not give up hope. God will help you, Gazan, and everything will fall into place."

"You sense these things. Did the Khan believe Aruz or not?" Gazan then asked.

"Gazan, how would I know if the Khan believed Old Aruz or not? I cannot enter the Khan's mind!" I replied. "I was not looking into the Khan's face. You saw yourself that my job was to write. I could see only the Khan's feet. He waggled his toes; I saw that."

"Then he must have been angry," Gazan said thoughtfully. "I know that if he waggles his big toe, he may keep quiet. However, in his heart, he is really angry."

"What do I know? Let us keep our mouths shut," I said. "God alone knows."

"Amen," Gazan nodded, ending the conversation on that topic.

The servants brought buttermilk. We were both thirsty and drained our cups. Soon after, Gilbash approached us. It was clear from his face that there was nothing pressing to report to us. "The Khan wanted you to rest. We shall continue our work tomorrow," he announced.

We agreed, and the three of us stayed talking a fair while in the shade of the elm tree, recalling the nobles' wager and Shirshamsaddin. Gilbash then looked at Gazan. "Has Uruz come?" He asked curiously.

"Yes, he has come," Gazan replied. "He went and looked at the horse you had chosen for him. He liked it very much. 'May my grandfather, the Khan, be in good health and enjoy a long and fruitful life!' he said."

Evening came and darkness quickly fell. A bright circle of moonlight shone upon the elm tree. The starless sky was a deep, deep blue. The three of us were still enjoying the evening together. Gazan looked at me sideways. "Gorgud, have you brought your gopuz[56]?" he asked.

"No, my Lord," I replied. "It is late; this is not the time for music."

"That's true. You are right. This really isn't the time for music. I don't know why I asked about the gopuz." With that, Gazan looked around. "What do you say, nobles? There is no music or storytelling. Let's go and rest. I am already weary. Are you?"

"You're right," I said. "Let's get some sleep, nobles."

"You go and rest," Gilbash replied. He looked over to where the slaves and servants stayed. Then he added, "I still have something to do."

We rose and wished one another good health. Then we went to our quarters. I lay down on my bed, but sleep ran away from me like wounded prey. I would catch it one moment, but then I would let it slip away and run off ahead of me. Anxious thoughts entered my mind: *The Khan has listened to everybody. He has heard words from everybody; nobody is left,* I thought. *Tomorrow will be the final day. The Khan will pronounce his decision, of course. May God himself help us! May God himself protect Oghuz. Amen!* With these thoughts, my eyes carried me away into darkness…

§ § § § § §

The first rooster woke me up. Morning had already come. I rose quickly and dressed, and then waited for Gilbash to knock on my door. I knew he would come for me. As predicted, Gilbash soon came, and we both went out into the Khan's courtyard up to the elm tree.

Morning mist had come down from the mountaintops, covering Gunortaj Palace. The chill of Mount Gazilig filled the Khan's courtyard. Gazan did not appear, though. I did not ask Gilbash about it. The servants quickly brought us food and drink, and we quietly ate our fill. Finally, Gilbash looked at me and shrugged. "It's time. Let's go!" he said. With that, we rose and left for the Khan's chamber.

---

[56] An ancient Azerbaijani string instrument, precursor of the minstrels' saz.

Bayindir Khan had risen at daybreak and was waiting for us in his place in the chamber. We greeted him upon entering his chamber, and he greeted us in return. We bowed and each of us then went and took our places. I positioned my paper and took out my pen. Then I patiently waited for the Khan to get started.

Bayindir Khan looked hard at my paper and pen. Then he looked at me. "Gorgud, my son, you have grown tired these last few days. Put them aside," he instructed. "I want to talk to you."

I sensed no anxiety or anger in Bayindir Khan's voice. My heart calmed down. I put aside the paper and pen and turned my attention to Bayindir Khan. Before starting the conversation, Bayindir Khan turned to Gilbash. "Gilbash, go. Leave us alone. I have to talk to Gorgud. Tell Gazan to be ready; once I have finished with Gorgud, bring him to me," he instructed. "Oh, and go and see if Shirshamsaddin is alive or dead, the scoundrel son of a scoundrel."

"Yes, my Khan," Gilbash replied. He turned and left the chamber.

The Khan smiled as he remembered Shirshamsaddin; he was aware of yesterday's competition. "Gorgud, son, sit closer," he then said. "Come sit opposite of me." I moved closer. Bayindir Khan looked at me a fair while before continuing. "What do you say, Gorgud?" he finally asked. "Is there anyone left who has not yet told us about the spy?"

"There is no one left, my Khan," I replied. "No one. Everyone has been questioned." I lowered my head.

"No, Gorgud, you are not right. One man is left," the Khan said.

"Who can this man be, majestic Khan?" I asked curiously.

"You," Bayindir Khan replied simply. "You are left, Gorgud, my son. Aren't you?"

My blood instantly froze in my veins. I kept silent, my eyes lowered, my heart pounding. Cold sweat trickled down my back to my undergarments. But Bayindir Khan's voice carried no wrath. This time, he clapped his hands and burst out laughing. "How Boghazja Fatma has wound these sons of scoundrels around her little finger!" he blurted.

I was bright red and ready to be swallowed up by the ground. I wished that the suspicions in Bayindir Khan's heart would come and go as quickly as the morning's mist from the mountaintops.

"Gorgud, my son, as I said, your turn has come. Let's talk. What do you say?" the Khan asked, struggling to suppress his laughter. He looked at me through narrowed eyes.

"Yes, majestic Khan," I began to speak so as not to lose time. "You are right. My turn has come. I would like you to know that whatever you want, I am ready to tell you."

"Gorgud, did you make Boghazja Fatma understand all this?" Bayindir Khan asked.

"Yes, majestic Khan. I made her understand," I answered.

"But why did you do it? Tell me," the Khan said. "Were you, too, caught up with Boghazja Fatma?"

"Yes, I was. Once in her home, I left the straight path and followed the crooked one. Now, I felt sorry for her wretchedness. May almighty God in heaven and you, Khan on Earth, forgive my sin, God willing," I replied.

"I like your answer. You said things as they were. You did not lose the straight path," Bayindir Khan said with satisfaction, looking into my face. After a short silence, he continued. "You have helped me very much during this inquiry, you know. Can you say what you understand of the matter so far? Why have I held this inquiry?" he asked.

I thought a little. Bayindir Khan was waiting for my response, not saying a word. I took a deep breath before giving him my thoughts. "My Khan, you wanted to learn who set the spy free," I said. "And you wanted to punish him so that he would be an example to the whole of Oghuz."

"Really?" Bayindir Khan asked, looking at me with interest. "Did you really think so?"

"Yes, my Khan, I really thought so," I replied.

"Gorgud, my son," Bayindir Khan said. "I already knew all of this before starting the inquiry. Couldn't you tell?"

> *Of course, I had been right. The Khan was not holding an inquiry; he had been conducting a test. What his real purpose was, however, only he alone knew.*

"Yes, Gorgud, of course, I was in the know. I had been told of the incident," Bayindir Khan said. He read in my eyes what was passing through my heart. He continued. "My main purpose did not concern the spy, you know, my son. My main purpose—let me tell you—was to find out who the scoundrel son of a scoundrel was who had been tearing Oghuz apart from within. I found this answer, Gorgud, my son. I found it; mark my words."

I was afraid to draw breath. The only sound in the Khan's chamber was the sound of silence. I wanted for him to fill me in on his findings.

"What do you think? Who can that scoundrel son of a scoundrel be?" Bayindir Khan asked slowly.

> *He was testing me again. We all know, don't we? No. It's not possible. Was I supposed to say Old Aruz? Again, no. Then who?* Don't say anyone, *I thought. The blood of mercy flowed from the Stone of Light into my heart.* Don't say anyone, *the Stone of Light told me.* The Khan

has come to his own conclusion. He does not expect an answer from you. He is talking to himself. *The Stone of Light sent me this sign. I remained silent and did not open my mouth.*

"Think about it, Gorgud, my son. Whomever I questioned said Old Aruz was to blame. I have never liked him, you know. Why don't I like him? There are many reasons. Did you see that Old Aruz was the only man who did not reveal his conversation with Boghazja Fatma?" Bayindir Khan asked.

"Yes, my Khan, indeed he did not," I said.

"What do you think about Gazan?" Bayindir Khan then asked. He fell silent, waiting for an answer from me.

I was confounded. "Gazan? Gazan is the pillar of Inner Oghuz, my Khan," I replied matter-of-factly.

"Yes, he is, but Gazan is also a wolf that gnaws at the whole of Oghuz from within. Were you confused? Do not be confused. Listen to me; I'll tell you. I won't tell anyone else, just you. I know that the time will come when you will need this," Bayindir Khan began. "Gorgud, my son, does a scoundrel go hunting and take all his army with him? If he does, then wouldn't he put his uncle in charge of protecting his kith and kin? When Gazan went hunting, Old Aruz was right to say, 'You are setting out on a long and dangerous journey. Who will you place at the head of your forces at home?' What did Gazan do? He did not appoint Old Aruz as head of his army, but his son, scarce more than a babe-in-arms. He offended Old Aruz in doing so. Is this so or not?"

The Khan continued. "Old Aruz wants to be first after Gazan. Gazan did not allow it. 'It's impossible,' he said. 'I don't respect you.' And what happened? The enemy lay waste our land and a great battle ensued. That is what happened! Next, he said, 'Let's invite Bakil from the marches, nobles, and go hunting.' They went hunting and ate and drank, right? What did he do? He disgorged his food on Bakil's head, praising the horse's skill above the rider's and offending Bakil. Did he do all this? Yes, he did," he said. He took a breath. "Then what happened? Bakil went back home angry. He wanted to revolt against Oghuz; however, he had no chance to do so. He went hunting to dispel his sorrow, but fell from his horse and broke his leg. Our enemy, Gara Takur, attacked Oghuz. The result? Another battle! This was all Gazan's doing, Gorgud. Do you understand?"

"I understand, my Khan," I said quietly. I waited for him to continue his thoughts.

"Then the scoundrel son of a scoundrel organized a plunder of his tent. He invited Inner Oghuz, but this time did not invite Outer Oghuz. What was the reason? Can you tell me? I would like to know. Is it what the nobles wanted? Could this be why? It's not possible, Gorgud, my son," Bayindir Khan said, shaking his head. "It's not possible at all…" The Khan fell silent. He was out of breath and rested for a short while.

Meanwhile, I gazed at the Khan. His face had turned a deep red. He bent his head to look out the window at the flower garden. After a while, he turned to face me again. "I haven't spoken yet about his other heroics. His mother is a prisoner; his wife is a prisoner; his son is a prisoner. That scoundrel desired that King Shoklu give back only his old mother, not his wife or son. 'Let them be your captive slaves,' he said," the Khan said disgustedly. "It was a trick of war. Go and tell the children of Oghuz this trick of war! Look at the wartime trick of the Noble of Nobles! Did I grant permission for Gazan to gather his troops and go hunting, leaving Oghuz open to the enemy? Did I grant permission? I'll have you know, Gorgud, that I did not!"

The Khan continued. "And then he hardly lets Beyrak out of his sight. What is there between the two of them? I don't know. I knew what Beyrak was capable of without you saying anything. He played his tricks with Lady BurlaeH. Can a woman be clever? She was like a drooling calf when she talked of Basat! Now she wants revenge on Old Aruz for Basat. Neither Gazan nor Beyrak understand this," he said. "Did I say women cannot be clever? Women have other qualities instead of cleverness; we can never understand them. As for Beyrak, he has his beautiful rose of a wife at home—I mean, Baybejan's daughter. Didn't she wait for him for sixteen years? And what do you think? He leaves his wife at home and goes cavorting across Oghuz! The scoundrel son of a scoundrel will be finished with the girl one day, I know. I knew before that scoundrel Shirshamsaddin told me…"

Everything that Bayindir Khan was saying made complete sense to me. I continued listening intently.

"Of course, we must find a way out of this. Old Aruz is a danger to Oghuz. Beyrak is a danger to my house, you know. This Oghuz that I have built—this tent that I have raised up—needs Inner Oghuz and Outer Oghuz and the whole of Oghuz—from suckling babe to warrior—to respect one another. If Oghuz does not first respect itself, will Arshin Dirak Takur or King Shokli show respect?" the Khan asked. "Take the day word came from the Kingdom of Trebizond, when Bayburd told of Beyrak's deeds there. What dungeon? What imprisonment? What hardship? Empty hearsay! They took Beyrak as a guest. Bayburd had a maiden daughter, and Beyrak lured her from the right path. Because of this, she sent back all the matchmakers, saying, 'Beyrak is mine. He will marry me. He has given his word!' Her father and mother were still waiting for the scoundrel when they went to their graves. He avoided joining the army to attack One-Eye by finding a cozy spot for himself in Bayburd!"

The Khan continued. "Misfortune will befall Oghuz—if not today, then tomorrow, Gorgud; mark my words. What are we to do? We must act. Outer

Oghuz has already bared its teeth. Old Aruz has moved aside and will go as far as war. I don't understand Old Gazilig. I know that after he returned from Duzmurd Castle, he often met Old Aruz, but I don't know what they talked about," he said. "Old Gazilig is also from Outer Oghuz; he can be considered Old Aruz's clansman. At that time, in order to please Outer Oghuz, I even appointed him Vizier. Now he and Aruz are sniffing around each other! So you see, Gorgud, son, this is how things are. We can say 'spy,' however much we want, but this spy, as I told you, is of little importance to me. The fault is ours, and the fault is Gazan's, Gorgud."

When Bayindir Khan had finished saying what had been weighing on his mind, he fell silent. I kept silent, too. Yes, this was what the Khan *really* wanted to find out: Who wanted what in Inner Oghuz? Where was Oghuz's weeping sore? Why had the unity of Inner and Outer Oghuz—which had been divided into two for a long time—become thin as hair? Who was at fault? Bayindir Khan did not speak empty words. Gazan was at fault. *Okay, so now what?* I wondered. *Our hope rests in the mercy of the Khan and in the Stone of Light...*

"Gorgud, son, listen to me carefully. Gazan is my son-in-law. I cannot do to Gazan all that I should. What do you think?" Bayindir Khan asked.

"You speak the truth, my Khan. If you vent your rage against Gazan, then Oghuz really will be shattered, once and for all. War will begin and never end," I replied.

"That is so. Then what are we to do?" Bayindir Khan asked. "We need the war to end before it has begun; it should be forgotten. We need to find someone else who is at fault."

"Khan, there is someone at fault," I said.

Bayindir Khan frowned at me. "Do tell..." he said, confused.

"Yes, majestic Khan. If Old Aruz is guilty, will this end the matter?" I asked.

"Gorgud, if someone is guilty, then he must be punished. What will you say to Old Aruz? He will gather Outer Oghuz, talk much nonsense, keep on talking, and a great battle will begin. But will it end?" the Khan asked. "You say Old Aruz, but he has not yet done evil."

"If he did?" I asked.

"What could Old Aruz do?" Bayindir Khan's black eyes sparkled. "Could he act against me?"

"My Khan, if Old Aruz killed an Oghuz noble without permission, would he be punished?" I asked.

"He would!" Bayindir Khan replied. "If he kills without permission, scores will be settled."

"My Khan, if Old Aruz is punished, and if the whole of Oghuz turns away from him, would the threat of war between Inner Oghuz and Outer Oghuz be finished?" I then asked.

"Finished!" Bayindir Khan replied decisively.

"Then, my Khan, Old Aruz must commit this sin," I said gravely.

Bayindir Khan looked at me attentively. He did not say a word.

I continued. "Yes, majestic Khan, a sacrifice is required. Let Old Aruz be this sacrifice. He will say, 'I have come to reconcile you and Gazan…'"

"And then?" Bayindir Khan asked, very interested.

"Then, my Khan, Old Aruz will sin. He will kill him. And after that, the whole of Oghuz will punish Old Aruz. The matter shall be over," I said.

"Really?" Bayindir Khan asked slowly. "Can you say who this sacrifice will be?"

Without thinking, I quietly told Bayindir Khan the name of the sacrifice, scarcely moving my lips. Bayindir Khan studied me again carefully. This time, I saw that the name had been hiding in the endless depths of Bayindir Khan's eyes before I even spoke it. A thought suddenly dawned on me: *The Khan had organized everything in advance, and his purpose was to hear the name from me.* Where did those words come from? Of course, they came from the Stone of Light itself.

"Man comes into this world, but this world will kill him, Gorgud. The hour of death strikes, and the earth conceals man and keeps its secret," Bayindir Khan said solemnly. "Can you bring this matter to its end?"

"The world is an old world, majestic Khan," I said. "Can a secret be kept or not in this world? I don't know. What have I become in gathering the secrets of Oghuz in my soul? Maybe this is the secret of secrets. It will be buried in the graveyard of my soul. But the world, you say, is like a man—here today, but gone tomorrow. If you are gone on tomorrow, to whom will you give your secret?"

"The number of your secrets would increase," Bayindir Khan said. "But the world is not old, as you say, Gorgud, my son. The world you talked about is a young world."

The Khan had spoken the truth. *But then, what has not happened in this world?* I wondered. *They have even invented catapults of fire…*

The Khan continued. "The world is a young world, Gorgud. The end of a man's long years is death. But the years of the world have no end. Do you know—do you know who told me this? It was my father! My father told me this, Gorgud; never forget it. You will need this," he said, kneeling on one knee. Then he squinted his eyes at me, focusing all of his energy into what he was about to say. "My father, Gamghan, said that…"

§ § § § § §

...That was the day when, with much weeping and wailing, the survivors of the earthquake gathered the bodies of the dead and laid them out in rows. When they had summoned all their strength, they took the corpses to the Sabzikar burial ground, an ancient plot on the north side of Ganja. Soon, there was no room left in the cemetery. It was impossible to move without treading on a fresh grave.

Clouds of countless birds, big and small, circled in the cemetery sky, striking fear into the hearts of the people. However, the fear was dissolved by the miraculous survival of an astrologer in the rubble of the earthquake. Though he had long since lost the trust of the people, he now declared with certainty, "These innocent souls of the dead are seeking peace. They will fly some more; they will fly, grow tired, and leave us..."

Epilogue

The Mark of Incompleteness

I promised the young Orientalist that I would return *The Incomplete Manuscript* to box No. A 21/733 to her or take it back to the Manuscripts Institute's strong room, which was located to the right of the main entrance. For some reason, I wanted to see the girl again, though. As I was carefully placing *The Incomplete Manuscript* in its box for the last time, I was suddenly startled by a thought that crossed my mind. *I won't see this girl anymore. Though I may look for her and follow in her footsteps, she no longer exists for me. She has flown away...disappeared...gone.*

I put on my coat and then picked up the box containing the manuscript, as well as the two exercise books the young Orientalist had transcribed for me. As I was leaving the room, however, I almost collided with the girl. I managed to quickly pass her the box from under my arm, and I felt almost a sense of relief, of relaxation, as soon as it was out of my hands. After I had expressed my thanks, the young Orientalist took the box and clasped it tightly without a flicker of expression on her face.

She stood and waited without asking me anything. I really wanted her to ask something, or at least briefly talk to her about my ideas and feelings about everything I had read, but she kept quiet. She didn't move. It was as though she wanted to see me leave for the last time with her own eyes. Without saying a word, the two of us slowly made our way toward the exit. I assumed that she would go straight to the strong room while I would simply leave the Manuscripts Institute.

I began to think about Khan's final conversation with Gorgud. I thought about the aged Bayindir Khan and the young Gorgud, and the world between them. I attempted to wrap my mind around the young world of the aged Khan and the aged world of the young Gorgud. *How did the Khan put it?* I thought. *"They have even invented catapults of fire." What else is left?* I suddenly understood that each of them was talking to the other in their own world; Bayindir Khan had his own Gorgud in his world, while Gorgud had his own Bayindir Khan in his world. They were not in the same place for one another.

Did the young Orientalist—a scrap of a girl who appeared before me with her heels clacking, and who seemed to be following my every move, hugging *The Incomplete Manuscript* in its box like a child—have her own world, too? Who was I in her world? Why did I see her silhouette so clearly in the scribbled notes? And why did the expression on her face when we collided in the doorway remind me of that same silhouette? *She was avoiding conversation with me—deliberately avoiding it,* I thought.

Is there any correlation or link, hidden or not, between the text about Shah Ismayil and Gorgud's text? If I asked, what would happen? I wondered. The Manuscripts Institute staff might get the wrong idea, however, and think that I was planning some investigative research—God forbid. At that moment, thousands of eyes were watching from holes and gaps, from visible and invisible places behind us. *What kind of a door is that? It's as though its shadow...*

The young Orientalist and I started to descend the wide staircase. She walked a few feet ahead of me. As I was preparing to bid her a proper farewell, and to express my heartfelt thanks for everything she had done for me, she suddenly turned and entered the manuscript strong room, disappearing entirely. I had lost my chance.

I frowned wistfully and exited the building. Once I was out on the sidewalk, I checked the exercise books the young Orientalist had given me (two thick books) in the pocket of my coat and sighed with relief. My doubts seemed to be at an end. *If this is ending,* I thought, *then it will end any old how, just as in* The Incomplete Manuscript. Everything now seemed to bear the mark of incompleteness—of course. Debating in my mind what to do, I began walking the long way home. Suddenly, I remembered what the young Orientalist had said to me...

CPSIA information can be obtained at www.ICGtesting.com
Printed in the USA
LVOW08s1854291013

359130LV00001B/306/P